MAXWELL'S RETIREMENT

Peter 'Mad Max' Maxwell, the 'dinosaur' Head of Sixth Form at Leighford High, doesn't know how to use a computer. However, it becomes vital that he learns when some of his female pupils begin receiving threatening messages, with the anonymous sender claiming to know intimate details about the girls' personal lives. Then Max starts to receive messages too ... and two of the girls go missing. When a body is found, it seems that the prank has taken a sinister turn. His wife is pressuring him to retire, but the chance of Mad Max reaching retirement looks increasingly unlikely.

MAXWELL'S RETIREMENT

MAXWELL'S RETIREMENT

by

M. J. Trow

Magna Large Print Books
Long Preston, North Yorkshire,
BD23 4ND, England.

British Library Cataloguing in Publication Data.

Trow, M. J.
    Maxwell's retirement.

    A catalogue record of this book is
    available from the British Library

    ISBN   978-0-7505-3250-1

First published in Great Britain in 2010 by Allison & Busby Ltd.

Copyright © 2010 by M. J. Trow

Cover illustration © Rolero 54/Fotolia by arrangement with
Allison & Busby Ltd.

The moral right of the author has been asserted

Published in Large Print 2010 by arrangement with
Allison & Busby Ltd.

Magna Large Print is an imprint of Library Magna Books Ltd.

Printed and bound in Great Britain by
T.J. (International) Ltd., Cornwall, PL28 8RW

Chapter One

The time capsule, faintly disguised as an office, waited, lifeless without its occupant. The movie posters on the wall reflected each other dully in their laminated surfaces. The coffee cup on the desk still held a brief memory of its warmth from the start of the day. The fridge hummed softly and the kettle clicked away its heat. The chair was pushed back from the desk, a pink and blue scarf thrown casually across the back. A pile of dog-eared exercise books teetered on its seat. The desk was not its usually neat self: a pen and a diary, a mark book, and a box of tissues, weeping girls for the use of, had been pushed to one side to accommodate a brown box.

In itself, the box was not particularly ominous. It was large, granted, but otherwise non-threatening. It had no labels: no lightning flashes to show it was live and shocking; no skull and crossbones to show it was poisonous; no sign of that meaningless biohazard symbol. It did not appear to contain dangerous chemicals of any kind, nor yet live animals, either tame or wild. But even so, as it sat, silent and still in the middle of the desk, it seemed to exude its own evil.

Every now and again the door to the room would open and there would be a sharp intake of breath. The door would then close again and leave the box to its own quiet thoughts. The hushed air of the room began to vibrate, on a very low wavelength, to the murmur of a growing crowd outside in the corridor. The voices rose and fell with the addition of each newcomer as every member of the crush whispered the news. Then, a hush so total that the word 'silence' could hardly accommodate it.

A voice, raised to normal speaking level, cut through the thickness of the quiet.

'Why are you all outside my office? You can't *all* be wanting to change courses. You had your chance last September and you muffed it. I want everybody other than...' there was a pause... 'Unman, Whittering and Zigo, to clear off to wherever you should be.'

There was a scuttling of feet and stifled laughter as the mob dispersed.

There was a pause. 'Why are you still here?'

'I'm Whittering, sir,' said a small voice.

'Are you?' There was a pause, long enough for a moderately tall man to bend down to examine a moderately short boy. 'So you are. Well, you are excused.'

There was a solo scamper, stopped short by a question.

'Why were you all outside my door?'

'I don't really know, sir. I couldn't get past, that's all. I was on my way to the library. I think someone mentioned...'

'Yes, well, don't keep it to yourself, Whittering. What did someone mention?'

'A box, sir.'

'A box?'

'Yes.'

The door handle turned and the owner of the voice stepped into the room. His name was Peter Maxwell. He was Head of Sixth Form. He was nearly four hundred years old in a metaphysical sort of way and today he was staring his future in the face.

'Oh, bugger.' He half turned to the Year Seven lad at his elbow. 'Pardon my French, Whittering. Could you pop along to the IT room for me, please?'

The boy stood there.

The man turned round fully. 'Still here, Whittering?'

'Why am I popping along to the IT room, sir?'

Just what Maxwell needed – a Year Seven lad with an enquiring mind. 'Sorry, Whittering. I've had a bit of a shock. Yes, tell Miss Thompson to come to my office at once. She is to bring scissors and a good excuse.'

The lad wanted to get it right. 'Scissors and an excuse, sir?'

'Yes. Scissors to open this box. An excuse to explain why she has seen fit to deliver to Mr Maxwell one laptop, technophiles for the use of.' He turned to the boy. 'Chop-chop, now, Whittering. Time's a-wasting. The sooner I get rid of this box, the sooner I can get on with other things. Like teaching you and yours the minutiae of the causes of the Black Death.'

'Fleas.'

'Pardon?'

'Fleas, sir. The minutiae of the causes of the Black Death.'

'Not bad, Whittering. I would have preferred a

11

bacillus and the specific flea *ceratophyllus fasciatus*, but still, not bad. There are two other things to remember, though.'

'Yes, sir?'

He closed to the boy. 'I do the jokes and nobody likes a smartarse. Now, run along, like a good chap and fetch Miss Thompson.'

The boy ran off – the Head of Sixth Form couldn't be arsed to tell him to walk – and Maxwell ran his hands through his barbed wire hair as he turned to confront his nemesis. This was the nearest he had come to having a computer thrust upon him and his footwork would have to be at its niftiest to repel it at this late stage. Ever since Charles Babbage had dreamt up his Difference Engine in 1822, Maxwell had been dreading this day. He sighed and walked round behind his desk to await his fate in the shape of Miss Thompson, of IT, an IT girl for her generation.

Chapter Two

Nicole Thompson was quite little and dark –
littler and darker than the Head of Sixth Form
certainly – and she put her head tentatively round
the edge of Maxwell's door. She had not been at
Leighford High School for long before she had
felt the hot breath of Tyrannosaurus Maxwellian-
ensis on the back of her neck as she bent over a
keyboard in her room under the eaves. She felt as
strongly as he did when it came to technology;
they were simply standing at the opposite ends of
a scale marked one to infinity, where one was
embracing everything Bill Gates could throw and
infinity was best represented by a piece of chalk
and a brain the size of the O2 Arena. Or the
Millennium Dome, as Maxwell had finally got
around to calling it, on the day after it had closed.
He and Jacquie could still end up not speaking
after another bout of the perennial 'when did the
century begin?' argument, first started when she
was only Woman Policeman Carpenter and he
was That Bloody Nuisance Maxwell.

'Max?'

He looked up, sharply, dragged from his contemplation of what he had begun to think of as
The Box. It was Nicole Thompson, funnily
enough. 'Clara! Thank you so much for being so
quick.'

'Faster than a speeding bullet, me, Max, as you

13

know. Now I'm on broadband. Ha ha.'

He smiled, a thin little smile. 'Oh ho, Clara. A technology joke. Very droll.'

'And you, Max. A silent movie reference. As ever.'

He looked her in the eyes and this time the smile was real. He was impressed.

'Clara, you have a mind like a...'

'Computer?'

'I was going to say razor, but whatever pleases you. Now,' he looked at her sternly, and tapped the cardboard, 'I notice you have not brought two hearty chaps to carry away this box.'

She stared him straight in the eye. 'That's because the box, or I should perhaps say the *contents* of the box, are not going anywhere, Max. You are joining us on the virtual highway, if I have to drag you there kicking and screaming myself.'

He looked grumpy. He knew it was his most endearing expression and had melted hearts from Leighford to Tottingleigh. 'I already know how to use a computer.'

'I'm not talking about a bit of surfing for research, Max. I'm not talking about checking the weather on the BBC news site.'

'Hmmph! I don't do that.' He looked even more truculent.

'No, Max, I know. Or at least, not our weather. The last time I looked over your shoulder you seemed engrossed in the weather in Uzbekistan.'

'I couldn't seem to escape from the former USSR,' he muttered. 'It goes with the territory in the teaching Year Thirteen stakes. However, Clara, I rest my case. I can use a computer. I have a Pea

14

Sea in my office already,' he waved extravagantly to where a dusty computer almost as old as the building glowered and hummed. 'I don't want a laptop. I don't need a laptop. So, ergo elk, my dear girl, you can take it away.' He smiled winningly and made half-hearted shooing motions with both hands. 'Can I carry it for you, perhaps?' After all, he had, in aeons gone by, been a public schoolboy. 'They use so much packaging these days, don't they? Makes it heavy.' He picked it up. 'Ooh, yes, very heavy,' He hefted it into a more comfortable position, stifling a groan, and made for the door.

She didn't move and he turned.

'So, where to? Your office, I expect. Hmm?'

'Max,' she said, her voice dripping patience. 'That laptop is not going back to my office. I would say that it is going nowhere, except that that would be inaccurate. It is going everywhere you go. It is going to lessons with you. It is going home with you at night. It is going to meetings. But before that, it is going on your desk and you and I are going to sit in front of it until I am happy that you are confident in its use. You were *at* the same staff IT familiarisation meeting as I was at, weren't you?'

He looked at her, open-mouthed. Not for a moment did he think that headmaster Legs Diamond's writ applied to him. The use of computers in schools was surely for the children or, at the very worst, the children on the staff.

'And that's final.' She relented and moved towards him to shepherd him back to his desk. She sat him down and slid the box to one side. She perched on the corner of his desk and looked

15

down at him. 'I'm not a bully, Max. Really I'm not. But the county has begun a paperless office campaign and Mr Diamond has decided to roll it out at Leighford High School as a matter of urgency. That means no memos, no printed minutes, no paper at all.'

'Lavatory paper?' he asked, weakly, household names like Bronco and Izal swimming in his memory.

'Only when totally necessary,' she smiled. 'But, seriously, Max. You knew about this, surely?'

'I didn't get a memo as I recall... Oh. I see.' He pushed himself back from the desk and sighed. 'I'm not a happy bunny, Clara. Not happy at all.'

She patted his shoulder. 'I can see that you're not,' she said. 'So let's try and make this as painless as possible, shall we?' A thought occurred to her and she tried to frame her next question tactfully. 'Your wife? Is she ... um, like you, at all?'

Maxwell considered the wonders that were Jacquie. 'Not really,' he said. 'Her hair is longer and a lovely chestnut colour. She's shorter than me and a different shape, of course. Thankfully. Our son can tell us apart, and so can the cat, so there must be enough differences between us. *"Vive,"* as they say over in Modern Languages, *"la différence".*'

'I think you know what I meant,' she said, icily. 'I meant, is she as computer-phobic as you?'

'No, not at all. She uses a computer all day at work and helps me out with anything I need. That's why,' he looked up from under cunning lashes, 'I think what I'll do is just take this home and let her sort me out.'

16

Nicole slammed her hand down on the desk and made them both jump. 'No!' she almost shouted. 'She won't be with you every minute, will she? You've really got to get to grips with this, Max. You won't even be able to register a class without this. You won't be able to write reports, mark exams... Need I go on?'

Maxwell was smiling. The thought of no marking or report writing was almost too wonderful to contemplate. He shook himself and looked her in the eye. He saw steel there and capitulated. Had it come to this? A slip of a girl without a teaching qualification to her name calling the shots? All right, Clara,' he smiled. 'Let's get on with this. I bow,' and he did so, stiffly, like George Peppard in his namesake film, *The Blue Max*, from the waist, 'to your expertise and to your dogged determination. I can give you five minutes.'

'We have all day, Max,' she said, grimly. 'I've covered all your lessons for today. Neither of us leaves this room until I have you at one with this machine.' *She* had covered all his lessons? Had the world gone mad?

'You'll turn me into a robot, Clara. Like C3PO.' The android voice was perfect.

'As I recall,' Nicole said, dredging her Old Films memory, 'C3PO was obedient. If you became a robot at all, I feel sure you would be more like the rebel one in *I, Robot*.'

Maxwell smiled. 'Do you think so? A rebel robot, eh?' He chuckled and reached into his drawer for a box opener. 'Let's do this thing.' It was as though Will Smith had just walked in.

As Nicole went to fetch another chair, she blew

outwards, silently. She had managed it. They had all said she wouldn't. But she had tamed Peter Maxwell, the dinosaur of the school. She would have him computer literate if it took all day.

The sound of the bell for the end of the day came finally. There had been tears. There had been silences. There had been silent tears, shed in the toilets. But, finally, Peter Maxwell could log on, log off, register a class and retrieve emails. Sending was a little ad hoc, but, as he said, he hadn't lost the power of speech, so he could always use the old-fashioned method of communication and yell down the corridor.

As if to prove that all was well in the world of the spoken word, the door crashed open and Mrs B entered on a waft of old cigarette smoke and ecologically friendly cleaner and the low hum of imprecations against an employer who banned both smoking and bleach. The woman was a walking stereotype.

Maxwell fell on her, if only metaphorically. 'Mrs B. How lovely that you're here. Clara, you'll be off, then, I imagine. It's been.'

The IT girl raised bleary eyes. 'Been what?'

He ushered her to the door. 'Nothing. Just been,' he smiled and waved as she walked down the corridor, back to the sanity of her own world. He turned back into the room, relishing the thought of clashing intellects with Mrs B. No one knew how old she was – rumour had it that she was the first cleaner in Robert Raikes' first Sunday School – but she was still as wiry as she was wily and could spread the dust into different places quicker

18

than you could say 'Would you like a cuppa?'

'Would you like a cuppa, Mrs B?' Maxwell was making for the kettle and spoke over his shoulder. What he saw froze his blood. Mrs B was standing over his still-open laptop, her face alive with a mixture of lively interest and faint contempt. 'Mrs B?' His lips were dry and his voice a croak. 'Cuppa?'

She raised her eyes to his and said, with a shrug of a shoulder, 'Don't tell me they're still palming off this old Leptis Three on you poor bleeders? It's not even got Intel and as for its RAM – well, Mr Maxwell, I don't know what you're going to do with a download speed of less than 6 megs per sec, I really don't. They should be ashamed of themselves, them up at County Hall.'

Maxwell leant against the fridge, his world disintegrating before his eyes. He cleared his throat and tried his voice out. It came as an awed squeak. He tried his usual technique, but he only just managed it, answering each remark in its turn. 'It seems they are. Has it not? I hardly like to think. Indeed they should.' He really only felt confident in the last answer County Hall should always be ashamed, for one reason or another.

Mrs B had pulled back his chair and installed herself in front of the laptop. She looked up at him. 'Are you logged on?'

He smiled, lopsidedly. He raised his shoulders in an elaborate shrug.

She narrowed her eyes at him. 'You don't know, then.' She bent to her task. 'Let's see. Hmmm. No, she's logged you off. She's a cunning one, that Nicole. She's done it to see if you can get back on again. What a cow, eh?' She gave a throaty chuckle. 'You game for a laugh, Mr Maxwell?'

Maxwell looked at her fondly. She reminded him of a kind of demented, shaven ferret, but not of the horrendous team from the TV show of the same name, so for that he was grateful. He went over to the desk and stood behind her. 'I believe I may be, Mrs B. What evil do you have in mind?'

She nudged him rather painfully, her sharp elbow digging in to a rather sensitive part of his upper thigh, but he tried not to mind. She coughed, dragging up memories of ancient ciggies from the depths of her lungs. 'Them up in IT, they think they're the bee's knees, they do. They leave coffee mugs all over the place, growing fur and all sorts, and I'm supposed to clear up after them. They spend all day on bleedin' eBay, selling county supplies as like as not and behavin' like they own the place. Any idiot can use a computer,' she twisted round and winked, 'present company excepted, o' course, Mr Maxwell.'

He acknowledged what he chose to take as a compliment with an elegant bow.

'So,' she flexed her knuckles with deafening cracks, 'what's yer logon?

'Hmm...'

'You'll be maxwep,' she said.

'That's the jobbie,' he said. 'Sounds familiar. I have people for that sort of thing. Helen Maitland for example...'

She tapped in the letters. 'Password?'

'Hmmm...'

She tapped again and the home screen flashed up.

'How did you do that?' he asked in disbelief. 'I

didn't tell you my password.'

'Well,' she said, and she looked so at home at the keyboard he could almost see the ghostly outlines of the smoke which had once wreathed her head, 'it didn't take much to work it out. It was either Nolan1, Jacquie1 or gallant600.'

Son. Wife. Hobby. All with that pointless number computers seemed to insist on.

Maxwell reached for a piece of paper and a pen. 'Which was it, in the end?'

'gallant600.'

He wrote it down. 'Next question, Mrs B. How did you...?'

'Easy, Mr Maxwell.' She was being a *little* smug. 'Most people use family names, sometimes they put a number in where it is the same as the letter or just add a one. So it could have been en, zero, one, ay, en, you see. Or jay, ay, sea, queue, you, one, ee. Do you get it?'

Maxwell was working it out on his fingers. He smiled as the light dawned. 'Yes,' he said. 'Yes, I do. But how did you come up with gallant600?'

'Easy,' she said. 'You've been using that in an alphanumeric code for everything since you worked here.'

'Mrs B,' Maxwell said thoughtfully, 'have you ever seen a film called *Invasion of the Body Snatchers?*'

'Can't say I have, Mr Maxwell. I don't watch many films.'

He looked down at her thoughtfully. He was looking, in a clandestine manner, at the back of her neck, to see if the telltale mark was there. Then he shook himself. Of course she wasn't a

21

doppelganger. She was just a woman he had known for years, who had always pushed a hoover, dropped fag ash, gossiped and moaned about everything from chewing gum under the desks to the state of the nation, where it impinged on the price of cigarettes, tea and Windolene. And now, suddenly, while he wasn't watching, she had become a computer whizz. She knew words like RAM. Well, he corrected himself, everyone knew *words* like RAM, but Mrs B seemed to understand it as well, in the sense of something other than a male sheep. In spite of himself, he bent his knees and looked again for the telltale mark.

'So,' she said, 'now I'm in, I'm going to send Miss Smartie and all her department an email from you to show how clever you are.'

'Absolutely, Mrs B,' he said, lost in admiration and thought in approximately equal measure.

She tapped away for a while and then, with a final and decisive tap, sent the emails on their way. She did some more esoteric things on the keyboard and then reluctantly pushed herself away from the desk. 'Well, Mr Maxwell. Must get on.'

The pain of the chair leg pressed firmly on his toe brought Maxwell back to reality. 'I hope you don't think me rude, Mrs B,' he said, 'but I really have to ask. How did you become so good on a computer?'

'Our Beryl's eldest – I think I told you about him – lovely boy, got in with a bit of a bad crowd, stockbrokers or summat, anyway, our Colin, pronounced Coe-lin, like that general, anyway, him, he taught me.'

22

'That was very sweet of him, Mrs B. The youngsters can't always be bothered these days, can they?' Maxwell knew that this was the kind of sentiment guaranteed to warm the cockles of her heart. It worked.

'Too right, Mr Maxwell. He's a good lad. He give me a bit of a crash course when he was with us a few months back. Well, the time hung heavy, with him not being able to go out.'

'Oh,' Maxwell's voice dripped sympathy. 'Was he unwell?'

'No, not really. The CCTV picture was real clear, they're usually a bit fuzzy, ain't they? Well, he had to stop in for a bit, so he got me up to scratch on the computer. Well, I have to keep a bit of an eye on things, while he's away.'

Maxwell knew he shouldn't ask, but he couldn't help himself. 'Away? Anywhere nice?'

'Ford Open Prison. Five years for fraud. As I said, a lovely boy. Lovely manners.'

Maxwell's smile appeared pinned on as he backed away. 'Well, that's lovely. Fraud, eh? I'm off now then, Mrs B. See you tomorrow.' And, brow furrowed beyond the help even of Pro-Retinol A, he made for the outside world, the familiar saddle of White Surrey, the newly blossomed leafiness of Columbine and sanity. Or at least, what passed for sanity. It never occurred to him to wonder what the email had said.

Up high under the eaves, in the IT Department, among their coils of leads, furry mugs and piles of bubble wrap and brown paper, eBay packaging for the use of, the computer techies looked at their screens in wonder.

From: maxwep
To: IT Department
Message:i done the practis and i can youse the computer alrite now. So dont cum down here cheking becuase im alrite.Yours Mr Maxwell.

'Nicole,' Mike, the least robotic of the geeks, called across the room. They'd named a musical after the slickness of his hair and he'd got a GNVQ in sitting around. 'You weren't supposed to take anything *out* of Maxwell's head. You were supposed to just put stuff *in*.'

'Perhaps he's like Homer Simpson,' she said, looking at her screen as though mesmerised. 'Something fell out to make room.'

'He's having a laugh,' Mike said, shutting down his screen.

'I had him at school,' said Ned, geek number two, in sepulchral tones, seemingly unaware that he was still sitting behind a desk in the same school. 'He put me on detention for a term once because I used an apostrophe in the wrong place. I can't see him using bad grammar. It'll be the last thing to go when he finally goes nuts.'

Nicole frowned at her screen and then looked up at her boys. 'Gents,' she announced. 'We've got us a hacker.'

Maxwell soared through the gates on the two-wheeled legend that was White Surrey, past the usual crowd of giggling girls. If they seemed less giggly than usual, he didn't notice, such was his

24

headlong flight from Nicole, computers and a strangely altered Mrs B. Today had been difficult, he acknowledged that. Usually, Maxwell didn't countenance difficult: challenges were for rising to, problems were for solving, he'd never met a shenanig he didn't want to go in. But the computer thing was different. He had been surfing ahead of that particular tsunami for some years now and it was a shock to find himself finally thrown up on the alien beach of technology. He could use a computer, of course he could. He could search on eBay and, should Jacquie be out, could even bid for things, but he had tried to avoid it ever since the heart-stopping day when he had bid £3,999 for a fifty-four millimetre plastic soldier kit because of a misplaced comma. He could find Wikipedia, and occasionally took notes from it (while advising Years Twelve and Thirteen never to do so), but he couldn't get it to print out anything but the adverts and so still resorted to that much maligned standby, the pad and pencil. He could receive emails, because they just appeared when he clicked on what other people were pleased to call the icon. It looked nothing like a highly decorated Russian religious picture to him, but whatever made them happy. He couldn't send emails, but he had either Helen at work or Jacquie at home for that, depending on his location at the time. Of course he could use a computer. Dinosaur? Peter Maxwell? The very idea.

His musings took him all the way home, through the wild wind of the Flyover and the chill nip from the sea. He was oblivious to Surrey's obvious shortcomings. The brakes squealed at that certain pitch guaranteed to make every hair on the body, no matter how tiny and no matter where located, stand up ready for flight. The front wheel wobbled and had a permanent tendency to lean to the left; the Leon Trotsky of the bicycling world. There had once been a bell, although with the noise from the brakes it had become redundant long before the top fell off. The saddlebag was a memory kept alive by two wizened leather straps. So many parts had been replaced that the conundrum was this – was this White Surrey still, as the only original bit was the left pedal? But it bowled along nicely, over the Flyover, down behind the shopping centre, along a few residential nonentities until it reached the haven that was home.

Far behind him, the girls were still clustering around the gates of Leighford High at that fag-end of the day. Closer examination by Peter Maxwell would have shown him that some of his Own were deeply upset. The mobile phones banned from school but smuggled in, secreted in the bowels of backpacks and sports bags, were now out and beeping. One was being anxiously passed round. The girls, wide-eyed, huddled together to read the messages which poured in, each one arriving as the previous one was still being read, each one more explicit than the last. They had looked with avid eyes as Maxwell pedalled past. Their watcher, their minder, their shoulder when everything got too much couldn't have helped them with this. Everyone knew that

Mad Max was crap at anything technical. He didn't do PowerPoints. He didn't do electronic retrieval for homework. He didn't do anything much that didn't rely on a pen and paper. For him a memory stick was something pink and sticky from long ago that would crack your teeth and had 'Leighford' written right through it. But if Maxwell couldn't help them, who could?

The question was unspoken, but one girl answered it anyway.

'I can't tell my mum or dad about this. They'll think it's my fault.'

'Come on, Leah,' another girl chimed in. 'Why is it your fault?'

'Yeah, come on. Your mum's cool.'

'Cool, is she?' Leah turned a tear-streaked face to her friends. 'If cool is going out clubbing and coming home with any bloke who buys her a Bacardi Breezer then, yes, she's cool.'

Her friends looked at their feet. Some had mums who stayed at home, baked cakes, had a nice hot meal on the table when their dad got home from the office. More had mums who worked all hours and came rushing in just in time to shove something instant in the microwave. Some had single parents; some had two; some, courtesy of second and subsequent marriages, had more parents than they could count on both hands. But none of them had a parent like Leah's mum.

Her best friend, Julie, known as Zhuzh, inevitably shortened to Zee, put her arm round the girl's shoulders. 'Come on, Lee,' she said. 'Tell your dad if your mum won't understand.'

Leah shook her off. 'Yeah, right. I'll do that,

shall I? He'll assume it's one of mum's lowlifes and take it out on me because I won't go and live with him and his posh new wife in their posh new house with their posh new baby.'

A girl from the back of the little crowd spoke for the majority. 'Why don't you go and live with him, Leah? His house looks great from outside. It's got those gates and everything.'

Leah dashed her tears away with the back of her hand. 'Electric gates. They're not to keep people out; they're to keep people in. And anyway, who would look after my mum if I don't do it? No,' she squared her shoulders and raised her chin. 'I'll deal with it.'

'Mad Max, Lee,' Julie said quietly. 'He'll fix it.'

There were quiet chuckles. 'He doesn't understand phones,' someone said. 'He calls them the Invention of Mr AG Bell and reminds us at every opportunity that even he refused to have one in his study after he had invented it.'

'He's got one, though,' a little fair girl at the front said. 'I've seen him with it.'

Leah smiled weakly. 'Yes, I've seen that as well. He looks down at it, kind of puzzled as if he doesn't know how it got there. Then he kind of stabs at it until something happens. Usually, he finds he has switched it off. No,' she picked up her bag and hefted it onto her shoulder. 'I'll have to do something myself. A new phone, maybe. New number.'

'You could get one of those cool new ones, Lee,' the fair girl said. 'A Blackberry or one of those sort of email ones.'

'Yeah, Alice. Leah's mum can so afford a Blackberry.' Julie was cutting.

'There's no need to be like that, Zee,' Alice snipped back. 'Her dad could buy her one.' She turned to Leah. 'Tell him you've lost the other. Tell him it was pinched. Tell him you need it for your school work. That always works with my dad.' She looked wistful. Her dad worked in Dubai and sent her loads of stuff, but they hadn't actually spoken in years. She found it hard to summon up his face these days.

Leah looked thoughtful. 'I don't like to ask him, really, but you might have something there, Al.' She looked more cheerful. 'That'll do it. He'll go for that, I think.' She looked at her watch. 'Time I wasn't here. I need to be home for Anneliese.'

'Your mum's not working just now, is she?' Julie asked the question before she even thought to put her brain in gear.

'No, but ... well, you know.' Leah and all the girls knew that her mum would be busy getting ready to go out. These days it took longer than it had a few months ago to repair the damage of the night before. Anneliese was a beautiful little girl, six years old, her parents' attempt at gluing together a marriage that was beyond repair. She had blonde curls, big blue eyes and a temper like Gordon Ramsay, though fortunately as yet, not his vocabulary. It was easier to be there for her than pick up the pieces later.

The group broke up, in all directions: to the town centre, The Dam, to their homes and in the case of just one, desperate girl, to 38 Columbine.

Chapter Three

Maxwell skidded to his usual stop at the kerb outside his town house in Columbine. The stop was rather more precipitous than usual, as Jacquie's car was parked there as well. Maxwell's heart did the little flip it always did when he knew he was about to see his wife. The word was still unfamiliar, but the woman wasn't. She had been in and around his life for years, in various roles from irritatee to lover to mother of his son, and now, wife, but even so a little shock went through him every time he came home and found that she was there. He was smiling to himself as he walked up the path, deciding as he went whether he would knock, ring or use his key.

A shrill voice cut him to the quick. 'Well, Mr Maxwell. That smile is a bit of a surprise to me, I don't mind telling you, what with one thing and another.' Mrs Troubridge popped up on the other side of the hedge, giving shape to the disembodied voice. She looked like a prune with hair.

A cold hand clutched Maxwell's heart. To be fair, it always did when Mrs Troubridge was in the offing, but something told him that this time there was a really valid reason for it. He licked his dry lips. 'One thing and another, Mrs Troubridge?'

'Yes, well, the accident. Presumably that's why you are home so early.'

'I'm not early, Mrs Troubridge. I'm a teacher.

We always get home early. And have long holidays. Our salaries are stupendous and we have total job satisfaction. We don't really know we're born. *What accident?*' The last two words were issued in a distant scream, as though from someone underwater down a well many miles away. Faint, but piercing.

The little woman visibly left the ground and clutched at where anyone else's heart would be with a claw-like hand. In the empty recesses of her head she remembered that Maxwell's first wife and child had died, long years ago for her, yesterday still to him and, in her selfish, addled way she was sorry for what she had said. 'Mr Maxwell, I didn't mean to alarm you. I'm sorry for what I said.'

This was almost as big a shock as he had already had and he wasn't sure how many more he could take. He drew a deep breath and tried to calm down. 'What accident, Mrs Troubridge?' He hadn't slipped off his cycle-clips yet in case he had to be away again and mentally noted the distance to Surrey, still saddled at the kerb.

'Nolan. Playground. Casualty. Not serious.' She had resorted to telegraphic speech, a decision arrived at as less likely to spread alarm and despondency. Her aunt had been incarcerated in the war for just that reason and she had never quite forgotten it.

But she was speaking to air. Maxwell had thrust his key into the lock after only the tenth attempt and was bounding up the stairs three at a time. He burst into the sitting room, to find Jacquie sitting in his favourite chair with Nolan asleep on

31

her lap and Metternich the cat on the chair's arm, glaring balefully at her. Her eyes brimmed with unshed tears and she was still wearing her coat. The smile she gave him was watery and the finger she raised to her lips was shaking.

He was on his knees at her side in a heartbeat, hat and scarf flying in all directions. Metternich gave him a cuff round the head for the look of the thing, but he wasn't giving it his full attention and it was a shadow of his usual offering. His slit eyes were fixed on the Boy. He was considering changing the help; he and the Boy just weren't getting the service they deserved. He had sent the little chap out in the morning, all neat and tidy, with a quick lick to finish him off, and they bought him back filthy, with a big white bandage and smelling of clean, which made the cat's nose ache.

'What happened?' Maxwell whispered, stroking her hair and reaching out a tentative hand to touch his little boy's cheek.

'Well, you know Nole,' she said quietly. 'Never does anything by halves. He was on the climbing frame at the afternoon break and he climbed up the ladder. Unfortunately, when he got to the end, he just kept climbing. Pitched right over and landed on his chin.' She pointed to the dressing. 'Five stitches and a bruise the shape of Australia. And the size.' She tried to smile, but failed and the quivering lip spilt over into crying. She stifled the sobs when the boy stirred and muttered in his sleep. A cloud went across his face as the pain stabbed briefly and then he was off again, twitching as he slept, like Metternich did. Maxwell

32

hoped that this didn't mean that Nolan was disembowelling rats in his dreams.

'So,' she continued, 'Mrs Thomas scooped him up and took him to the nurse. It was bleeding everywhere.' She moved her protecting arm and Maxwell saw the front of his son's T-shirt, soaked in blood and his mother's tears. 'They waited until it stopped and then realised it would need stitches. They called me and I met them in A&E. He was so brave, Max. He didn't cry at all. His chin was so small they couldn't give him a local, so they just stitched it up. And he didn't cry. Not once.'

'You made up for it, I suppose,' he said, looking as though he might join her.

She compressed her lips and nodded. She took a deep breath through her nose and calmed down. 'They said it was a really common injury. One of the nurses and both of the doctors said they had scars under their chin.'

Maxwell lifted his head and pointed.

'Oh, Max, I had no idea you had a scar there. When did you get that?'

'Crécy, was it? Poitiers? Agincourt? No, I tell a lie. I was coming up to five and I fell out of a tree.'

'You were up a tree when you were five?'

'Four.'

'Even worse.'

'Different days, darling, different days. I'd climbed the Matterhorn before I was twelve. Metternich has one as well. Don't you, Count?'

Oh, the old buffer was whittering again. The huge black and white creature couldn't understand what he was going on about, but if they had

33

asked him, he could have assured the Boy's mother that anyone who was anyone had a scar under their chin. He had a fine example, the result of a rather overzealous use of the cat flap when he was only knee-high to a vole. And it was only his lustrous fur that hid all the other wounds of battle. Under all that black and white he looked like Moby Dick.

'Why didn't you let me know?' he asked her. 'I nearly had a heart attack when Mrs Troubridge collared me outside with tales of death and destruction.'

'Max, I *tried* to let you know. I rang school but you'd gone. I got Mrs B. Then I tried your mobile, and guess what?'

'What?' Maxwell was almost certain he knew what was coming.

'Well, surprise, surprise, I got Mrs B again. Your mobile was in your desk drawer. I suppose I should be grateful that you are improving. At least it was switched on.'

'I wondered where it was,' he said sheepishly.

'Well, never mind,' she said. She was too relieved that her son was safe to be angry at his father. 'But, Max,' she looked seriously at him. She saw her opportunity and she took it. 'This could have been a bad accident. I might have been unavailable. You really have to carry your phone.' Then, as an afterthought, 'And have it switched on. On your person and switched on. That's nice and easy to remember, isn't it?'

'I do understand that,' he said, stroking Nolan's cheek with the back of his fingers and ignoring Jacquie's rather patronising tone. 'I know I ought

34

to be contactable. But I can't have my phone switched on in lessons. I have banned all phones in my class.'

'I thought they were banned at school in general.'

He drew back from her and looked at her as though she was a new and interesting animal just invented by David Attenborough. 'Dear girl, I had always been led to believe that you were a Woman Policeman. Can you really be that naive?'

She shook her head, smiling. 'Sorry, I can't imagine what I was thinking. But, seriously, Max, can't you have it on silent?'

'I don't know. Can I?'

'Of course you can. Or, you could let messages go to voicemail and pick them up in breaks.'

'Again, I must respond – can I?'

'Max, do you know how to use your phone?'

'Of course I do. I've phoned you with it.' He sounded triumphant.

'Yes. I remember those rare times. And, before you say, I have phoned you. Texting?'

'I've had texts.' Triumph was giving way to truculence.

'Sent one?'

'I may have done.' It was pure Homer Simpson.

'To the right person?'

'Who knows?' To Maxwell, a text was something historical. They'd called them gobbets in his day; people were rather more unpleasant in his day.

She sighed and hefted Nolan into a more comfortable position. 'I tell you what, Max. What if

35

you go and make me a cup of tea? I've been sitting here for what seems like hours. I just can't bear to disturb him. I'm absolutely parched. Then, we'll have a lesson in how to use a mobile phone.' He opened his mouth to reply but she was quicker. 'Properly. In all its web-surfing glory.'

He tried to change the subject. 'Is it all right that Nole is sleeping like this? He hasn't got concussion or anything, has he?'

'No, he's fine. They gave him a paediatric painkiller in A&E, just to get him over the first few hours. He'll be right as rain in the morning, but I think I'll sleep in his room on the futon, just to be in range if he needs someone in the night. So,' she made flitting motions with her free hand, 'off you go and make my tea and then we'll talk phones.'

'Ah!' He raised his finger in badly disguised glee. 'My phone is at school.'

'Ah!' She was equally gleeful but with more reason. 'Our phones are the same and mine is here and juiced up and ready to go.'

'Ah!'

'Yes?' She smiled the smile of a woman who has won.

He sighed. 'Nothing. Just "Ah!"' And he went into the kitchen and began to gather the makings of tea together. Then, like a peal from heaven, the doorbell rang. He stuck his head round the sitting room door, stifling a grin. 'I'll get that, shall I?' he said, and positively skipped down the stairs.

Closing her eyes in resignation, Jacquie settled herself more comfortably under her sleeping son and rested her free hand on her cat-by-marriage.

With luck it would just be someone from Kleeneze, a nosy Mrs Troubridge or, at worst, a Jehovah's Witness. Maxwell was particularly effective in dealing with all three – 'Not today, thank you', 'I was just about to have a shower – join me?' and ... but luck was not on her side. Above her son's soft breathing and the cat's reluctant purr, she could definitely hear sobbing, and whilst it was not uncommon for Jehovah's Witnesses to sob as they left the doorstep of 38, Columbine, it usually took longer than the few minutes Maxwell had been at the front door. Using the wriggling technique that all mothers subliminally learn as they give birth, she extricated herself from beneath Nolan and left him sleeping in the chair. Metternich, with the speed and cunning native to all cats everywhere, was in the warm space left like a rat up a pipe, although that was not necessarily the analogy he would have personally chosen, given the option.

She went to the head of the stairs and stood back in the shadows. Maxwell was filling the doorway from her vantage point but the voice told her that their visitor was a girl, Sixth Form no doubt. She tuned her ears to maximum Woman Policeman mode and didn't think she recognised it. So, not one of the elect babysitting brigade, then. But even so, she sounded quiet and not argumentative, so it wasn't one of the drop-outs who littered their doorstep briefly halfway through every year, arguing the toss as to why nail extension technology should be an AS subject. Leaving school had seemed such a Utopian dream at the end of Year Eleven. Six months filling shelves at Morrisons killed all that. Jacquie hesitated, not knowing whether to go down and defuse a situation which might not exist. In her line of work, she was fully aware of how unwise it was to allow a male teacher to be alone with a distressed adolescent girl, although 'alone' was probably not the way to describe their front step, with Mrs Troubridge just a hedge width away. But, on balance, Mrs Troubridge was probably not a witness to rely on, as she had long ago decided that Maxwell, although handy for putting up pictures and carrying out heavy rubbish, was, underneath a pervert, no better than he should be. She decided to go down.

At the sound of her step, he turned. 'Darling, we were just talking about you. Is Nolan awake?'

'No, no, he's still sleeping. I tucked him up on the chair. Metternich is watching him for me.' She smiled at the girl, standing there on the path with tear stripes down her cheeks. 'Who's this?'

'How rude of me,' Maxwell muttered. 'Julie,' he gestured to Jacquie, 'this is my wife. Mrs Maxwell,' he added, perhaps a tad redundantly. 'Darling, this is Julie, who seems to have a bit of a problem but doesn't seem able to explain what it is.'

'Julie,' Jacquie smiled. 'Why don't you come in? Perhaps it will be easier for you when we are inside. I'm afraid our son has had a bit of a bump at school today and is asleep in the sitting room. Shall we go into the dining room? I can leave the doors open and then I'll hear him if he calls, but we won't wake him up.'

The girl looked from Maxwell to Jacquie. These

two were difficult to read, not like her parents, who left no doubt about what they felt; mostly anger. But Mad Max made it easy for the girl by stepping aside and gesturing her upstairs with a courtly wave.

'After you, ladies,' he said, adding, 'I was about to make some tea, Julie. Would you like some?'

'Have you got any Coke?' she asked, not really knowing if old people had such things in the house. 'Diet, if you've got it. Citrus Diet for preference.'

'Goodness me,' Maxwell said. 'My very own favourite, in the soft drink line. Well, well. We must have been separated at birth or something. Coke it is. Is that all round, heart?'

Jacquie smiled at Maxwell and then at the girl, standing uncertainly on her landing. She ushered her through the door into the dining room. 'I'd rather have tea, if that's still on the cards,' she said. 'Can there be biscuits?'

'I'm sure there can,' he said. 'Abyssinia,' and he went off to the kitchen, with a sneaky check on his two boys. Nolan was curled up with his fingers in his mouth and the cat was curved into him, like a spoon. See it every day though he might, Maxwell could still hardly credit the sight of the hard-bitten assassin sleeping with the enemy. He just hoped that Metternich wasn't playing the long game and was not planning a major coup, such as eating Nolan one evening when everyone's back was turned.

Shouldering the dining room door open and balancing a tray, Maxwell could only marvel again at the woman he had married. She was sitting next to Julie, who was now noticeably calmer. They were looking through the thin volume of Maxwell and Jacquie's wedding photos. Julie was cooing and pointing wordlessly, to emphasise some esoteric fashion speciality invisible to Maxwell and to men everywhere. She looked up as he came in and set down the tray, her eyes still red-rimmed but her mouth now in an uncertain smile.

'These are lovely photos, Mr Maxwell,' she said. 'You look very smart.'

'Oh, yes,' he said, passing her her Coke, with ice and a slice. Jacquie got her tea just as she liked it; in a mug and thick enough to stand on. He sat down opposite and smiled. 'I polish up quite well, don't I?'

Julie was one of the Sixth Form girls who actually thought that, ancient as he was, Mad Max would stand up quite well with the likes of ... well, that was always a difficult list to start, but with the old actors her mum liked – Sean Connery, that was one. Pierce Brosnan, he was all right. She looked up under her lashes and admitted that Mad Max wasn't quite in their league, but he looked very nice in his wedding photos and very proud as well. Mrs Maxwell was nice as well. Really understanding.

Tears stood in Julie's eyes again and Jacquie patted her hand.

'Come on, now, Julie. Explain to Mr Maxwell what you have just told me.'

The girl looked at Jacquie doubtfully. 'But, Mrs Maxwell ... will, I mean, does Mr Maxwell...?'

Jacquie smiled and looked at her husband, sit-

40

ting in a posture of confused alertness opposite. 'I think what Julie means, darling, is that she isn't sure you will quite get what she is talking about. It's a bit technical.'

'Technical?' Maxwell was puzzled. 'You're not doing CDT, are you, Julie? IT? Anything like that?' Encyclopaedic though his knowledge was, Maxwell could not keep *all* his students' time-tables in his head.

'No, Mr Maxwell. I'm doing English, Geography and History. It's nothing to do with my subjects. It's this.' She held up her mobile phone, which obediently bleeped for an incoming message. She dissolved into tears again. 'It just keeps on and on. I can't stand it.'

If Maxwell was confused before, he was totally at sea now. 'Can't you just turn it off?' This was, after all, his own preferred method.

'That doesn't help, Max,' Jacquie said, absently patting Julie on the back. 'The messages are there when you switch the phone back on. They're not like calls. They are automatically stored on the phone.'

'I think I knew that,' Maxwell said, uncertainly. A distant memory from a long-ago reading of an instruction manual rose to the surface. 'I seem to think you can block a caller.' His hatred of the moronic interrogative prevented him from making the statement a question, but it was one, nonetheless.

Julie and Jacquie looked at him, their eyes big with concern. Their worlds had rocked on their axes. Jacquie was the first to recover the power of speech.

41

'Yes,' she said, only just biting back the 'well done, dear'. 'You can do that, but not when the caller withholds their number. You can block all withheld numbers, but of course that means that anyone you *know* who habitually does that would be blocked as well.'

'Yes,' Julie said. 'That's the problem. My step-dad is a doctor and he withholds his number. He often has to ring me, or text, and so I can't block withheld numbers.'

Maxwell seemed to see a simple answer just in front of their noses. 'Can't he *unblock* his number when he texts or rings you?' It seemed too simple to be true.

'It's a bit of a faff,' Julie said. 'He wouldn't always have the time. Anyway...' she looked at Jacquie, asking for help.

'Julie hasn't told anyone about this,' she said, giving Maxwell what he had learnt to consider The Look. 'She hasn't even told her friends. The texts are not very friendly, Max. In fact, they are really very disturbing.'

'Can we see one?'

'I delete them straight away,' the girl said. 'I just don't want to have them on my phone. It's spoilt everything, you know,' she burst out. 'I used to love it when I got a message.' She looked at Jacquie. 'I had a little bird tweeting for when I got a text. It made me really happy, somebody wanted to say something to me, even if it was just "Hi". But now, I just dread it. I don't have my little bird any more. Just a beep.'

Maxwell reached across the table. Political correctness be blowed, he just wanted to hold her hand. He racked his Head of Sixth Form brain to try and recall her family situation. Stepdad, obviously, she had just told them that. But, who else was part of her family? Slowly, the details emerged. Stepfather, quite high-powered at Leighford General and very driven. Had clearly had a radical humourectomy at an early stage. Mother, blonde, socially mobile from the Barlichway estate to a detached executive home and looking for more. She used her one brain cell for that sole purpose. One sister, older and at university. Two half-brothers, twins and as precocious and unpleasant a pair of seven-year-olds as Maxwell had met in his many long days marching. They had come to the Christmas concert and had almost single-handedly – perhaps 'double-handedly' was more appropriate – led one of Santa's little helpers the rest of the way to the nervous breakdown begun by her being Head of Social and Religious Studies. They reminded him of the Boys from Brazil. But he didn't say any of this.

'Julie, I know you find it difficult, but your friends love you and so do your family. You must let them know what's happening.'

The girl snorted. 'Friends! Well, they wouldn't care. And as for family – I don't think they'd notice if I just disappeared. Puff of smoke. The first thing they'd know would be when they needed someone to collect Neeheeoeewootis and Vaiveahtoish from skating or riding or swimming or any of the other million things the little dears do.' Bitterness dripped from her as she spoke.

Jacquie laughed. 'Great nicknames. What are

43

their real names?' As she spoke she caught Maxwell's expression and tried to claw back her question. 'I mean, ah ha, we called Nolan Nolan, but we call him Nole and...'

'Don't worry, Mrs Maxwell,' Julie said. 'It's a common mistake. They *are* their real names. They are Native American and Neeheeoeewootis means "high-backed wolf" and Vaiveahtoish means "alights on a cloud". Don't ask me what they were thinking when they chose those names. Everyone calls them Nee and Vee now. Except me. I don't see why they should be let off the hook.'

'Don't your friends call you Zee?' Maxwell asked mildly.

She rounded on him. 'Yes, they do,' she snapped. 'But that's my *friends* do that, not my family. They call me Julie. Or, my mum calls me Jules, because that's what Jamie Oliver calls his wife and they went to his restaurant for an anniversary and so she likes to think they're mates. Oh,' she buried her head in her arms and her voice came out muffled, 'I hate my family.' She sniffed and raised her head. Jacquie and Maxwell could almost see her physically pull herself together. 'I'm sorry to be such a nuisance.' She reached round behind her for her coat on the back of the chair. 'It's nothing, just a bit upset about stuff. I'll go home now.'

Jacquie put a hand on her shoulder, half Woman Policeman, half mother, all Jacquie. 'You most certainly will not. You got a text just then. I can't let you go without seeing it. I'm sorry.'

The girl clasped her hands tightly round her

phone. 'No!' she cried. 'You can't.'

Maxwell leant forward. 'Julie, Mrs Maxwell is a police person, as I'm sure you know. If she lets you go without looking at the text, she could be in a lot of trouble down at the station.' It had started out as an impression of George Dixon, but he remembered the girl's age and swapped, in mid-sentence, to Gene Hunt.

Julie looked from one to the other, checking.

'He's right, Julie,' Jacquie said. And then, because she preferred the truth, 'And anyway, I want to help you. Let me see. I won't show Mr Maxwell if you don't want me to. I promise.'

Reluctantly, the girl opened her hand and Jacquie took the phone. It was quite a new model, rather more sophisticated than many, but simpler than some. Jacquie clicked a key and the screen sprang to life. She touched the jog wheel and the text appeared.

'Hi Z. Bin an wile. RU doing wot I sed? Wdnt like 2 think UR still wearing panties. I no wt U do. I'm watching U.'

Jacquie looked at Julie and then tilted the phone towards her. Gently, she said, 'It's not that bad, is it? Might it be one of your friends, messing about?'

The girl read it. 'That's one of the mild ones. He's been on and on about ... well, what it says. The other things are worse. And he says he's watching me. I'm so scared.'

'Of course you are,' Maxwell said. 'But how can he watch you all the time?'

'He can,' she whispered. 'He knows where I've been, who I speak to, everything.'

45

Jacquie raised an eyebrow at Maxwell and he nodded. 'Look, Julie, Mrs Maxwell will go outside and have a look. She is trained in this, she will know if there is anyone watching. Trust me.' He tapped her hand and she looked up. 'Trust us, Julie. It's all right.'

Jacquie got up and left the room, then they heard her feet on the stairs. She went through the lobby and out of the back door.

'Cheer up, Julie. Mrs Maxwell is really good at her job. I'll tell you what, let's go and see if Nolan is stirring. He'll be up for a game if he is.'

'I've seen your little boy,' Julie said, without much enthusiasm.

'He's not like your two little mon– brothers,' Maxwell said. 'Not at all. Come and meet him,' and he ushered her into the sitting room, where Nolan was just stirring, unlike Metternich, who was asleep on his back with his legs in the air, one eye disconcertingly half open.

Nolan woke up as he did everything, with calm good humour. The crying started when he forgot his little adventure and rubbed his chin with the back of a podgy fist.

'Whoops,' Maxwell said, scooping him up. 'OK, mate, let's be like brave soldiers, now. Look, Julie has come to see you.'

''Lo, Julie,' the boy muttered, wiping his eyes and nose lavishly on Maxwell's shoulder. 'Are you a babysitter?'

'No,' said Julie, smiling in spite of herself. 'I've just come to visit your mummy and daddy.'

Nolan's eyes clouded. 'Where is Mama?' he asked.

46

'Don't worry, Nole. She's out running an errand for Julie. She'll be back in a minute. Do you fancy a game of any sort?'

Nolan wriggled down out of his arms and made for the TV 'Mario Kart?' he said, pulling out the Wii from the drawer in the TV table.

Maxwell made a face. 'Oh, come on, Nole. You know I'm hopeless at that sort of thing. I had in mind three-dimensional chess, something like that.'

But Nolan knew an opportunity when it presented itself and he held up the handset to Julie in mute query.

She had plumped herself down beside him in seconds and they were off, leaning round the corners, accelerating into the bends, skittering off the obstacles before Maxwell could plug in his Atari II ping-pong console.

'Right,' he announced. 'I'll just sit over here then, shall I?'

'Uh huh, Dads,' said Nolan absently. 'I'm a bit thirsty, could I have a drink?'

'Of course,' said Maxwell the butler. 'Anything else? Crisps? Caviar? Roast suckling pig?'

The boy chuckled and risked a quick glance over his shoulder. 'Crippies, please, Dads. And some for Julie, please.'

'Your wish is my command, oh master,' and Maxwell, transformed from Jeeves to the Genie of the Lamp, went off in search of food and drink. He found Jacquie in the kitchen, the phone cradled in the crook of her neck. She put her finger to her lips. The tinny sound of an answerphone could just be heard through her

47

head. She seemed about to leave a message, then decided against it and replaced the receiver.

The Genie wafted out with the refreshments but was back in the twinkling of an eye. 'Well?'

'I was trying to reach Henry.'

The image flashed into Maxwell's mind. Henry Hall was Jacquie's boss, the DCI up at the nick, the *capo di capi*, all blank glasses and solemn, immobile face.

'I guessed that much. Why?'

'Well, to see if we've had any complaints from parents about the Internet, or texts, that sort of thing. I've been busy with this burglary case and I haven't really had time to keep my ear to the ground. I just wondered if Henry knew anything.'

'I gather he wasn't there.'

'Well, not picking up the phone, anyway.' They stared at each other with wide eyes for a second. She immediately corrected herself. 'That's right. Not there.' Neither of them could countenance for a moment the idea of Henry Hall sitting calmly and letting the phone ring and ring.

'So, what are your thoughts on who this is, without Henry's input?' Maxwell said, casting a glance over his shoulder.

Jacquie drew a big breath and let it out slowly. 'Obviously, my first thought was kids being nasty.'

Maxwell put in an understanding nod. In his experience, *all* kids were nasty. 'But, on the whole, I don't think so. I think the text was a bit adult in its content, the whole panties thing rather smacks of a flasher in a mac, or perhaps I am being ageist. And sexist too, I suppose.'

'And weatherist?'

She gave him a flick with a tea towel. 'That too. Also, the text-speak was rather half-hearted. A text from a youngster really is like a foreign language. There isn't a single whole word in the thing. This was rather stilted, not followed through.'

'It's a shame we don't have it.'

'We do.'

'Well, yes, heartsease, I am not denigrating your memory...'

She waved her mobile at him. 'I forwarded it to myself.'

'I didn't see you do that.'

'Ah, the quickness of the Woman Policeman deceives the Head of Sixth Form,' she said. 'I went on the suofam course.'

'Suofam?'

'Sneaky use of a mobile,' she smiled. 'Anyway, I'll try to get a meeting with Henry and a few of the IT mob tomorrow. I'm assuming Nolan is awake?'

Screams of hilarity filtered through from the sitting room.

'Correct.'

'And playing with Julie?'

'Again, right on the button.'

'What are we going to do with her?'

'Well, help her sort herself out, if we can. It would be nice if we could show her rather horrible family that she is worth more than being an unpaid babysitter to the Midwich Cuckoos.'

'I mean now. This evening.'

'Oh, I see. Well, what if we invite her to do a bit of proper babysitting, with a proper boy. You can get her away from her phone perhaps and then you

49

can watch for texts. Is it possible to trace a sender?'

'I'll have to ask the IT guys. I suspect more than one phone is being used, though.'

'More than one person sending these things. Might that explain why they are sometimes worse than others?'

'No, just more than one phone. You can buy a pay-as-you-go in any supermarket for around twenty pounds. It's a stalker's charter. And while we're on the subject of phones,' she pointed at hers, sitting on the table, 'pick that up and join me in the study. Lesson One is about to begin.'

'Awww, miss,' Maxwell whined. 'I've got a stomach ache. I've got a bone in my leg. It's my granny's funeral. The dog ate my homework. Anyway,' his expression became one of low cunning, 'you know that my phone is at school.'

She pointed at the door. 'If you haven't brought a note from home, you can't skip this lesson. And no, before you ask, I am not going to write you a note! Now, scram,' and they made for the stairs, not forgetting to look in to check on their injured son on the way. He was bouncing up and down on the spot with his legs crossed, in a way that can only be done by contortionists and those under six. He was winning – whether by skill or Julie's good offices – they couldn't tell.

'We're upstairs in the study, Nole,' Jacquie announced.

'Laters,' he said, waving his fingers at her.

'Right, then.' She went up to the study, laughing. 'How old is he?' she asked his father.

'Twenty. Three. Forty-two. Who knows? He's a human being, and that's the important thing.'

'Every child is a human being, Max,' she said.

'My dear, dear girl,' he said, pushing open the door of the study. 'How sweet of you to think so. And how incredibly wrong. Now, no more shilly-shallying, you. Just get that walkie-talkie out and tell me how it works. What does this button do, for example?'

'That switches it on and off, Max. And let's be honest, you don't have any trouble switching it off, do you? Just sit down there and don't let me hear another peep or there'll be trouble.'

'Have you ever considered teaching, at all?' he asked, head on one side and a winning expression on his face.

'No,' she sighed, sitting down beside him. 'I've seen what it can do.'

And so, little by little, with much sighing and sobbing, mostly from Jacquie, Peter Maxwell learnt all he would ever know about mobile phones. Which was about half of what most people knew, but at least three times more than he knew before. He could already send a text, but after these lessons it would now usually get to the right destination. When he rang someone, the chances now were that they would get the call, rather than someone rather puzzled in Turkey. He had the phone set to vibrate so he would never miss a call. He had privately designated the very desk drawer where it could vibrate itself to death and no one would ever know. He had agreed to check messages and voicemail in every break and before he set off home. He had worded the promise very carefully, and at no time had he undertaken to have it with him.

'Right then, sweetheart,' Jacquie said, leaning over and kissing him on the nose. 'I think we're all set.'

He smiled sweetly up at her. 'You betchya,' he agreed.

'Oh, and by the way,' she added.

'Yes, oh queen of my heart,' he smiled.

'Having the phone with you is understood – just because you didn't positively say you'd have it doesn't mean you can leave it behind.'

'Well, really!' He looked outraged. 'As if I would do such a thing!'

'Yes, well, just so you know that *I* know,' she said. 'Tell you what, just to check your skills. The Chinese restaurant takes orders by text. Go and ask Julie what she'd like and we'll have a take-away as a treat.'

'I'll phone it in,' he beamed.

'Text it in.'

'Phone.'

'Text.'

'Do you *want* five portions of special fried and a side order of duck's feet, hold the guano?'

He had a point. 'Phone it is, then. But only because I'm hungry.'

And chuckling quietly to himself, Maxwell headed downstairs to take the order. By the time he reached the sitting room door, he was virtually indistinguishable from Charlie Chan himself.

The house was still faintly redolent of Hung Woo's Special Dinner for Three as Maxwell and Jacquie got ready for bed. Julie had eventually been prised from Nolan, who had welcomed a playmate so accommodating with open arms, and had been driven home by Jacquie. Nolan had been put to bed, with another dose of paediatric painkiller hidden in his bedtime milk. His chin had taken on a rather attractive shade of lilac, shot with navy blue, and by morning would be twice its normal size; he'd look more desperate than Dan. Metternich had mooched off in search of amusement. No one really wanted to know the details, but it probably involved rodents.

'Well, tiddles,' Maxwell said, snuggling up to Jacquie in the lavender-scented dark. 'What do you think?'

'About what?' she asked. 'Surely, you can't want my opinions on the aberrant apostrophe again?'

'My good woman,' he said, 'your opinion on that is surely in no doubt. Should there *be* doubt in your mind, I suggest that the place to think it over is the spare room.'

She poked him in the side, with her specially trained Woman Policeman's forefinger.

'Ouch. No, I mean about all this texting lark. What is going on?'

'Hmm.' He heard her scratch her head in the darkness. 'I don't know, to be honest. My first thought was that it was kids, as you know, ganging up. Then, when I saw it, I thought it was an adult, but who, and how did they get the number? Now, I'm thinking... I'm not sure. But Julie did tell me something on the drive home which I am going to share with you on the very strictest understanding that you won't tell a soul. OK?'

There was no reply. Surely, he hadn't dropped off?

'Max? OK?'

'Yes. Of course.'

'Well, answer, then.'

'I was nodding.'

'In the dark?'

'I thought you would be able to tell. That your extraordinary hearing would be able to discern the slide of my golden tresses on the pillow. But I understand now that you can't, so, yes, I promise not to tell a soul.'

'Good, because Julie was most insistent.'

'Fire away.'

'Well,' Jacquie snuggled closer and tucked her head just under Maxwell's ear. He obediently bent his legs to make a chair and she sat in her favourite place, knees bent, ankles crossed, hands clasped at her waist. 'Apparently, Julie is not the only one getting these.'

'Really?' He pulled his head away as if to look at her. Although the thick curtains made the dark as deep as a well, he could see her face as clearly as if she was on stage, lit by limelight. Her presence, there in his arms, in his bed, was so intense he almost felt that he could smell her face changing as she smiled, frowned, cried.

She pulled his head back into position and made herself comfortable. 'Yes. Someone called Lee.'

'A boy?'

'Oh, that's a thought. I didn't get that impression. Is there a girl called Lee?'

'No, not in the Sixth Form at any rate. But these days, with that great blurring of names that has accompanied political correctness, gender neutralisation and global warming, who knows?'

'Lower down the school? Perhaps a neighbour she travels with.'

'No, no. Julie has gone up in the world. She gets brought to school by her mother, driving a huge behemoth fit to climb Everest. Not so much a four-by-four as a forty-by-forty. No, no, let me think.'

She almost dozed off there in the warm bed as he put his cogs to work.

'I've got it!' He leapt as he said it and nearly catapulted her onto the floor. 'Oh, soz, heart. Did I make you jump?' She was lying on her side of the bed, the cold side of the bed, making little whimpering noises and clutching her chest histrionically. 'Leah. That must be who she means.'

'Leah? Yes, she may have said that. But I was accelerating over traffic lights and I may have misheard.'

'Bit of amber gambling, dearest?' Maxwell was only half scolding. He was a nervous-driver husband and she was a bit of a chancer.

'Oh, possibly. But, yes, Leah. That sounds right. She has a bit of a feckless mother, rich dad, new stepmother.'

'That's the one. As Julie has gone up, so Leah has come down in the world. I understand from Sylv that she looks after a young sister much of the time. Her grades are slipping.'

'Well, it might not be because of the baby minding. Julie says Leah gets far more texts than she does and they are much nastier.'

'Poor kid. She tries her best to look as though she's coping, but her mother is really the child in the relationship. The father, I think I'm right in saying, is in business somewhere along the coast and was a bit of a ladies' man. Probably still is, but at the moment is managing to hide that behind a new wife. Possibly a baby as well, I can't quite remember.'

'Can't remember, Max?' Jacquie was genuinely surprised. That wasn't something he often said.

'Well,' he expelled his breath in a sigh, 'there are so many in this situation now. When I was first Head of Sixth Form...'

'...when Adam was in the Militia...'

'I only had a few single-parent families.' He completed the sentence. 'In fact, we had so few, I don't think we even had a phrase for it. But now it seems they outnumber the other sort of family.'

'Our sort of family,' Jacquie chimed in. He gave her a squeeze.

'I hate the stereotyping of so-called "broken" homes. Some are better off broken, when you meet some of the parents who have snapped off, so to speak. But there are some, Julie's, Leah's, which don't seem so bad when you look in from the outside. Plenty of money. New mobiles, new shoes. Cars as soon as they are old enough and often before. But no love, from anywhere. They often end up being quite desperate and that's why you see these beautiful girls walking along with tattooed louts with only one brain cell.'

'Bit sexist, Max,' Jacquie protested.

'Count them next time you're out and about,' he said. 'Look into their eyes and see what's in there.'

'What will I see?' she said quietly.

'Nothing, that's what. Their mouths are smiling, with their perfect teeth, but their eyes are empty. Poor little girls.'

'They wouldn't want to be called little girls, I don't think,' said Jacquie. 'They like to think of themselves as women. That's why we have to patrol the city centre every night, to pick women up off the pavement where they are lying passed out from bingeing.'

'What little right-wingers we sound, here in the dark,' muttered Maxwell.

Jacquie patted him absently on the arm. 'No, not really,' she said. 'Long as I've known you, I still don't know your politics, do you know that?'

'And nor will you, madam.' He was suitably outraged. 'Since William Gladstone brought in the secret ballot in 1872, no one has known my politics. Of course, I had only been voting for a while at the time. It was such a pain putting your arm in the air every seven years, but the free beer was good.'

She chuckled and turned over on her side, pummelling the pillow into a comfortable shape underneath her head. He turned to kiss her goodnight and inhaled a strand of hair. By the time the coughing had more or less subsided, she was asleep and the subject of the lost girls was shelved for the day. But they were on his mind as he closed his eyes and his dreams were of looking for something lost, in a place he didn't know.

Chapter Four

The seamlessly organised morning chez Maxwell was not taking its usual course. For one thing, Nolan's chin had indeed swollen overnight and now taking off his pyjamas had become a major issue, involving cajoling, threats and, ultimately, scissors. He was inordinately proud of his stitches, sprouting like a witch's whiskers from his lilac chin, and the offer of a day off school – usually a popular choice – was instantly rejected. So, late and more than a little testy, Jacquie had driven off with her wounded soldier in the child seat in the back of her newly acquired Doblò, chosen for two reasons, both Maxwellian – his bike would fit in the back without having to strap Nolan on the roof, and it reminded him of his first train set. He inevitably referred to it as the Hornby, to the confusion of all.

Maxwell and Metternich still had time for a quiet cup of something when the pair had driven away. 'Well, Count,' Maxwell remarked. 'Once more unto the breach. Now, where did I leave that mobile phone?' Metternich obligingly lifted his head and looked around in a desultory fashion. This was a trick learnt by accident in kittenhood and even now was still good for an extra pouch of something in gravy. 'Thank you for looking, Count. But in fact I know it is in my office. I'm just getting used to asking. Something in gravy?' Maxwell got up and reached for the cat food cupboard, an interrogative eyebrow raised. What a sap this man was. The cat extended both arms in an extravagant stretch and walked over to his bowl, the general impression being that he would indeed do Maxwell the honour of eating his kindly offered food. It was usually a messy job, but somebody had to do it.

Maxwell raised his voice for his next conversational sally, to be heard over the noise of one pouch of unidentified abattoir sweepings disappearing into a cat. 'What do you know of mobile phones, Count?' The cat stopped gulping for a microsecond, but this was long enough to express his contempt that Maxwell could even ask the question. 'Yes, exactly,' Maxwell agreed. 'Me too. But I think that I know enough in this instance. Julie and Leah must have given their numbers to someone, because this isn't like an old-fashioned heavy-breathing call. In the good old days, if anyone wanted to ask a random housewife what colour her underwear was, he would dial numbers at random and if he struck lucky that was a bonus. The more organised of them would write the number down first, so that if he *did* strike lucky, he could always try that one again. Are you with me so far?'

Metternich gave the bowl one last, lingering lick and looked up. The old geezer had paused and had that hopeful expression on his face again. Better humour him. He jumped, a blur of white and black, onto Jacquie's only recently vacated chair and licked one paw, he hoped intelligently. Perversions of the past weren't really his thing, but he could blag it along with the rest of the feline community.

'Good,' Maxwell said. 'I thought I'd lost you for a minute there. Well, the old-fashioned heavy breather knew he had struck lucky, of course, because he had a reply from the other end. A little horrified scream, an answer, whatever he wanted. But someone *texting* gets no reaction. They just send the text and that's it. Nothing.' He looked the cat in the eye. 'I know what you're thinking. When I send a text and get nothing it is often because I haven't sent it at all. But that's not what I mean. I happen to know,' he said proudly, 'that you get a little message on your phone saying "message sent" but you don't know if the person to whom you have sent it has received it. So, why would you send it in the first place? But even if there was a reason, why would you send more? They might be going to a docker in Glasgow, an all-in wrestler in Ynysybwl or a bouncer in Scunthorpe. You wouldn't know it had gone to a rather sad girl in Leighford, would you?'

For some reason, Metternich did not reply to that one and Maxwell had to concede that he probably was not very up on mobile phones, even for a cat.

'You wouldn't, anyway. Take it from me. So, what we've got to find out is, how has the sender – let's call him a "he", shall we, because I just can't picture it being a girl somehow – got their numbers? And to do this I will have somehow to think of a question I can ask Julie and Leah without letting Leah know that I know that she has had these texts.' There was a pause. 'Don't just look at me, Count. Do you have an answer – yes or no?'

Metternich flicked an ear and, jumping from the chair, was down the stairs and out of the cat flap before you could say 'vole'.

'I'll take that as a no, then.' Maxwell yawned, stretched and, rather more slowly than the cat and, this time, not using the cat flap, made his way into the big wide world and beyond. Spring-time in Leighford. What could be nicer? How long have you got?

The morning light, filtered through the blackthorn blossom and unfurling leaves of the woodland, stroked the man's cheek with its pollen-sparkled fingers. The catkins shook and trembled above him, but in the wind, not because of any disturb-ance he made. His chest was still, the one half-open eye did not flicker as the sun struck the pearly cornea. His lips were parted over his teeth, as if a smile had been frozen in the making. A beetle walked over his lip and investigated the edge of his nostril. An early fly, drowsy in the still chilly spring morning, walked round the spiral of the ear and, without a moment's hesitation, disappeared inside. Either this man was a very determined naturalist, or he was dead.

Jacquie made her way to her office through a thicket of concerned women. As she had barrelled out of the station the afternoon before, the tales had grown and spread and so by the morning it was common knowledge that Nolan had been squashed by a runaway steamroller whilst being

61

mauled by a rabid Komodo dragon, despite both fates being rather unusual in Leighford.

Her desk was in an even worse state than she had feared. A report that she had been annotating was in the middle, with the pen still in place where she had been underlining a witness's non sequitur which might be vital. A coffee cup with a greasy slick on top of its grey contents stood in the dried spill caused when she had leapt to her feet, flinging on her coat and grabbing her bag. Someone had pushed the chair under, but that was all. Otherwise it was a testament to her flight. She sat down, picked up the pen and tried to gather her thoughts again. She had only just got back to understanding the gist when Henry Hall's head popped round the door.

'Jacquie? Have you got just a minute?'

'Yes, guv.' She put down her pen again. One day, if she was lucky, she would finish that report and also, with luck, it might get to the court before the subject had completed his tariff.

Henry Hall was already behind his desk when she went in, closing the door behind her. In a cruel light, the DCI was beginning to look his age these days. An old fart like Maxwell could see something of the old copper in Henry Hall, with a whiff of Hilaire Belloc's lion – 'his shoulders are stark, and his jaws they are grim, And a good little child will not play with him'. All very apt.

'Are you in the middle of something?' Hall asked as soon as she had sat down.

'Well, I'm trying to do a report on that robbery last week. He's got a sheet as long as your arm and he was caught with all the stuff in his lock-up, but he also has a damned good brief and we want to be sure of getting him this time.'

'Who is it?' Hall was not known for his expressive voice or, come to that, his expression, but Jacquie was trained in the small nuances and knew that this was just a courtesy question.

'Oh, whatsisface, Enfield. No bother, guv. Anyone can do it.'

'Fine. Because I want you to concentrate on something else now, Jacquie. And, look, this is a bit awkward, really, but I have to ask. HR are wondering whether Nolan has ... well, anything wrong with him?'

Jacquie flew straight up out of her chair; had she had feathers, they would have been filling the room. '*What?*'

Hall held out his hands in supplication. 'Please, Jacquie, don't shoot the messenger. It's just that you've had a lot of odd half days and things lately – yesterday, for example.'

'I'm sorry, guv, about yesterday, but he fell over and had to have stitches. I tried to get Max onto it – Sylv would have helped out, but ... well...' her voice trailed away, 'I couldn't reach him, and Nole needed to go to A&E.'

'I do understand, Jacquie,' Hall said. He wasn't exactly a hands-on dad, Heaven knew – his boys could testify to that – but Maxwell seemed to dodge the column rather more than he would have expected. 'But Max has short days and–'

'Yes, I know, long holidays. Yes, yes.' Jacquie was beginning to feel quite cornered. 'And he has Nolan all through those holidays, in case anyone hasn't noticed. But his days aren't all that short.

He has meetings. He has detentions.'

Had Henry Hall had the necessary muscles, he would have smirked.

'And before you say anything, he isn't *in* detention himself. And – I can tell you, Henry, for goodness' sake we all go back far enough – he never has his phone on. Well, that's not true, he does sometimes, but it is becoming a bit of an issue, I will admit.'

Hall sat immobile, the strip-lights on his glasses obscuring his eyes, windows to what he probably thought of as his soul.

'So, last night we had a little lesson and now he will be using his phone, carrying it at all times. He will be able to take his turn at any emergency. And, to get back to HR,' Jacquie almost spat, 'no, there is nothing at all wrong with my child, unless being bright is wrong. And a bit on the clumsy side, possibly. Two left feet, bless him.'

Hall breathed a sigh of relief. He knew Jacquie and he knew Maxwell and he knew Nolan. A brighter trio would be hard to find. He also knew that Jacquie could morph into an outraged mother tiger at the drop of a criticism and he despised the lily-livered HR manager for giving him the task of asking if Nolan had a problem. Why not just put his head in a vice and be done?

'Well, that's excellent, then.' He made a note, which Jacquie tried, unsuccessfully, to read upside down. 'How busy are you right now?'

'Just the Enfield thing, ongoing. There is plenty else I could be starting, but they are still in my "to do" pile. I suppose a few more days in there won't hurt them.' She smiled up at him, to show

64

there were no hard feelings. He looked back. Probably, in his head, thought Jacquie, he thinks he is smiling. 'But that's it.' She spread her arms, palms up.

'Well, that's good, because I have a job here which is right up your street. I've got this file here,' he picked it up and let it fall, 'of reports and complaints from concerned parents about mobile phone abuse. Apparently, someone is sending rather nasty texts to a whole lot of girls in Leighford.'

Jacquie's mouth fell open with surprise and it took her a moment to recover her composure. 'Guv, that's amazing,' she finally said.

'Why?' He felt a Maxwell problem raising its ugly head and his stomach plummeted. Why did his favourite sergeant have to be married to his least favourite meddler? In fact, even that wasn't fair. At all other times – at their wedding, at the occasional staff party – he found Maxwell perfectly good company. In fact, at the occasional staff party, he and Maxwell were often to be found glorying in their shared wall-flowerdom. Maxwell's idea that pubs should have two seedy gazebos out back, one for smokers and one for people who hated staff do's, struck an echoing chord with Henry Hall.

'Well,' she hesitated. 'Oh dear, Henry. This is so difficult. It means betraying a confidence.'

'What, a confidence from Max?'

'No, no. Well, I suppose in a way. One of his students came round last evening. She was totally desperate. She has been getting unpleasant texts and she doesn't know who from. From whom, perhaps I should say.' She gave a little chuckle. She wasn't just married to Maxwell. She was turning into him.

Henry Hall knew what she meant. He was pretty sure that Maxwell had inserted a clause into the wedding vows pertaining to the use of correct grammar at all times.

'She didn't swear me to secrecy about her texts. In fact, she seemed quite relieved to get it off her chest. But she did tell me about a friend of hers who is getting even worse stuff and *that's* what she asked me to keep secret.'

'That's not too bad,' he conceded. 'We can perhaps work on the first girl. Did you see the texts?'

'Only the one that came while she was at our house.'

'Just one? In how long?'

'Ooh, let me think. She arrived around about four-thirty, I suppose. She left about eightish.'

'That seems a long time just to tell you about nasty texts.' Henry Hall was pedantic by nature and also nurture. He left no pernickety bit of gravel in a story unturned, even when the teller was one of his staff.

'Well, yes, I suppose it does. But she was very upset and we wanted to calm her down. She started a computer game with Nolan and then we had Chinese. I took her home and got back just as *Panorama* was starting, so I suppose she was with us until about quarter past eight, something like that.'

'So, in nearly four hours, she only got one text?'

'Yes.'

'Was her phone still switched on? She wasn't

trying to hide things from you?'

'I don't think so, guv. Why would she want to? She had come to us about it, after all. And I must admit, the text wasn't all that horrible. It was a bit seedy, you might say. Real heavy breather stuff. Except one thing; he said that he knew what she was doing. That he was watching her. Obviously, that bit was worrying, although thinking it over there was no way in which he could actually do that. But it *has* worried her, naturally. The fact that someone can send you texts from a number you don't know is creepy enough.'

'Did you copy it down?'

'Better. I forwarded it to myself.' She fished in her bag and pulled out her phone, pressed a few keys and passed it over.

'Nice phone,' Hall remarked. 'Fancy.'

Jacquie shrugged. 'It came with the tariff. To be honest, I'd be happy with something simpler.'

Hall raised one eyebrow. 'Max?'

'He'd be happier with a pigeon, or failing that, two baked-bean cans and a nice long string. But he's managing.' She hoped that was true, because she was going to test him later.

Hall finally found the right angle to view the screen, turning it first so the light didn't reflect off it, then to accommodate the extreme edges of his varifocals and then back again to rid it of the reflection. 'Hmm,' he said at last, refocusing on Jacquie with difficulty. 'Text speak isn't my forte, of course, but I would say that this is a bit of a hybrid at best.'

Jacquie just forbore from applauding and crying 'Well done!' Instead, she said, 'Yes, guv. I thought that. Definitely not a kid. Their texts don't have any full words in and I don't think anyone under forty uses the word "panties", do you?'

Hall handed back her phone and thought for a moment. Nothing Henry Hall said was off the cuff. Maxwell often said that if Hall was caught in a towering inferno, he would think many more times than twice before shouting 'Fire!' 'It could be someone trying to fool us,' he said at last.

'But why would anyone do that, guv?' Jacquie said. She and Maxwell had been over this already and she had all the bases covered. 'She's not supposed to tell anyone.'

'That's a valid point. But he might assume she would.'

'I think we're reaching a bit, there, if you don't mind my saying so, guv. I think that this is some kind of game that the sender of these texts is playing, and I don't know what it is, or even who he is playing it with.'

'Sorry,' Hall said. 'I assumed he – or don't forget, it could be a she – is playing it with these girls, if it is a game.'

'I think it is definitely a he, and can we keep to that, so we don't go bonkers?'

He inclined his head. It would certainly make it easier.

'I think he *is* playing with the girls, but I find it strange that he is doing it without any feedback. We all remember the old days, with the anonymous calls. I don't remember any of those where they would just leave a message. What would be the point? No, I think he is playing with *lots* of girls, not just these two. And he knows at least

68

one in his net, so he can get gratuitous feedback. If Julie just got one text in all that time, I'm assuming the other girl she told me about, Leah, probably gets about the same. So I'm tempted to think that the gaps between are filled with him sending merry little messages to other phones.'

'I agree.'

'Just like that?' Jacquie was a little taken aback. 'That's nice, Henry.'

'I'm glad you think so, Jacquie. But in fact, not only is it nice, I agree because I have had rather a lot of reports of similar texts coming in from all over town. Some of the girls have parents who are either much nosier, or perhaps just more hands-on than the families of your two girls.'

'Well, they both come from single-parent families.'

'Well, so do some of my complainants,' Henry said, rather acidly. He was tired of hearing that as an excuse. Only the previous week, in court to give evidence in a rather unpleasant fraud case, he had listened with growing amazement as the accused blamed the whole thing on his broken home. Since the man in this case was sixty-three and his home had been broken only two years before when his ninety-two-year-old father had died and left a widow of ninety to mourn his passing, Henry Hall had found the excuse rather a lame one. So he wasn't really all that sym-pathetic to the broken-home excuse.

'Max and I wondered whether he might be targeting lonely kids from … that kind of family situation.' Jacquie could recognise a sore subject when one bit her on the leg.

Hall looked down at the open file on his desk and flicked over a page or two. 'Let's see.' He kept a count under his breath and after a moment looked up at her. 'Right. Twenty-five complaints.'

'Twenty-five!'

'Yes, and I suspect this is the tip of the iceberg. Of that twenty-five, we have fifteen with two parents, by which I mean the original pair. Another four have two parents, but one is a step. The other...' he quickly checked his maths in his head, 'yes, the other six have one parent, that's five with a mother, one a father.'

Jacquie shrugged her assent. 'Right, so that blows our first theory out of the water.'

'Never mind.' Henry Hall knew how irritating that could be. 'What was your second theory?'

'I don't think we had one, as such.'

Hall pushed himself back from his desk and picked up the folder. He handed it across the desk to Jacquie and, as she took it, she felt it momentarily turn into a poisoned chalice.

'Is anyone else working on this one, guv?' she asked, hopefully.

'Not as such,' he admitted.

'So, I'm on my own?'

'Well, obviously you can have help as and when you need it,' he said magnanimously.

'Lovely,' muttered Jacquie, and turned to the door. 'Who is taking my burglary off me?'

'Look, Jacquie,' Hall said. 'I don't want to over-burden you, but I must admit I have a sneaking suspicion even now that this might be a hoax. Don't rush on this. Do your burglary first.'

'Thanks, guv,' she said. 'Any chance of a quiet

room to work?'

'Of course, of course,' he said, ushering her out. The feeling that the whole thing had gone quite well wouldn't quite come together in his mind. He felt like a bit of a shit, truth be told, and someone would be getting it in the neck, just to pass it on. 'I'll get Matt out of his office. He doesn't need it now he's finished that drug thing. I'll go and tell him now.'

'Oh, thanks.' Jacquie wasn't happy with getting the rough end of the stick, but the rough end of the stick had fewer splinters when you were holding it in the corner office one floor up from the hoi polloi. As she went back to her desk, she heard the door to the stairs swing to behind Henry Hall. Fortunately, she couldn't hear the shouts when Matt was thrown out of his nest; he was calling her a lot of things, but 'cuckoo' wasn't one of them.

Maxwell made his way to his office through a thicket of concerned women. The rumour of the content of Jacquie's calls trying to reach Maxwell had spread schoolwide. It had not reached the dizzy heights of the nick, having stopped short at the steamroller. The reduced severity was offset by the fact that whereas Jacquie worked with about seven women, Maxwell had a total of around five hundred to wade through.

'Sir, sir, is your little boy all right, sir?'

'Is it true you were in hiding, sir, when your wife tried to phone you?' This one from one of the boys, of course.

'Sir, sir...'

Maxwell turned to face the mob. He knew they

71

meant well. He knew that if he had a Kalashnikov right now, Leighford High School would be another victim of falling rolls. 'Ladies and...' he looked around. Just the one boy. Not much of a surprise. 'Gentleman. Nolan is fine. He took a bit of a tumble at school and needed a few stitches. That's all. There will be another press statement on the hour.'

'Aaah,' came as a general comment from the crowd.

'He hasn't hurt his face, has he?' said a mascaraed ghoul midway back in the press. 'He's ever so pretty.'

'No, Holly-Jane,' Maxwell said. 'Thank you for the compliment, though I think he might prefer handsome. He'll just have a scar under his chin.' Two hundred heads tilted back to salute the club. 'Yes, exactly. Just like yours. At the moment he's a bit sore, but he's back at his pre-school, so don't worry. I'll pass on your regards. Now, off you go. You must have *something* you should be doing. Even here.'

Muttering mumsily, the crowd dispersed and Maxwell made his way to the staffroom, that haven of sanity in the middle of Bedlam. While the doors were still swinging behind him, there was an indrawn breath as everyone prepared the same question. He got in fast with the stock answer and, grabbing a coffee from the machine, went to sit next to Sylvia Matthews, a calm centre in an hysterical world. On the walls around him the NUT posters demanded a four-day week, a ten per cent pay rise and a whole squadron of flying pigs. Alongside that a photograph of the

Secretary of State for Education beamed down benignly and someone had written the legend 'Edward Testicles' under it. The Family Trust stats facing the door, which placed Leighford High somewhere other than the bottom of the league tables, continued to give frazzled staff the false impression that their daily toil had *some* purpose.

'Sylv,' Maxwell acknowledged, throwing himself down in the chair.

'Max,' she replied. Since her marriage at Christmas, she had become even more Madonna-like, serene, peaceful to be with. There were some days when Maxwell just wanted to be near her, to soak up some of the atmosphere. The days when she pined for him were long gone, but they had left a cool shadow where he could recharge his batteries. 'Nolan's OK, then?'

'Fine,' he said and gestured vaguely to his chin. 'Few stitches. A bit of swelling.' He fought down the memory of the screaming that morning as Jacquie and he had struggled to part the child from his pyjamas.

'Very common injury,' Sylvia offered. She hadn't been the school nurse for three decades for nothing.

'So I gather,' sighed Maxwell. 'The whole thing got me into a bit of hot water, actually.'

Sylvia paused mid-sip. 'Why? You didn't push him over, did you?' She twinkled at him. 'I thought that you were just AWOL, not lurking in the bushes having done the deed.'

He smiled at her. 'No, no. I just didn't have my phone with me.'

'Of course you didn't.'

He waited for the next comment, but for some reason she seemed to consider the statement complete.

'Oh, sorry,' she said. 'Perhaps you expected me to be surprised.'

'A bit of empathy might be nice.'

'Oh, no, Peter Maxwell. You'll get no empathy, sympathy or any other athy from me. You have a small child and a wife who might be up to her neck in other peoples' entrails at any moment of the day.'

'Sylv, I must just stop you there. You seem to have a glamorised view of police work. This is Leighford, not Fort Apache, the Bronx.'

'Glamorised?'

'Well, perhaps that's not the right word, but I can assure you that Jacquie is rarely up to her neck in entrails. I'm more likely to be in that situation than her.'

'I'm talking literal entrails here, Max, not metaphorical.'

Mavis, the rather shy little woman from the Textiles Department who had been about to join them, backed away. Entrails had never featured in her conversational gambits thus far and she had no wish to add them to her portfolio at this stage in her life. She had just fancied a little chat about her impending retirement, which had been her sole topic of conversation since the decision had been made on the day before they had broken up for Christmas. It had not been made so much as thrust upon her; Diamond had decided in the previous year that, should she be sewn up in Santa's sack and left in the car park

74

one more time, she'd have to go.

'Mavis,' Maxwell nodded in a friendly fashion as she retreated.

'Don't!' hissed Sylvia out of the corner of her mouth. 'Don't encourage her. She'll start talking about retiring. And,' she added, in the nick of time, 'don't say the R word, or she'll come over.' She raised her head and smiled at Mavis, just to convince her that the hiss was not about her.

'Can I spell it, like w-a-l-k-i-e-s for a dog?' asked Maxwell.

'She may only teach Textiles, Max,' said Sylvia, 'but I do believe she can spell.'

'Oh?' Maxwell was surprised but pleased to hear it. 'Anyway, to get back to entrails... I know what you mean. You mean that she can't leave her entrails, however metaphorical, at one bound, whereas I can leave thirty twelve-year-old homicidal maniacs to wreak whatever havoc they wish every time there is an emergency.'

She leant back and looked at him long and hard. Then, 'Got it in one, Max.'

He deflated, beaten. When Sylvia Matthews was not on your side, you didn't have a side. 'I'm not that much help, though, Sylv. I don't drive.'

She smiled at him ruefully and patted his hand. She knew that and she knew why. The battered photos in the Great Man's wallet were a permanent reminder of what it is to drive. And to die. A family one moment. Old photos the next. Unfortunately, Maxwell's hand was holding his hot coffee at the time and after much mopping and soothing, she spoke. 'I know that, Max, and no one is expecting you to start. But if you were

75

only contactable, it would save a lot of time with Jacquie phoning round to find you. I can imagine how it looked yesterday. That particular injury bleeds as though your throat's been cut. She just needed the moral support.'

'I know.' He looked as contrite as he felt. 'I'll try, Sylv. Old habits, you know.'

'I know,' she said. 'But give it a try, eh?'

'All right. I'll do my best.'

'Where is the phone now?'

'Mrs B answered it last night so I am assuming it is in my office somewhere.'

'Mrs B answered your phone? It's a smart-phone, isn't it?'

Maxwell made a noise which was difficult to quantify. It somehow encompassed amazement, confusion and mild distress.

Sylvia made it easier for him. 'Is it one of those phones with a little keyboard?' she asked in the tones she usually kept for her grandmother, ninety-seven, still going strong but without a functioning synapse to her name.

'Yes,' he smiled happily. 'It has got a little key-board. Yes, it has. And I have to say – perhaps I should say that *even* I have to say – that it makes the occasional text I send much easier. None of that silly tapping at one key all the time.' He had never really understood why the people who invented the earlier type assumed it was all right to reduce twenty-six letters of the English alpha-bet to eight buttons.

'Well, there now!' Sylvia could not have been happier had his ears sprouted multi-coloured bal-loons to the strains of *Cavatina*. 'That's excellent!

76

But I am surprised that Mrs B tackled one of those.'

'You can't miss the ring,' Maxwell said. 'It's *The Bum of the Flightlebee.*'

Mavis from Textiles bridled as she walked behind his chair. They were talking about bums now. Thank *goodness* she was retiring soon.

'Very lovely,' Sylvia patronised. 'But I meant she might not know how to answer one of those.'

Maxwell tutted. 'Don't get me started on Mrs B and technology. She seems to be morphing into Bill Gates. It gave me quite a turn.' He was interrupted by the bell, yammering away in the corner of the room. He slurped his remaining coffee. 'Ah, *la* damn bell *sans merci*,' he said; it was a mantra for him. 'Oh well, time to face Ten Oh Zed Pea. Or is that Oh Zee Pea, if my television watching is any guide.'

'Don't despair, Max,' Sylvia chuckled. 'American pronunciation will never invade your little corner of England.'

He shook his head sadly. 'It will, Sylv, but I'm going down fighting.' He made for the door and ended up holding it open for Mavis. The last thing Sylvia heard was his merry, 'Mavis, dear thing, I understand you are leaving us...'

The door swung closed and she heard no more. But she thought to herself as she watched through the glass door as his barbed wire head disappeared down the corridor, bent in fascination to Mavis's Seventies perm, that greater love hath no man.

Chapter Five

Briefly dropping into his office before the delights of Year Ten, Maxwell found his phone where he had left it, in the drawer. His detective's nose smelt polish and old cigarettes and so he knew that Mrs B had indeed been the answerer of Jacquie's call. Trying to remember his masterclass of the previous evening, he tentatively probed a few buttons and found that his wife had not lied; the phone was indeed easy to use, and so he set it to silent and put it back in the drawer. As an aide-memoire he wrote a Post-it note to himself and stuck it on the top of his desk. He left the room, a bewildered Al Pacino as Serpico looking at him in disbelief from his poster on the wall.

Seconds later, he was back. Perhaps 'Phone in top right-hand drawer' was a little obvious. So, instead, he wrote 'custard, rhs'. He was pretty sure this would not alert anyone to the presence of what he understood was called a blackberry in his desk. On another wall, The Duke in *The Shootist* was already cocking his forty-five.

A few strides along the corridor and he was with Ten Oh Zed Pea.

'Damian.' The Head of Sixth Form collared the smallest boy in the class, a pasty-faced weasel who would have looked more at home in Year Five. 'Stand out here, could you, dear boy?'

Damian pointed silently to himself.

'Yes, Damian. You. That's right. First one foot, then the other. Good. Good.'

The hapless lad had reached the front. Anything could happen now and Ten Oh Zed Pea were more than up for it; they had just had two hours of General Science.

'Now, Damian,' Maxwell broke every rule in the Modern Teachers' Handbook by placing his hand lightly on the boy's shoulder in order to position him, metaphorically, somewhere in central Europe. 'You are Serbia. All right?'

Damian didn't have a clue, but if Mr Maxwell said so, it must be all right.

'Jake.'

A lumbering lout with pecs like body armour clambered to his feet.

'Here, dear boy, front and centre.'

Jake complied and even let Maxwell place him alongside Damian.

'Right, you two. Face each other.'

They did, Damian frowning into Jake's chest, Jake looking into the middle distance over Damian's head. There were giggles all round.

'I was going to ask,' Maxwell said, 'what differences you notice here, boys and girls, but I see you are way ahead of me. Damian,' he turned to the lad. 'You have upset Jake here. You are Serbia, remember, and you're possibly responsible for the murder of Jake's archduke, Franz Ferdinand. Jake – who as you have all worked out by now, I'm sure, is Austria – of course is much bigger than you. He's upset. You're going to get it. What do you do?'

'Run!' half the class shouted, hoping to see

79

blood on the mat.

'There's only one way to settle it.' Maxwell, to the delight of the class, had turned into Harry Hill, climbing on his desk. 'Fight!'

The rest of Ten Oh Zed Pea joined in with a will, but Maxwell's hand was already in the air for quiet.

'Or...' he beckoned Luke forward. The boy was in fact bigger than Jake, but probably slower on the turns. He stood him next to Damian. 'Now you've got a mate,' he said. 'Serbia, say hello to Mother Russia.'

'Mother?' Luke was going through his most macho phase.

'Figure of speech, dear boy,' Maxwell calmed him. 'Figure of speech. Father, if you prefer.'

'He'll never be a father!' a class wag piped up.

'Quite,' Maxwell smiled. 'Mother it is, then. Now, Jake,' the Great Man turned to Austria. 'Not so easy now, is it? What do you do?'

'Er ... I get a mate too,' the boy said.

'You'll never have a mate.' The wag was on good, if repetitive form today.

'Excellent, Jake. You've got realpolitik written all over you. Who do you want?'

'Er ... Jimbo.'

'Jimbo!' Maxwell echoed. 'Excellent choice.' He waited until the lad was in position alongside Jake. 'Germany stands with Austria. How do you feel now, Damian?'

The little lad looked at Luke alongside him. He looked at the two opposite. All in all, he didn't like the odds. Are there any more mates allowed?' he asked.

'There are indeed,' Maxwell smiled. 'Who would you like to be France?'

'Um ... Tommy.'

Poilou would have been better, but that would have gone over the class's heads and anyway, there wasn't a *poilou* in Ten Oh Zed Pea.

As Tommy made his way to what was rapidly becoming the Front, a girl's voice piped up. 'Why are they all boys, sir?'

Maxwell beamed broadly. 'Sophie, light of my life; well spotted. What we are doing here, dearly beloved, is to build up the two armed camps in Europe in 1914. This was a man's business – killing usually is. But don't worry, Sophie. We'll be looking at Edith Cavell – she was a brave nurse, and a woman by the way, shot by Jimbo here. And Mata Hari, she was a spy. Now, just a few more volunteers and we're ready to play World War One. Nobody wants to be Belgium, I suppose?'

Nicole Thompson was still mulling over the events of the day before. School systems were not the most sophisticated in the world, she had often had to accept. But, so far, she had never felt the need to increase security in any way. But the email she had received along with her department yesterday was so clearly not from Peter Maxwell that she felt sure she had a hacker in the school. The problem was ... who? She couldn't think of a single staff member who had both the skill and the residual humour to do it. There were quite a few kids who could do it, but she knew who they were, and if they went a-hacking, the directgov or inlandrevenue sites were where they liked to make merry. Many was the heart-stopping tax demand that they had engendered. Sending an only slightly amusing email purporting to come from Maxwell was beneath their contempt. She didn't go along with Mike's theory that Maxwell had had a sudden overload. Ned was right. When Maxwell was waiting for the last trump and Peter was twirling his keys in his face, he would be insisting on correct grammar and spelling. So, she tapped her teeth with the key to the mainframe cupboard; who was it? Who *was* it?

She pushed herself off from her desk and shot across the room, to the not very well stifled chuckles of Mike and Ned. The mind of a computer geek is a simple one and prat-fall jokes were still their favourite.

She stifled them with a look. 'Put the WD-40 can on my desk by the time I get back and if any of it gets into the office again, there will be trouble. I mean *serious* trouble. I mean,' and she rested on her knuckles on Ned's desk, 'permanent staff record trouble.'

The two managed to look crestfallen while she was in the room. As soon as she had left they both shrugged. How much trouble could a computer-stored record be? Bless James Diamond and his paperless office. With a casual high five they both bent to their tasks: reading *What Computer?* in the case of Ned, listing old county laptops on eBay in the case of Mike. Another day, another dollar.

Nicole strode along Maxwell's corridor. She was pretty sure that that was where the answer lay. She knocked on his door but there was no reply. Listening carefully, she could hear his voice along the corridor in the hell-hole that was the History Department and so now she had a dilemma: should she go away and come back later, or should she go in and say nothing? Obviously, the right thing to do would be to go away and come back later but, oddly, her hand was on the handle and she was on the threshold of the room.

To her surprise, his laptop was not in evidence. So there went one plan of action; to open it up and check when he had last sent an email from it. She went round behind the desk, expecting to find it stashed under there. But no, nothing. Perhaps, against all the odds, Peter Maxwell was actually intending to register classes electronically! Then, she saw the Post-it on his desk: 'custard, rhs'. Surely he didn't keep custard in what she correctly guessed was his right-hand desk drawer? Looking round furtively, she slid it open. No ... no custard, just a rather spiffy mobile phone. Probably one he had confiscated from a kid. She couldn't really picture Peter Maxwell with a Blackberry. But the custard note was a bit worrying. What if he *was* losing it? What if the email had actually come from him? Nicole wasn't a malicious woman, but she was a woman on the make. There were many opportunities within the school for advancement, if you knew what moves to make. County directives were always chopping and changing and she had seen a preview of the latest bulletin from on high.

Human Resources were leaving the ivory tower of County Hall and were coming to a school near you. £35k a year – she almost rubbed her hands together in glee but stopped herself in the nick of time – in the warm, no heavy lifting. No spending hours trying to get these antiquated dinosaurs of computers to work for just one more day. She sighed happily and shut the drawer. Yes, a little visit to James Diamond's office, a casual mention of Peter Maxwell's odd behaviour and bingo! She would be down there in Diamond's brain as a caring colleague and a definite definite – Nicole didn't do maybe – for the new job. She almost skipped out of Maxwell's office and down the corridor, pausing only briefly to listen outside his classroom. The kids were actually *singing*.

'We're 'ere because, We're 'ere because, We're 'ere because, We're 'ere.'

And over it all, Maxwell's belting baritone; 'I shall kiss the sergeant-major...'

She raised her face to heaven and murmured, 'Thank you.' She loved it when a plan came together.

Back in Maxwell's office, underneath the carefully arranged pile of marking on a chair, the laptop slumbered, dreaming its silicon dreams. As always, Maxwell had used the tried-and-tested technique of hiding in plain sight. It hadn't let him down in four hundred years of teaching, and it hadn't let him down now.

Jacquie's quiet office was not quite what she had hoped. It was quiet. It was an office. And that was more or less as far as it went to fulfilling her dreams. There were eight filing cabinets ranged against one wall, each with only two functioning drawers. Should anyone accidentally pull out one of the broken ones, the others all fell off their runners, trapping the unwary hand. Along the top of the cabinets were a range of dead plants. They reminded Jacquie of a sequence puzzle in an IQ test. The one on the left was so totally dead that only the pot remained. The next one along had a brown stick poking out, the next had three leaves, also brown. And so it went, until at the extreme right it was still just about possible to identify the poor wilted thing as a *pogonatherum*, should anyone care to take the time.

The window, which had a rather good view of the Downs once the eye had negotiated the car park and the low-rise office blocks, was so filthy that the view was a suspicion, rather than a fact. Jacquie extended a cautious finger to see which side of the glass was dirty and discovered that it was both. The desk, recently vacated by the cursing and spitting Matt, was covered in a kind of gritty dust, left behind when his paperwork had been unceremoniously swept into a black bag. Jacquie felt rather sorry for him. She hadn't meant to get anyone thrown out in order to have her quiet space, but then again, she couldn't understand why he was so upset. After all, the place was a tip.

Down in the main office, DS Matt Carter was happily reintegrating with his peers. He had managed to hang on to the office longer than anyone so far and he knew he had already won the sweepstake based on tenure, which finished on the Labour Day Bank Holiday. If Jacquie thought she owed him a few cups of coffee and a chocolate biscuit now and again, he wasn't going to disabuse her. He had only gone up there to do his expenses and had been forgotten about for seven peaceful weeks.

Jacquie had found an almost empty can of Pledge thrown in a corner, wrapped in a cloth which on closer inspection turned out to be a pair of boxer shorts, torn beyond repair. Suppressing a shudder, she weighed up her options. Either work on a desk so filthy she would need a total strip and a shower before she left the nick, or risk the underpants. She convinced herself that the pants had been a duster for longer than they had been used for their proper purpose and, spraying happily, spruced up the space. Soon, it was a bit more like an office and a bit less like a pesthouse.

She popped downstairs for a coffee, making a note to self to bring in kettle and comestibles from tomorrow. Matt Carter was standing by the machine, looking disconsolately through a handful of small change.

'Matt,' she said, with extravagant bonhomie. 'Let me.'

He shook his head and foraged through the change again.

'No, really. It's my treat.'

'Oh, as long as you're sure,' he said, with a small smile. 'Cappuccino, then, please.'

'Of course.' Jacquie fished out another coin. Froth was extra. 'Biscuit?'

'That's very good of you,' he said, trying not to

smirk at his mates over her shoulder. A Kit Kat would be lovely. Ooh,' he feigned surprise, 'they do Chunkies in this machine. One of those would be smashing.'

Jacquie threw him a suspicious look but put in the necessary coins.

'Thanks, Jacquie. I appreciate this. Enjoy the office.'

'I've thrown your plants out, I'm afraid,' she said. 'They were dead.'

'Not my plants,' Carter said. 'I thought they were part of the decor.'

'Not any more they're not,' she said. 'I'm afraid I've binned your grit as well.'

He smiled. Women, eh? Can't live with 'em, can't live with 'em.

'I thought you would like this back, though,' she said and delved into her bag. 'It was in the drawer.' She waved the girlie magazine in the air as she handed it over. *Best of Barely Legal* Bumper Edition.

He recovered quickly. 'Not mine,' he said, with a nervous laugh.

She snatched it back and flicked through until she found what she wanted. 'No, I definitely think it's yours.' She pointed to a page. 'That *is* your writing, isn't it?'

He grabbed it from her and tore it down the spine. He was so red in the face he matched the Kit Kat wrapper. He might be a cappuccino and a chocolate bar to the good, but she had definitely won that round.

She pointed to the paper cup. 'Enjoy,' she said and, taking her coffee with her, made for the stairs. Henry Hall, watching from his office, allowed himself a small and private chuckle. Jacquie Carpenter, Jacquie Maxwell, it didn't matter what she was called; she was his favourite DS and, every now and again, she reminded him why.

Back in her office, she arranged her desk as she liked it. The file dead centre, the coffee to the right. She got out her sandwiches and her mid-morning snack and put them in a drawer, top right as always and known to her colleagues as 'the pantry'. She plugged in her laptop and flicked it open and set it to one side. Reaching further into her bag, she encountered her mobile phone and sat there for a moment, weighing it and her options up.

She was tempted to ring Maxwell, or to text him to tell him what an odd turn the day had taken. But, she reasoned, it would only wind her up; he wouldn't answer, he wouldn't reply to the text. She would end up grumpy and that wasn't the way to start a new case. She tossed the phone up and down in her hand a few times and then, deciding, put that on her desk as well, just behind the coffee.

She opened the file and began to see the size of the task in front of her. At first glance, it seemed to have quite a lot in it. Then, as she turned the pages, she realised that in fact all it was was a collection of contact sheets from the front desk, brief details of phone calls and, in a few cases, a drop-in complainant. There were names, times, brief descriptions of the issue and that was it. Added to that, every one was basically the same. Précised, it came to the fact that twenty-five

Leighford and Tottingleigh parents had seen fit to look at their daughters' phones and had discovered texts on them that they found disturbing. What was not there, and what Jacquie would have to unravel, were the stories behind it. Why did the parents check the phones? Were these girls troublesome kids or did they have abusive parents, either psychologically or physically? Did these parents dig in pockets, pick the locks of private diaries, have the passwords to their daughters' email accounts? She flipped the file shut and took a slug of coffee. Cheers, Henry. The upside was that she would probably be in this office until Christmas. She might bring in a plant.

She drew a notebook towards her and started to make a rough plan of where the girls lived on a very basic map of the area. No help – they were spread widely and randomly around. This probably meant that they went to several schools. At least she could start by ringing Leighford High School and checking to see if any of the girls went there. She could secretly check up on Maxwell at the same time, since she and Thingees both One and Two, switchboard operators extraordinaire, had struck up quite a relationship since she spent so many hours of the average term making small talk with them whilst they scoured the school tracking down the elusive Head of Sixth Form.

She had the number on speed dial.

'Good morning. Leighford High School.'

Jacquie drummed her fingers waiting for the rest of the recorded message.

Instead, she got a slightly testy Thingee One. 'Leighford High School. How may I help you?'

Jacquie jumped and stammered into the phone, 'Oh, you're a person. Oh, sorry, of course you're a person, it's just that I was expecting the list of numbers to press and ... sorry. It's ... er ... Mrs Maxwell.' It still sounded strange in her ears, but equally it made her smile.

'Oh, hello, Mrs Maxwell.' Thingee One went into her Pavlovian response. 'I'm not sure where Mr Maxwell is, but I'll try and get him for you.'

'No,' Jacquie almost shouted, as Thingee One was particularly quick with her button pressing. 'No, actually I think I want Student Services, Emma. I have a list of names I want to check off against your roll.'

There was a silence, in which Jacquie could sub-liminally discern the brushing of cloth on cloth, the whisper of skin on skin as Thingee beckoned to someone. Another voice, altogether less friendly than that of the redoubtable Thingee, came on the line. 'Help you?' it barked.

Jacquie felt she should straighten those seams and push back her shoulders. 'Well, I certainly hope so. This is Detective Sergeant Carpenter. I–'

'I distinctly heard Emma call you Mrs Max-well.'

'Yes, that's right. I *am* Mrs Maxwell.'

'You said you were Detective Sergeant Car-penter.'

'Yes, you see, I... Do you mind telling me who you are?' Jacquie suddenly snapped. After all, *she* represented the police state in this conversation.

'Yes, I do mind. After all, I know perfectly well who I am already whereas you don't seem to have the first clue who you are. This is a school, you know, and I can't have people who can't identify themselves cluttering up my switchboard. Good day.' And before Jacquie could protest, the phone was slammed down and that was that.

Jacquie sat staring at the receiver for a long minute. Who in heaven's name was that? It sounded as if the school had been taken over by the Gestapo. Where were the Home Guard of Warmington on Sea when you needed them? There was only one thing for it. She scrolled down her contacts list until she reached 'Maxmob' and pressed the bar to connect.

After a short pause, after which she expected to hear her own voice tell her that Maxwell was unavoidably detained and would get back to her as soon as possible, the unexpected happened.

'Peter Maxwell, no job too small, weddings and bar mitzvahs a speciality of the house.'

'Max? Is that you?' She was stunned.

'Heart! How scrummy to hear from you. I was just this instant about to check to see if I had any messages.' He told this lie with perfect aplomb and she was still so shaken by her experience that she didn't detect it.

'Max, who is that vile person in the front office?'

'You can't mean Thingee? She's a dear girl.'

'Of course not Thingee. A woman who sounded like ... well, I'm lost for words.'

Maxwell's chuckle echoed down the phone. 'You mean Irma Grese?'

'She's foreign? She didn't sound it.'

'No, no, honeybunch. Her name's, oh, I don't

know, I can hardly keep up, it's Mrs Dominatrix or something. Donaldson, that's the one. I call her Irma Grese after the most hated concentration camp guard in Auschwitz. Albert Pierrepoint hanged her, bless him. She's not exactly like her, of course. She's much nastier.'

'I agree.' Jacquie's reply was heartfelt. 'But who is she?'

'What. I think you mean *what* is she? Well, she's the new office manager.'

'Is that an answer?'

'Good question, Woman Policeman. We'll make a detective of you yet, or your name's not Dalmatia Entwhistle. There have been, as I think I may have ranted to you at some length, various Cost-cutting Measures here at the funny farm.'

Jacquie had memories of Maxwell, splashing gravy about willy-nilly as he gestured with his knife and fork, to the glee of Nolan and the despair of Metternich, who liked to keep his coat looking nice and not bespeckled with Bisto. Heads had been rolling since September, but she hadn't heard of anyone new being appointed. That didn't seem a very sound cost-cutting measure to her. She replied, 'I do recall, yes.'

'Well, that's what she is. She is a cost-cutting measure. By getting rid of three staff earning twelve thousand pounds a year and replacing them with Irma on a mere forty-five thousand pounds a year, Legs has contrived to save oooh, let me think, the old mental arithmetic isn't what it was, that will be minus nine thousand a year, or thereabouts.'

'Max, you work in a madhouse!'

'Again, I refer you to my rants, 1995 onwards.'

She chuckled. 'Indeed. Anyway, look, I didn't actually ring to be yelled at by a psycho. And I wasn't checking on you, although I admit I was going to later. I really wanted Student Services.'

'You remember the three staff I mentioned just now?'

'Yes ... oh, I see. No Student Services any more, then?'

'Not so's you would notice. Can I help?'

'I have a list here of girls whose parents have complained about...' she paused to look around. This was confidential stuff. 'About ... you know.'

'You'll have to be a little more precise, my little cabbage. I know such a lot of things.'

'Max! Behave. About our visitor last night. That thing.'

'Oh, *that* thing. Well, that's quite good, isn't it? That the two of them are not alone.'

'I didn't think for a moment they were. But I need to know if the girls on this list – which doesn't include ours, by the way – go to Leighford High.

'Fire away.'

'Come on, Max. You can't know all of them.' He did, of course, have his school list somewhere, still, mercifully, on paper. But it was a point of honour with him to do without it.

'Try me.'

'All right, I will! Hang on while I get a pencil to check them off on my list. While I'm doing that, you could order your crow from the canteen for later.'

'Let's meet for lunch and I can watch you eat

93

your humble pie.'

Jacquie snorted. 'OK, eyes down, look in.'

'Two fat ladies, Mrs Donaldson.'

'Is she fat? She sounds thin.'

Maxwell kept quiet. Female logic was an odd creature and he preferred not to rattle its cage.

'First name, Eleanor Capstick.'

'Now, that's an interesting one. No relation to Charlie Artful, by the way, that doyen of Scotland Yard when detectives were all men – oops, sorry.'

'Don't hedge, Max. If you don't know, just say so.'

He chuckled. 'I'm not hedging, sweetness. It's just that she was with us, then went to Brighton Grammar, courtesy of Grandma.'

'Kind of her.'

'Well, she was dead, but doubtless she was a nice old dear and would have approved of a vast amount of her money being spent on her only granddaughter for school fees. Next.'

The list ground on until all twenty-five had been docketed and accounted for. Three were current Leighford Highenas, three had been, but had moved on, though not necessarily up. The rest Maxwell didn't know. Jacquie was convinced.

'That was amazing, Max. How do you do it?'

'It's a blessing...' It was a perfect Mr Monk.

'...and a curse.' Hers wasn't so good and she laughed gently. 'I still can't get over you,' she said fondly.

'You'll just have to get up and go round,' he said and she could hear the smile in his voice. 'May I ask a question, delight of my life?'

'Knock yourself out.'

'Are you in the Big Boy's office? I only ask because, as a rule, you don't get the leisure for endearments.'

'Ooh, I forgot to say. I was so excited that you answered your phone it went out of my head.' It was just as well that she couldn't see his face, a perfect mixture of pride and relief that he hadn't been caught out. 'I have the corner office up-stairs.'

'Next stop Pennsylvania Avenue,' he said proudly. 'How did you get that?'

'I just asked Henry for somewhere quiet and he came up with this. I must admit,' there was a pause as she looked round her little domain, 'it's not the Ritz, but once I sort out the filing cabinet drawers so they aren't so lethal and get rid of all the dead plants and a rather strange smell I'm having trouble identifying, then it will be really nice.'

'Can I give you a bit of help on the smell?' he asked. 'But first I'll need some extra information. Was the previous incumbent popular? Is he, I hope I should say. Dead men's shoes are one thing, dead men's offices something else entirely.'

'No, he's not dead,' she said. 'He's a bit of a lout, but nothing wrong in the main.'

'Has he been having a bit of a fling with anyone in the station?'

She lowered her voice. 'Are you bugging the place, Max? He had a bit of a knee trembler, rumour has it, with one of the desk sergeant's wives just before Christmas.'

'Thank you, Miss Lemon,' Peter 'Hercule' Maxwell replied. 'Just look under the chair.'

'I'm just putting you down a minute.' He heard the phone go down on the desk and then the scrape as she got off the chair and turned it over. Distantly, he heard, 'Eeuwwhh. What in God's name...?' The phone was picked up again. 'Oh, God, Max. There's what looks like a rotting kipper under this chair!'

'I suggest you ring the desk sergeant in question and get him to come up with a new chair and take this one away. He won't argue.'

'You're scary, you know that?'

'Oh, go on! You're only saying it because it's true. Anyway, heart, must go. I have– Oh, Leah waiting in my doorway.'

'Leah? What, as in–?'

'Well, must go, dear.' And the phone went dead.

Jacquie stood staring at the phone in her hand and could have yelled with frustration. But she trusted Maxwell. All she could do was wait.

Chapter Six

'Come in, Leah,' Maxwell invited. 'Don't just stand there, wearing out your knees or whatever the health gurus are saying these days.' He gestured to a chair.

She sat on the very edge, hugging her backpack on her lap. She licked her lips and then said, in a very small voice as though the world was listening in and she only wanted Maxwell to hear, 'Were you on a mobile just then?'

He looked down at the thing in his hand as though he had only just realised it was there. It was probably a hanging offence in some countries. 'I seem to have been, yes.' He smiled disarmingly. 'It was the wife.'

'Everybody thinks you don't know about mobiles and computers and stuff.'

'Everybody thinks I don't know about the coefficient of linear expansion, but what the hey?' Maxwell plumped into a chair opposite and flung one leg extravagantly across the other knee. There was a faint twanging noise and he carefully adjusted his position. He smiled again at the girl. 'I really should stop doing that,' he said. 'Cyclist's knee.'

She smiled momentarily and then went back to minutely examining a buckle on her bag. The clock's intermittent digital click sounded like the crash of cymbals in the quiet room. Somewhere out there was a school full of life, chairs screaming back on wooden floors which had long since lost their polish, markers squeaking on whiteboards, the massed whisper of five hundred tongues muttering into five hundred ears as the seconds before the bell clicked slowly as a watched kettle boiling, sounding like waves on a distant beach. Doors slammed, but they were muted as if they slammed against marshmallow, toilets flushed distantly, but their water was molasses, slow and silent. Eventually, the sound of one tear splashing onto a sad girl's hand broke the mood and Maxwell was out of his chair and holding that hand. Breaking the rule-book again.

'Come on, Leah. It can't be that bad. This too shall pass, as Abraham Lincoln almost said.'

The girl sniffed and scrubbed at her teary cheek with the back of her hand. Did they know, wondered Maxwell, how like a baby that made them look? That angry denial of the tears which gave away their age. 'It is that bad, Mr Maxwell,' she said. 'I ... I've been bad somehow, I know I have. And someone has found out.'

He let go of her hand and rocked back on his heels. 'How can someone find out something you don't know you've done?' he asked, a little testily. He sometimes wondered if these girls liked the drama or whether they really thought there was no sadness in the world but theirs. He had to bring this to a stop right now.

'Don't be cross, Mr Maxwell,' she begged him. 'It's just, well, I've been getting these texts.' She looked up at him. Despite the fact that she had seen him using a mobile, she still wondered if he could follow the plot.

'Yes, Leah,' he said. 'I know about texts.'

She scrubbed at her cheek again. 'Sorry,' she muttered. 'Well, I get these texts and they say all sorts of things. They say that the person watches me, that they know where I am, what I do. They say I ... do stuff that I really don't do, Mr Maxwell. Honestly, I don't. They say they'll tell my mum, the school. They say I won't get into university. Oh, please, make them stop.'

He knew that this moment hung by a thread. There could be no flippant throwaway like 'Well, it's only Leeds Metropolitan, after all'. His answer was to take the simple way out, to change her phone number, to only give out the new number to certain people, then if the texts resumed she would at least have a small chance of finding out who it was. But that wasn't what she wanted to hear.

'I think you need to talk to someone who really understands technology,' Maxwell said in the end, rather lamely. 'I can only just use these things. I used to be a technophobe. You need a technophile. I'm only a technOK.'

'But I don't want to talk to anyone else, Mr Maxwell.' She grabbed his lapel. 'You are quite literally the only person in the whole world who I know isn't doing this.'

He chose to take it as a compliment, although in fact he fully realised that she only meant that he couldn't have done it for technical reasons. He was still framing an answer when she went on.

'Even now I've seen you with a phone, I know you're rubbish at computers.'

He bridled slightly, but it was nothing if not the truth. Then he grasped her point. 'You mean that you've been getting emails as well?'

'Emails, instant messages, things like that. Messages on my wall.'

'Your ... you mean someone has been leaving graffiti on your house?' It would be spirit writing next.

She looked puzzled, then she cottoned on. 'No, no, Mr Maxwell. My wall. My cyber-wall.'

'Ah.' Maxwell didn't know a lot about these computer communities, but he did know you had to join and get a password and everything. 'But you must know who is doing that, surely. An email says who it is from, and I suppose the others are the same.'

'No, Mr Maxwell.' She spoke slowly, as though to a small child. 'An email says who the sender says it is from.' She looked into his eyes to see if it had sunk in. Nothing. 'When you set up the account, you say who you are. You could set it up to say you were, oh, I don't know, the Duke of Wellington, say.'

He brightened up. 'I could?'

'Well, you could if you, like, wanted to hide who you are. It's easy.'

'Where did you find all this?'

'What do you mean?'

'Well, did you find it out online, in a ... chat room?' The words were ones he used, but not usually linked together. He felt the real world recede and he didn't like it.

'No. It really is so basic, Mr Maxwell.' Leah was relaxing now and the words flowed better. 'I don't know how I got to know about it. I just, like, *do*.'

He clambered slowly to his feet, knees cracking like pistols. 'I think you need to talk to someone other than me, Leah. I understand people. I don't understand the technical stuff.'

She jumped up as well and fetched him a smart one under the chin with her bag as he attempted to straighten up to his full height. 'Sorry,' she muttered and ran from the room, bowling over Sylvia Matthews as she went. Maxwell rushed to haul her to her feet and they staggered into his office and collapsed on chairs. Sylvia looked closely at him.

'Max, you appear to have "Hello Kitty" printed on your chin.'

He felt it, gingerly. 'Is that what it is? I just prefer to think of it as a painful bruise,' he said huffily.

Sylvia took a deep breath. 'Max, I have to ask this, and obviously, you can stop me if you want but–'

He sighed. 'Nothing, Sylv. She was upset about something and I didn't give her the answer she wanted.'

'No one ever gives them the answer they want at that age, Max. Surely you know that by now.'

'Sylv. Can you keep a secret?'

'I'm horrified you need to ask.'

He reached over and patted her arm. 'Soz,' he said. 'I know you would never share a confidence, but I think you might be a bit conflicted with this.'

She drew back, making the sign of the cross with the forefingers of both hands. It warded off vampires, by all accounts, but would it work this time?

'What is it?' Maxwell asked, rather taken aback.

'You just used psychobabble,' she said. 'From that I can only deduce, Sherlock, that you are not yourself, but some kind of clone.'

He looked at her with his head on one side. 'There's a lot of that about,' he said. 'I wear my armour of righteousness whenever I go near Bernard Ryan, but obviously something creeps through sometimes. I will rephrase.'

She patted her chest and fanned her face with relief. Nobody ever went near the Deputy Head without *some* form of protection.

'I think you might find yourself, Sylv, between a rock and a very hard place.'

'That's better. But what are they, the rock and the hard place?'

'Leah and, I happen to know, Julie and at least three other girls in this school are receiving unpleasant texts and, I have just discovered, emails and other cyber stuff which I don't really understand, to be truthful. Leah and Julie have only told Jacquie and me about it. The other three have either told their parents, or their parents found out somehow and they are known to the police.'

'So,' Sylvia wanted to get it right, 'Jacquie officially knows about all of them. You know about Julie and Leah.'

'Yes. But Julie told Jacquie about Leah and Jacquie told me, though Julie asked her not to tell me. But now, Leah has been to see me, so I know.' He looked up to the ceiling and muttered to himself, pointing at invisible list items in the air. He looked back at Sylvia. 'Yes, that's right.' He'd always found the 'he said, she said' enormously complicated at the best of times.

'Max, you know the old saying about webs and tangles?'

'Yes, yes, I know, Sylv. But this has moved on somewhat quickly. I'm glad that Leah came to me, because at least that's one secret I don't have to keep any more. But unless the other three do, I'm a bit hamstrung.'

'Do you think it is only three others?'

'I haven't really thought about that. Do you think there will be more?'

'I should think there will be *loads* more, Max. These kids spend half their lives on computers, phones and what have you. You see four girls walking down the road and they will all be on the phone, talking to four other people. Communication has gone mad.'

'Sylv!' Maxwell was ecstatic. 'I'm not alone!'

'Well, you are, Max, pretty well.' Illusion shattered. Moment gone. She chuckled. 'I at least use my phone and computer.'

'So do I.' He did a little wriggle, learnt from Nolan, who had learnt it from Metternich. Although in the latter case, it was a precursor to a pounce on a small and unsuspecting rodent. 'In fact, I had a call from Jacquie just this morning. That's how I know about the other girls.'

'You mean you checked your phone?'

'Umm...' Maxwell could lie with the best of them, but never to Sylvia Matthews. Her skills had been honed over years of games-evaders, faux headaches and the occasional mock broken leg, although the last did not really take that much expertise to spot. 'I was passing the drawer and it rang.'

'Passing the drawer?' The buck she had heard of, but this was a new one.

'Looking for a biscuit, if you must know. My small and secret stash is in the next drawer down.'

Sylvia smiled. 'Your secret is safe with me.'

'I know.' He looked at her fondly. It occurred to him that of all the people he knew, she had known him for the longest. She knew him when the loss of his wife and daughter was a gaping wound he wore for the world to see, because to hide it would be an insult to their memory. She had seen it scab over, she had seen it heal. She was one of the few who knew that there was still a scar, a silver thread now, all but invisible, which wound around his heart.

'Computer?'

'Yes. I have one of those.' He looked round the room and awe crept into his voice. '*Several* of those.'

'Logged on today?'

'Not so's you'd notice, no.' His tone was airy, but wary. 'My name is Peter Maxwell and I am not a technoholic.'

'So no one knows where anyone in your classes have been this morning.'

'I know.'

'I don't think Pansy will think that that is good enough. I would imagine she has put Nicole on your case already.'

'Pansy? Who, for heaven's sake, is Pansy?'

104

'Pansy Donaldson. In the office.'

'Mrs Donaldson is called *Pansy?*'

'Max, let's not get sidetracked.'

'But–'

'I really think you're going to have to come to terms with this laptop business, Max. Just let's say ... well, I have overheard a few things as I make my quiet way around the school.' She held up one foot to display her rubber-soled shoes, nurses for the use of. 'I think there is an element here who are out to get you.'

He flung himself back in the chair and laughed until she thought he would never stop. Finally, wiping his eyes, he said, 'Sylvia Matthews. You always know how to make me laugh. Of *course* there is an element trying to get me. I wouldn't be doing my job properly as Leighford High School's Official Subversive if there wasn't. Legs could have wallpapered his office a dozen times with complaints about me. I am the fly in the ointment, the African-American in the woodpile, the wind in the willows, whatever. But we're always all right in the end.'

'Yes, but now you're up against something bigger than Diamond and a few miffed staff. You're up against Health and Safety, you're up against the No Paper Lobby, you're up against...'

He sighed and shook his head ruefully. 'I know, Sylv. But if I give in to this techno-rubbish, where will everyone be, come the deluge? If we all go down that road, when the crash comes, we'll be up shit creek without a paddle, digital or otherwise.' He'd lost track of the metaphors he'd mixed.

'Crash?' Sylvia's smile looked a little pasted on.

'Don't worry, Sylv,' he said. 'I'm not going paranoid. But, let's face it, we rely so heavily on the chip that if anything goes wrong, we really will be doomed. Look what happened to the Irish in the 1840s.'

'Max, do you remember the Millennium Bug scares?'

'You know my views on the Millennium, but yes, I do. Planes were going to fall out of the air, everything on computers would be wiped as the hard drives thought it was 1900 and so nothing had been invented yet. And yes – before you tell me – nothing happened. But if it had, civilization would have not crashed but would certainly have gone over a very large pothole.'

'But these things don't happen, Max.'

'They haven't happened *yet*,' he said darkly. 'You mark my words, young lady,' Sylvia gave him a rudimentary nod of thanks for the compliment, 'I make a point of still writing everything down, against the day. Someone has to.'

'And we all know that person will be you, Max.' She got up to go. 'But please be careful. Just register classes in the first instance. For me?'

He gave her a brief hug, which was half affection and half a means of getting up out of a low chair. 'Yes,' he said. 'I will. But only for you.'

Nurse Sylvia Matthews went back to her office feeling in some ways better, in others worse. She had passed on the warning. There was no more she could do. But she knew, with her long years of experience of human nature and Peter Maxwell in particular, that it was unlikely to be heeded. There was more interesting quarry to hunt and Maxwell was off on the scent while the rest of the hounds were still in the kennel.

The little line of whingers would get short shrift today. 'I'm busy,' she said tartly. 'Anyone with verrucas?' Four hands went up. 'Get back to classes, all of you. No,' she held up a hand to stop their protests at source. 'I don't care if it's Games. Wear plimsolls. Right. Headaches, anyone?' Two hands went up, but tentatively. 'Any flashing lights?' One head nodded vigorously. 'If you can do that, you're fine. If you don't have flashing lights, you're fine. Off you go.' There were two left in the queue. She spoke to the first one, a lad who clearly wished he was anywhere but there. 'And you would have symptoms of what, Michael? Ebola? Smallpox? A bad case of *burkholderia mallei* perhaps?'

Michael wasn't stupid. It was just that he was more stupid than Sylvia Matthews. He knew about Ebola and smallpox. He hadn't heard of the other thing, but he thought he'd give it a go. 'Yes, that one. Burkhold's Mallet. It's in my thigh. I can hardly walk.'

'Well, you surprise me, Michael. You don't have enough legs. *Burkholderia mallei* is the causatory bacillus in a disease of horses. Off you trot.'

He knew when he was beaten and he slunk off to the horrors of Maths. Looking on the bright side, he had missed half of the lesson, so it wasn't all bad news.

Sylvia turned to her last customer. 'And how can I help you?' she said.

The girl immediately burst into tears. 'Oh, Mrs Matthews. I'm so worried. I keep on getting

107

these emails.'

Sylvia put her arm round her and ushered her through into the privacy of her back room. 'Come in,' she said. 'I think we need to talk, don't you?'

Nicole Thompson knocked on the door of the Headteacher's office with a smart little tattoo. She didn't realise that she did that on every door and that the sound was one which many people had come to dread. She was so immersed in computers that she also didn't realise that she was rapping out the Windows opening sound.

James Diamond was trapped. And he had been ever since he'd gone into education. He was a superficial, sound-bite sort of chap, forever blowing in the wind of County Hall directives, a prey to nervous disorders and desperately trying to balance books and climb higher in the league tables. Teaching? He'd have to leave that sort of thing to people like Peter Maxwell. Except that there weren't any people like Peter Maxwell. Not any more. Diamond looked frantically behind him; no luck there, the window had been painted shut by over-zealous County operatives some years before. He could see the outline of Mrs Donaldson's head, surely too large for any normal human – the woman was a different species – looming through the frosted glass in the adjacent office. No help there. He even peeked under his desk and quickly assessed the likelihood of getting away with hiding in that dark, stale-smelling cubbyhole. But no – he could only imagine the embarrassment should his ruse not succeed.

There was only one thing for it.

'Come!' He hid his trepidation beneath a peremptory tone.

Nicole's head peered round the door. 'Do you have a moment, Mr Diamond?'

He grasped the opening, small as it was. 'Well, just a very small moment, Nicole,' he said. 'I am expecting a phone call.'

'Well, I'll just get as much of what I want to say said, then,' she said, sliding round the door and sitting down, 'before the call comes through.' She gestured behind her. 'I've slid the "engaged" sign on your door across. I hope you don't mind but what I want to say is really rather private.'

His heart leapt. Resignation? Oh, joy. Perhaps she was going to go and make IT mayhem somewhere else. He hated himself for it, he liked to think that he was at one with modern trends, but there was something about the IT Department in general, and Nicole Thompson in particular, that made his short hairs stand on end. She was a pleasant enough woman on the surface. She even had a sense of humour, or so he had been reliably informed. But she was so clearly on the make that it made her a very abrasive colleague. Even though he knew that she wasn't qualified to steal his job, he wasn't sure that she knew it. As for her staff, he wasn't sure why they were there. They were to be seen around the school, sure enough, but even so, computers didn't work and if they did it wasn't usually for long. Sabotage was a big word, but Diamond couldn't help suspecting it.

He laced his fingers together and pressed the sides of his hands firmly down on the desktop, to stop them trembling too much. 'How can I help you, Nicole?'

'It's about Peter Maxwell.'

Oh, for pity's sake, Diamond thought. If he had a quid for every time someone had sat in that chair and said that selfsame sentence, he wouldn't still be in teaching, and that was a fact. But he said, 'Maxwell? What seems to be the problem?'

'I think he's losing it, Mr Diamond.'

'Can you be more precise?' Diamond knew full well that not everyone understood Peter Maxwell. He himself had more than a little difficulty getting on his wavelength, but he knew that the man could get results out of the kids that everyone else wrote off, was as loyal as Lassie and that he would move heaven and earth to help any of God's creatures. He didn't care whether he liked a lame duck – he was going to help it over the stile, even if it didn't know it wanted to go. He had a vague idea that he might have got his metaphors a bit mixed, but if he couldn't take a few short cuts in his own head, where could he? And anyway, he had been a Biology teacher once.

'He sent a very strange email last night.'

'An email? Well, that's excellent,' Diamond beamed. 'I thought we'd never get him online. What else?'

Nicole was confused. This wasn't going according to plan at all. 'He left himself a note about custard on his desk.'

'Custard on his desk? That must have been annoying. I'll have a word with the Premises Manager.'

'No.' Nicole could feel her dander getting ready to get up. 'The note was about custard. The note was on his desk.'

'I see. Probably a shopping list, something of that nature.'

'And then I went past his classroom just now and it sounded as though World War One had broken out.'

At this, Diamond snapped. 'Miss Thompson,' he said, with an acid smile on his anonymous features. 'Peter Maxwell consistently gets the best results in the school. And that is in a subject generally considered to be one of the most difficult at both GCSE and A Level. If he wants to teach in a bear garden, I don't care. I don't hear any complaints from his fellow *teachers.*' He couldn't help putting the emphasis on the word, it just slipped out. 'So I don't expect unqualified staff to get involved. Now, if you'll excuse me...'

'But, I wasn't complaining,' she said, leaning forward, 'I just wanted to–'

'Yes, Miss Thompson. I'm sure you did.' And then, like a small miracle, his phone began to ring. Diamond tried not to look too smug, or surprised. 'Thank you. Can you see yourself out?'

She got up reluctantly and made for the door, aware in her ambitious little heart that she had made the biggest mistake of her working life so far, even if you included the day she had crashed the entire computer network of Southern Water.

'Good,' he smiled as she went. He picked up the phone. 'Diamond.'

The phone quacked in his hand.

'Doctor Melkins. How are you?'

111

Quack.

'I'm so sorry ... Mister ... of course. Umm, how can I help you?' He listened intently. 'I have no idea why Julie should have missed her dentist appointment today. I'll look into it. Yes, immediately. At once. Yes. Goodbye.' He didn't so much put the phone down as hurl it back onto the cradle. What did these people think teachers did all day? Just played nursemaid? How should he know where she was? He took a deep breath and picked up the phone again and dialled an internal number.

'Mrs Donaldson?' Through the frosted glass he saw her head turn from grizzled brown to pink as she instinctively turned towards him. He just resisted the urge to wave. 'See if you can track down Julie ... umm, her name isn't Melkins, is it?'

'No,' her voice came, rather disconcertingly in uneven stereo through the glass and through the earpiece. 'I'll check, but I'm almost certain it's Jackson. Why do you want to know?'

'I need to find out if she's in the school at the moment.'

'I'll check the computer records,' she said. There was a brief and bitter laugh, 'Unless she should have been in Mr Maxwell's class, of course.'

But Diamond was feeling a bit pro-Maxwell at that moment, a condition he was in but infrequently. 'In that case, Mrs Donaldson,' he said, 'I could ask Mr Maxwell and he would know. The world isn't all about computers, you know.'

Again, he slammed down the receiver. He wiped his lightly sweating forehead with a handkerchief. He must be coming down with some-

112

thing. He had stuck up for Maxwell twice in the last five minutes. There was a tap on the door and a grizzled head popped round the edge.

'Headmaster? Do you have a mo?'

Diamond froze, but at least he knew one thing. This latest intruder would not be here to complain about Peter Maxwell. 'Come in, Max, How may I help you?'

Chapter Seven

Maxwell threw himself into his usual chair. He tried to spend as little time as possible in Diamond's company and, of that little time, he preferred to spend the greater part of it in public fora. But, with all of that said, he had still spent enough time facing Legs over a desk to have a usual chair.

'You're looking a tad frazzled, Headmaster,' the Great Man said thoughtfully.

Diamond drew a deep breath and let it out shakily. 'Max, you have no idea.' This was unfair as it was still less than a year since Maxwell had found himself Acting Headteacher while Legs languished in hospital. But they both knew what he meant. 'Do you want me about anything...?' What was the word he wanted? 'Major' could mean anything. 'Important' sounded very condescending.

'Vital?'

Yes, that was a good one. 'Yes, Max. Vital. Do you want me about anything vital?'

'That's a bit of a tough one, Headmaster,' said Maxwell. 'I have several layers, as it were, to my reason for being here today. The topmost layer is concern for some of my girls.'

Diamond looked up from his introspective examination of the mock wood grain on his desk. 'Girls? Max, you know we don't use gender-based descriptions of the students at Leighford High.'

One of these days, Maxwell pondered, Diamond's political correctness would choke him. Or he would; it was a close thing which would come first. 'I don't see how I can avoid it in this instance,' he said, quite snappily, 'since all the students involved are girls. Would "female persuasion" be better?'

Diamond tried out a few ripostes in his head and once or twice got as far as moving his lips, but no sound came. In the end, he spread a conciliatory hand across the desk and muttered, 'Sorry, Max. Please go on.'

'Thank you. I am, as I say, concerned for some of my girls. Well, perhaps there are also causes for concern lower down the school, but I suspect that Sixth Form girls are the main target.'

'Target? For what?' Diamond felt his ulcer lurch. He had been told to avoid stressful situations and here was one, sitting right in front of him.

'I think they call it grooming. Except that I had always assumed that that implied someone being nice in order to get the girl's trust.'

Diamond had attended the workshop. Since it had been advertised to the staff by email, obviously, Maxwell had not. 'Yes, you're right. It is usually an adult male posing as either a younger male or another girl. It is said to be rife.'

'Indeed. This particular problem doesn't quite fit the pattern, then. The texts are unpleasant and threatening. The emails, I understand, although I haven't seen one, are worse. But the general tone is that someone knows what they have done, and that they are watching.'

'Done? What do you mean, done?'

'I have no idea, Headmaster. But you know what these girls are.' He looked closely at Diamond. It was obvious from his face that he didn't. 'They sometimes ... well, go a bit too far, with boyfriends, after nights out and so on. We have to be realistic.'

'So you're saying that these texts are spelling out...?'

'No. That's exactly what they *don't* do. They just seem to imply things, but the girls are rattled and the police are involved.'

'*Police?*' Diamond's screech was almost off the scale of human hearing. 'Police? Do you just mean Detective Sergeant Carpenter? I mean, Mrs Maxwell? Oh, dear. Police?'

Maxwell could not help a wry grin. 'Headmaster,' he said. 'Surely the idea of the police at Leighford High School can't really come as too much of a surprise? I'm only amazed that they don't have a satellite police station somewhere on the grounds.'

Diamond was on his feet. 'What can you mean?' He would have shouted, but he seemed to be having difficulty getting his breath.

'Don't get in a state, Headmaster.' Maxwell was also on his feet by now and making his way round behind the desk. He needed to be nearer to catch the man when he fell over in a faint. 'I just mean we are not strangers to police investigation, are we? Last year. Year before. Then the year before that...'

Diamond waved him away with a flapping hand and sat down heavily. He patted his forehead

116

again with a handkerchief he seemed to keep ready for the purpose. 'I'm sorry, Max. I've been under a lot of strain.'

'You still seem to be, Headmaster, if you don't mind my mentioning it. Is it something you can tell me about?'

Diamond fell under the Maxwell charm as easily as generations of bolshie sixth-formers had done since time immemorial – immemorial to everyone but Peter Maxwell at least. 'It's all these cutbacks, staff redundancies, new initiatives. Sometimes I think they'll never end. League tables, SATs, AFL.' He looked up at Maxwell and apologised. 'Assessment for Learning.'

Maxwell looked affronted. 'I do *know* what AFL stands for, Headmaster. That I consider it and its myrmidons a waste of time is my own affair. I personally prefer the AFQL initiative.'

Diamond tried to look intelligent. This was one he thought he should know but, what with the stress and everything, couldn't call to mind. He settled for a generic, 'Ah.'

Maxwell smiled and leant forward. 'Don't worry, Headmaster,' he whispered. 'You don't have to know this one. It is a favourite of mine because it stands for Anything For a Quiet Life.' He leant back. 'You should try it sometime.'

Diamond tried a smile but it came out rather a poor, crooked affair and it was all Maxwell could do not to start back in horror.

'Anyway, Headmaster, if you don't mind getting back to the main reason for my visit. Time's a-wasting, you know. Helen will have poured the boiling water on my Pot Noodle by now and I

117

don't want it to go soggy and lose its huge nutritional value. We need to think of a way to speak to all of the sixth-form, boys as well, I suppose, so as to start fewer hares, and just make it clear that this email and text thing is pretty widespread and people who know what to do are on to it.'

Diamond looked thoughtful. That sounded a reasonable idea and one he could, with luck, leave to Maxwell to arrange. 'Sixth Form assembly might be the right place, Max, don't you think?'

'Excellent idea, Headmaster.' Maxwell stole a look at his watch. Not a bad decision to have arrived at in only twenty minutes. He looked up with a smile. 'I'll get onto it, shall I?'

'If you would.' Diamond felt a little more in control again. 'Oh, but, wait a minute.' He felt he had to at least take into account the comments from Nicole Thompson and Pansy Donaldson. 'It has been brought to my attention that you are not ... um, how shall I put this? *Embracing* the enhanced IT ethos of the school.'

'Me, Headmaster?' Maxwell splayed hurt and amazed fingers on his chest. 'But I am legend wherever IT gurus gather.'

'That could be taken both ways, Max,' Diamond was quick to respond.

Darn. The man was back to his nit-picking self. 'No, really, Headmaster. I have come on in leaps and bounds.' Distant music grew in volume and filled the room. *Diddle iddle diddle iddle diddle iddle iddle iddle iddle iddle.* Maxwell looked around, confused.

'It's your phone,' said Diamond, raising his voice over the noise.

'Ah, yes,' Maxwell said. *'The Bum of the Flightlebee.* I thought I recognised it.' He pressed the right button first go and looked up at Diamond proudly. 'Maxwell.' His salutations were usually much more baroque, but he was trying to impress the Headmaster. It was never too late to start that kind of thing.

On the other end of the phone Jacquie, with lightning reflexes honed as both DS Carpenter and Mrs Maxwell, realised he was somewhere rather more public even than his office. 'I assume you're with someone.'

'Absolutely on the money as always, heart,' he said.

'Right. I was just wondering how it went with Leah.'

'Not wonderfully, to be frank.'

'Ah. Have you spoken to anyone?'

'Yes.'

'Diamond?'

'Again, spot on.'

'How did it go?'

'Umm...'

'Sorry. One, two, three, four...'

'Let me stop you there.' Out of ten, that was a reasonable score for the success of his interview with Legs, he felt.

'Oh, rats. I was hoping you might have got somewhere. It's a bit of a dead end here, really. I'm tracking down the other names I have via the parental contact details but, surprise, surprise, they're not in, or they wish they'd never been to the police or the other million excuses we always get.'

'Great. Well, that's wonderful. Give the little

119

chap a kiss from me and I'll see you at home. Bye now.' Maxwell clicked the right button for the second time in a row and ended the call. He looked at Diamond. 'Jacquie,' he smiled. 'Just giving me an update on Nolan.'

'Yes,' Diamond said, concern wiping across his face on cue. 'How is the little one?'

'Bruised. Loves his stitches. Hopefully, he will have learnt that when the steps run out on a ladder, it's a good idea to stop climbing.'

Diamond gave a half-hearted chuckle. If only Nicole Thompson could learn the same lesson.

Maxwell opened the door and made to leave, but turned in the doorway. 'You're sure you're all right?' he asked. 'Because, obviously, if you're not I would be more than happy to help out.'

Diamond was round the desk and behind Maxwell with his hand in the small of his back like a rat up a pipe. 'Ha ha,' he laughed mirthlessly. 'Oh, yes, always the jokes, eh, Max? Well, can I leave that assembly thing to you, then? Excellent.' They heard movement in the adjacent office and through the frosted glass both men saw the unmistakable shadow of Pansy Donaldson, and she was coming their way.

Maxwell showed the whites of his eyes and was away up the corridor with a turn of speed creditable in a man half his age. James Diamond stayed where he was, transfixed like a rabbit in the thrall of a stoat, albeit the largest stoat in the whole world.

The door opened. 'Mr Diamond. Glad to have caught you.' She looked up the corridor and said with some venom, 'Was that Mr Maxwell in there with you all that time? He should know better than to waste the time of someone as busy as you.'

'No, no, Mrs Donaldson. It was an important meeting. Now, how may I help you?'

She snorted in Maxwell's direction and tossed her head. Then she turned what she liked to think was a calming and professional countenance on Diamond. In fact, her face looking, as it did, like a particularly malevolent currant bun, made him feel quite queasy. 'I just thought I'd bring you up to speed on the Julie Jackson scenario.'

Diamond compressed his lips and suppressed a remark along the lines of the fact that it was his lunchtime and she was being paid almost what he was and why couldn't she just update the Julie Jackson scenario herself and leave him alone? The words that crept out were different. 'Thank you, Mrs Donaldson.'

She stood there complacently, hands clasped over what she no doubt considered to be her waist.

He nodded at her encouragingly. 'So, what is the speed up to which you wish to bring me?'

'I'm sorry, Mr Diamond,' she said with a barely discernible bridle. 'I assumed you might want to continue this in your office.'

'Why?' he snapped. 'Everybody seems to want to come into my office today. Just tell me.'

'All right,' she said. What she didn't say, but was thinking it so obviously that she might as well have spoken aloud was – you ungrateful pig. I was just trying to stop you getting bad news out here in the corridor. But OK, here goes. 'She seems to have disappeared.'

'What?' The corridor walls and ceiling spun

round and he closed his eyes. That was worse, as they were then spinning round in the dark. He raised his lids quickly and there was the doughy face of Mrs Donaldson, much closer than it needed to be. 'Aaghh. Oh, sorry, it's the strain.' He drew himself up and took a deep breath. 'Mrs Donaldson. I want Bernard Ryan and Peter Maxwell in my office now.'

'But, Mr Diamond, you don't look at all well.'

'I wouldn't expect to, the way I feel,' he spat. 'Just fetch them and then come in yourself. I think this thing just got bigger than all of us.' He looked in horror at her size thirty bulk and wished he could eat his words. But she had not noticed as she hurried away, excited to be in on an adventure, even if it was to include that sarcastic so-and-so Peter Maxwell. That he had sunk to getting people to make prank calls to her switchboard wasn't something she was going to forgive in a hurry, oh no. Her door swung to behind her and James Diamond, feeling rather less than sparkling and using door jamb and sundry furniture to support his wobbling legs, made his way to behind his desk and waited for the chaos to begin.

Peter Maxwell hummed snatches from other Rimsky-Korsakov ditties as he trotted along the corridor to his office. A Pot Noodle wasn't terribly exciting, but he found pleasure in the small things these days and to find that the thing was edible on even a basic level was always a nice surprise, for all Nostradamus had not had the foresight to warn us about them.

He walked in, hand outstretched for the comestible, lovingly prepared by Helen Maitland, the Fridge, safely re-ensconced as his deputy after a short stretch in the madcap world of the SLT. But there was no noodle-based snack to hand.

'Helen? Where is my Satay Pot Noodle?'

'I've eaten it,' she said. 'It was going soggy. Anyway, you wouldn't have had time to eat it. Legs wants you in his office.'

'Just been there,' he said, shouldering past her to the real fridge to see if the cheese that he had stashed there some time ago was still remotely edible.

'Yep. I've eaten the cheese, by the way. He wants you there again.'

'That must be about what Pansy wanted to tell him.'

'Pansy?'

'Yes. Upsetting, isn't it? There were so many other less attractive plants after which Mrs Donaldson's parents could have named her.'

'Bladderwort,' suggested Helen.

Maxwell laughed. 'I literally cannot top that one, Helen,' he said. 'But I'm sure you won't mind if I claim it as my own from now on. I hope Pansy hasn't been called to the presence. I won't find it easy to face her after that.'

Helen patted him on the shoulder. 'Off you go,' she said. 'There's no one better than you at keeping a poker face. If you're good, I'll buy you a sandwich for later.'

'You're a star. Where will you leave it?'

'In the drawer where you keep your custard,' she said, with a questioning lift of an eyebrow.

'Have you been reading my desk?'

'Not particularly. But I understand that Nicole Thompson has.'

'Clara? Why should she be behind my desk?'

'She's everywhere, Max. Behind every Great Man's desk. Don't trust her an inch. I certainly don't. Don't put anything personal on your laptop, she'll be reading it in a flash.' She looked up to see him staring at her. 'Oh, sorry.' She gave him a push which nearly broke his arm. 'What was I thinking? Off you go, don't keep Mr Diamond waiting.'

'I don't suppose you know what it's about?'

'Not a clue. BLT?'

'Another initiative? Like AFL?'

'No, Max. Stop it, now, and be serious. BLT. Bacon lettuce and tomato. Sandwich.'

'Oh, yes. Just practising.'

She spirited a large chunk of chocolate from somewhere amongst her clothing and bit into it with frighteningly efficient teeth. 'See you later,' she mumbled round it.

'I hope so,' Maxwell said. 'I'll try to come out alive.'

Helen waggled her fingers at him and sat down at her desk and flipped open her laptop. The faint grey light that lit her face seemed to turn her into someone else, someone of a species other than the one to which Maxwell happily belonged. She double-took something that pinged up on her screen and, deciding it might be amusing rather than horrendous, turned to tell Maxwell. But he had already left the office and was on his way back down the corridor. And he wasn't humming now.

Jacquie had grown tired of her eagle's nest fastness and had wandered back down into the scrum of the main office. She had had rebuff after rebuff, phones ringing with no reply, several brushes with cleaning ladies and au pairs from unspecified and unidentifiable EU member countries of which no one has heard. She had had just one conversation that she counted as a success, with a very tearful and unhappy mother who she was visiting later in the afternoon. She wondered what the woman's motive had been in going to the police. She felt that it was largely because of the disappointment she felt that her daughter had not shared everything that was happening with her.

'I thought we were such good *friends*, Detective Sergeant Carpenter. We used to do *everything* together. And now this. She hadn't said a word.'

Jacquie was of the school of parenting which believed that your child could have loads of friends, mates, acquaintances, later on many boy-friends, girlfriends, lovers, even multiple wives and husbands. But only one mother. Only one father. But if that was what this woman, Daisy Wilkins, wanted, then that was fine. She would never find out from the questions Jacquie asked that her opinions were not the same.

'I think it would be easier if I popped round this afternoon,' Jacquie had suggested. 'So I can speak to your daughter ... er...' Her finger slid down the list.

'Maisie.'

Of course. 'Yes, Maisie. Do you have a good time for me to visit?'

'Well, she has tennis on Wednesdays.'

'But today?'

'She used to have oboe on Thursdays, but it was giving her lines around her lips.'

'So ... a good time would be?' Jacquie persisted.

'Any time after five,' Daisy said. 'But not too late, because she has homework, of course. And she sometimes goes out. And, of course, she spends quite a lot of time on the computer.' There was a little silence, full of unspoken regrets. 'Looking up things for school, I expect.'

'Yes, possibly,' Jacquie said. She had to wind this up before Daisy drove her potty. No wonder Maisie spent time elsewhere. 'Will your husband be home from work by then?' she asked, innocently.

'No,' Mrs Wilkins said tartly. 'He hasn't been home for the last ten years.'

'So it's just the two of you, then?' Jacquie asked and immediately wished she had not spoken.

'Yes.' The woman dissolved into fresh tears. 'Just the two of us. My baby and me.'

'Right. Well, I'll be round after five, then. Try to keep her at home until I arrive, Mrs Wilkins, won't you? 'Bye for now.' Jacquie wanted to suggest that Daisy didn't tell Maisie that Jacquie was on the way. But, of course, she reminded herself, they shared everything. She sighed and put down the phone. Some days she wondered whether she shouldn't have just gone in for social work and be done with it.

A voice in her ear brought her back to earth. 'Jacquie. How's the office?'

She turned and found that the speaker was one of the WPCs from Traffic along the hall. 'Fine,

126

thanks, Yvonne. How did you know about it?'

'I heard from Steve.'

'Steve?'

'Front desk.' The woman looked for signs of recognition. 'Kipper?'

'Oh. Yes. Well, it did smell really horrible.'

'Nothing quite like it, is there? But you know something? Matt couldn't smell it. He's got hardly any sense of smell.'

'Oh,' Jacquie said, a bit bemused. 'I'm sorry, Yvonne. It's been a bit of an odd day so far. Why is that funny? Surely it spoilt the joke.'

'No, no, Jacquie.' Yvonne poked her in the ribs. 'Think about it. He's sitting in there, smell enough to choke you. Someone goes in. Does Matt say, "Phew, can you smell that smell?" No, he doesn't say anything. So ... everyone assumes he is responsible. Now do you get it?'

The light dawned. 'So everyone thought he had...'

'Yes.' The WPC's laugh rang out around the room. 'And with his surname being Carter, of course, well, he's got a whole new nickname now! Anyway, I must be off. Just thought I'd pop in and see if I could have a chat. How's Nolan?'

'Oh, fine,' Jacquie said. 'Just a bump at school.'

'They will do it,' Yvonne said. 'My kids are in the Sixth Form now and not quite so clumsy, but they make up for it in being miserable little sods.'

Yvonne's twins were legendary in the nick as being the tearaways to watch and, if possible, remove from the scene before they got their mum into trouble.

'I thought they were quite...' Jacquie had to

127

think for a second for a word that wouldn't give offence and finally found it, 'boisterous.'

'Yes, that was them all right. But now they just mope about. I'm at my wits' end, tell you the truth.'

Jacquie thought fast and didn't like the results she came up with. 'Yvonne, have you got a minute? If the guv'nor is free, I think we'd like a word with you. You probably won't like it, but you may well be the answer to a maiden's prayer.'

Yvonne looked at her quizzically. 'Why won't I like it?'

'It may be nothing. But if it's what I think, we may have found ourselves a very useful mole. Are you game?'

'I'll tell you later, can I?'

'Of course.' Jacquie took her by the elbow and led her across to Henry Hall's door. She tapped on it and listened for his murmured response. She put her head round the edge and Yvonne heard her say quietly, 'Guv, I think we may have a bit of a breakthrough in the phone and Internet thing.'

The traffic cop's heart constricted in her chest. It was an instinctive chain reaction, built into the synapses of any mother of the twenty-first century. Internet. Paedophile ring. Her little girl. Oh God. She was almost in tears already as Jacquie opened the door and ushered her in.

Chapter Eight

The bus reached the end of its journey. When it had begun, edging out of Leighford bus station, it had been almost full, its passengers representing the many and various sections of the population. There was the obligatory little old lady sitting at the front, smugly ensconced in the 'Please give up this seat to anyone who is elderly or disabled' seat. Her bad leg was prominently displayed in front of her in the best position to get kicked by anyone joining the bus. This gave her a perfect opportunity to wince and clutch her calf, whilst muttering imprecations against babies in buggies, babies not in buggies, toddlers, school-age children, mothers, fathers, other old people and anyone else not covered by her rather comprehensive list. There were many from the babies and mothers camp. Some were screaming, some just whimpering. Some of the babies were also making a reasonable amount of noise. Add to the mix the tinny flick of the iPod earphones screwed into ears so pierced it was a miracle there was still an unimpeded hole to take the plugs. Apply on top the whine of the motor as the driver changed gear as he crept through the daytime traffic past the shopping centre, and it was easy to see why no one noticed their fellow passengers. The aural and olfactory overload was such that everyone just battened down their personal hatches and tried to bear the journey until their stop.

Soon, the town was left behind and the passengers got fewer and fewer. The bus wound over The Dam and up onto the Downs, its destination a village so remote that only the most determined tourists ever went there. The driver was alone with his thoughts for the last five miles and that was how he liked it. He switched on his radio and sang along lustily with the Golden Oldies of Coast FM, mercifully devoid of DJ diddle-daddle as it was. So he didn't know about the two abandoned mobile phones on the back seat of his bus, although they had been bleeping and ringing throughout the journey. He found them along with empty crisp packets and a particularly nasty-looking half-chewed Wispa when he did his lost-property sweep after he had turned his empty vehicle round. He hefted the phones thoughtfully in his hand and considered what to do with them. He had several options and they needed careful thought. He could hand them in at the depot. This would result in paperwork. He could toss them in the waste basket at the bus stop where he was parked for the regulation ten minutes as he waited for the phantom passenger who never came. No paperwork. He could keep them and see how much they would net him on an Internet site. Again, no paperwork, save a few boxes to tick and possibly a few quid in his pocket.

He was sitting in his seat looking down at them and had just decided to go with option three when a voice made him jump.

'Hello, driver.'

A passenger after all this time. He straightened in his seat and looked up, blinking. 'Hello. We don't usually get anyone getting on here. Sorry if I seemed rude.' All the drivers on the Leighford routes had gone to customer services courses. He, along with all his colleagues, had found them a complete waste of time, but the constant threat of customer feedback had kept them all on their toes. Even on the school runs when they had to battle with those psychos from Leighford High.

'Not at all. I don't usually use the bus myself, but my car is off the road. You do go straight to Leighford, don't you? Not the scenic route or anything?'

'As straight as the road is,' the driver said and, looking again at his passenger, added, 'Vicar.'

The man smiled. He always liked to know that he could trust the ocular powers of a man who was, albeit briefly, to be responsible for his life. He looked down at the phones in the driver's hand. 'Two mobiles? My word, you like to stay in touch, I can see.'

The driver knew when he was beaten. Option three might be all right, but God seemed to have weighed in for option one. 'Lost property, Vicar,' he said. 'Going to hand them in at the depot.'

'Well done,' the vicar beamed. 'Honesty is the best policy. Now, how much is a return to Leighford?'

'Six pounds twenty, Vicar.'

'*How much?* No wonder no one uses these buses.' The man of God moved off down the bus, inspecting and rejecting seats as he went for various reasons ranging from smears of rusk to smears

131

of something unidentifiable. When he reached the back, he decided to settle. He braced himself in the corner as the bus lurched away from the stop; these seats were really not terribly comfortable. Something was sticking into what his mother had always called the top of his leg, but which he more prosaically, despite his calling, called his bum. He wriggled to make himself more comfortable and the small notebook was pushed down even further between the cushions. Its secrets were pressed tighter together as his weight and the vibrations of the bus wedged it more firmly into its hiding place. Would anyone find it now?

Maxwell sat in Diamond's office, not in his usual chair, which had been snaffled by Bernard Ryan, and tried not to lose his temper. Bernard Ryan defied description really. As Deputy Heads go – and they usually do – he was just the acceptable side of God-awful. Tipped for the top he would never reach, he looked increasingly burnt out these days. Like Maxwell, he knew where the bodies were buried, but, unlike Maxwell, he wasn't talking. As always he was trying to minimise the problem. Yes, the girl could hardly be called 'missing' when she had only been off the radar for a couple of hours at most. But, there were extenuating circumstances, which Ryan didn't seem able to grasp. Mrs Donaldson sat at Diamond's right hand, with a pad on her knee. Maxwell wished that he had been there to witness the small power struggle which must have gone on before she bagged the pole position from Ryan. Finally, he could take it no longer.

'Bernard,' he cut into the man's droning. 'I don't know about you, but I have work to do, even though it is only teaching, which I appreciate is very little of your day. May I recap, Headmaster?'

Diamond was spread too thin to argue.

'Imagine these remarks as bullet points, Bernard. It might help you cope better. Bullet One is that there is something going on in this area in general but, for our purposes today, in Leighford High School which is potentially serious. Bullet Two is that our girls and only the girls are being targeted by someone who has their mobile numbers and their email addresses. Bullet Three is that one of the identified girls, which I think we have already agreed may be the tip of the iceberg,' he glanced across at Mrs Donaldson, who flicked over a page or two and then reluctantly nodded assent, 'now seems to be, if not actually missing, not where she ought to be. And Bullet Four, I have to add, is that I think we ought to call the police.'

Diamond and Ryan both chorused, 'Police? No.'

Maxwell looked at them, both professionals, both allegedly intelligent, and not able to make a simple decision to save their lives. Or anyone else's life. 'Compromise, gentlemen?'

Diamond was quicker on the uptake than Ryan, who was mulling over what trick Maxwell was trying to pull. 'Mrs Maxwell?'

'The same.'

'That reminds me, Mr Maxwell,' Mrs Donaldson piped up. 'I had a rather annoying call from a woman this morning who claimed to be your wife but didn't seem at all sure what her name was.'

133

'I heard about that,' Maxwell said. 'Detective Sergeant Carpenter, as she is still known at the nick, is also Mrs Maxwell. Confusing old world, isn't it?'

'I had no idea...' she blustered.

'Did you ask Thingee? She knows Jacquie. They go way back.'

'Thingee?'

'He means Emma, on reception,' offered Diamond. He and Maxwell went way back too.

'Well, why didn't he say so?' she muttered, annoyed that she had been made to look silly. 'I prefer my staff to be called by their proper names, not some stupid nickname. It is very demeaning.'

Maxwell snorted quietly. Bernard Ryan, every cell in his body screaming against it, spoke up for him. 'Mrs Donaldson. If Max started calling people by their real names, we would think the world had come to an end. They are just terms of endearment, Max, aren't they?'

'Mostly,' he conceded, with ice in his smile.

'For example,' Diamond chipped in, 'behind my back, Max calls me Legs, after Legs Diamond, the famous gangster of the Thirties.'

'Well done, Headmaster.' Maxwell's admiration and amazement almost cancelled each other out. 'And Nicole Thompson from IT is Clara.' He paused. 'After Clara Bow, the It Girl.' Their faces remained blank. 'Never mind. You won't remember him, Mrs Donaldson, but we used to have a caretaker, Mr Martin. So I called him Betty, after "all my eye of a yarn and Betty Martin", a phrase whose meaning is now lost to time and even to me. Do you see how it works?' They clearly

134

didn't. He was dreading the next question and, right on cue, it came.

'What do you call us?' Mrs Donaldson asked, indicating her ample self and Bernard Ryan.

Maxwell's brain, working overtime as it had been, folded its tents and left the oasis. He longed to come out with a merry quip to cover the fact that Ryan was too boring to have a nickname and he had christened her after a hated concentration camp guard. But there was just a void where that merry quip should be. He resorted to mimicry, the true last resort of a scoundrel. 'I've got nothing.' His perfect Randy Disher was wasted on them. If they had Hallmark on their TVs, they were clearly not aficionados of *Monk*. Heaven knew, they could do with a preternaturally talented private investigator now. And they'd all thank him later.

The silence ticked on for a few more seconds. Then, 'So, Max, perhaps you'd like to ring your wife,' Diamond suggested. 'Just in the first instance. Unofficially, as it were.'

'Why not?' Maxwell said and proudly brought out his mobile phone. He hit the speed dial and they all sat waiting as the connection went through.

Yvonne Thomas could hardly sit still. Jacquie took a seat to the side of Hall's desk, unconsciously mirroring Pansy Donaldson, miles away across town. The traffic woman policeman sat facing them, perched on the edge of her chair.

'For God's sake,' she burst out. 'What's going on? Are my kids OK?'

Hall never lied. 'We don't know, Yvonne. There

135

is a problem which has only just come to our attention, but could or could not be extremely serious. Someone is targeting girls of about the age of...?' he paused. He had no idea what her daughter was called, but it seemed only polite to at least suggest that he had the name at the tip of his tongue.

'Amanda. Seventeen, nearly. What do you mean, targeting?'

'They get texts on their phones, emails. That kind of thing.'

'I would know if she was,' the woman said, her throat tight with indignation and fear. 'She tells me everything.'

'I think we have to accept,' Hall said patiently, 'that no child tells its parents everything. I'm not sure it would be good for any of us if they did.'

'I'm already glad that Nolan keeps things to himself,' Jacquie said. 'If I knew half of the things he did at school, my hair would be white.'

'Do Amanda and her brother share a computer?' Hall asked. He gave himself a pat on the back for remembering that she was a twin.

'Yes. Well, we all share it, really. I didn't want them to be hiding away upstairs on chat rooms and things so it is in the dining room. Well, study, now, I suppose.'

'But she has her own email account?'

'We all do, yes. You have to give them *some* privacy.'

'Of course you do,' said Hall.

'Is it password protected?' Jacquie said. 'Can you access it from any computer?'

'We all have the same password,' Yvonne said.

136

'For the same reason we didn't want them to have a computer in their rooms. But I wouldn't pry. We've promised them that.'

'I suggest you pry now,' Hall said. 'Are they close, the kids?'

'They're twins,' she said simply. 'Although I know twins of different sexes aren't always closer than ordinary brothers and sisters, these two are. They are hardly ever apart.'

'So he will know, then? About this, if she is getting these texts and emails?'

'Certainly. His name is Josh, by the way.' She knew Hall was waiting for the information.

'Josh. Of course.' He sounded as though he had always known.

Jacquie turned Hall's laptop towards Yvonne. 'Can you log on to Amanda's email account, please?'

'You can't get it from this server,' the woman said, naively. 'It's blocked.'

'Yvonne,' Jacquie said. 'This is DCI Hall's computer. Nothing is blocked from here.'

'Oh, yes. Silly.' She tapped a few keys and waited. She looked up at them, gnawing her lip. 'A bit slow,' she said, with a nervous laugh. 'Oh, here it comes.' She tapped in a few more letters, then frowned at the screen. 'Hang on, I've probably put it in wrong.' Hall and Jacquie exchanged glances. 'Oh, God!' She pushed herself away from the desk and stood up, her hands to her mouth. 'Why has she done that? She's changed her password. I can't get in.' She looked frantically from one to the other, her eyes wide and filling with tears. 'What does it mean? Is she all right? Has anyone...?' She couldn't finish the sentence. Even in traffic, a police person was well aware of man's inhumanity to man.

Jacquie went over to her and put her arm around her shoulders and pulled her gently back into the chair.

'Come on, Yvonne. Calm down. We have no reason to assume that whoever is doing this is hurting the girls or even meeting them. But we need to get in touch with Amanda and get into her emails.' Her phone rang out with Rimsky-Korsakov's finest. She foraged in her bag and pulled it out. She looked at the display and hit a button. 'Not now, Max. I'll ring you back.'

The phone rang just a few times before it was answered. Before he could speak, Jacquie said, 'Not now, Max. I'll ring you back,' and the line went dead.

'Sorry, gents and lady,' Maxwell said. 'It appears the little woman is busy. Probably with entrails or something, if we are to believe Nurse Matthews. I'll ring back later and then get back to you, if that is acceptable?' He beamed round the room. On each face relief was written large, particularly large in the case of Pansy Donaldson.

Bernard Ryan was the first on his feet. He didn't want the police trampling through the school again. Sometimes it seemed as though all they had were police enquiries. In these days of falling rolls and parental choice, these things were best avoided. 'Perfect, Max. I'm sure I speak for us all when I say that we will happily leave it in your capable hands.' He hoped that Maxwell didn't hear Mrs Donaldson's snort. No point in antagonising him unduly. And, in Bernard Ryan's sterile little world, if the police had to be called in, Jacquie Carpenter, or Maxwell as he tried not to think of her, was at least rather more attractive than Andy Dalziel.

The meeting seemed to have ended, so Maxwell drifted away. Baulked of his Pot Noodle, his stomach began to growl. He thought he ought to appease it, if only with Helen's BLT. But it was not to be. As he passed the door to Sylvia Matthews' domain, she poked her head out and hissed at him.

'Max. Can you come in here a minute?'

'Matron.' An impeccable Kenneth Williams would usually have her in stitches, but not this time.

'Be serious, Max. What we were talking about earlier.'

'Yes.' It could be any one of a number of things, but he knew which one it was.

'I think you should come into my treatment room and have a word with Alice.'

'Alice. Any particular one?' It had been a popular name circa 1993 and the Sixth Form seemed stiff with them. Not one of them knew Christopher Robin.

'Alice Thistlewood.'

'Any relation to the Cato Street Conspirator of the same name?'

'Alice?'

'No. Arthur. And now who's being frivolous?'

'Sorry. It's just something you do to people.' She lowered her voice. 'Alice came to me very upset.

139

She's been here since the middle of the morning, having a lie down and a bit of a cry. She's on the verge of quite a serious bout of anxiety and depression, Max. Because of these dratted texts and so on.'

Maxwell stuck his head round the door, and in the subfusc lighting of the treatment area, he could see a girl lying precariously on the narrow bed, covered with a single off-white cellular blanket, medical treatment rooms the world over, for the use of. Her back was turned and at first she seemed to be asleep. But then he heard the tiny sobs which went with the subliminal shudders of her bony shoulders and he realised that she was softly crying. He nodded over his shoulder to Sylvia and crept into the room.

'Alice?' he said quietly. 'Alice? It's Mr Maxwell.'

The girl didn't turn to him, but he heard, thick with tears, her answering whisper, 'Hello, Mr Maxwell. Sorry.'

'What are you sorry for, Alice? You haven't done anything.'

'Sorry for crying. Sorry for being a nuisance.'

He checked behind him that Sylv was within sight and risked a hand on the girl's shoulder. 'A good cry does the world of good. I often treat myself to one when the going gets tough.'

The girl gave a tiny laugh and half turned round. 'I can't imagine you crying, Mr Maxwell. When did you last cry?'

'Yesterday,' he said promptly. 'When I saw my little boy with bruises and stitches in his chin.'

'He's all right, though?'

'Yes, he is. I shed a few tears because I realised

140

that I won't always be able to pick him up and dust him down. He'll have to do that for himself one day. But for now, he comes to me or his mum when he is hurt or sad. It's always better to share.'

'S'pose.'

'You know it is. Have you told anyone else about this texting thing except Nurse Matthews?'

'No. Some of the other girls are getting them as well.'

'I know. But in that case, why didn't you tell them? Someone?'

'Mine are different. He knows things about me. Things I've done.'

He looked down at the girl. She was a stringy little thing, not six stone wringing wet, with fine mousey hair pulled back in a brutal pony-tail from her sharp little features. Whatever could she have done to get her in this state? But there were no words to frame the question which wouldn't demean her and make the situation much worse. Somehow, 'You're a flat-chested and not particularly attractive girl, Alice. What do you think you would have had the opportunity to do that someone would be interested in?' didn't quite fit the bill.

He decided not to pursue it. He patted her shoulder again and backed out of the room. Once outside, he said, 'Look, Sylv. This has gone far enough. I'm sure there are all sorts of data protection, human rights and goodness knows what other bills passed through the European Parliament to prevent me, but I have to make this public. I want names, I want details and most of all I want this ... I'm lost for words, Sylv ... this

141

shit-head found before someone gets hurt.'

The nurse looked at the closed door as if she could see the sobbing girl behind it. 'Or hurts themselves, you mean?'

'That too,' he said. 'Entrails or not, I'm ringing Jacquie.'

'Entrails?'

'It was you who brought them up. She might be up to her knees in entrails, you said.'

'Oh, yes. I think that it was this kind of entrail I had in mind.'

'Fair enough. I'll ring her from my office, I think.' He tossed his head towards the treatment room. 'I wouldn't want Alice to overhear anything. Make matters worse.'

To her own surprise, Sylvia Matthews reached up and planted a kiss on Maxwell's cheek.

'Sylv!' he said, looking down at her. 'That was nice, though possibly a tad ill-advised within snooping distance of the main office. What was it for?'

'Oh, just. Because we all should do that more often. To whoever needs a kiss, a hug or a quick pat. We've become too self-contained, too self-centred to notice when people need our help, need our thanks. So, that was for all the times in the past and all the times still to come when you deserve a kiss. Tell me when my credit runs out and you can have another.'

He gave her a squeeze. 'It's hard to do that in a text, I'll agree. I'll send regular statements in future.' He brandished his phone at her. 'Off now to ring the little policewoman. Look after Alice...'
And he was gone.

Chapter Nine

On his way down to the foyer, Maxwell's mind was whirring. Phoning Jacquie was still a bit of a one-way street. What on earth could she be doing? But he still had myriad choices when it came to the rest of the afternoon: he could go and see Jacquie in person; he could track down some of the other text victims, such as Julie or Leah; he could go home and, although this went seriously against his grain, do some research on the Internet to fill in the gaps in his knowledge, which were not so much gaps as huge fissures; or, and this was the least appealing what with everything else that was going on, he could do a bit of light teaching, like what they paid him for.

But whatever choice he made – and he knew that it would never be the last one, with so much going on – he first had to negotiate the reception desk. Security had never been lax at Leighford, but then again, it had never reached the CIA-compliant standards of some other schools. But, in accordance with County policy, now no one got in without signing in, no one got out without giving their inside leg measurement and three forms of ID – 'Even I have to follow this procedure,' Legs Diamond had said in one staff meeting, as if Zeus had come down from Olympus. Pansy Donaldson had embraced these tactics to the manor born and no one was

143

exempt. Maxwell had often derived innocent pleasure from the sight of Legs trying to think of a reason for bunking off early. The fact that the man was often still in his office at ten o'clock at night didn't wash with Pansy. In the phrase 'flexible working practices' she recognised all of the words as English. She recognised 'working' as an all-round good thing; she recognised 'practice' as a useful precursor to effective working; what she didn't have in her vocabulary was 'flexible'.

He planned his body-language strategy as he went down the stairs. Was he to wander out casually, as though going to check on the status of White Surrey, languishing alone in the staff bike shed? Would a better plan be to jog vigorously to the door and, flinging it open, hail the sun, flap his arms around, rip off his clothes, breathe in deeply through his nose three or four times and then just leg it? Or should he go in to the office, like an honest citizen, and sign out, looking Pansy and Thingee Two square in the eye?

In the event, he opted for Plan Z_2. He lurked round a corner until the office staff were all looking the other way and then, collar up and hat pulled way down, like Flash Harry in the St Trinian's films, he just ran like mad down the drive and didn't stop until he reached the pavement. A goodish plan as far as it went and it certainly saved him the third degree. But he didn't have his bike and, he discovered after patting his pockets feverishly, he didn't have his wallet, either. But, to his amazement, he did have his mobile phone. He pressed a button. And it seemed to have battery still left. And ... what did this mean? There was a rather small and faint picture of an envelope flashing in one corner. He cast his mind back to his lesson of the night before. Easy – he had mail. Tentatively and with the phone held at arm's length to accommodate his rather unreliable focal length these days, he pressed some buttons. He could hardly suppress a little whoop of joy when text appeared on the screen. A woman walking her peke, who happened to be within earshot, rapidly crossed the road. What was the world coming to when drunks had mobile phones? Shouldn't they be spending their money on drink?

'The ancient work will be accomplished,' the message said. 'And from the roof evil ruin will fall on the great man. The girls will get it now, Maxwell.'

He stared at it for a moment, amazed. Everything seemed to have gone into slow motion. His vision was through a tunnel, the walls of which were multi-coloured and black, swirling away to an infinitely distant vanishing point. The rushing in his ears filled the world. It was a text. A threatening text. Someone, somehow, knew not only that the girls had been in touch, but what his mobile number was. Hell, he didn't know himself what his mobile number was.

The world came back, rising out of the maelstrom, and he looked again at the screen, willing the words to have disappeared. But no; although they had gone darker (to save the screen, Jacquie had explained) with a click of the elusive 'any' key, he could bring them back. Now, whatever

145

she said, no matter how busy she might be with any amount of entrails, he must get Jacquie. After only a few moments fumbling and trying to get rid of the text, whilst not getting actually *rid* of the text, Maxwell was listening to Jacquie's answerphone message. Jumping from foot to foot with frustration, he left a short message after the beep, remembering to speak clearly.

'Hon, petal, listen, are you there? No, of course not. Oh rats, bugger and poo. I've had one. I've had a text. Ring me – no look, I'm on my way. I don't have Surrey. I'll get a taxi. I've got no money, so someone at the nick will have to help me out on that one. How long is a short message? I was going to try and forward it to you but, look, hon, I might lose it doing that so ... anyway, I'm on my way. I hope you're there. At the nick, I mean. See you soon. Abyssinia.'

Jacquie had switched her phone off. She was glad that Maxwell had embraced a tiny corner of cyberspace, and she would get back to him and pat him on the back – one day soon when she had time. But just now, she felt that this case had exploded in her face. And it wasn't even a case, not really. A few disparate examples of kids getting texts, which hadn't seemed too desperate in the scheme of things, had suddenly grown tentacles reaching far and wide. She had left Yvonne with Henry Hall, to plan the next few moves. Not freaking out her daughter was her main aim, but she had gone beyond frightened to furious and so that might not actually happen.

Meanwhile, Jacquie had places to be. Daisy and

Maisie. Oh, boy. She wasn't looking forward to this at all. She got in the car and switched the phone on. She only intended to make a quick call, but she had messages and it wasn't in her nature to ignore them. One was from her mother, asking whether she thought that petunias would look a bit common on the front border. Delete. Another was from the garage, asking if she was happy with the car. Happy? As in delirious or in not standing on a hard shoulder in the dark in the pouring rain with a smoking engine? Either way, they wouldn't be getting an answer. This was customer care gone mad. The third one was from Maxwell.

'Hon, p ... sen, are you there? No ... Rats, bugger and poo. I've had one. I've had...... Look, I'm on my way. I don't ... Surrey. I'll get ...... so someone at the nick will have to help me... How long is a short message? I was going to try and forward it to you but, look, hon, I might lose it ... anyway, I'm on my way. I hope you're there ...... you soon. Abyssinia.'

Where was he when he sent that, Jacquie wondered? It could actually be Abyssinia, to judge by the reception. It was really hardly any use at all as messages went. He was on his way to some-where, but where to and where from? Why was he on his way anywhere at this time of the afternoon? He should still be at school. She stabbed the return call button and waited while it connected.

'Hello?'

'Max? Where are you?'

'Did you get my message?'

'In a way,' she said. 'I have no idea what it was

147

about. More than half of it was missing.'

'I'm in a taxi, on my way to the nick. I need to speak to you.'

'What about? What is so urgent that you have left school?'

He sounded puzzled, even over the flattening effect of mobile phone technology. The explanation was so obvious that he didn't waste airtime. *Anything* was urgent enough for him to leave school! 'I just needed to show you something. But I haven't got any money.'

Jacquie rummaged for her purse. 'What are you – the queen? I'll leave some at the desk,' she said. She opened the door and stepped out, reaching behind her to stow her bag. 'How much do you think it will be?'

'Four pounds twenty-five, heart,' said Maxwell's voice in her ear. 'Plus a tip, the man's been very helpful.'

She straightened up and found herself nose to nose with her husband, who was ringing off with a flourish. 'God, Max! You'll kill me one day, doing that.'

'Boys will be boys,' he said. 'Shall we make it a fiver?'

She handed it over and he leant in the window of the taxi parked alongside. The driver made a half-hearted turn to look through his change bag – aren't they good at that? – but Maxwell brushed it aside. The driver threw the car into reverse and screeched off. He didn't like to linger in the car park of the nick.

'Excellent timing,' Maxwell beamed at Jacquie.

'Well, not really,' she said ruefully. 'I'm just off

148

to interview someone.'

'Anyone I know?'

'No. It's a mother and daughter. I've spoken to the mother already and I think it is going to be a bit of a mission, to be honest with you. She's her daughter's best friend, I'm sorry to say.'

'Oh, dear. Called Jane and Janet? No, no, too old-fashioned. Hold on, Amy and Mamie?'

'Close. Daisy and Maisie and that's more than I should tell you.'

'Oh, snookums. You can't go to interview the terrible twins on your own. Why isn't Henry going with you? You know he loves your driving.'

'I'll have you know,' she bridled, 'that Henry has actually gone to sleep in my car before now. *That's* how relaxed he is when I am driving. In fact, he is going off with a colleague to interview her daughter.'

'Ouch. Shoplifting?'

'No. Another text victim, we think. Look, Max,' she got in the car and closed the door firmly. Through the window he could just hear her say, 'That's enough. I can't tell you any more.'

He pulled the door open again. 'But I have got things I need to tell you. I've had a text. I told you in my message.'

'Of which I heard one word in five.'

'All right, all right. That's technology's fault, that is, not mine.' When the moment arose, Maxwell could be petulant for England.

'Interesting.' She chewed her lip, always a sign that she was close to caving in. 'But even so, you can report that inside.' She pointed at the nick.

'But who to, petal? Look at the state I'm in,' he

149

said, slapping his forehead. 'To whom? To whom should I report it, dear Liza, dear Liza?' His Harry Belafonte was lost on the woman.

'The desk,' she said. 'They've had lots of reports coming in. They will know what it's about.'

'They'll think I'm crackers.'

'They already think you're crackers, Max.'

'Oh, come on,' he wheedled. 'What if you take me home and I'll tell you on the way?'

'It's in the opposite direction.'

'Not if you go round the pretty way,' he smiled. 'Or, better yet,' he held up his finger as if to point at the twinkling light bulb above his head, 'why don't I just come with you and I can tell you all my news, like my text and,' and he lowered his voice and waggled his eyebrows, 'Julie going missing.'

'Julie is missing?' Jacquie was aghast. 'Max, this is no time to be frivolous.'

'Oh, no, really,' Maxwell said. 'She is missing in that no one knows where she is. But she isn't *missing*. It's only since this morning. She was registered first lesson. Then she missed an outside appointment and we're not sure where she is. But, after what she told us, love, I don't expect she is in the habit of going home early.'

'No,' Jacquie agreed. 'But, even so ... hang on a minute.' She got out of the car and trotted in that girlie way of hers, knees together, feet splaying out to each side, back into the nick. After a minute or two she was back.

'Pee?' Maxwell enquired in a friendly enough tone.

'No. I've left a message with the desk. If any

parent, or anyone at all really, phones in with a missing teenaged girl, he rings me straight away.'

'Makes sense. Well, now you've done that, I don't expect you've got time to take me home or to the bus station or anywhere, have you? So I'll just come with you, shall I?'

'Smashing idea,' Jacquie said. 'Jump in.'

Maxwell was in the passenger seat before he realised his mistake. 'Umm, where are you taking me?'

'Bus station. Look in my bag and you'll find my purse. Help yourself to a tenner and get yourself home. I can't take you with me, Max.' She didn't look at him – she knew that to do so would be to lose her advantage.

'But I'll stay in the car,' he whined. 'I will. I won't be a nuisance. And I will be company on the journey.'

'It's ten minutes.'

'I know. But there might be traffic. Your satnav might not be working.' He flicked it with a finger. 'Look, nothing.'

'It isn't switched on. I know where I'm going.'

'In that case,' and he pressed a button, 'let's confuse you and use the computer, eh? I'm trying to embrace technology.'

'Don't be silly. Even *I* don't embrace satnav. I want to get to where I'm going.'

Maxwell smiled and leant back in the seat, eyes closed. This was nice. Doing a bit of sleuthing with his wife, bunking off school on a nice spring afternoon, the long-suffering Helen Maitland no doubt holding the Sixth Form hordes at bay.

'Don't you go to sleep on me, now,' she said,

poking him in the ribs. 'You're supposed to be providing entertainment on the journey.'

He straightened up and, adjusting his tie, burst suddenly into song. 'Daylight. See the dew on the sunflower. And a rose that is fading. Roses wither away.'

'How do you know the first lines of that? No one knows all the words of "Memory".'

'And rightly so. But the Count is rather fond and so I have seen the video rather a lot of times.'

'Cats don't necessarily like *Cats*.' She knew he was just giving her a little light relief before Daisy and Maisie.

'No, indeed. And, again, rightly so. But the Count likes a little musical theatre as you know. For some reason, management prefers not to sell him one of the better seats, so he watches at home.'

She laughed. 'Max, what would I do without you?'

There was no answer. She glanced sideways and wished she hadn't spoken. There was a spectre at their happy feast and that was the age gap, of which she was scarcely aware. But she knew and he, the historian, knew even better, that their days together would not be too long in the land. Nothing like long enough. She took his hand and squeezed it and he squeezed back. 'Historians can do it for ages,' he laughed and salvaged the moment. 'But, listen, let me tell you about my–'

But she had turned a corner into a small cul-de-sac. '*Et voil*à,' she said. 'Without the help of a satnav of any description, either digital or human, here we are at Daisy and Maisie's house.'

She looked at the small bungalow at the end of a short drive. 'Oh, good heavens above. Will you please look at that.'

Maxwell craned round to see and his eyes popped. He had never seen so many gnomes in one place in all his life. They all but outnumbered the blades of grass in the lawn. In amongst them, as if their happy, apple-cheeked faces weren't nauseating enough, were wishing wells, windmills, large daisies with smiling faces and unlikely eyelashes and one rather beleaguered-looking rabbit, twice the size of the largest windmill. 'Oh.' He had never been so very lost for words.

'"Oh" is right. She sounded a bit ... twee, but I never expected this.'

'No wonder young Maisie is kicking over the traces.'

'How do you know she's kicking over the traces?' Jacquie wondered if she had accidentally said more than she had meant to.

'I'm just hoping she is, I think. Can any sixteen-year-old girl feel she can fit in to this little grotto? Do I mean grotto?' he mused. 'Anyway, heart. Knock yourself out. I'll just wait out here for you. Mwah.' He pulled his hat over his eyes and settled back, flicking the station to Radio Four.

'Oh, no, sunshine.' Jacquie was getting out of the car and coming round to his side. She wrenched open the door. 'Out you get.'

'Precious, surely I can't barge into a police investigation?'

'Get out of the car, Maxwell,' she said between her teeth. 'I don't think I can manage Snow White on my own. I need a sane – well, the nearest to sane I can get at this late notice – person with me in case I drown in Golden Syrup. If she asks, you are my ... stenographer.'

He looked down at his mildly disreputable trousers and his tweed jacket which was older than many of the children he taught daily. His bow tie had once been bow-tie-shaped, now it tended to look a bit more like a piece of fat string. Everything was clean, but that was about all that could be said for it. Added to which, he had to admit, he was a bit long in the tooth to be a police stenographer. 'Do you think she'll buy that story?' To be fair, David Jason had got away with posing as a policeman for years.

She tugged his shirt collar a bit straighter and resisted the urge to lick her hankie and polish up his chin. 'I've never seen anyone look more convincing,' she said. 'Do you have a pen?' He whipped open his coat and showed the veritable arsenal of every colour ballpoint Staples could provide. 'Pad?' The other side of the jacket, flung open, revealed a spiral-bound notebook. 'No wonder your coat is such a peculiar shape,' she told him. 'I thought it was your old trouble. Right. You're armed and not terribly dangerous. Let's go.'

They walked up the drive in line abreast and Jacquie pushed the bell button. It didn't come as too much of a surprise when it dutifully played the tune of 'April Showers' in a tinkling cascade.

When the door was opened, Maxwell thought for a moment that perhaps the woman was in rehearsal for an amateur production of *Little Shop of Horrors,* for there, surely, stood Audrey.

154

From her back-combed, bottle-blonde hair to her white stilettos, she was femininity through a distorting mirror. 'Hello,' she trilled. 'Detective Sergeant Carpenter? And this is...?' She literally batted her eyelashes at Maxwell. He fancied he could feel the draught.

'Yes,' Jacquie said, stepping inside, hoping her warrant card would do for them both. 'This is Mr Peters. He is a civilian stenographer. Community Police Service. Here to take notes,' she added, when the woman appeared to have passed out on her feet, for all the reaction she showed.

'Oh, I see,' she said. 'I thought you had tape recorders.'

'Data protection act,' Maxwell chimed in quickly. 'Some people don't like their voices being recorded.' He smiled at her and Jacquie turned to him gratefully. 'They think they steal their souls. Ow.' He dutifully reacted to the dull ache resulting from Jacquie's heel pressing down on his toe.

The woman looked at him and it was possible that her expression changed slightly, but it was hard to tell. She stood aside and extended an arm. 'Do come in,' she said and led the way into what at first Maxwell took to be a frill factory. It turned out to be the lounge and, after a little searching, Maxwell found a chair and perched on the edge. He extracted a pen and the pad and sat in an attitude of extreme alertness, eyebrows raised, pen poised, ready to jot down every phrase that fell from Daisy Wilkins' glossy lips.

'Mrs Wilkins,' Jacquie said, sitting down on what she hoped was a sofa, despite the fact that it looked like a random pile of cuddly toys. 'Is Maisie at home?'

'Please, call me Daisy.' She simpered at Maxwell. 'Everyone does.'

Maxwell raised one eyebrow a fraction further at his wife. He knew he would be in trouble later when he noticed the nerve jump at the edge of her jaw, which always meant she was about to laugh in an inappropriate situation.

'Thank you, Mrs Wilkins ... erm, Daisy. Is Maisie at home?'

The woman raised her eyes to the ceiling and pointed. Despite themselves, Maxwell and Jacquie both looked up, as though the girl might be actually there, suckered to the stucco like a huge gecko. She lowered her voice to below the threshold of any normal ears. 'In her room,' her lips said.

'Wonderful,' said Jacquie. 'Can you get her to come down?'

'She's just changing,' her mother said. 'She finds school uniform very demeaning. She prefers her own clothes.'

Jacquie and Maxwell could imagine the vision that they would be honoured with when the girl came down. A clone of her mother, down to the American Tan stockings and the small pearl clip-on earrings. Maxwell also expected her to be mildly overweight. His experience over the millennia had taught him that doting mothers tended to dote with chocolate as well as other less fattening things like clothes, computers and syndromes needing years of therapy. He had also noticed they didn't tend to dote with books. His

156

mind wandered; he was looking forward to his dotage. He would like the doting to take the shape of more plastic models for his diorama, Southern Comfort, and banana sandwiches. He was brought back to earth by the sound of a door slamming overhead and galloping feet on the stairs. Daisy smiled indulgently in the direction of the door. The Princess was at hand.

Maxwell just had time to wonder why the girl sounded so heavy on her feet when the door crashed back and a vision in black stood there, feet in purple Doc Martens planted aggressively apart, black-nailed fingers curled into loose fists resting on the well-padded vinyl-clad hips. There probably was room for more piercing on the face, but Maxwell was hard-pressed to identify it. The eyes were ringed with kohl, which had the disturbing effect of making them appear even closer together than they actually were. The hair was dyed, certainly, but in many shades from pale magenta to midnight blue. The vision spoke in a nasal whine.

'Quickenoughforya?'

Daisy sprang to her feet and hurried over to give the girl a hug. 'Thank you for hurrying up, sweetie,' she cooed in her ear. She turned to Jacquie but mainly to Maxwell. 'She'd do anything for her mummy, wouldn't you, baby?' She reached up and, finding a non-metallic area of cheek, kissed the girl. 'She usually takes a long time to get ready, but she has cut a few corners for us, haven't you, love?' She tugged the girl's arm to bring her into the room. It was as if a sparrow had suddenly decided to drag the cat in

157

through the cat flap, instead of the other way round. The girl's dark bulk remained stationary and so the mother gave up and went and sat back down, settling her skirts around her calves in a modest and yet unsettlingly provocative way.

'Hello, Maisie,' Jacquie said brightly. 'I don't know how much you know about my visit, but I gather you've been having some upsetting texts and emails.'

'Notupsettin,' muttered the girl. 'Anythin-toeat?' she suddenly demanded of her mother, who immediately leapt to her feet.

'Sandwich, poppet?' she asked. 'Cake? Crisps?'

'Yeah,' the girl nodded and came into the room, flinging herself onto a chair, scattering cushions and frills left and right. Jacquie caught Maxwell's eye and knew that he, like her, was remarking to himself that now he knew why they were called that.

Daisy turned to Jacquie and smiled. 'She can get so cranky when she's peckish, can't you, sweetheart? Do you have children, Sergeant?'

Maxwell almost answered for her but remembered in time that he was Mr Peters, police stenographer.

Jacquie smiled and said that yes, she had one small son, but before she could go into any detail, hoping to bond with the woman in shared parenthood, Daisy had closed her eyes in horror and one small, exquisitely manicured hand was pressed to her chest to still her beating heart.

'Oh, I am so sorry,' she breathed. 'Never mind,' and her eyes flew open, sparkling with hope for the future, 'next time it might be a girl.' And with that, she trotted off to the kitchen to prepare a small banquet for her little chick.

The room seemed emptier after she had gone by more than the sum of her parts. Maxwell was reminded of the strange silence that follows a firework display. The air was almost fizzing with the ghosts of her relentless sparkle.

Jacquie thought they had better get this show on the road. Nolan was staying, until she fetched him, with his best friend in the whole world this week, Spencer, and she had learnt that there was a sell-by date on these after-school get-togethers that could be scarily short. 'Maisie,' she said, 'I know you just said that your texts and emails weren't upsetting. Did you just say that because your mum was here?'

Maisie turned her cavernous eyes on Jacquie. It was as though Mount Rushmore had suddenly decided to make eye contact. 'No,' she said, perfectly clearly. 'Why should I do that?'

Maxwell wished he could pat his own back these days. He certainly deserved it, for having pigeon-holed this girl so well. Schizophrenia of parental embarrassment, he called it. He saw it all the time.

Jacquie did a double take. 'Well, she did say you two were ... extremely close, and I just wondered...' she said, her voice tailing away.

'Close?' The Goth girl looked both amazed and amused. 'Do you think we look close?'

'Well, no,' Jacquie conceded. 'But appearances can be deceptive.'

'Not this time,' Maisie said. 'I can't really be arsed to get out the baby pictures, but she's got them all around if you can see them through all this frilly crap. Take a look. You'll see.'

Jacquie got up and wandered round the room. There were indeed photos everywhere, of Maisie at every age from newly born to yesterday. And in each and every one, she looked like the cuckoo in the nest that she so clearly was. Dark spiky hair adorned the head of the cross-looking baby in Barbie doll's arms, a truculent toddler with fat thighs making her feet splay out was half-throttling a patient-looking cat, an eleven-year-old in a Black Sabbath T-shirt was holding a repelling hand out to the camera. On and on through the years, Maisie was definitely not a chip off Daisy's block. Looking at her now, she seemed poised to sack Rome.

It was difficult to coo and it was clear that Maisie would not have relished it. She was revelling in her difference to the general public; perhaps it was all she had. Maxwell knew he shouldn't ask questions, as a humble stenographer, but couldn't resist it. 'Is your dad in any of these?'

'No,' the girl replied. 'Mum pretends he left us when I was small, but to tell the truth, he was never here. I don't know whether she was with him for long before I was born, but he was gone before I was a month old.' She saw the surprise on Jacquie's face. Daisy didn't seem the kind of mother to tell her daughter that. 'Don't worry. It wasn't the Fairy Liquid Mum who told me that. It was my gran. Her mum. She knows how to call a spade a spade.'

Maxwell was relieved that someone in the

family had that simple skill, as well as poor Maisie.

'So,' Jacquie said, as the sounds from the kitchen started to sound a bit final, 'how did your mum come to find out about your texts and emails if you didn't pour your heart out to her whilst painting each other's nails?'

Maisie threw her a look of pure gratitude. It was obvious she wasn't used to being understood. 'She goes through my pockets. She goes through my drawers. I lock things when I can, but when I put a password on *my* computer and a PIN on my phone she threatened to kill herself.'

'Pardon?' Jacquie's eyes were wide.

'Yeah.' Maisie was laconic. 'She's a bit melodramatic.'

The sounds of a trolley were heard in the hall. Maxwell just knew it would be highly varnished wood with a faux brass gallery round the top level.

Jacquie knew she must be quick and gave the girl her card. 'Can I see you tomorrow at the nick?' she hissed. 'Will you be at school?'

'School?' she laughed. 'I haven't been there in months. I'll come to the nick, sure.'

'Do you know where it is?' Jacquie asked, and immediately knew she was wasting her breath when Maisie gave a short bark of laughter.

The trolley was pushed triumphantly into the lounge and it was exactly as Maxwell had suspected. It was laden with cakes, home-made jam in little Wemyss pots, scones, kettle-chips of umpteen different varieties in bowls printed with pictures of crisps. It was enough food for twenty, but Daisy put it pointedly alongside her daughter. This was love food and not for strangers.

'Have you been having a nice chat, poppet?' she asked her daughter, trying to tuck a wiry wisp of hair behind a much-pierced ear.

The girl tossed her head and squirmed away. 'Goinout,' she muttered and slouched out.

Daisy gave a small, regretful shrug and then smiled up at Jacquie and Maxwell as though nothing had happened. 'Was she any help?' she asked.

'Loads,' Jacquie said brightly. 'What a lovely girl. You must be very proud.'

Maxwell was proud as well ... of his lovely, caring wife. He thought of what she could have said, the calls to social services she could be making; but no – she knew they were both interdependent, no matter how it looked and she would leave well enough alone. But she also knew that Maisie could be a deep mine of information, if tapped the right way. Now, how to get away from Daisy? He looked forward to seeing how she accomplished that.

'Oh, I am,' Daisy gushed. 'Only the other day–'

The Bum of the Flightlebee rang out in the airless room.

'Excuse me,' said Jacquie, smiling. 'It's the station. I must answer it. DS Carpenter,' she said into the phone in her hand. She stood up and then stiffened. 'What?' She looked at Maxwell, who pocketed his notepad and stood up obediently. 'On my way.' She rang off and turned to Daisy Wilkins. 'I'm afraid there is rather an emergency at the station, Mrs Wilkins. We'll have to go. Thank you for your time and please thank Maisie for me when you see her.'

'Oh,' carolled Daisy. 'She'll be in shortly.' She dropped her voice and wrinkled her nose at Maxwell. 'It's our night for washing our hair.'

'Lovely,' he said. 'Girls' night in.'

She patted his arm. What a wonderful man. She loved tweed on a bicep; so manly. Her pat became a stroke. Jacquie grabbed his other arm and pulled.

'Well, Mr Peters,' she said. 'We must be away. Goodbye, Mrs Wilkins.'

They forced themselves to walk, not trot, down the drive. Only Maxwell looked back. Daisy Wilkins was standing in the doorway, wiggling her fingers at them, a brave smile on her face. It was enough to break your heart.

'Good work there, Juliet Bravo,' he said. 'That trick with the phone.' He snapped his seat belt on. 'Now, let me tell you about my–'

'Yes, a good trick,' she muttered, interrupting him, turning the ignition. 'Only it wasn't a trick. That was the nick. Leah's little sister has just knocked on their neighbour's door.'

His throat seemed to have just gone very dry. 'Why?'

'Leah hasn't come home from school. She seems to have disappeared.'

Chapter Ten

The drive back to the station was quiet, as they both wrestled with their thoughts. Maxwell had taken Julie's 'disappearance' lightly. If he had a quid for every girl whose parents had thought she was missing, only to have her turn up, crestfallen or dishevelled according to the reason for her absence, he would almost be able to buy himself an ice-cream on the Front in high season. Jacquie was tuned to a slightly different level. Her experience had taught her that the length of disappearance had no bearing on its severity. If someone had been abducted, they were missing from the second they were snatched and that could be within a minute of their being last seen. If someone wanted to disappear, they could mask their departure by means of messages, phone calls and false trails until they had time to burrow into whatever parallel world they had chosen as preferable to the one they were leaving. But when two girls, friends, sharing the same trouble, went missing on the same day, then the alarm bells rang. She didn't know whether they had been taken, or if they were in hiding. What she knew for certain was that she was about to be immersed in the world of crying mothers, shouting fathers, press and tension.

She also had to get rid of Maxwell as soon as possible. When they had set off to interview the Wilkins pair, the plan had been that Jacquie could drop Maxwell off at home, or very nearly, and then go on to finish her day. And although that was still theoretically possible, she didn't want to waste even those few minutes.

Maxwell had also been thinking and along very similar lines. He cleared his throat. 'I haven't told you about my text,' he said.

'Max,' she said, a little testily, as she took a bend rather too wide for anyone's comfort. 'I'm glad you've mastered the phone, but really, I can hear about this later, at home.'

'Two things, heart,' he said. 'The first is that I can't see you getting home any time soon today and you know how I need my beauty sleep.'

She glanced at him and gave a small laugh. He was the only person she had ever met who could get by on the same few seconds a night that she could. 'If you say so. And the second thing?'

'I thought you understood about my text. I told you in the message and I've been trying to tell you since. I've had a message like the girls'. Threatening and rather disturbing.'

'Max!' He didn't know whether this came out as a scream because she was angry or because a lorry was bearing down on them from the right. 'Why didn't you tell me sooner?'

'I did try,' he said mildly.

There was a pause as she reran the last hour or so. 'Hmm, all right. Perhaps you did.'

He silently mouthed, 'Yes, I did,' but her eyes were on the road and she didn't see.

'But...' She looked at him. 'I'm sorry. I wasn't concentrating on what you were saying. Tell me now.'

165

'It said "The ancient work will be accomplished, and from the roof evil ruin will fall on the great man. The girls will get it now, Maxwell."'

'Like that? No text speak?'

'No. Everything was spelt out in full. They even included punctuation.'

'That's odd. Most people don't bother. But what the hell does it mean?'

'There's something about it that's familiar and I can't put my finger on it. The great man's me, of course – who else?'

'Yes, dear, of course it is. I rather thought it was referring to Sherlock Holmes and it's obviously someone who knows you because you don't text, or use abbreviations.' She thought for a moment, drumming her fingers on the wheel as she waited for a traffic light to change. 'So are we back to kids?'

'No, I still don't think that. And that's not just because the kids who would find this funny wouldn't be up to the grammar or the emailing and what must be a quotation. A kid who *could* do this, *wouldn't* do this, if you see what I mean.'

'I do see,' Jacquie said. 'But I think that perhaps you and I have a different view of kids.'

'Perhaps,' he turned and smiled at her. 'Perhaps we had better agree to differ.' Then, as if he had read her mind, 'What do you want me to do when we get to the nick?' This was a timely question, as she had just turned into the car park.

'I was going to go back to the first plan of the afternoon, before you talked yourself into being a stenographer.' He ignored the obvious injustice of this – he had been perfectly content to stay in the car. 'You should get yourself home and I'll see you later. But now...' She turned off the ignition and the car clicked quietly as the engine started to cool. 'I think you ought to come in and give a statement.'

He looked dubious. 'To anyone in particular?'

Jacquie ran through the list of people who Maxwell hadn't annoyed at the nick. It was very short and only one was on duty. 'I suppose it will have to be Henry,' she said.

'Isn't he out?'

'Oh, damn. Yes, he is. Or at least, was. It might just be that he's back. We'll go in and see, anyway.' She unbuckled her belt and got out of the car. She turned and faced him over the car roof. 'We could do with a holiday, you know,' she said.

'Half-term, now, I suppose,' he said. 'No last minutes for the Easter holidays left, I shouldn't think.'

'When you retire,' she said, 'we can go away whenever we want.'

'True,' he agreed. 'As long as it only costs fourpence three farthings.'

She laughed and clicked the key. The car warbled back at her and flashed its lights in a friendly fashion. Falling into step, they walked up the back steps of the nick.

Henry Hall drove to Yvonne Thomas's house, following her. She was at the end of her shift and he saw no reason to make her come back in just to get her car. As a father himself, he knew she would have a difficult evening ahead of her. As

167

they walked to their cars, he had chatted to her of this and that, mainly trying to find out a bit about her home life. He liked to think he kept his ear to the ground, but there was a limit; not even he could remember everything about everyone. He realised that he perhaps should have known that her husband was a desk sergeant at another station, but he just chalked that one up as a failure. He would be home before they got there.

He got out of his car, which he had parked at the kerb over the end of the traffic cop's drive. At least he knew he was probably safe from a ticket there. She was waiting for him by her vehicle and set off down the drive to the front door as soon as he had locked his doors.

It was a nice house, Henry thought. Well kept, a basketball hoop on the door frame of the garage, a cat flap in the panel beside the double-glazed front door. The door knocker was a tiny truncheon, in brass. Someone had a sense of humour at least.

The door opened and Yvonne's husband stood there, framed from behind by sunlight filtering through from the kitchen. The house sounded too quiet to have two teenagers in it, especially the two that Hall remembered: forces of nature, red-haired, freckled kids, always throwing a ball or catching a Frisbee. They were always the ones who played the funny jokes, not the cruel ones. They went to school out of Leighford, going in every morning with their dad, coming home on the school bus. Nice kids, from a nice home.

Their parents spoke together.

'Kids home?' their mother said.

'They're upstairs,' came from their father. Then he added, 'They wanted to go out but I said they had to wait for you.' He looked past her to Henry. 'DCI Hall,' he extended his hand for him to shake, 'I wasn't expecting you.' The subtext said – you're a bit high-profile. What's going on?

'Don't worry, Pete,' Yvonne said, thus relieving Henry of the problem of not knowing the guy's name. 'It's just that DCI Hall was free and the DS who is running the case had an appointment. I'm sure it will all be something and nothing.'

'I'm sure it will,' Hall said. He turned to the husband. 'It's just that Amanda and Josh might be able to give us a unique insight into the issue that we're dealing with: nasty texts and emails.'

'We're getting them as well, over at Littlehampton,' Pete said: 'We've had about five complaints.'

'Get ready for more,' Henry said darkly. 'Ours seem to be increasing on a ridiculous scale.' He knew there was a word for it, but couldn't bring it to mind.

'Exponential,' a voice came from over his head.

Yes, that was it.

'It means that the more there is of something, the faster the amount increases.' The voice was coming nearer, in time with soft footfalls on the stairs.

'Meet my son, Josh,' Yvonne said. 'He's something of a mathematician.'

Henry Hall's spirits rose. Maths went with computers, as often as not, in his experience.

'I'm sorry to disappoint you,' the lad said, reading his mind, it seemed. He stopped on the bottommost stair. 'It's Maths and Music with me.

169

Maths and Dance with Mand. It's a bit of a rhythm thing.' He rocked his hips and clicked his fingers.

Hall nodded. 'Hello, Josh. I assume you know why I'm here, then?'

'We guessed, me and Mand. It was only a matter of time, you know, with the pezzers being Old Bill and that.'

There was a sound of a door closing quietly on the landing and the same soft footfalls came round the corner of the stairs. Suddenly Josh had a shadow, slighter, paler, with longer hair, but otherwise they made Hall feel as though the focus had slipped, like it used to on the old-fashioned TVs of years ago. He had never seen twins of different sexes look so alike.

Yvonne saw his expression and gave a small laugh. 'Yes,' she said. 'It does that to people. It's just a family thing, though. Plus the red hair; the face, the freckles, the slight build seems to go with it.'

'Yeah,' Amanda said, pushing past her brother and standing one step below him on the hall floor. 'You'll see our type all over. We would have been exposed on a hillside years ago, wouldn't we, bro?' She tossed her flaming curls and turned to look up at her brother. 'They'd have called us changelings.'

Their father called the meeting to order. 'Shall we go into the dining room?' he said, pushing open a door.

'Family conference?' the girl said. 'Wassup?'

'Come on, Mand,' her brother said. 'You know what's up. They,' he indicated his parents with a

170

toss of the head, 'aren't stupid. And we've been behaving like a pair of total spazzes. They were bound to cotton on sooner or later.'

She tried to keep up the pretence. 'Cotton on? What to?'

He gave her a gentle push in the small of the back. 'Just get in there. Sooner it's done, sooner it's done.'

Yvonne gave Hall a small smile. 'He's the eldest,' she said, by way of explanation.

'How much by?' Hall asked.

'Two minutes, but it's important to them.' She stood aside and let Hall go into the dining room first.

This was not a room out of any of the home-improvement shows on the television. There was no rather self-conscious flower arrangement in the middle of a highly polished and barely used table, no throws over the backs of the chairs. This was a room where a family ate, played games and, yes, used the computer. It sat, not exactly state of the art, in a corner on a small desk. A shelf of CD-ROMs was attached rather haphazardly on the wall above it. Hall leant over to read the titles: garden planners, Scrabble, Sudoku; not even a shoot-em-up game in the little collection. He turned back to the family and saw they were smiling.

'Sorry, DCI Hall,' Pete Thomas said. 'We are really boring parents when it comes to our kids and computers. No shooting here. We've both seen enough in real life.'

Hall thought – but didn't say it – in Traffic? Things must be wilder on the streets than he remembered. His face, though as stone-like as ever, must have shown it, because Yvonne looked at her husband before she spoke.

'We haven't always lived here, DCI Hall. We used to live in Nottingham.'

Hall understood. The drive-by shooting capital of Britain. And he also understood why these parents were taking this problem, which might not be a problem, so seriously. 'I see.' He sat down and looked round the table at them. 'I'll just give a quick recap, mainly for the sake of Amanda and Josh,' he began.

'No need,' Josh said. 'We know why you're here. Mand has been receiving texts and emails which scare her.' He looked over at his mother and, reaching out, covered her hand with his. 'Don't worry, Ma. She hasn't been meeting paedophiles behind the bike sheds. No one has touched her. They mostly suggest that she has done something wrong that the person on the other end knows about. That they will tell if she tells, that sort of thing. Usual sort of thing.' The last statement was on the edge of being a question, and it was directed at Hall, who nodded.

'I was scared,' the girl said. 'I had to tell Josh, he always knows when something is wrong anyway, so there was no point in hiding it from him.'

'How long have these messages been arriving?' Hall asked.

The twins looked at each other and pursed their lips, thinking. Amanda answered. 'Since just after Christmas, I think,' she said. 'Yes, that would be about right. Still in the holidays, but after all the Christmassy bits, you know. Say around the fourth of January, that kind of time.'

'Not that long, then,' said Hall. 'How many have you had? Ten? Fifteen?'

Josh gave a harsh laugh. 'Make that ten or fifteen a day,' he said. 'And that's on a quiet day. Sometimes it's far more.'

His parents stared in horror. No wonder their children had become rather quiet. Yvonne looked ready to speak, but Hall held up his hand and she shut her mouth again.

'Was it that many from the start?' he asked.

'No,' she said. 'At first it was just the odd one or two. In fact, I thought it was a friend messing about. Because it was the school holidays, you know? I had had a new phone for Christmas and I thought it was because of that.'

'So it was a new number,' Hall said thought-fully.

'Of course not,' Josh said, with the laugh that teenagers reserve to reward a cute old fogey who knows nothing. 'She kept the number. Can you imagine the chaos if she had to change her number?' He snorted. 'It would take, like, weeks to let everyone know.'

'I'm sorry to hear you say that,' Hall said. 'Because that's exactly what I want you to do. I want you to change your number. Get this one suspended temporarily so that whoever this person is knows you are not getting the texts. Then, get a new one,' he glanced across at the parents. Pete nodded. 'Don't let anyone have the new number, except your parents and Josh. Then, if you get more texts, let me know.' He didn't say as much, but his plan, as far as it was formulated,

173

was to find out where the information was coming from. Did the texter have some way of finding out telephone numbers other than from friends and general calling circles? This would be the way to find out.

'What about the emails?' It was a fair question.

'Yes, well, I need to see those. Have you kept them?'

'No. Of course not,' the girl said. 'I wouldn't open them, only he sends them from different addresses all the time, so I don't always know it is one. There'll probably be one now, though. I haven't logged on for a while.'

'Oh, yes,' Yvonne chipped in before Hall could stop her. 'What's with changing your password, my girl?'

'I don't know how you could even ask,' Josh spat. 'She didn't want you to know.'

'But you always tell us everything,' their mother wailed, and burst into tears.

Hall had been through this learning curve, as every parent did. It made it no easier to watch someone climb its slopes. He glanced at Pete Thomas, who looked stricken; he didn't know which way to jump. Hall decided to save them from themselves. 'Yvonne,' he said. 'You know that's not true. You know kids have secrets from the time they can talk. Before, probably. They didn't do it to hurt you, you know that.'

'I'll tell you what, though,' Amanda said, stroking her mother's arm, 'it's amazing you only found out today. That means you haven't been checking. That means a lot to Josh and me.' The boy nodded. Their mother blew her nose and wiped her eyes. The smiles they exchanged made even Henry Hall's cynical heart lurch a little.

To break the somewhat schmaltzy mood, Hall cleared his throat and said, 'Can you get logged on, Amanda, and we'll see what our friend has for us?'

'This will take a while,' Amanda said ruefully. 'This computer is old and a bit cranky.'

'It does for us,' Pete Thomas said, rather defensively. 'You don't need state of the art for what we use it for.'

'State of the ark, this is,' Josh said, and Hall had to admit that, as jokes went, and as circumstances went, it wasn't bad.

'Excuse me,' Hall said to the Thomas family in general. He had felt the preliminary stirrings of his mobile phone and almost at once, they all heard the growing tones of a very simple, basic ring. Not for Henry Hall the merry Rimsky-Korsakov extravaganza of the Maxwells. He didn't even like the more restrained and very popular Mozart tune. He just liked a nice, simple, regular ringing phone noise. The fact that it drove his wife mad and that every bird in his garden had the sound off to a tee didn't matter – he knew what he liked and what he liked was, *ring, ring. Ring, ring. Ring, ring...* He looked at the screen and pushed a button. 'Yes?' He turned his back on the assembled family and sidled out of the door. They heard him say, 'Yes. I see. Can you cope at the moment?' Then the door closed behind him and they couldn't hear any more.

Josh grimaced at his mother. 'Is he always like this?' he whispered.

'God, no,' she said. 'Usually he's a lot more strait-laced than this. He's trying to relax a bit, you know, being in our house and all. He likes to make people feel at ease.'

'Blimey!' her husband said. 'I wouldn't like to see him when he was being a bit po-faced, then. I'd heard the rumours, but I can't believe they are actually true.'

Yvonne elbowed him in the ribs. The door was slowly opening and Henry Hall was coming back in. 'Sorry,' he said, looking round. 'Something has come up and I'll have to go back to the station. Thank you all for your time. Yvonne, I wonder if I could ask you to just jot down anything that Josh and Amanda can remember about form of words, general content and the rest.' He turned to the twins. 'If you can remember any of the email addresses the mails came from, I would be very grateful.'

'Well, we can look now,' said Amanda. She pointed to the computer. 'Look, the poor old girl is up and running at last.

'Ah, yes, that. Well,' Hall turned to Pete, 'I would be very glad if you would turn that off now and sign a piece of tape across the keys with time and date. There will be someone along later to pick up the whole thing. I hope that isn't too much of an inconvenience – homework, that sort of thing.' He looked round and they all nodded or shook their heads. They weren't quite sure what the answer was. 'I'm sorry to dash off,' he said. 'It's a good job you're the job,' he said to the parents, standing there one behind each child's chair, hands on their shoulders. 'Otherwise I'd have to get someone in. As it is, we're going to be a bit short of personnel.'

'What's happened?' Yvonne couldn't help herself.

'One of the girls we had already worked briefly with,' Henry crossed his fingers behind his back, for now he was counting Maxwell in the magic 'we', 'seems to have disappeared. She hasn't been gone long and I'm sure it's going to turn out to be a misunderstanding, but, as I'm sure you both know, you can't be too careful.' He turned to go, then spoke over his shoulder. 'If I could have that report, Yvonne, as soon as possible.' He looked at the computer. 'Longhand will be fine.' And with that, he was gone.

In the silence that was left when the front door slam had echoed its way to nothing, Josh asked the inevitable question. 'So that was po-faced?'

'No, no,' his mother said. 'Of course not. That last bit was a joke.' She looked around and saw that no one was laughing. 'He does take a bit of getting used to,' she said.

'You've got that right,' her husband said, going off to the garage for a piece of masking tape to take his own computer into protective custody. 'It's a shame I can't tell this story tomorrow at work.'

'Well, you can't,' said Yvonne. There was a pause. 'But I can. It can go in the Book of Henry.'

'What's that?' Amanda asked, although she thought she knew the answer.

'*The Wit and Wisdom of Henry Hall.*'

'And how many pages does it have?' Josh was a loving son and liked to feed his mother her lines.

177

'Just the one,' she said. She looked around her family, bent but not broken. The computer was out of bounds and she didn't feel like letting her kids out of her sight. 'Scrabble, anybody?'

'Not really, Ma, to be honest,' said Josh.

'Scrabble, followed by takeaway...' there was still not too much enthusiasm, 'followed by a DVD.'

The twins looked at each other, then at their mother. 'It's a deal,' they said, and each kissed a cheek. The weight on their minds had lifted and if it took Henry Hall to do it, then, they considered, he was a Good Thing.

The Good Thing sat in his car outside the Thomas house. It could have gone many ways, but in the end it was all right. Now, he was going to have to face parents who had lost their child. Hopefully, she was just temporarily mislaid. But Henry Hall couldn't help wondering when they had lost her. When they found she was missing today? Or at the moment when, with one click, she had received her first text? Before too long, Henry Hall intended to find out.

Maxwell was waiting patiently for Henry Hall in Jacquie's only slightly kipper-smelling office. He had read all the paperwork on her desk and arranged it into alphabetical order. He had twirled round in the chair until its twirl stopped working and was trying to mend it when his wife stuck her head round the door.

'Henry's back, Max,' she said, 'but he's got a bit ravelled up with another case.' She winked to tell him she thought she might be overheard and he winked back, in a friendly enough fashion.

'I'll wait,' he said, settling back gingerly in the chair.

'Have you broken my chair?' she asked. 'You have, haven't you?'

'Not broken, as such,' he said hurriedly, avoiding the obvious observation – why was he mending it? He changed the subject. 'So, Henry's busy. What next, then?'

'I don't want you to freak out now,' she said. 'Henry has asked that you send a copy of the text of the ... um, text, to him as an email. Don't forget to put the time you got it, that kind of thing. As he says, that's all the statement needs, really, and it would be a shame to keep you longer.' She was nodding her head slightly as she spoke, encouraging him to agree. Maxwell noted with a smile that it was how she spoke to Nolan when getting him to eat Brussels sprouts, cauliflower and vegetables of that kidney.

'I'll certainly try,' he said, non-boat rocking being the order of this rather busy day. 'I assume his email address is at home somewhere?'

'It's in the address book,' she said.

'The one with the Degas on the front or the one that Nolan chewed that time?'

'The one in the Windows Mail ... oh, right. It's – have you got a pen? Of course you have. Right, this is all lower case with no spaces. Hall aitch at,' she sketched the @ sign in the air, 'leighford-police dot gov dot you kay. Got that?'

'Yes. I'll give it my best shot.' He got up and the chair fell into two halves. He looked at the destruction. 'It was probably that kipper. It rotted something, I expect.' He walked past his wife and risked a small kiss on her nose. 'What about Nole?'

'Darling, I'm sorry.' She tore her eyes away from her ex-chair and tapped her forehead. 'I'll forget my head next. Spencer's mum will drop him off in about half an hour at home.'

'I can't get back home that quickly.'

'Cinders, you shall go to the ball.' Jacquie waved an invisible magic wand. 'There's a car outside for you. Don't say we don't spoil you.'

'I would never say that,' he said, and meant it. 'I'll see you when I see you, then?'

'That's about the size of it.'

'Night night, then.' They were in the corridor by this time and he reduced their leave-taking to a pat on the shoulder. 'Abyssinia.'

'Love to Nole,' she said.

'Of course.'

They walked down the stairs together and parted on the landing, he to carry on to the foyer, she to enter the mad world of a new situation, which might go so many ways.

Chapter Eleven

The police driver was suffering from the virtually
epidemic Curmudgeon Disease and after a few
conversational sallies had been drowned at birth,
Maxwell sat back and let the drive wash over him.
He was aware that being brought home in a squad
car would probably turn heads in quiet Columbine, but he was used to the curtains twitching
whenever he came home. Despite its genteel
veneer, the whole road was a hotbed of seething
underground vice, according to Mrs Troubridge,
who was an expert on such things. For example,
her at number 35, across the road and down a
few, spent her entire day drinking cheap sherry.
She then buried the bottles in the garden before
her husband came home. Since Maxwell happened to know that the woman was a freelance
upholsterer who, when not out measuring up
sofas, spent her time with a mouthful of tacks and
a staple gun in one hand, he had tried to put the
record straight. This had made things rather
worse, as Mrs Troubridge added the interesting
fact to the mix that she wandered around armed,
and so he had stayed out of it after that.

But Mrs Troubridge came into her own when
telling the entire street of the goings-on chez
Maxwell. She was disappointed that he didn't
seem to be a wife-beater, but everything else was
grist to her mill. Jacquie often told Maxwell that

he should be grateful that Mrs Troubridge was so fond of him; had that not been the case, he would have been on the front page of every Sunday rag for sure – MY NEIGHBOUR, THE MARTIAN, ATE FREDDY STARR'S HAMSTER ... or something like that. As it was, she just kept it local and everyone knew to take things with at least a small pinch of salt. But, they all said to each other over their respective back fences, there was rarely smoke without fire. Except when him at 16 had one of his bloody bonfires – there should be laws or something.

Maxwell was used to seeing a little old lady crouching behind a hedge as he approached his house. She seemed to have a preternatural ability to anticipate his arrival. He had never considered the truth; that she spent almost all of the afternoon lurking by the front door, ready to leap, or at least lurch, out at him when he came down the path. The usual picture was the same but somehow different this particular afternoon. As the squad car turned into Columbine, Maxwell could, by craning round slightly, see Mrs Troubridge 'weeding' her flower bed, waiting to collar him. But he could also see an unexpected little old lady sitting on his doorstep, like a down-and-out in Victorian Whitechapel, sleeping rough. That little old lady was Mrs B. And she appeared to be crying.

He could hardly wait for the car to stop and he leapt out and slammed the door without his customary courtesy.

'Ignorant bastard,' muttered the driver as he sped away in a squeal of rubber. 'I thought you were supposed to be a gent.'

Maxwell was kneeling at Mrs B's side before the car was out of sight. 'Mrs B. Whatever is the matter? And why didn't you let yourself in, for goodness' sake?' If only to keep that nosy old trout next door from seeing this, he felt like adding, but didn't.

Mrs B gave a colossal sniff which almost lifted Maxwell's hat off his head. 'I din't like to,' she said. 'It's not my day or anything.' Mrs B did for the Maxwells once a week and did them proud. She didn't just move the dust around, she actually removed it, which was against her principles usually. Only the attic was off-limits to her.

'Let's get inside,' Maxwell said, leaning heavily on the woman as he got to his feet. 'Have a cup of tea.'

'That'd be nice,' she said, wiping her nose with the back of her hand. Maxwell made a mental note of which hand she used, should patting be the order of the day later on.

Mrs Troubridge bobbed up just as Maxwell was shutting the door. He saw her open her mouth to speak but a man has to know his limitations. One old dear behaving funny was enough for anyone, even on a fine spring afternoon.

'Up you go,' he said to Mrs B as they stood at the bottom of the stairs, in the gloom of the hall. This early in the year it could strike a bit cold, but in the summer, it was bliss to walk in out of the heat and glare and wait just a few seconds to let the cool wash over hot eyes and itchy skin. There were usually at least three days like that every year. 'Make yourself comfy in the sitting room.' He glanced at the doormat; no post. This didn't necessarily mean that they had no letters. It could be because Mrs Troubridge had coerced the postman again. Time would tell. Their mangled correspondence would arrive by night-fall, if she had managed to divert it.

Mrs B went ahead of him and he noticed for perhaps the first time that she was getting old. She pressed on her thigh with each ascending step, as if to lever herself up the stairs. With the other hand, she grasped the banister as if pulling herself out of Great Grimpen Mire. Her breath came in short gasps, interspersed with racking sobs. Whatever could have got her into this state? Time, obviously, accounted for the aching limbs and varicosed legs. Forty roll-ups a day since kindergarten. But the crying? This was not the real Mrs B at all. Maxwell couldn't help but wonder how many other layers there could be in this matryoshka whom he had thought he knew.

He went into the kitchen and put the kettle on. He had probably made her tea before, but he couldn't remember when or how she took it. He stuck his head round the sitting room door. She was sitting on the very edge of one of the chairs, feet together. Her hands were screwing a hand-kerchief to death in her lap and he set aside the rules of the house without a second thought. 'Do have a cigarette, Mrs B, if you'd like one.'

'Oh, no, Mr M. I couldn't, really. Not with the little one.' She looked around. 'Not back from school, yet?' She thought it was cruel that the poor little chap seemed to spend so much time away from home. The place for little ones was in

184

front of their own telly, in her opinion.

'Due any minute,' said Maxwell, mentally adding another layer to his multi-tasking. 'But one cigarette won't hurt him and I imagine you could do with one. I'll see if I can find you an ashtray.'

'Kitchen, last drawer on the left as you go in,' she came back immediately with the information. 'It's a Queen's Silver Jubilee one. I expect it was a present, wassnit? I can't see you goin' out and buyin' one of those.' She gave a hoarse chuckle, but it was a shadow of her usual bonhomie.

'Thanks.' He had no idea he possessed such a thing. Or that she knew he was broadly of the Republican persuasion. 'How do you like your tea?'

'With a drop of whisky in it, if it's all the same,' she said. 'I know you don't usually keep it, but there's still a drop left from Christmas. Back of the cupboard one along from the cooker, right-hand side.'

Maxwell withdrew back into the kitchen, where the kettle was beginning a rumbling boil. It must be like this to actually meet your stalker, he thought (he allowed himself the luxury of a split infinitive every now and again, but only in his darkest thoughts).

Her voice floated through from the other room. 'No sugar and just a splash of milk, if that's awright.'

He raised his voice to carry over the noise of the kettle. 'Message received and understood. Over and out.' He put the mug, milk jug, whisky bottle and ashtray on a tray and made a precarious entrance into the sitting room. He put the whole lot down on the coffee table and let her make her beverage as she liked it: a whole lot of whisky, about a teaspoon of milk. She sucked about half the mugful down in one go and topped it up with whisky.

'I'm not much of a drinker as a rule, Mr M,' she assured him. 'But I'm that upset.' A cigarette had appeared by magic in her mouth and she lit it and inhaled appreciatively between sentences. 'I've had my sister on the phone. My nephew, you know the one I told you about, the one what's so good on computers? Our Colin?'

'Ford Open Prison?' Maxwell offered the only fact he could recall.

'That's the one. Well, he's been reported missing.'

'Missing? From prison? That's a bit major, isn't it? Why wasn't it on the news?'

She cackled into her tea. 'Bless, Mr M,' she said. 'If they reported every con what goes missing, there'd be no time for other news.'

Maxwell had the feeling that he was about to wade into uncharted waters. 'Oh, I didn't realise,' was all he said.

'Well, it's not as if our Colin is a dangerous lunatic, nor nothing,' she said. 'I don't see why they make such a fuss over the white-collar stuff. It's only money.'

Again, Maxwell forbore from comment. It may be only money, but it was someone else's money; a concept obviously foreign to young Colin and his ilk.

'Well, it wasn't even money, in the end,' she sniffed and inhaled together, a clever trick only

186

mastered by a few really dedicated smokers. 'He was gathering some venture capital together. They got most of it back.'

'Venture capital, Mrs B?' He was totally unused to tackling only one of Mrs B's startling remarks at once. He realised he had never actually sat down and had a conversation with the woman before. It was rather unsettling.

She looked a little uneasy as making an admission didn't really suit her. 'I can't say as I understand it, Mr M,' she said. 'It was all about networking or summat. They didn't have nothing to sell, it was just... It's no good me trying to tell you. I'd get it wrong.'

Maxwell had heard of these computer scams, without understanding a thing about them. The apple of Mrs B's eye had probably set up some sort of spurious website, www.colin.con or something similar. 'So, when you said you were looking after his interests...' Maxwell remembered her computer skills from the previous day and wondered how she was using them.

'Oh, I just make sure his money goes to the right place...' Her face suddenly shut up like a clam that had sucked a lemon. 'I don't know whether I ought to tell you any more.'

'That's quite all right, Mrs B.' Maxwell patted her hand and hoped he had chosen the right one. 'Tell me about his disappearance.'

'He just din't come back from work. They did the roll-call and he wasn't there. It was the driver's fault, o' course. He should have noticed when he din't get on the coach, but I s'pose he wasn't concentratin', or something. Anyway, they done the roll, he ain't there. He keeps a bit to himself, our Colin. So nobody really could say when they'd seen him last.'

Maxwell finally managed to get a word in. 'Work?'

'Well, that's the plan, innit? They lock them up but only at night. Later on, he'll be having weekends at home.' She paused and the tears came back to her eyes. 'Well, he would've. Not now.' She leant forward and clutched Maxwell's arm. 'He would've come to me, Mr M. Or his mum. He wouldn't just go off. He was just doing his time.'

Maxwell looked at her. She was clearly distraught and, after years of seeing her unmoved, except by a knee-jerk cynical response, by the most devastating upheavals, he found it cataclysmic. It was as though the Isle of Wight, just visible from The Dam, mistily distant over to the right, had suddenly lifted its skirts and moved to Aberdeen. 'I assume they have been in touch with his employers?'

'First thing next morning,' she said. 'They didn't answer the phone till nine o'clock.'

'Not straight away?' He found it incredible that a firm employing a prisoner, albeit from an open prison, albeit a nice boy, fond of his family and guilty only of a bit of light fraud, should not be contactable out of hours.

'Administrative error,' she said. 'Well ... more a case of– This won't go any further, will it, Mr M?'

He shook his head. He hoped Jacquie would forgive him.

'Our Colin had hacked into the computer at the prison. Easy as falling off a log, he says. They should be ashamed. He only did it for a laugh, though, Mr M. He changed all the out-of-hours contact numbers.'

'For a laugh?' Maxwell raised one eyebrow.

She looked embarrassed. 'He's not very...' She was stuck for the word. She wanted to say that Colin was a nice boy, not the brightest apple in the barrel, not really a people person, just happy with his computers. Not simple, you understand, just not very...

'Sophisticated?' Maxwell helped her out of her linguistic hole.

'That's right. If somebody asked him to do it, he'd just do it. He was always like it, from a little 'un. Always did what the bigger boys told him.' She gave a phlegmy chuckle, which seemed to remind her to light another cigarette. She held it up with a querying expression. He nodded and she drew on it hard. 'He jumped off a roof, once, 'cos they said to. Broke his leg.'

'Boys, eh?' Maxwell laughed. The doorbell rang, breaking into the conversation. 'And talking of boys, that's mine, I think. Will you excuse me a minute, Mrs B?'

'Aah, love him.' Mrs B went into dote mode instantly. 'I'll just say hello to him, Mr Maxwell, and then I'll get along. I feel a lot better.'

'Nonsense, Mrs B,' Maxwell said from the doorway. 'Nole can always go and watch the telly in another room. He'll be fine for a while.' He clattered downstairs and the woman could hear cries of welcome in the hallway below. These were followed by the scamper of little feet up the stairs.

'Mrs B?' called Nolan. 'Where are you?'

189

'In here, ducks,' she said, hurriedly stubbing out her cigarette and moving the ashtray out of range.

He ran into the room and flung himself into her lap. He gave her a fierce hug and stood back. 'Dads says you're a bit sad,' he said, gazing into her eyes with his big brown ones. 'Do you need hugs, or do you need to 'scuss it, because if you do, I can go to my room.'

Poor little mite, she thought. It was no wonder he sounded as though he'd swallowed a bleedin' dictionary, always on his own, reading books, no doubt. She put an arm round him and gave him a squeeze. 'I just want to talk to your daddy a minute. Then you can come in here and watch the telly. All right?'

'I don't watch much TV in the evenings,' he announced.

Her heart bled for him. She couldn't begin to picture a typical evening in the Maxwell household, with Nolan playing games with either or preferably both parents; the bedtime stories which sometimes took so long the bedtime was theirs, not his, by the time they were complete. As Jacquie often said to Maxwell, if they had wanted to spend all the time watching a cute infant, they should have got a kitten. But of course, she had to whisper, in case Metternich was in earshot.

Maxwell came in behind the boy and shooed him off upstairs, via the kitchen for a drink and a biscuit. He had had a faintly acrimonious exchange at the front door with Spencer's mother, who had a zero tolerance to smoking. Since Maxwell had a zero tolerance to women who ranted first and asked questions later, Jacquie would have a lot of bridge-building to do. 'How's Spencer?' Maxwell asked as he and the boy raided the cupboard.

'Hnh,' Nolan said, all the derision in the world in that one sound. 'We're not really friends just now, Dads. He's a bit childish sometimes.'

Maxwell gave him a kiss, not just for being a great kid, if sometimes rather middle-aged, but because he had got his dad off the hook with both Spencer's and his own mother. 'Kit Kat?' He waved it tantalisingly.

'Yes, please!'

'Only if you can promise me you won't get it on your bedclothes, clothes, curtains or Metternich.'

''S OK. The Count just licks it off.'

Maxwell lifted the child down from the work surface where he had been sitting like a small, skinny, bruised Buddha. The cat and he had a private life of which Maxwell knew nothing; he felt faintly jealous. 'Off you go then, mate. I'll give you a shout when Mrs B is going. You can come down and say bye-bye, we'll have rubbish for supper and then a game or twelve.'

'Uh huh. 'Sinya.' And the little chip off the old block was off up the stairs like a rat up a pipe.

'Abyssinia, toots,' Maxwell muttered and watched as his son's heels disappeared round the corner into his bedroom. There were distant sounds of a large black and white cat putting up with a hug from a small and already chocolaty boy. Maxwell wasn't sure he believed in God. He wasn't even sure he believed in atheists. But there had to be someone nice up there somewhere, if

191

such small things could make an old curmudgeonly teacher so happy.

Back in the sitting room, Mrs B was making up
for the stubbed-out fag with a new, fresh one.
Maxwell sat opposite her. 'Where were we?' he
asked. 'Sorry for the interruption.'

'Oh, no, he's a lovely little chap,' she said. 'He
reminds me of our Shawn a bit, when he was
little.'

'Shawn? I don't think I–'

'No, you wouldn't know him. He lives abroad.'

'How lovely. Do you visit?'

'Nah. He's on the Costa. Too hot for me.'

Maxwell suddenly saw the world through her
eyes. Family everywhere but here. In prison, on
the run, on the Costa. No quiet evenings chewing
the fat for her; just checking the text on the television to make sure no one she knew had been
caught or escaped or, he tidied up the thought,
escaped and been caught. He forced a smile.
'Don't worry about Colin, Mrs B,' he said. 'He's
probably just gone to a friend or something. He'll
turn up.'

'He ain't got no friends. He's only got his mum
and me.'

'Might he have gone to, well, Shawn, for
example?'

'They don't get on.' The statement was not for
discussion.

'Well, even so, I'm sure he'll turn up.'

She finally got to the point. 'Can you ask Mrs
Maxwell to find out if there's any news? They
don't tell us, in case he's in touch.'

'I don't know whether–'

'I know she shouldn't tell you anything, but I know she does. Everybody knows that you can get anything out of anybody. Tha's well known.'

He needed her to feel better. He needed her to be gone in enough time for him to open a window and air the house before Jacquie got home. He needed to think. Computers seemed to be coming at him from all sides. But before she went, she could do him a favour. 'Mrs B? Could you just do me a favour? I need to send an attachment later in an email. Could you just remind me how to do it?'

She struggled to her feet from the embrace of Maxwell's favourite chair. 'Have you got your laptop?'

'No, I came away from school a bit suddenly today.'

'I heard. We'll have to use your PC, then.'

He nodded and ushered her up the stairs to the study, where she was soon sitting at the desk, waiting for Maxwell's aged computer to wake up.

'It's slow, innit?' she remarked.

'It is a bit thoughtful,' he said. He found himself becoming rather defensive on its behalf. 'It will be ready hourtarily.' Finally, it proved him right and the wallpaper appeared, a baby photo of Nolan. Desktop icons reluctantly populated the screen and it was as ready as it would ever be.

'Do you want to bring your emails up?' Mrs B asked, bringing all sorts of images into Maxwell's head.

'No, you do it,' he said. 'It's just click on that there.' He pointed to the icon and she politely decided not to comment. The pane came up on the screen, followed by the familiar page.

'You've got messages,' she said, trying not to read anything.

'I'll read those later,' he said. 'Can you just show me how to attach something?'

'It's easy,' she said. 'Look, you click "Create" and the box comes up. See.' And sure enough, there it was. 'You put the address in, see, there, for who you want it to go to – see, it says "To".' It was Maxwell's turn to be polite now; this much, he could do. 'Then, when you've written the email, and you want to attach something, you click on this paper clip, here.' She suited the action to the words. 'Then, you can choose from the documents, look, or pictures, whatever you've got there, and click open and you've done it.'

'That looks easy.' And he was right – it did *look* very easy.

'Well, Mr M, it *is* easy. Do you want to try it while I'm still here?'

'No, Mrs B. I'm sure I will manage. If not, Nole can probably help me.'

Mrs B gave a throaty chuckle and smacked him on the shoulder. 'He could as well. He's bright, that lad.'

'I'll just tell him you're going,' said Maxwell. 'Nole!' he raised his voice. 'Mrs B is off now, darling.'

Mrs B gave vent to a mental tchah! Calling the boy 'darling' – he'd grow into a right girl's blouse if they weren't careful. Telly and some nice videos, that's what he needed. The boy came whizzing out of his bedroom in full Spiderman costume and gave the old woman a hug.

'Night, night, Mrs B.' He dashed back into his

194

room and, by listening carefully, the adults could just hear a very private rendition of a boy, armed only with his superhuman powers, saving the world.

They went down the stairs in silence, pausing only to pick up her coat, bag, fags and umbrella, without which she felt inadequately dressed. At the bottom, she turned to him.

'You will talk to Jacquie ... I mean, Mrs Maxwell, won't you?' She lifted her face to him and he saw the vulnerability, the naked trust in her eyes. He needed to get her back on an even keel, back to her machine-gun delivery, her impartial hatred of the world in general. He wanted to turn the world right-side up.

So he agreed. 'Yes, I'll talk to her. But I can't promise anything.'

'Thank you, Mr M. I knew you'd help me if you could.'

'I can't help you on this, Mrs B, but are you all right to get home? Do you want me to call a taxi or anything?'

'No, I'll call our Jean's eldest from the top of the road.' She patted her pocket to check if her mobile was in place. 'He'll pick me up. Bye, then, and thanks.' She beetled off up Columbine, her cares lightened slightly by sharing them with the mad old bugger. She studiously avoided the lurking shade of Mrs Troubridge. In Mrs B's opinion, she ought to keep her old nose out of other people's business, old besom. As she got to the end of the road, she looked back. The old trout was knocking on the door, now. Nosy old so-and-so.

Maxwell had just toiled up the two flights to Nolan's bedroom and was giving him the all-clear when he heard the soft tap at the door. Only Mrs Troubridge knocked rather than rang. It reminded him of Edgar Allen Poe and the raven, someone gently rapping, rapping at his chamber door. Unfortunately he had found, over the years, that it was never the lovely Lenore, but always the ghastly, grim and ancient Troubridge, wandering from the nightly shore. He decided to ignore it.

He and Nolan decided to plump for pizza. It was quick. It was round. It claimed to be food and, followed by ice cream, did them both very well. Bath time was slightly cursory, but Nolan was still a little fractious about washing, with his sore chin, and didn't really mind its foreshortening. When he was tucked up in nice loose-around-the-chin pyjamas, Maxwell craved his indulgence.

'I've got to do some work tonight, old mate,' he said. 'Ma is running late, trouble down in Dodge City.' Nolan chortled at his perfect Gary Cooper. 'I'll just be in the study. You can watch a DVD. Guns, knives, chubs, all the same to me.' Maxwell had morphed into Lee Marvin out of *Cat Ballou*. 'All right with you?'

Nolan offered a silent high five and went over to his shelf to choose a DVD. He finally settled for a cartoon. Maxwell started it for him and left him curled up in bed, sucking the fingers of one hand and absent-mindedly twirling the fingers of the other in Metternich's coat. The cat responded by laying an admonitory paw on his leg, as if to say, 'Watch it. Too many liberties, my lad,

196

and it's not just the chin that will have stitches.' But for now, all was peaceful and Maxwell retired to the study.

The email inbox page was still up, obscured by floating bubbles. He would happily have sat and watched them for hours, but he was against the clock, really. He should have sent this email ages ago. He opened a new document and typed a short and succinct résumé of the text: when he got it, what had happened just before and just after, what it said. He managed to avoid mentioning things he was not supposed to know. He saved it as text.doc and then thought that Henry Hall might ignore it if it was called something so innocuous. He renamed it importanttext. doc and saved it somewhere. He was quite good at starting tasks on the computer; it was finishing them that gave him trouble. He opened a new message in his email. He even remembered where he had written down Henry's email address. He copied it meticulously into the relevant place. Things were going well so far. He chose a nice, middle-of-the-road subject for the email. 'Text received today by Peter Maxwell.' He wrote a friendly but short note for Hall and then, tentatively, clicked on the paper clip. Calooh, callay, he chortled in his joy. He couldn't have been happier if he had indeed slain the Jabberwock. There was the self-same page that had popped up so obediently for Mrs B. Now, where had he saved that document?

A mere half an hour later, he had tracked it down. He clicked 'open' and, to his amazement, the title of the document appeared in the right place on his email. He was delighted and horrified at himself for being so pleased. This was *technology* for goodness' sake! He clicked 'send' and his blood, sweat and tears disappeared, hopefully to wing its unintercepted, crashed or otherwise filtered way to Henry Hall's Inbox.

He turned his attention to his received emails. One was from Helen Maitland and was marked 'urgent'. He opened it and scanned it quickly. She had thoughtfully forwarded an email from Legs – news of a team-building exercise, dated some weeks ago. Why on earth...? Oh, because it was taking place the next day, which was a development day, no kids, just disgruntled staff. Paintballing? Maxwell was about to claim a bone in his leg when he reconsidered. Guns. Diamond. Ryan. Oh, joy – Pansy! This could be just what the doctor ordered.

The next one was from eBay, telling him his watched item was finishing shortly. He had another five minutes by this time to decide whether he really wanted another forage cap – his modelling one was getting a little painty round the edges and, anyway, it was only a matter of time before Nolan would need one. But he'd let it pass, this time. The bid was already up to eight times his salary.

The third one made his eyes open wide, then wider. Without taking his eyes from the screen, he groped for the phone and pressed speed dial.

'Leighford Police. How may I help you?'

Chapter Twelve

Things were not going well at Leighford Police Station. Jacquie had walked into the foyer to be met with a scene from Dante's Inferno. People were yelling, people were crying. There was a lot of posturing, strutting, arm throwing and general alpha male behaviour. She waited for a moment in the doorway and then resorted to response 7.1.1.a in the latest manual on Crowd Control.

'Oy!' A simple enough sound, but at enough decibels it seemed to reach into the hind brain of most humans and shut them up, if only for a short while. Everyone turned to face her and she felt like telling them to line up in an orderly fashion, lines of policemen, Julie's family, Leah's family, all separately and not talking until the bell went. Instead, she used technique 7.1.1.b, which was to lower her voice so that they all had to keep quiet as they strained to hear.

'I am Detective Sergeant Carpenter,' she said. 'I am working on a case I think may be connected with the disappearance of these two girls. I think it would be best for everyone if we all calmed down and then I can assign rooms to the families and we can go from there.'

There were mutters of agreement, although not wholehearted, and Jacquie turned to the desk sergeant. 'Do we have anyone available at the moment? I know DCI Hall is out.'

'DS Carter is available,' the desk sergeant said, with barely disguised contempt in his voice. Jacquie remembered the kipper and forgave the man. 'Would you like me to call him down?'

'If you would,' Jacquie said. 'Are the interview rooms free?'

Before the desk man could reply, a man pushed forward and stood in front of Jacquie. 'I am Gregory Melkins,' he said, as if that explained everything.

'Are you?' Jacquie asked mildly. She turned back to the desk again.

'I don't think I want my wife to be shut up in an interview room. She is in a very fragile state and extremely worried about her daughter.'

'I'm sure she is, sir,' said Jacquie. 'But I think that you have misunderstood the interview room situation. We're not on the set of *Waking the Dead*. Trevor Eve is not going to come in and shout at anyone. There is no two-way mirror. Our interview rooms are light, clean and well furnished. We need to speak to you in private. I don't expect you want your family business conducted in the foyer of a police station, do you?'

The man looked at her as if she was something on his shoe, but his wife, hanging on his arm and with her face swollen with tears, curtailed his behaviour into something approaching acceptable. 'What I want is that you should speak to my wife about her daughter at our home. We have younger children who shouldn't be left.'

Jacquie didn't miss the use of the terms 'hers' and 'ours'. This was Julie's stepfather, then. 'If you would like to wait at home for one of our officers to come and interview your wife, Mr Melkins, then by all means that is what we will do. Let me see, today is Thursday. I think we should be able to free someone up by...' She turned to the man behind the desk and raised an eyebrow. He slowly turned and consulted a calendar, then bent to his computer and tapped a few keys. She smiled a tiny smile. Steve was a good lad and could understand subliminal messages with the best.

'Tuesday,' he said.

'That's outrageous,' the man exploded. 'Tuesday? Tuesday? With a girl missing.'

'Sorry, sir, my mistake,' the officer said. 'That's Tuesday week.'

'And that's two girls missing.' Another man had joined the circus. 'My Leah is missing as well as your kid. I won't get pushed around by the likes of you, you can bet on that.' He turned to Jacquie. 'You can interview me when you like, but I don't know if I will be much help. Leah lives with her mum and her sister. I live ... somewhere else.'

Melkins snorted and turned away. Jacquie spoke to Leah's father quietly. 'I understand your younger daughter reported her sister missing. Where is their mother?'

'I don't know,' he said. 'She's not ... well, she's not very reliable.'

'A tart, that's what my Julie says,' the weeping woman burst out. 'My Julie wouldn't have gone off without your daughter encouraging her.'

Leah's father turned on her and the whole bear garden started to reassert its dominance. Jacquie opened the doors to the interview rooms and pushed the crowd through as though they were one animal. Somehow, she managed to sort the families into different rooms and, when this was done, she realised that, in fact, the crowd had not been so big after all; they were just incredibly noisy and awkward.

Julie's mother and her stepfather sat side by side but not communicating. There was no sign of her father. Jacquie watched for a moment through the window in the door. The mother was an attractive woman trying perhaps a little too hard. She had not had an easy life in her first marriage and was now living in the lap of luxury. She didn't intend to let that go; her body was testament to hours in the gym, her face was blank and smooth and full of bacterial toxins. Her lips were just the right side of trout. He could have been used in a pictorial dictionary to define 'prosperous'. Or 'pompous'. Jacquie heard Maxwell in her head remind her of other 'P' words. 'Prat' was the one that came immediately to mind. 'Pillock', that was a good one.

She moved to look through the other window. Leah's father and her stepmother sat close together, foreheads touching. A carrycot with a small baby in it was at their feet. Occasionally, a chubby arm waved in the air and they automatically turned their heads and one of them would reach in to touch the child, as if for reassurance. Of Leah's mother, there was no sign. She assumed the younger sister was with the neighbour who had helped her to raise the alarm. She turned from the window with a sigh. Families, eh?

As she turned she found herself pressed into

the blue serge front of Steve from the front desk. After some muttered apologies and scuffling, they managed to get her hair unentangled from his buttons and dignity was almost restored. He stepped back.

'Are you thinking what I'm thinking?'

She doubted it. She was thinking, *What an oaf to come creeping up behind a person like that.* 'I don't know. I was thinking how odd that they have kicked up a stink so quickly when two girls have been missing for a matter of a few hours and in broad daylight.'

'That's more or less it,' he agreed. 'Except that I am also thinking, where are the other parents in this? The father of one and the mother of the other. And – and you can probably help me on this one, Sergeant – why are we taking it so seriously, also at this early stage? Hmm?'

'Steve, we'll have to get you out of that uniform and upstairs. You've got me.'

'Well?'

'I said you've got me. Not that I'm going to tell you. I'm sure a bright guy like you can sort it out for yourself. Now, then, I think we'll wait until DCI Hall gets back before we tackle the Melkins family. I have a feeling he is the kind of bloke who takes no notice of women as a species.'

The desk sergeant looked through the window and whistled under his breath. 'He was taking notice when he picked that one,' he said.

'Trophy,' Jacquie said. 'Not a brain in her head and it shows. I expect he ditched the wife he had had all through the hard times. I have him pegged, Steve. He took on Julie because his new wife

203

wanted her. I expect he fought the father for her through every court he could so easily afford. Now, as I understand it, they have two new kids and Julie is probably surplus to requirements. But now her father doesn't want her either and they're stuck with her.'

The sergeant looked at her with awe in his eyes. 'Blimey,' he said. He looked in through the window again but couldn't see any of that. 'How did you work all that out just by looking at them?'

She realised that she had dropped a possible clanger. Oh, what a tangled web we weave, when first we practise to deceive. Maxwell would have also added to her poetic maunderings that none by sabre or by shot, fell half as flat as Walter Scott. Her deception skills certainly would take more practice. 'It's just a sixth sense, Steve. It comes from being a detective.' Before she let out any other random pieces of unofficial information, she fled into the other interview room.

The couple looked up as they heard the door click.

'Mr and Mrs Booker?'

The man stood up. 'Yes. I'm Mark Booker. This is my wife, Meriel. She's ... er ...she's not Leah's mother. That's our baby, there. Apple.'

Ah, a Coldplay fan, Jacquie mused. And, at a top age of twenty-two, not likely to be Leah's mother. You didn't have to have specially honed detective skills to tell that. But she just said, 'Hello,' and nodded at the girl, who stayed sitting. Jacquie gestured her husband back into his seat and took one opposite.

'Firstly, let me reassure you that your daughter

has not been missing for long enough to spark off a full police inquiry under normal circumstances. I appreciate that her behaviour is out of character and that normally she would be at home to look after her little sister.'

'She never misses,' Mark Booker burst in. 'She has always looked after Anneliese. Since I left, really.'

Jacquie took in the age of the baby and did a small calculation. 'So that would be about two years ago?' she asked.

'More than that. I didn't leave my first wife for Meriel.' He cast her a loving glance and put his arm round her shoulders. 'Leah's mother, Pam, had been...' He swallowed and dipped his head. This was obviously still raw for him. His wife patted his leg and he carried on. 'She had been playing the field for some time before I left. I had to go while I still could. I had even thought of suicide. I'm not even sure that Anneliese is mine, although I always treat her the same. I begged Leah to come with me, but she wouldn't. Pam said she would fight me in the courts for Anneliese, and Leah wouldn't come without her.'

Jacquie could see a horrible and infinitely sad pattern emerging. 'She didn't want Leah?'

'I wouldn't say that. She loves her, I'm sure. It's just that, well, having a daughter that age stops her from lying about hers. She was only twenty-three when Leah was born. That doesn't leave her much wiggle room when her men friends find out about Leah. Also, of course, Leah is what she thinks of as competition.'

Meriel Booker snorted and spoke for the first

time. 'I don't think Leah would go for the rough stuff that Pam brings home, do you, hon?' she said, addressing the remark to her husband. Then, to Jacquie, 'She's a lovely girl, Sergeant, and I would love to have her live with us, I really would. But she won't hear of it and her mother has more or less poisoned her against us. Mark pays Pam far more than he needs to, but the kids don't see much of it, I'm thinking. Clubbing and trying to take fifteen years off your age doesn't come cheap.'

Julie had told Jacquie all about Leah's rich dad on the drive home and this was another side to the story.

'I'm not complaining,' Booker added, as though reading Jacquie's mind. 'I can afford it. But I wish...' He buried his face in his hands.

'Has Leah spoken to you lately?' Jacquie asked. 'Perhaps about some problems she has been having with nasty texts on her phone? Possibly emails?'

Meriel spoke for her husband, who had just shaken his head without looking up. 'She hasn't. But she should've. Mark owns a software company. He has just started a sideline in mobile Internet devices. It's going well. He could have helped her.'

'*Can* help her,' he suddenly shouted. 'Can help her, when she turns up.'

'Ssshh,' his wife stroked his back as though he were a baby. 'Sshh, listen, you're upsetting Apple.' And the baby had indeed started a thin wail which, even after the almost five years since Nolan had made that same noise, went straight to the nerve in the pit of Jacquie's stomach that prepared her for fighting off a sabre-toothed tiger. It was a noise from prehistory, pre-speech and it had a hotline to the hindbrain.

'Pick her up and soothe her,' Jacquie said, making for the door. 'I'll get someone in to take a statement, just contact details really, in the circumstances, and then you can take Apple home.'

They smiled their thanks and bent over the carrycot.

Jacquie paused outside the door of the other interview room and peeped in. The two were now in the throes of a vicious argument, he was leaning over her and she could almost see the light glinting off his bared teeth. She was apparently giving as good as she got, but it was hard to tell from the outside, because her smooth face gave nothing away and her words were indistinct. Jacquie gave a shudder and, bottling out, made for the stairs. From her office, she rang the desk and asked for someone to go and take the statement from the Bookers; it could be a civilian. She almost asked for Mr Peters, the stenographer, because she could certainly do with him here now, but didn't, in the cause of not looking like an idiot. She asked that Henry Hall should be told where the Melkins were and that they were waiting for him. She felt like a worm, but a relieved worm, which had managed to offload its responsibilities and wasn't feeling that bad about it, really. After all, she had had Daisy to contend with.

She was quietly getting on with some more paperwork, getting ready to link the cases, and was almost finished when the door opened and

Henry Hall's bland face looked in.

'Oh, hello, guv,' she said. 'How did the interview go?' He'd been quick, she gave him that.

'Oh, well, you know, quite well. They're great kids. How was yours?'

Wires crossed, she thought, or were they? Henry could be very devious, but with the light on those damned glasses, how could anyone tell? 'Not so great, but the girl is coming in tomorrow to chat without the mother.'

'Yvonne's computer should be with the boffins tomorrow.' He rubbed his hands together in a simulacrum of enthusiasm. 'Well, see you tomorrow. Sorry, Jacquie,' and with an unusual turn of speed, he was gone.

Jacquie was hampered by being behind a desk and also the fact that she was sitting in a chair which fell in half every time she got up from it. By the time she had made it to the stairs, all that could be seen of Henry Hall was a clean pair of heels.

Steve, the desk guy, was smiling. 'Gotcha, Sergeant,' he smiled.

'Well, of all the...' She was lost for words. It was so unlike Henry to dump on his staff a job he didn't want to do – he was as much of a gentleman, in his policemanly way, as Maxwell.

'Don't think badly of him,' the sergeant said. 'He's gone off to track down the parents who aren't here. He's left the Melkins to you. Better the devil you know, eh?'

Jacquie had to concede that that was true. Henry could be up all night trying to find them, especially the mother from what she had heard.

And then he would have to put on an alert and intelligent face for the inevitable press conference. And that would be a minefield; if he spooked the parents of the area, the nick would be besieged. She shrugged her shoulders and turned to meet her fate at the hands of the pompous, pretentious, pillocky prat. She suppressed a smile. Instruction 8.1.1.z in the *Jacquie Carpenter Interview Handbook:* if they piss you off, imagine them naked or give them a silly name. Gregory Melkins looked a bit too upholstered to look very appetising naked, so the names it would have to be. She looked over her shoulder. 'No calls, Steve,' she said, and the doors swung closed behind her.

The phone rang. 'Leighford Police Station. How may I help you?' God, how he hated saying that! He felt like a drone selling double glazing. 'Oh, Mr Maxwell, hello. I'm afraid DS Carpenter has just gone into an interview. Can I take a message?'

But there was no message. How can you explain the inexplicable? Quote the unquotable? 'No,' said Maxwell. 'No message. Thank you.'

'You're welcome,' said the desk sergeant. May as well be hanged for a sheep as a lamb. 'Have a nice evening, Mr Maxwell.'

'Oh, er, thank you. I'll try.' Maxwell put the phone down and shook his head as though to resettle his brain. He briefly toyed with the idea that he had rung the wrong number and had just been speaking to the gas board, BT or similar, but decided he had struck lucky and had got through to the only policeman in Leighford in a good mood. He wasn't to know that being in a position to inconvenience Maxwell put any policeman in

Leighford in a good mood, they just didn't always choose to share it.

He turned again to the screen. The message was still there, so it hadn't been a mirage.

'A family,' it began, 'will be almost overcome by death.' Whose family was this? Maxwell's one rainy Saturday on a tight bend? And who knew about them, Maxwell's loved ones, Maxwell's dead? But the next line threw him completely. 'The red red ones will knock down the red one.'

Maxwell pushed back his chair and blew out a long breath. He was by no means a cryptic expert, but it rang distinct bells. Was this all part of the game? Were the girls getting nonsense like this too? Then, like a flash on the Damascus Road ... he got up from the desk and went to the bookshelf behind him and ran a finger along the tightly packed spines. He knew Jacquie had bought him a book on dear old Nostradamus for Christmas a year or so ago; now, where was it? Jacquie had offered to list his library on her system, but to Maxwell the old ways were always best. He remembered it as a blue paperback... no, here it was. A black hardback with red writing; just as he thought. The tome was huge, but so was Maxwell's capacity for speed reading. Yes, he was right – these lines had been taken from Century VIII, Quatrain 19. So, not too difficult to get hold of; the prophecies of the Seer would be on millions of websites and even, if his memory served, in this very book in the school library.

So, as clues went, not very helpful. Which was why he needed Jacquie home. There must be other clues embedded in this thing which might help. Emails had to come from someone; no doubt there was some clickage which could be done which would show who that person was.

But it was no good mulling over that. He didn't want to mess about with it in case he deleted it altogether. It had been known to happen and to better men than he – Bernard Ryan, though not one of the better men of whom he was thinking, had once deleted the entire school's record of every child there had ever been through its doors with one uninformed keystroke. Maxwell wasn't going to risk a similar happening. But he was awaiting his moment to shop the incompetent bastard to the *Mail on Sunday*.

The best thing to do, he decided, was to pour a nice large Southern Comfort, check on Nolan and go up into the attic to work on his latest project, the half-finished figure of Private John Swiney of the 17th Lancers.

He went into the kitchen to pour the drink and wash up their pizza-smeared plates. He topped up Metternich's bowl while he was at it, and then went to the top of the stairs to switch on the outside light for Jacquie when she got home. He looked down to the half-glazed door at the bottom. This time of the year, with the blossom just breaking on the trees that lined Columbine, was one of his favourites. The street lights gave odd shapes to the most mundane things. For example, it sometimes looked as though someone was waiting just outside the door. He had often mistaken the silhouette for Jacquie coming home and had dashed downstairs to meet her, only to realise that it was a blossom-laden branch across

211

the lamp which had caused the illusion. He went into the sitting room to draw the curtains and keep the night out, as his mother had always said – he looked out and noticed that the tree across the light had been pruned. The branch wasn't there any more; victim, no doubt, of the credit crunch or swine flu, whichever came first.

He went back to the head of the stairs, the soles of his feet buzzing with the tension. He looked down. The bubbly glass of the door just showed a wavy image of the path, the green of the hedge, the pale glow of the slabs heading to the pavement. No ghostly figure at the door. Scalp prickling, he went down and flung open the door. There was no one there. He shook his head and pushed back his shoulders to ease the tension which had built up in his neck and spine.

Back to Plan A, he told himself. A drink. A quick check on the Boy and a nice evening of modelling, until the Mem got back. Just the ticket. But, even so, he checked the door was locked before he climbed the stairs.

Drink in hand, he eased open Nolan's bedroom door. The DVD was long finished and the TV had been turned off. What a good boy, Maxwell mused. Unless the cat had done it, of course. He raised an eyebrow and the glass at the Count, who rose carefully to his feet and stretched, whiskers forward in the aftermath of an enormous yawn which showed his razor-sharp fangs to perfection. He kissed the Boy's hand in farewell with his cold, pink nose and followed Master II up the stairs to the attic room. They did their best thinking up there.

Maxwell's attic was the War Office, an Inner Sanctum where only two members of the family were allowed. All right, Jacquie could pop her head over the parapet to tell the Great Modeller near the sky that supper was ready. And Nole could stay as long as he didn't touch anything.

'Anything' meant Maxwell's Light Brigade. For years now, man and boy, he'd been lovingly recreating all 678 riders bound for the half a league that turned them into legend back in the autumn of 1854. With glue, a magnifying glass, small pots of Humbrol and a lot of patience, he turned Messrs Historex's white plastic 54mm figures into real people, and positioned them as they might have looked to the north of the Woronzoff Road that chilly October day.

Maxwell sat in his creaking old swivel chair and began gluing Private Swiney's lance to private Swiney's hand.

'Well, Count,' Maxwell began. 'It seems a coon's age since we last talked. It's hard to believe it was only this morning. Does that look like nine feet of bamboo to you?'

Metternich crashed over onto his side and began to nuzzle his flank looking for his pet flea. Sometimes it just had to be told who was boss.

'I know.' Maxwell shared the cat's amazement. 'It's hard to credit, isn't it? Well, I suppose you missed the Mrs B fandango, as she would doubtless call it in her more frivolous moments. She's in a bit of a state, I don't mind telling you. Count?'

The cat looked up with a chirrup. The old coot had made him jump; he had been really concentrating then. He so wished the old fool would just whitter and stop just saying his name like that. Did he not know that cats were hard-wired to hear their own names, and respond, even if they had trained themselves to generally give no outward sign?

'Are you listening? This is important. If I collapse with Humbrol fumes, you'll have to repeat all this to the Mem. Anyway, where was I?' He laid the lancer on his back to give the glue time to work. 'Yes. Mrs B is in a bit of a flutter over her nephew, who has obviously just done a runner. But he is a computer nerd, which is a bit of a coincidence, bearing in mind our main problem of the hour.' Impatiently, he sat the all-white Swiney astride his horse. 'This poor bugger lost an arm at Inkerman,' he told the cat. 'Swiney, that is, not the horse. He eventually died in Chingford – nothing else to do there, I suppose. No, it's no good asking me, Count, because I really don't know the links between all this. Texting, emails, it's all Greek to me. Well, let's call it Serbo-Croat because I do read Greek up to a point. I'm not just a member of the κοινή αγέλη you know.'

As a paid-up member of the *un*common herd, Metternich kept his counsel. As everyone knew, cats walked by themselves; except when in need of the odd bowl of cat food, in which case there would be a human on tap to pander to them and they'd walk with anybody. A cushion was nice. A warm room with no draughts. But, no, essentially, a cat was definitely not a herd animal. He licked a paw derisively.

'Ah, you old softie,' Maxwell said, prodding

214

him with a slippered toe. 'Thank you for agreeing with me.'

Whatever, Metternich thought, yawning again and licking the slipper grime off his flank. *He means well. Oh, hello, he's off again.*

'So,' Maxwell crouched to line up Swiney in his place on parade, behind Captain Morris on the left of the line. 'Jacquie and Henry are on the case, now. I don't think that Julie and Leah are missing in the police sense. I think they have just decided not to be around at the moment. It's all got too much. I mean, look at little Alice today at school.'

The cat obediently twisted his head round in both directions as far as it would go.

'No, I don't mean look at Alice as in look *for* Alice. She isn't here, Count. I was speaking metaphorically. And, by the way, it's really scary when you do that with your head, has anyone ever told you that? Like *The Exorcist 28*.'

Metternich lay back and closed his eyes to the smallest slit. That way, he might shut the old fool up, but could still watch for any movement in the shadows and, possibly, kill it.

'Am I boring you, Count?'

The cat opened one eye and made his feelings so clear that he might as well have said it aloud – you have no idea.

'Well, tough. As I said, little Alice today, obviously one of life's goody two-shoes, even so she's scared to death that someone knows something bad about her and that that someone will "tell". That's the schoolkid's fear, Metternich. That someone will "tell" on them. There is a web of

215

fear around, and I don't mean that as a joke, although I could work it into quite a good one given time. Someone is sitting in the centre of it pulling the strings and I'm going to find out who it is before some poor little girl does something stupid.'

No. He didn't want Swiney there. He put him next to the ex-factory grinder William Purvis, who didn't seem to mind.

'And now, Count,' the Head of Sixth Form said, loud in the enclosed space, 'I'm getting the things as well. Who knows my phone number? My email address? I don't know them myself.'

The cat sat up and stretched out to his full length. He yawned, showing pink gums and tongue and teeth that wouldn't shame a tiger. He let go the tension in his muscles and sprang back like an elastic band to a sitting position, where he stayed for a few seconds, licking his lips and twitching the skin on his back. He'd dropped off for a minute there. He blinked the sleep from his eyes and touched Maxwell's bare ankle with his freezing cold wet nose. It was the nearest he would ever come to an apology for his rudeness, but it was enough between old friends. Maxwell bent to his gluing again and muttered, 'Abyssinia. Don't do anything I wouldn't do.'

That left him with an extremely short list of night-time activities and so he had no intention of following *that* instruction. The cat pattered down the stairs, checking on the Boy on his way through. To take first things first, it was highly unlikely that Maxwell would enjoy the cat food he finished up on his way to the cat flap. And as for the rest – best not go there. The cat oozed out of the cat flap just as Jacquie drove up to the kerb. Out of politeness, he waited until she got out and came down the path.

'Hello, Count,' she whispered, in view of the lateness of the hour. 'Are you coming out or in?'

He brushed her legs with his silky flank and was off through the hedge and away.

She laughed quietly. 'Out, I see,' she said and, straightening up, put her key in the keyhole and turned it as quietly as she could, easing the door closed behind her.

Mrs Troubridge, waiting in her hallway, had gone to sleep on her hard chair where she usually put the Maxwells' accumulated post. She muttered and twitched and woke herself up and dropped back off again, but all too late to realise that her vigil was now pointless. All the Maxwells were present and accounted for and soon would all be fast asleep in their beds.

Chapter Thirteen

Mornings in the Maxwell house were always the most stressful time of the day. Jacquie and Maxwell were not morning people, or night people, nor even midday people – they were twenty-four-hour, round-the-clock people. Jacquie had always had the knack of waking instantly as soon as she had to, whether it was to answer the phone, the door, the alarm clock or a call of nature. Nolan had never had to cry as a baby; the first indrawn breath would have one of his feather-light-sleeping parents at his bedside.

So it seemed cruel and ironic to them that they had seemed to fuse their genetic material in such a way that their son was a curmudgeonly grump when he woke up. It didn't last long, and it had no bearing what time this happened. He always burrowed under the covers in search of just five more minutes. They had got into the habit of taking it in turns to wake him up and, Jacquie having taken the brunt of the bruising aftermath, it was Maxwell's turn this time.

It was a testament to the thought he had given to his paintballing clothes that Nolan had hopped out of bed without a murmur and was sitting at the breakfast table, mutely spooning in the Coco Pops without taking his eyes off the vision.

Maxwell was also sitting spooning in the Coco Pops. He didn't usually eat cereal, but he had heard that carbohydrates were essential before physical activity and he wanted to be prepared. He was also having scrambled egg on toast with bacon and was hydrating with water rather than coffee. Jacquie was preparing his eggs, but kept stopping to leave the room and laugh hysterically on the landing. He was a rather arresting sight, dressed in camouflage from top to toe, and with random black stripes on his face to break up the outline. The black lines were to have been shoe polish, but Jacquie said, between hiccoughs, that it might make him come out in a rash, so he had compromised with eyeliner. He had sunscreen on his nose and lips, rapidly being rubbed off by breakfast and his nose rubbing, caused by the odd feeling of having sunscreen on it. He didn't have a camouflage hat, so was wearing his usual pork-pie, complete with bedraggled fishing fly in the band. For once, the feather looked at home.

Jacquie controlled herself long enough to speak. 'Is this get-up compulsory?'

'I understand from Helen's email,' he paused to give the phrase its full significance, 'that dress code is optional. We can wear any casual clothing we wish. Since my pelisse, dolman and overalls are in the wash momentarily,' he swept a hand down the length of his body to draw attention to his outfit, 'this is what I wish to wear.' He looked at Nolan and leant forward, raising an eyebrow. 'Nolan likes it, don't you, mate?'

His reward was a spray of flying brown cereal. 'Leave those in your hair,' Jacquie advised. 'It breaks up the outline.' She turned away and gave the eggs a cursory stir. Her shoulders were shaking. She gave a small cough and collected herself. 'Why did I not know about this until this morning?' she asked.

'A reasonable question,' he said, buttering some toast to fill the gap before the bacon was frazzled enough. 'I didn't know until last night. No, that's not quite right. I should have known, but it came in one of Legs's email memo things ages ago and I didn't read it. Helen reminded me last night. In an email.'

'That woman has a sense of humour all right,' Jacquie smiled.

Maxwell looked thoughtful. 'That's true.' He brightened up. 'She'll get a nice surprise, then, when I turn up.'

'I think they'll all get that, I can guarantee,' Jacquie said. 'Rambo Maxwell, at your service.'

'I'm glad you can see the resemblance,' he said smugly, in his best Sly Stallone. 'Nole noticed it straight away, didn't you, chap? And Metternich did. Where is the Count, by the way?'

'Last I saw, he was out of the cat flap and off up the road doing about ninety miles an hour. Even that cat can be freaked out, you know. Even after all these years of living with you.' She gestured with her spoon and he sat back. 'Eggs coming through,' she said. She brandished the spoon at her son. 'Scrambled egg, Nole?'

'Plah!' he grimaced.

'Same old, same old there, then,' she said.

'He'd probably be all right if you put a bit of smoked salmon in it,' Maxwell said. He wouldn't have minded some himself. Fish. Brain food. 'But enough of this tomfoolery, heart,' he said, shovelling in the egg. 'What time are you going in this morning? You were back really late last night.'

'I know,' she said, sitting down and picking up her orange juice. 'I'm going in usual time, though. I've got to drop Nole off, for one thing – and you, practically speaking. You can't ride through Leighford like that... Oh, and anyway, Surrey's at school still. And I want to see Henry. He hadn't come back when I left last night and he had been to see the other parent of each girl, the ones who didn't come in to the nick.' She took a sip of the juice. 'I'm sorry I wasn't up for chatting last night; I was just so tired. That Melkins man is a menace.'

'Melkins? Remind me.'

'Julie's stepfather. What a piece of work.'

'Involved?' Maxwell had started on the bacon and was feeding illicit bits to Nolan.

'No. He's only involved with himself. He wouldn't have bothered us, I don't think, except that his wife's eyes were getting puffy. Honestly!'

'Have you read my email?' he asked her.

'Yes. I've compared it with the full quatrain in your book and I think it at least shows he doesn't mean anyone any physical harm. I mean, the whole thing is nonsense. The joke about the Pot Noodles.'

'True, but some people believe every word of it – both World Wars, Hitler, the Holocaust, the Kennedy assassination. They say it's all there if you know where to look. I assume you've forwarded it to yourself, something like that?'

'Yes. It's possible that the IT boys will be able

221

to track down the sender, but I doubt it. These people just set up different emails on free providers and then abandon them after a few days. It's the same system spammers use.'

Maxwell had often wondered why they had chosen, out there in IT hand, to hijack the name of a perfectly innocuous canned meat to cover emails which could range from the banal to the frankly disgusting. Monty Python had once done an entire sketch on it. 'Well, I know you'll do your best. Any light on where the girls might be?'

'No, none. But I'm pretty sure they've just ducked out of sight for a while. They aren't answering their phones, which is perhaps understandable in the circumstances. And speaking of which, can I have your phone today?'

Maxwell pulled a face at Nolan. 'Mummies, eh?' he said. 'First it's "take your phone with you" then it's "don't take your phone". Where do we chaps stand? Hmm?' Nolan looked at his mother and raised his shoulders one by one in a rather inept shrug. He wasn't taking sides.

'I'll watch it for texts, you nit,' she said, swiping with the dishcloth at his head. 'Anyway, you'd only get it all painty.'

'I'll have you know, madam,' he said, adjusting his webbing belt, 'that I do not intend to get one single drop of paint on me. I will be the last teacher standing, you can rely on that. Well, me and Walter Willis.'

'Yes, well, if you insist. But no one will get anywhere if we don't get going. Everyone finished?' There were nods from both her men. 'Right ho, then. Dishes in the sink. Nolan, clean teeth please and bring your blazer down with you when you come. Rambo – well, I don't know what to say. Perhaps just a little touch up with the sunblock and I'd say you were good to go.'

Maxwell was trying to see a clear reflection in the cooker hood. It was testament to Mrs B's hard work that he nearly succeeded. It was the high gloss that reminded him. 'Oh, heart of my heart, did I ask you to check for Mrs B? Her missing nevvie, I mean?'

'Yes, you did,' said Jacquie, shrugging into her jacket and simultaneously wiggling a foot into a shoe. Maxwell always admired her ability to multi-task. He found that unless he concentrated, he was likely to put both legs down one leg hole, a tendency he had bequeathed to his son. 'I'll look into it, Max, if I have time. It all depends on whether the girls have turned up. I must stop trying to put them in one pigeonhole. They might not be together, even.'

'No, but I bet they are,' Maxwell said. 'And thanks for checking for Mrs B. She's in a right state.'

'Bless her,' said Jacquie fondly. She and the cleaning lady had struck up a rapport. Jacquie could find it in her heart to be fond of Vlad the Impaler if he cleaned her toilet, but she had a genuinely soft spot for Mrs B. 'I will check, but I don't think I'll be able to tell her much she doesn't know already, as family.'

Family. There was that word again, Nostradamus's word, reaching out from the grave. He sketched a kiss at her. Somehow, he didn't think she would appreciate a print of his camouflage on her cheek at this late stage of the morning.

The kitchen door swung back and Nolan appeared in the doorway. His shining morning face was beautifully adorned with black. 'Da daaaaaaa!' he crowed, throwing his arms wide and bending one knee.

All in all it wasn't a bad Al Jolson for one who had only ever known PC. Keeping a straight face but only by a whisker, Maxwell said, 'Don't you "da daaaaa" me, young man. Upstairs and wash that off and report back as soon as possible and as shiny as a new pin. You'll make mummy late.'

Nolan stamped a foot, but only half-heartedly and went to do as he was told. Jacquie dropped her voice and kept the laugh quiet too. "Da daaaaaaa" indeed,' she said, and poked Maxwell's brown and green shoulder. 'That's your fault, that is.'

'Don't make me laugh,' Maxwell begged. 'My eyeliner will run.'

They had managed to regain their composure when the boy came back. 'All right?' he said, offering up one cheek at a time for inspection. 'It's very boring.'

'Boring is good when it comes to school uniform,' his mother said. 'If you're good, we'll dress you up in full gear for tomorrow. If we can get Dad's bike back in time, we'll go for a bike ride and see if you can hide in the sand dunes. I bet we won't be able to find you for ages and ages.'

'Yay!' The child bounced up and down. 'Way to go, Ma,' and he raced down the stairs. There was a crash as the door was flung open and a 'Morning, Mrs Toobidge,' followed by galloping feet up the path.

'Good morning, Nolan,' they heard her say faintly. 'Are Mummy and Daddy at home?'

'Inna house,' they heard from a distance. They looked at each other with horror. Not Mrs Troubridge, not now, not when they were running so late. They took a deep breath and went down the stairs as quickly as possible without actually measuring their length in the hall. Jacquie was out first.

'Morning, Mrs Troubridge,' she said, taking the path at a run. Thank goodness for remote unlocking, she thought, as the car winked and beeped at her. She gestured Nolan to get in and he, trained since infancy in the esoteric art of Troubridge-avoiding, was in and buckled without being asked twice. She looked behind her for Maxwell. He should have been on her heels.

He had caught some webbing on the banister post and was looked up in a most uncomfortable-looking way. He struggled to get free as Mrs Troubridge regrouped and turned to the open doorway. As she waited for her eyes to adjust to the gloom of the hall, Maxwell suddenly loomed out at her, a vision in his jungle camos and warpaint. With a cry, she fell back, clutching her chest.

'Morning, Mrs Troubridge,' he called as he barrelled past. 'Development days, eh? Don't you just love 'em?' Jacquie had the door open and he was in and buckled in seconds. Jacquie gunned the engine and they were off. They all sat in silence for a few minutes, before Nolan spoke.

'Was that rather rude?' he asked the passengers in general.

225

His questions were often stunners, usually at difficult moments. His parents looked at each other. Maxwell tried an insouciant laugh. 'Not really, old mate,' he said. 'We are in a bit of a hurry.' He twisted round in his seat but Nolan still looked rather stern. 'Mummy? What do you think?' Maxwell asked hopefully.

'Well,' she said. 'I wouldn't usually recommend being that rude to people, no, Nole, you're right. But today was special.'

'Special Be Rude Day?' the boy asked hopefully. He could think of a long list of people to use it on, should it prove to be the case. Miss Spinks, his teacher, for one.

'No. Just We're In A Rush Day. I'll make it up to Mrs Troubridge later. Perhaps she can come to tea tomorrow. What do you think of that?'

'Not much,' Maxwell was quick to reply. 'Perhaps a bunch of flowers this evening? She'd like that.'

'Good idea,' Jacquie said. 'So, you see, Nole, if you don't mean to be rude, you can make it up by doing a nice thing later.' As she spoke, she knew she was storing up trouble. Elephants and her son never forgot a thing. She could just picture the years of Parent Teacher evenings when she would have to retell this incident, to her detriment as a competent parent, she was sure. 'Anyway, here we are at the bus station. Dads is going to catch the bus to the paintball park.'

'Is he?' Maxwell was frankly amazed. He thought he was going to be taken to the gate at least, if not the actual door of the training hut. Senior officers like him had chauffeurs and batmen. 'I haven't got any money.'

Jacquie pointed to the knapsack on the floor at his feet. 'Sandwiches, drink, money. I checked with Helen what you would need. Now, off you go, have a good time and play nicely with the other children.' Maxwell got out of the car and stood there, looking like an overgrown toddler, as the car pulled away. Jacquie turned briefly to her son as she waited to pull out onto the main road.

'Tuh,' she said, with a toss of her head. 'What a fuss about a school trip, eh?' And the last that Maxwell saw of his wife and son before he went to face the multicoloured bullets of his colleagues was their laughing faces and, in Nolan's case, a pointing finger. Good job they were nominally on his side, he thought.

Maxwell was not a natural bus traveller. He was used to the freedom which White Surrey gave him, to go anywhere, by virtually any route. He found it more than slightly irritating to be within sight of his destination, then to take a sharp left and meander around a housing estate for another hour, only to be deposited at a bus stop further away from his intended target than he had been when the bus had turned off. But, needs must when the devil drives. He did find, though, that if one had to use a bus, it was a darned good idea to do it wearing full jungle camouflage. The bus driver spoke very slowly and clearly to him and gave him change for a twenty-pound note with hardly a flicker. Also, seats were amazingly plentiful when he turned from paying to find somewhere to sit. He decided to be a bit cussed, though, and made his way the length of the bus, smiling benignly at everyone as he went, clouting the odd head with his bag as he passed. Finally, he came to the perfect seat, the back corner. He could sit here and watch the world go by, all around the town and out over The Dam to the wooded area set aside for Paintball Ltd. Parties and Corporate Our Speciality. He wriggled down, trying to get comfortable on a seat made stiff with years of chewing gum and the lord knew what else. Something was sticking into his bum through the thin polyester camouflage trousers. He delved down the back of the seat and came up with a small, spiral-bound notebook with a very girly picture on the front of a kitten in a bow. The teacher in him kicked in and he was about to check for a name when the driver turned round and shouted, 'Oy, Terminator, Rambo, what's yer name? This is your stop.'

'Oh.' Maxwell stuffed the notebook down the front of his knapsack and dashed down the bus, giving the heads he had missed on the way onto the bus a series of little buffets as he went.

'What a nutter,' one woman said to the world in general as the bus gathered speed.

'You're right there,' answered another. 'He was my teacher up at the school. Mad Max we called him. I knew he'd end up like this, part of some barmy army.'

'You weren't wrong,' said the driver. 'He was lucky I let him on.'

Maxwell was standing at the bus stop, waving gaily. 'See,' said the first woman. 'Nutter.'

Maxwell toiled up the drive to the reception hut of Paintball Ltd. He was exhausted already. Perhaps this was some sort of test, this cruel gradient, to sort out the old men from the boys. There were a few cars in the car park, unsurprisingly those of Legs, Ryan and Pansy Donaldson. Sylvia Matthews was sitting in a faded canvas chair on the edge of the clearing and burst into hysterics at the sight of his camouflage gear.

'Max,' she said, getting up and walking towards him. 'I knew I could rely on you to make this day faintly bearable.' She turned his face this way and that with a finger under his chin. 'You look positively gorgeous. Does your wife know you're out?'

'Why thank you, ma'am.' Maxwell sketched a curtsey, straight out of *Gone With the Wind*. 'Yes, she does, thank you very much. I have to ask you though, Sylv, what on earth are we doing here?'

'Team building,' she said, looking him straight in the eye, daring him to laugh.

'Team building? What team? Legs has demolished almost every team in the school that was working well.'

'Ah,' again her face scored ten out of ten on Maxwell's Buster Keaton sliding scale, 'that's why we have to build some more.'

'Didn't he get rid of people to save money?'

'Correct.' She smiled, but it was the smile of a crocodile. 'But since taking on,' she glanced behind her and seeing nothing continued, 'Mrs Donaldson that saving went west; I suppose he doesn't care any more. Anyway,' she made an expansive throwing-away gesture, 'new financial year, what the hey.'

'Sylvia,' Maxwell admonished. 'You're being very cynical.'

'Who, me?' she asked. Then, 'Sshh, we're no longer alone.'

Maxwell turned and saw the Big Three approaching from the reception hut. In fact, he mused, Pansy Donaldson was the Big Three on her own. The other two were just for decoration. Diamond opened his mouth to say something but he was beaten to it.

'Mr Maxwell!' the woman boomed, as though they were three miles away, not three yards. 'I looked everywhere for you yesterday afternoon. Where were you?'

'Pansy, dear thing,' the Great Man gushed. 'I had no idea. Where did you look?'

'All over your floor. I asked your class, the one you should have been teaching...' she paused for effect but no one spoke, 'and they said you had gone out.'

'Little tinkers,' Maxwell chuckled. 'That's Year Twelve for you. They meant I had gone out to get some books from the library, I expect. The Corn Laws – tchah! You have no idea how many corroborative texts you need to teach those well. If I left them to their own devices, the little dears would merely Google everything and copy it all down from the aptly named Nickipedia.' He smiled and was amazed to see the corner of Legs Diamond's mouth twitch in sympathy.

'Well, I won't call you a liar, Mr Maxwell,' she said.

'That's good,' he said, voice dripping ice. 'Otherwise, you may find yourself hearing from my solicitor.' Not that Maxwell had one, of course, but Pansy didn't know that.

'Steady on, Max,' Sylvia said, out of the corner of her mouth.

Pansy Donaldson was rocked but not beaten. 'As I say, I will not call you a liar, but I *will* be watching you, mark my words.'

'Ah,' Diamond cried, desperate to change the subject. 'Here come the others.'

A whole flotilla of cars was making its way up the rutted drive, packed to the doors as the staff of Leighford High School took car-pooling to new heights. Pansy Donaldson metaphorically rubbed her hands together. She looked forward to refusing a good eighty percent of the mileage claims on Monday morning.

A motley crew soon stood in front of the reception hut. Some had followed Maxwell's thinking and were wearing fatigues or at least really, *really* old leisure clothes, including one rather distressing turquoise tracksuit being worn by Paul Moss, Maxwell's Head of History. Paul had been a young man when he started at Leighford, but the gruelling demands of AFL had turned him into a wizened prune. The Head of Sixth Form sidled over to him, an interrogative eyebrow raised high.

'I know, I know,' Moss said. 'It was a moment of madness. I will say no more.'

'I should think not,' Maxwell agreed, then bounced up and down excitedly. 'Can I be on your team, can I, can I?'

'I understand that Pansy has allocated teams already,' Paul said despondently.

'Oh, well then,' Maxwell said. 'Goodness knows

where she will have put me. Digging latrines has got my name all over it.'

Bernard Ryan was clapping his hands together for quiet. It appeared that he had been doing it for some minutes, but no one was taking any notice.

'Hush!' Maxwell shouted and made almost everyone jump. 'Sorry, chaps,' he said to the staff. 'But poor old Bernard here has been trying his best to make you shut the hell up.' He gestured to Ryan. 'Off you go, then, Bernard.' *Band of Brothers* it was not.

'Er, thank you, Max. Yes. I have these health and safety sheets which the company has asked us to read. I will be needing your signatures and your names printed at the bottom before we are issued with our paint guns. If you would all like to just get one of these...' he handed a pile to Pansy Donaldson, 'yes, that's right. Pass them round. Has everyone got a pen?'

'No,' came a voice from the crowd. 'We were told to come in old clothes or something we didn't mind being spoilt and not have anything sharp in the pockets.'

'Yes, that's right,' came from several quarters. The situation had all the potential to turn ugly.

'Oh, um, yes...' Bernard Ryan patted his pockets helplessly.

'Why don't we form an orderly queue up to the reception desk,' suggested Maxwell, 'like pay day in the real army, and while we wait to get to the front, read this paper, and then we can sign it when we get there? Then, they can give us the guns and we can come out here and form into teams?'

'Great idea,' said Paul Moss staunchly, noting that Maxwell had just given everybody Alistair Sim's Miss Fitton, straight out of *St Trinian's*. And it had worked.

Reverting to infant school, everyone dutifully queued up and, with only a few sets of lips moving, mostly among the CDT and PE staff, proceeded to read the health and safety instructions. Maxwell was, as if by right, at the front of the queue. It was generally accepted that he wouldn't be reading the instructions anyway, so he might just as well be first.

He signed the paper with a flourish and handed it to the rather etiolated youth behind the counter.

'What colour team are you in, Mr Maxwell?' asked the lad.

Maxwell peered closer. An old Leighford Highena, as he lived and breathed. 'Quentin? Quentin Marjoribanks, is that you? I always had you down as ... I don't know, a merchant banker or something.'

'It's the name, Mr Maxwell. It was your little joke. I got three GCSEs A to C and was lucky to get them, you put on my final report.'

'Ah, yes.' Maxwell remembered now. 'That's probably why I had you down as a merchant banker, lad. Anyway, I'm afraid I don't know what colour team I am in.' He turned to the queue. 'Could someone ask Mrs Donaldson whose team I am in, please? Thanks.' While he waited for the answer he smiled at Quentin and drummed his fingers on the counter. The answer came back along the queue like Chinese Whispers.

233

Paul Moss was right behind him and so it fell to him to give the news. 'Pansy says she has you down as a joker, Max. Whoever wants you can have you.'

Maxwell chose to take it as a compliment, and if Pansy Donaldson had meant it to be otherwise, she had made a mistake, because arms were in the air all along the queue. Maxwell decided to be merciful. 'I'll be on your team, Paul,' he said, patting him on the back.

Paul Moss leant round and told the lad behind the counter, 'That will be green, then, Quentin.'

He reached behind him and took down the gun, which was marked with a green circle on the butt. 'Be careful how you point it, Mr Maxwell. Don't aim at the head. Don't shoot at less than a ten-foot range. Always wear your own goggles. The rules are that if you are hit you are out. When you have hit someone stop shooting...'

'Quentin, lad. Surely, these rules are all on the piece of paper I've just signed?'

'Yes, Mr Maxwell, but...' He wanted to say that Maxwell clearly had not read the sheet, but somehow the words wouldn't come. 'Sorry, Mr Maxwell. Next? Hello, Mr Moss.'

'Quentin. How's things?'

'Mustn't grumble, Mr Moss. Green, was it?' And so it went on for the poor hapless lad, until all the staff of Leighford High School were tooled up and ready to go.

Paul Moss clung to Maxwell as his name suggested. The old bugger may be slow on the turns but he was a military historian and tactics were second nature to him. He also led a charmed life,

234

as became obvious as the Head of Sixth Form downed his first victim minutes after Quentin blew his start whistle. Bill Grogan was Head of PE, a first-class lout who had put the mach into macho, but he looked decidedly under par with a splodge of green ooze where his belt buckle might have been.

'Na na di na na, Bill,' Maxwell chuckled and rolled into the damp bracken to his left, Moss flinging himself down too.

'Jesus, Max, I didn't hear him at all.'

The Generalissimo tapped the side of his nose. 'Precisely,' he said. 'It's all done by sense of smell. Which team is Pansy in?' He checked his gun. 'Head shots may be banned, but in her case I'll make an exception. Besides, it'll miss her brain by miles.'

'No team known to man, Max,' the Head of History told him. 'She's overseeing the whole thing, a sort of umpire. Or do I mean vampire? Die Mavis!' Moss was on his feet, blasting away at the diminutive teacher of Textiles. He missed by half a wood and Mavis's missile splattered his shoulder with yellow goo. He gasped in disbelief. 'Oh, dear,' he muttered.

'Mavis,' Maxwell trilled in an eerie voice, still lying as he was in the woodland greenery.

'Who's that?' she hissed, frantically looking to left and right and seeing no one but a rather crestfallen Paul Moss, wiping his turquoise top. She fumbled to reload, only to come face to face with Maxwell. She jammed home the cartridge and aimed at him, but the Head of Sixth Form poked his finger down her muzzle.

'Don't, Mavis,' he said softly. 'Don't make me kill you.'

'All right, Max,' she said and lowered her gun.

There was an awkward moment.

'What happens now?' Moss asked.

'What happens now is that Mavis here retires – oops, there, I've said it – and goes down to the gate to tell Pansy how bloody silly all this is. And shut up, Paul. You're dead.' He looked down at the man and shook his head, chuckling. 'Gunned down by Mavis. Oh dear, oh dear.'

He watched them both go, the Head of History and the retiring little seamstress. She was apologising for spoiling his nice blue top and Maxwell could have sworn he heard the 'r' word as they reached the bluebells. Now he knew he was on his own. So much for team-building. Maxwell knew these woods well. Apart from being lovely, green and deep, he used to wander here often, lonely as a cloud, before Nole, before Jacquie, before Metternich and certainly before Paintball Ltd had got their clutches on it. He crawled towards the ditches he knew lay away to his right, his rifle cradled in his arms like everybody did, from *All Quiet on the Western Front* to *The Thin Red Line*. It had to be said, he made Lew Ayres and Sean Penn look like amateurs.

Peering above the tall grass, he had a clear view of the car park, the entrance gates and Sylvia's First Aid centre. The Florence Nightingale of Leighford High had fixed a rough red cross flag above her car. Bless. One by one, the damned and the dead who were Maxwell's colleagues drifted back covered in paint to the disapproving clucks of Pansy Donaldson, out of luck, out of the game of life. He could see her clearly and drew a bead on the woman's head, much as he had once drawn a beard on her photo in the staffroom. But this was no *Enemy at the Gates*. His gun didn't have Joseph Fiennes' range. He'd have to get closer.

A curly blonde flashed across his vision. Sally Greenhow, Head of Special Needs, could still turn heads and she turned Maxwell's now. He hadn't had time to notice it before, but she was Green by team as well as by name. One of his own. She hit the bracken feet from him, but too far away to risk calling out. Maxwell could see the crouching figures of Mike and Ned, the IT nerds, moving out of the undergrowth towards her, like the Ghost and the Darkness. 'Beware the Geeks, Sally, my love,' he whispered to himself and risked a hand in the air.

Mike spun towards him, but held his fire. Maxwell rolled sideways, scraping his cheek on the rough bark of an oak. He waved at Sally and held up two fingers, pointing in Ned's direction. Happy, simple soul that she was, Sally just waved back.

Ned's scarlet shot hit her in the chest as she tried to run backwards and he beamed in triumph as she shouted, 'Bugger.' IT, One; Special Needs, Nil.

But Maxwell, of course, was a public schoolboy, bred in the fine tradition of cruel revenge and petty spite. He popped up out of the grass like the Guards at Waterloo and watched as Mike's scarlet whistled past his arm.

237

'Tut, tut, Mike,' the Head of Sixth Form said, 'and me a sitting duck.' He strode forward, fully aware that his gun was empty, and laid a friendly hand on the lad's shoulder. 'It seems to me you two boys don't know the rules.' And as Ned opened fire on him, Maxwell hauled Mike in front of him and a scarlet stain spread over the geek's back. Suddenly, there was a scream. It hadn't come from Mike, dead though he was. Nor from Ned, appalled at having gunned down his oppo. Sally Greenhow was silent. And Maxwell hadn't screamed like that for years.

Chapter Fourteen

The scream seemed to hang in the air for far longer than normal physics would dictate. Depending on their personalities, the staff of Leighford High School either froze in their tracks or ran towards the sound. Maxwell dumped Mike unceremoniously and ran. Paul Moss was hurtling up from Pansy's circle of shame. Bill Grogan, Action Man once more, was first on the scene.

Nicole Thompson stood rooted to the spot, on the edge of a shallow ditch, her mouth still open as if to catch its own echo. Her breath was coming in harsh gasps and her face was the colour of putty. She was pointing at the ground and, with every breath, they could hear a little whimper.

Paul Moss put his arm round her shoulders and tried to lead her away, but she just twisted in his arms as though she had been hypnotised by the thing at her feet. The men all looked down. Even Maxwell, considered by most to be an old stager in the finder-of-dead-bodies stakes, felt the lurch in the pit of his stomach as he looked down at the face of a man so clearly dead.

He was quite young, not more than twenty-five or so, and a stranger to them all. Therefore not a Leighford Highena, therefore probably not local. He looked quite peaceful, and if it wasn't for the beetle walking across his eyes, and the teeth marks around his ears, he could have been sleeping. Looking closer, Maxwell could see that his head was at a rather strange angle to his shoulders and guessed at the cause of death being a broken neck He manoeuvred round between the growing crowd and the body.

'Everyone back,' he said. 'Keep back. We need to stay away as much as possible. Forensics.' He walked towards them, arms outstretched, a one-man cordon. The crowd, acting as one as crowds often do, decided to obey him. He was, after all, Police-by-marriage and so would do until the real thing arrived. Heads appeared above bushes and from behind trees as the tiny guerrilla army realised that, for them, the war was over.

Paul Moss passed the by now weeping and trembling Nicole into the care of Sylvia Matthews, who had made her way from the reception area in response to the screams. She and Maxwell stood out from the crowd as being the only people there, apart from the body, to have no paint on them. She and Mike took the girl back to the safety of the hut, where Quentin was positively agog. He had put the kettle on when he heard the screams, having decided that it was probably safer to establish his role as refreshment guru, rather than hero.

'Have you phoned the police?' Sylvia asked the lad, rather tartly.

'Um...no,' he said. 'I didn't know what was going on. We often have screaming, Mrs Matthews.' He looked puzzled. 'It's a paintball event. People get excited.' He had to admit to himself that this woman, quite tasty if a bit old for his own personal predilection, she must be all of forty-seven, didn't look excited. In fact, she looked like shit. 'I'll phone now, shall I?'

'I think you should,' Mike said. 'There's a dead body out in your woods.'

'Somebody's died?' Quentin was horrified. His heart was in his mouth and going nineteen to the dozen. In his panic, his brain was suffering from tunnel vision; did he get everyone's signatures on the health and safety policy? Had they all signed their proper names? He knew what teachers were – had one of the buggers signed in as Mickey Mouse? Oh God, oh God, why had someone died on his shift?

'Calm down, for heaven's sake, Quentin.' Sylvia Matthews could recognise incipient hyperventilation at a thousand paces. 'It's a dead body. Not a dead punter. Unless, of course, he is from a previous group?' She raised an eyebrow.

'We always count people in and out, Mrs Matthews. He can't be left over from another time. And anyway, surely people would look for him ... wouldn't they?' He was picking the phone up and putting it down in an agony of indecision. He should ring his boss first. But how would that look to the police? Would it look as though Paintball Ltd had something to hide? *Had* Paintball Ltd something to hide? Oh God, oh God... He felt the phone being taken from him and firm hands on his shoulders bent him over until his head was between his legs. He heard a voice from above his head.

'Just breathe, Quentin. Nice deep breaths, now. One, two, three, four, five, go on, as slow as you can. That's it. Now out, two, three, four, just keep going. That's the ticket. Good chap.' Sylvia remembered Quentin as a bit of a vomiter when he was in Year Ten, a veritable martyr to panic attacks. She could do without that right now. She turned to the IT bloke standing beside Nicole. 'Mike, ring the police, will you?'

'Nine nine nine?'

'Hmm, good question. Where are we?'

'Ah... Paintball Ltd?' Mike didn't know what else to say.

'No, no. I mean, where *are* we? Are we still nearer to Leighford than anywhere else? I'd rather keep it local, makes it easier for questioning afterwards.'

Mike wasn't a Leighford Highena. He wasn't even Leighford born and bred. Like many of his kind, he kept abreast of everything except what mattered, surfing, surfing, always surfing that net and yet missing the things which would affect him directly. So he had no idea how many times Sylvia Matthews had brushed shoulders with police procedure. He just assumed she was a bit of a *Midsomer Murders* fan or something. 'We're still closest to Leighford, I would have thought. Just villages for miles inland.'

'Fine. Nine nine nine it is, then,' she said brightly.

Nicole made a slight whimpering noise and jumped convulsively, and started to cry.

'Ah, that's better. She's coming out of her shock. Perhaps we ought to have an ambulance as well,' she said over her shoulder to Mike, who was giving directions to the emergency services.

'That's right,' she heard him say. 'Police and an ambulance. In fact, make that two ambulances.'

242

He put the phone down and came over, putting a hand on Nicole's shoulder. He dropped his voice and mouthed to Sylvia. 'I thought two; one for her and him, one for ... well, you know.'

'Good idea,' said Sylvia. 'Hold on to her. I'll check on Quentin.' She felt like a ping pong ball, bouncing between the two. Who'd be a school nurse?

Maxwell and Legs Diamond were standing by the body, the Headteacher with his back resolutely turned, spattered with yellow paint as it was. Ryan and Paul Moss had marshalled the other staff back to the car park where they were standing in disconsolate groups waiting for the inevitable arrival of the police. From the high ground, it looked faintly like a fire drill at school. Some were so covered in paint as to be virtually unrecognisable and, standing around without the thrill of the chase, were beginning to realise just how painful paint pellets could be when they made contact with a delicate area. Personal scores had been settled, vendettas pursued and no teams whatsoever had been built. Maxwell, standing shoulder to shoulder with Legs, would have loved to take the opportunity to remark that, for the price of a Kit Kat and five minutes' sit-down, he could have told him what the outcome would be, but it seemed inappropriate.

Diamond shuffled his feet in the damp grass, looking down at the crushed violets and primroses on the bank. 'Do you recognise him, Max?' he asked.

'No,' Maxwell said. 'He's not one of ours, if

that's what you mean.'

Diamond bridled. 'I like to think I can recognise my own staff, Max,' he snapped. 'And the students. Especially by this time of the school year.'

Into Maxwell's head came an unbidden picture; it was the entire cohort of Year Nine girls and they were all standing with their weight on one leg, with their arms folded at the waist and, with one voice, they were all saying, 'Oh, purrllleeease!' He shook his head to rid himself of it and smiled faintly at Legs. 'Naturally, Headmaster. I wasn't implying to the contrary. I think what I meant was none of ours in the past. As in, an alumnus of the school.' His grin was an exact facsimile of the last thing many a solitary surfboarder sees on the Great Barrier Reef, just before being bitten in half. 'No one would expect you to remember all of the students who have passed through.'

Diamond looked at him sharply. Maxwell was famous for never forgetting a face. What was the man saying, as such? He sighed and relaxed. What was the point of trying to second-guess Maxwell? It could only come round and bite you on the arse. 'Sorry, Max.' He passed a paint-encrusted hand over his face. He was probably the only person there that day who had every colour represented on his clothes and skin. Even, and perhaps especially, the colour of his own team. 'It's been a bit stressful, today, one way and another. And now, this ... the police, the missing girls, just everything, really.' He paused and rather disconcertingly put out a hand and clutched Maxwell's sleeve. In everything they had gone through together, there had been very few examples of actual *touching* and it showed perhaps more than anything else the depths he had plumbed.

Maxwell was surprised. It wasn't often Diamond got to an idea before he did. 'Do you think there is a link between him and the girls, then?' he said.

Diamond shook his head. 'No, no, of course there isn't. I was just counting my blessings.' He gave a short, mirthless laugh.

It was true that Legs Diamond was way down on the list of Maxwell's favourite people. In fact, had that list been written down in five columns on a sheet of narrow-feint A4 paper, it was unlikely that he would be on the first page at all. But Maxwell's sympathy button could be pressed by almost any of God's creatures and so he said, 'Look, Headmaster. There is no need for us both to be here. I don't mind waiting by myself. Off you go and help with the staff. I expect they could do with a bit of guidance about now. The police will be here soon, anyway.'

It would have been nice if Diamond had at least made a pretence at wanting to stay. But he was off down the slope like Eddie the Eagle, calling over his shoulder, 'Are you absolutely sure, Max? That's very good of you.' In a matter of seconds, Maxwell and the dead man were alone together.

The Head of Sixth Form looked down into the dead face. 'Who are you, I wonder?' he said to it. He filled in time by practising his Sherlock Holmes techniques. He looked at the clothes. Chain store, cheap end he would guess, he who was by no means a fashionisto. The shoes were cheap as well, black trainers that could pass for smart footwear at a pinch. They were typical of someone wanting to look well turned out on little money. He could only see one hand, as the body was lying twisted round on one side, but the nails looked clean, trimmed and well looked after. The hair was auburn, short and neat, not tending to anything that could be called a style. There were no bruises or cuts on the face or hand, nothing that implied a fight or struggle. In fact, at a cursory glance, there didn't seem any reason why he should be dead. Except that head, twisted round to an impossible angle.

Maxwell raised his head. Was that fairy music coming from the direction of The Dam? Or was it sirens? He would certainly prefer it to be sirens; it would mean he wasn't going mad. Yes. He turned his head, triangulating on the sound; it was definitely sirens, the broken noise of ambulances and the higher-pitched wail of police cars. The Seventh Cavalry. They could always be relied on. He moved away from the body, a little way down the bank, distancing himself from it and trying to stop caring about this dead man, almost a boy, really, lying there in the ditch, with beetles walking over his eyes.

At Leighford nick, Jacquie had the surprise of her life waiting for her when she signed in at the desk. The desk sergeant, in formal tones said, 'Detective Sergeant Carpenter. You have someone to see you.' He indicated, with the smallest imaginable nod of his head, the chair in the corner of the foyer. His eyes said – a bit of lowlife over there; do you want me to get rid?

Jacquie turned to follow his indication and saw, to her surprise and delight, Maisie, slouching in such a way as to show that she didn't have to be there, she just thought she might drop in. 'Thank you,' Jacquie said to the desk man, 'I was expecting Miss Wilkins. Maisie, would you like to come up to my office?'

'Yeah,' the girl said and, bending forward and not taking her hands out of her pocket, slumped herself upright and stood by the doors, waiting for Jacquie to be buzzed through. It was not a comforting thought that she seemed to know the drill. They climbed the stairs in silence, Jacquie's court shoes tap tapping, Maisie's Doc Martens shaking the building. Jacquie opened the door to her office, sniffing for lingering kipper, but thankfully the plug-in air freshener had taken control.

''Snice,' the girl remarked, flinging herself into a chair.

'Thank you,' Jacquie said. 'I haven't had it long. It's nice to have a bit of privacy.'

'Hnuh,' snorted the girl. 'You're not wrong. She goes through my pockets, my bag, my phone, everything. She comes in while I'm asleep and just, you know, like, *looks* at me.'

Jacquie resisted the urge to ask how she knew if she was asleep. She wanted to tell her that all mothers looked at their sleeping children, whether they were one day, one year, ten or twenty years old. It was a comfort thing, that this human that you had made was still alive, still well, that you hadn't broken it or mislaid it. It was an instinct that was as old as the first two cells that ever joined together, back in the primeval ooze.

But Maisie wasn't going to believe that. It was snooping, pure and simple.

'It's because she went through your phone that you're here,' Jacquie reminded her. 'Other girls are in a bad way about this, Maisie. Two are missing, we think because of it. We've got to catch who is doing this texting, emailing and stuff because it will have serious consequences soon, if it hasn't already.'

The girl looked thoughtful. When her face was in repose, and if you looked past the piercings, the make-up, the residual truculent expression, Maisie was actually quite a pretty girl. She wouldn't welcome that information, Jacquie thought, but she will be grateful one day, when she takes all the metal out and becomes a swan. Assuming the holes heal up and assuming she doesn't leave it so late that all her tattoos have dropped with gravity and become a series of demented lines and whorls instead of the no doubt rather distressing images they were intended to be. She looked up. 'OK,' she said. Without the whine, her voice was quite pleasant and the intelligence shone through. 'You can have my phone if you want. I'll just need it back tonight, yeah, because my boyfriend will be ringing when he gets off work. I'm getting, like, twenty of these things a day. I just delete them. They don't bother me.'

'What kind of things do they say?' Jacquie asked.

'Mostly they know what I've done, things like that. Well,' the girl laughed, 'they've chosen the wrong one with me.'

Jacquie laughed as well. It was doubtful there

was much that Maisie hadn't done and she couldn't see her being ashamed of any of it.

The girl closed her mouth and pointed at Jacquie. 'I know why you're laughing. You're thinking that I've done the lot, drugs, sex, you name it. Well,' she shrugged her shoulders, 'you're wrong, see. I dress like this to annoy Mum. That's my hobby, you might say. But I don't do drugs, I don't do sex, I hardly do rock and roll. I prefer a nice bit of Mozart any day of the week. So whatever the sicko doing these texts says, I know he doesn't know anything, because there's nothing *to* know. So they really, really don't bother me a bit.'

Jacquie leant back in the chair and as she fell back, hitting her head on the wall, she knew that was a bad idea. Maisie was on her feet and round behind the desk like lightning.

'Don't get up,' she said, rather superfluously. 'That was a really hard bang there. There'll be feet on the stairs in a minute. They'll think I'm knocking you about.' Jacquie gave a small laugh and struggled to rise. 'No. I'm a first-aider.' As far as it was possible with her face against her own chest, Jacquie expressed mute surprise. 'I'm a senior Girl Guide, actually, but if anyone finds out I'll know it was you who told them. Now, can you wiggle everything?' Jacquie dutifully wiggled. 'Right, let's get you up, then.' With an expert heave, the girl had her on her feet. 'Whatever happened to your chair?'

'My husband broke it,' Jacquie said, sitting on the edge of the desk, for lack of anywhere else.

'Oh, the bloke who was with you at ours?'

Jacquie was staggered. 'Ummm, no, that was–'

249

'Well, let's hope he is your husband,' Maisie said, straight-faced. 'Or otherwise you're playing away from home, DS Carpenter.'

'He is my husband, yes, but how did you know?'

'You straightened his tie before you came in. You don't do that to just anyone.'

'Have you ever thought of joining the police when you're old enough?' Jacquie said, impressed.

'What, and blow my cover?' the girl laughed.

'I think your mother would hate you being a WPC,' Jacquie said. 'Think of how hideous the uniform is.'

'You've got something there,' Maisie agreed. 'I'll think it over.'

Jacquie cricked her neck back into place. 'To get back to your texts, then. Are you on any networking sites?'

'The usual,' the girl said.

'Any not usual?'

'No, Facebook, Bebo, MySpace, all those. The school one.'

'Your school has a chat room?'

'Yeah. We've got a really great IT Department. They've set it up. You can only use it on the school intranet, but it's great if you've missed anything, stuff like that. Good essays get put up on the noticeboard, it's good.'

'I thought you were a famous truant.'

Maisie laughed and ducked her head. 'Part of the image. I'm there most days.'

'And you can chat on the school site?'

'Yeah. We've all got log-ins that disguise us. It's fun, because you don't know who anyone is. You can chat to someone in another year, that kind of thing, and no one knows. You can literally be chatting to the person next to you in class, and neither of you would know.'

'Has anyone talked about the texts?'

'No. I didn't know anyone else was having them. It's not like I've got loads of friends.'

'Except in the chat room.'

'Well, yeah. I'm good with words when I can write them down.'

'What's it called, this intranet site?'

'It's a bit naff really. We log in to wwwitsgoodto-talk.sch.uk. We can only access our own school, though.'

'So other schools have these things?'

'Never thought about it. Suppose.'

Jacquie made a note. 'Well, thanks for coming in, Maisie. Keep in touch, I'll—' Jacquie's phone rang. 'Excuse me while I answer this. Carpenter, hello?' She jumped down off the edge of the desk. 'What? Oh, hello, Steve.' She hoped she sounded calmer that she felt. 'Yes, thanks for letting me know ... yes. I'm on my way.' She looked up at Maisie, her eyes dark with worry. 'Look, I'm sorry, I'll have to go. I'll see you out.'

The girl got up and reached out to touch her arm. 'DS Carpenter, what's the matter? You look terrible.'

Despite the rings, swords and various other piercings, despite the laddered tights and the purple Doc Martens, Jacquie felt oddly at ease with this strange girl. 'Um, I've had a bit of a shock. My husband was off paintballing today.'

'Bit long in the tooth, isn't he?' The question was out before the girl realised how rude it sounded.

'Yes, I suppose he is. He hasn't noticed, though. Well, there's a report of ... well, of someone dead at Paintball Ltd.' She suppressed a sob. 'No details. I'm sorry, Maisie. I've got to go.'

'I'm coming as well,' the girl said. 'My Quent works at Paintball Ltd.'

Jacquie was about to say– So? He's not likely to have keeled over with a heart attack, is he? But something in the girl's face made her stay silent. Here was someone who didn't open up willingly. Her Quent must be something pretty special, Jacquie decided. 'OK,' she said. 'Let's go. But if anyone asks...'

The girl mimed zipping her lips. Or at least, Jacquie hoped she was miming. They made for the stairs and this time their feet drummed in perfect time until they reached Jacquie's car. Maisie was still shutting the door as it barrelled away.

Up on his hill, Maxwell felt distanced from the hullabaloo below. He could see the cars and ambulances as they swept into the drive from the road, but they were invisible once they reached the car park. He wondered why they needed two ambulances; someone being overzealous, he supposed. He noticed Henry Hall's car, just a few minutes after the two squad cars. He had to chuckle – Henry would have jumped at this chance to get his teeth into a proper crime. He would have been chafing at the bit, following leads on the missing girls who Maxwell was still convinced were mislaid rather than missing. He could hear the car doors slamming and voices coming his way. Then, out of the corner of his eye, he saw Jacquie's car taking the turn into the drive on what looked like two wheels. He was surprised to see her, especially with a passenger; surely, she was too busy for this. Never mind, she would doubtless tell him all about it later. He heard a shout.

'Max? Mr Maxwell? Where are you?'

Oh, for goodness' sake. Surely someone was bringing the police up to the spot? They couldn't be that squeamish, not even Legs. 'Up here. Follow the path round to the left. I'm at the top of the bank.'

Through the undergrowth came Henry Hall followed by a phalanx of policemen, in Indian file. They stumbled and crashed about as they came; Yul Brynner and Burt Lancaster they certainly weren't. It was as if a herd of elephants were drawing closer.

'Over here,' he waved and Henry waved back. Finally, puffing and panting, the police squad were lined up on the bank. 'He's down there,' Maxwell pointed. 'I kept people back as well as I could but I wasn't the first on the scene, sadly.'

'No,' Hall said. 'I've left someone down there interviewing her. She's badly shocked. Well, they both seem to be.'

'Both?' Maxwell was pretty sure he hadn't missed anyone, up here on the bank.

One of the policemen consulted his notebook. 'Quentin Marjoribanks.'

'That's Marshbanks,' Maxwell said automatically.

'Oh, damn.' The policeman scrubbed out the name with the rubber on the end of his pencil.

'He spelt it for me as well.'

'No, I ... never mind.' Maxwell decided that least said was soonest mended in this case. He turned to Henry. 'Quentin wasn't here at the time. How is he involved?'

'Oh, I don't think he is,' Hall said. 'He's just got a bit over-involved.'

'Yes, that's Quentin,' Maxwell said. 'I'll just go and join the others, shall I?'

'Do you have any ideas?' Hall asked. It sounded as though the words were being ripped out with red-hot pincers.

'I can't say that I do, no,' Maxwell said. 'Except that I don't know him, which is unusual around here. Most locals his age have been Leighford Highenas at some stage in their school career.'

'I take it you haven't touched the body.' The statement came out as more than half a question.

'No, I haven't. And you can take it that if I haven't, then none of the other squeamish lot will have done. Although, if you're thinking in terms of DNA, I wouldn't be surprised if you find traces of Nicole Thompson's. She was screaming and gagging fit to burst.'

'Good point.' Hall gestured for his note-taker to take a note. 'Anyone else get near?'

'Only to glance down and back away. But we've been all over these woods today, ducking and diving.' He suited the actions to the words. 'Some people may have been near without realising it.'

'We'll check for paint,' Hall said. 'That will help pin people down.'

'It depends how long he's been here, though, doesn't it?' Maxwell asked.

'It's the beginning of the paintball season,' said Hall.

'I have to interrupt you there,' Maxwell said. 'Do you mean to tell me paintballing has a season? Like grouse?'

'I think it simply means that people don't tend to do it when the weather is cold,' Hall said. 'After Easter is when they get busy. So in fact, you lot are the first punters this week. And I'm sure your wide reading and even wider experience would have already told you that he wasn't in place as early as last week, Wednesday to be precise, when the management level of Leighford Tyres were here on a team-building exercise.'

'There's a lot of it about,' Maxwell muttered. 'On another subject altogether, I'm surprised you've got Jacquie in on this one.'

Hall looked suitably bewildered. 'I haven't.'

'I just saw her car,' Maxwell said. 'And if, as you may suspect, I am not too good on car makes and models, I would recognise my lovely wife's driving anywhere.'

'She does have a certain flair,' Hall conceded. 'But, really, I haven't called her in on this one. She has enough to do on this ... other matter.' He suddenly realised that the rest of the team might not understand about Maxwell and exactly where they all stood, vis-à-vis him knowing every fart that flew.

As he spoke, there was a crashing in the undergrowth. 'Unless we are having a spot visit by David Attenborough and a couple of rogue silverbacks, we will have our explanation in very few seconds.'

The bushes parted and Jacquie stood there, twigs in her hair and smears of various paint on the front of her best jacket. 'Peter Maxwell,' she snapped as best she could when so out of breath. 'I come over here, driving like a maniac,' Maxwell and Hall exchanged a fleeting glance, 'and I find you fit and well and talking to Henry. How dare you scare me like that? Well?'

The whole wood held its breath. The wrong word now could be fatal.

Maxwell stepped up to the plate. 'Darling, I'm so sorry.' He extended a hand and pulled her the last few feet up the slope. 'It was thoughtless of me. I wouldn't worry you for the world.' He put his arm round her and gave her a peck on the cheek. 'Look at you,' he said fondly, 'all painty. Shall we go back to the car park? Then perhaps I can cadge a lift with Sylv, save you dropping me off. Hmm?'

She fell into step as they slithered down the slope and onto the path.

The policemen watched them go. Then one of them let out a long-held breath. 'God, he's good,' he said. 'I've seen her reduce grown men to tears because they put sugar in her coffee. I take it all back, the things I've said about him.'

'I wonder if he gives lessons,' said the other.

'I would imagine so,' Hall said drily. 'He's a teacher.'

'I mean in … whatever that was.'

'I think you can either do that, or you can't,' said Hall. 'Right, now. We'll do what *we* do best, shall we? Where the hell are the SOCOs?'

Chapter Fifteen

On the short walk down the slope to the car park, Jacquie reflected on recent events. She accepted that she had over-reacted, that she shouldn't have blamed Maxwell for something he hadn't even known he had done. Hadn't done, if she was being brutally honest. She knew that he knew that it was her fault for not checking first but the mad old bugger had put his life on the line before. He was a risk-taker and she had to live with it. The apology had been a calming-down exercise. She now had two options: she could yell at him for condescending to her and agreeing that he was in the wrong; or she could just pretend the last ten minutes had never happened and take it from there. By the time they were with the others, she had chosen Option Two and would stick to it through thick and thin.

One ambulance had discreetly withdrawn to the edge of the car park. It was unlikely to be used any time soon; forensics would take ages. But ambulance drivers are used to being called by people who spent too much of their leisure time watching *CSI* and so took these kind of calls in their stride. The other ambulance was parked near the reception hut with its rear doors open. Nicole Thompson could be dimly seen, lying down on one of the beds. A paramedic was taking her pulse and a drip was being prepared; there was no doubt that she had had a severe shock. At the doorway, Quentin Marjoribanks was leaning against Maisie, looking pale and wan. He nevertheless was also looking smug. His woman had come running to his side; as far as he chose to understand it, she had hijacked a police car to achieve it. He was blessed.

Jacquie turned to Maxwell and he smiled down at her. He was ready to receive more lambasting or an apology – he wasn't really fussy, he knew that both of them were the equivalent of being told she loved him. So, what she actually said was a surprise. 'Well, I must be getting back, I suppose. Maisie had some quite useful information which I ought to follow up. Are all the schools in the area on development days today?'

Ah, he thought. We're on Option Two. He went along with it; it was too tiring, especially on a day like this, to swim against that particular tide. 'I'm not sure,' he said. 'I'm sure Mrs Donaldson would be able to help you on that.' Before Jacquie could stop him, he raised his voice a notch. 'Pansy?' She turned. Many was the Greek warrior who saw that sight, his last on earth, as the basilisk turned him to stone.

'Mr Maxwell?' It was the first time he had heard his name used as a curse. She did it very well.

'My wife would like a word with you, if you have a moment.' She came over reluctantly. 'Mrs Donaldson, Pansy, this is Mrs Maxwell, Jacquie, also known as Detective Sergeant Carpenter.' He smiled benignly at them both. 'I'll just go and see what's going on over there.' And he wandered away. He hadn't been keeping score, but he

258

thought they must surely be at deuce right now.

He ambled over to where the ancillary staff had made a rather exclusive huddle. This was where the best gossip was to be found. 'Hello, chaps and chappesses. How're tricks?'

The disconcerting sight of both Thingees in one place made the universe spin. They usually only met in the car park as one left and one went in at lunchtimes, like the Weather Man and Woman in those old barometer toys of Maxwell's childhood. Various Teaching Assistants stood around, paint caked and tired looking. Most of them had evening jobs to eke out their pathetic wages and were getting rather anxious that they would be late. It didn't do to turn up for the night shift at Tesco with your hair thick with multi-coloured goo. There was a general melee of greetings.

'Did anyone recognise the chap, you know, the dead one up in the ditch?' he asked.

Heads were generally shaken. But one person disagreed. 'No,' one of the dinner ladies said. 'I've seen him before, but I'm blowed if I can remember where.'

'In school?' Maxwell asked.

'That's just it,' she said. 'It's kind of school *based*, but not in school, if you see what I mean.'

'With someone from school, perhaps?' the Great Detective probed.

'Hmm, I really dunno, Mr Maxwell,' the woman said. 'It's no good werriting it. I'll never remember that way.' She wandered off to get a bit of peace. Things often popped into her head if she did that. These days she found that she had to walk round the post office once or twice before she could remember her PIN.

'Anyone else?' Maxwell asked.

'We didn't really see him,' said a Thingee. 'We were already shot and down with Mrs Donaldson.' She made it sound as if she had actually said 'doing twenty to life at Parkhurst'. Maxwell could empathise. 'She wouldn't let us go, even when we heard Nicole scream. She hadn't logged us in.' The two receptionists exchanged glances. Life wasn't the same, now they were ruled by Pansy.

'But you saw him briefly?' Maxwell checked.

Thingee Two giggled. 'We managed to get away,' she said. Then her face fell. 'We didn't know why Nicole was screaming. We thought ... well, we thought that someone good had been shot. Like Mr Diamond.'

'Or you, Mr Maxwell,' piped up Margaret, from Reprographics.

Maxwell merely swept an arm down his immaculate person. As if he would have been shot, indeed. The very idea. He was a Superhero to the core. Perhaps not the Silver Surfer, but any one of the others.

'So no one recognised him, except perhaps Doreen.' No one stopped to marvel at Maxwell's recall of names; it was just the way he was. If only Doreen's memory was half as good.

With shaking heads, they moved away. Maxwell glanced across to the main crowd of people, over by the door of reception. Jacquie was talking to one of the uniforms and was making her preparing-to-move gestures. Patting her pockets, rummaging in her bag for her car keys. Maxwell could read the woman like a book. Finding them, she looked up and caught his eye.

'I'm off now,' she said. 'Did you mean it about cadging a lift with Sylvia?'

'She may be a while,' he said. 'A lot of people are feeling the after-effects and knowing Sylv, I don't think she'll leave until the last one is sorted. I'll get a lift with someone, though. I ought to pick up Surrey, while he still has wheels. You could take my knapsack, though, if you don't mind.'

'Of course.' They were still being a tad polite with each other. This would pass, when one or both of them forgot about it.

He went over to the pile of bags near the door and moved them aside until he found his. As he picked it up, he remembered the notebook he had found on the bus. 'I suppose I ought to hand this in,' he said to her, pulling it out of the front pocket.

'What is it?' She looked at it, albeit upside down. 'Where did you find it?'

'On the bus.' There was just the tiniest hint in his voice that it was her fault he was on the dratted vehicle at all. 'It was down behind a seat.'

'May I?' She held out her hand. The notebook was quite small, with a girly picture on the front of a kitten in a bow. The bow was attaching a label to its neck, and on the label someone had written in glitter pen, 'Zee'. She pointed to the name. 'Have you looked in here at all?'

'I hardly looked at it,' he said. 'It was sticking in my bum and I hoiked it out. That's it. Why?'

She pointed again, jabbing the cover of the book.

'Zee.' He looked at her. 'Why does that ring a bell?'

'Because Zee is what Julie's friends call her. Julie, who is missing.' She flicked open the first few pages. 'Julie who is missing, and seems to have left her diary behind.'

He reached out to take it, but she stopped his arm with her other hand. 'Sorry, Max,' she said. 'This is evidence. I think we'll be needing you to give a statement.' She gestured to a policeman standing nearby. 'Kevin, Mr Maxwell has found some evidence in the case I am working on. Have you been asked to take names from these people yet?'

'Yes, DS Carpenter,' the man replied. 'I have a list, though. That ... lady over there had one all made out, with times of arrival, times they were "shot", everything.' He waved a thin sheaf of paper.

'Ah. Right. You've got a minute to take this down, then, have you?'

'Yes, I should think so.'

Jacquie turned to Maxwell. 'That's best, then. You give Kevin your statement while it's still fresh in your mind.'

'I'm an historian. Everything is still fresh in my mind.'

Jacquie smiled and patted his arm. 'Enjoy, Kevin,' she said. 'I'll see you at home, Max. Nolan is sorted this evening.'

'Spencer's mum?' Maxwell asked with trepidation.

'No. Baby minder. Apparently, Spencer's mother has pollution issues. We'll talk about that. Anyway, laters.' And she was gone.

'Shall we pop into reception, Mr Maxwell?'

asked the policeman. 'Or shall we sit in the car?'

'Car's quieter,' Maxwell said. And besides, there was often a police radio left switched on. It was wonderful how much information you could pick up that way.

Jacquie resisted the temptation to open the diary in the car. It really had to go to forensics. They had a way of opening books page by page, collecting anything that fell out. It was a moot point, though, whether it would be of any help. This notebook had been down the back of a bus seat, possibly for weeks, but hopefully only for one day. It had been in the front pocket of Maxwell's knapsack for only an hour or two, but since his trusty bag had been with him since his, admittedly brief, Boy Scouting days, the DNA in there would be enough to tax Quantico. But, nevertheless, rules are rules and so it had to go to the lab. She found that she had taken the turn which would take her to Chichester and the main laboratory. She had to take a chance that the person left on duty when the team went out to Paintball Ltd would not be Angus.

'Angus. Hello.' Jacquie stood just inside the doorway of the laboratory looking with a sinking heart at the long streak of piss that was the representative of God's forensic scientist on Earth.

'Jacquie. DS Carpenter. Mrs Maxwell.' Angus always perked up when he saw Jacquie, although it would take another forensic technician to tell. He took casual to a new level. It would be interesting to pit him against Maisie, thought Jacquie, in a slumping contest. She wouldn't care to bet on the ultimate winner.

Angus was a more than competent forensic scientist; he simply looked like a brainless moron and chose to sound pretty much like one too. His white coat and his PVC gloves were absolutely according to guidelines. His hair was pulled ruthlessly back in a scrunchie and the whole thing was covered with a white paper cap. He wore disposable theatre scrubs under the coat and on his feet he had a pair of Crocs, ultrasounded every day and encased in a fresh pair of paper slipovers. Despite this, had Jacquie been asked as she left the building to describe him, she would have been precise and to the point and, as far as her memory went, accurate. She would have said that he had curly hair falling all over his face. He was wearing a very old and rather grubby Soundgarden T-shirt, jeans with the knees out and motorcycle boots with the toes out. He was smoking the biggest joint she had ever seen. This was because Angus had a very strong self-image and, despite his white and clinical clothing, he still *felt* that he looked like that, and belief can be catching. 'Bones' he was not.

'DS Carpenter will be fine,' she said crisply. 'I have been handed this,' she proffered the notebook, rather belatedly in an evidence bag, 'by a member of the public. Can you go through it, please? We have reason to believe it belongs to a missing person.'

'Right. Cool. As you see, I'm a bit understaffed at the moment. Body up at Leighford. Well, you probably know about that, eh?'

'Um, yes. I'm on this different case, though.'

She tapped the notebook for emphasis.

'Yeah, right, but a body, eh? Paintballing accident, they reckon.' He rubbed his hands together. His eyes went misty. 'I love a bit of paint analysis, me. Gas chromatography. Microspectrophotometry. Lovely.' He smiled at the ceiling. 'Loads of overtime.' He came back to himself with a start. 'Sorry. Went off on one there for a minute. Where was I?'

'My notebook.'

'Gotta requisition?'

'Come on, Angus.' Jacquie had learnt most of her wheedling techniques from Maxwell. 'We understand each other, don't we? We don't need requisitions.'

'Now, come on, DS Carpenter. You've got me in a lot of trouble in the past with this sort of behind-the-elbow sort of stuff.'

'Behind the elbow?'

'Erm ... Dutch phrase. My girlfriend uses it. I like it. Did you know that you can't kiss your own elbow?'

'Dutch girlfriend? Goodness, Angus. You've become very cosmopolitan.'

'We don't get to see each other much,' he confided. 'She lives in Amsterdam. We met when I was over there last year. We talk a lot on the Net. Words like "dank u vell" and "slagroom".'

For heaven's sake, thought Jacquie. If I could just go one day without the dratted web getting in my way. 'Lovely, Angus. But ... my notebook?'

'I'll give it my best shot, DS Carpenter. But I can't promise.'

'Missing persons, Angus. Should take precedence over a dead body, surely?' Jacquie leant over his countertop. She knew she was reaching in more ways than one.

'Requisition, DS Carpenter. Takes precedence over you coming in here and trying to get round me.'

Jacquie straightened up, feeling a little ashamed that she had played the breasts card so blatantly. 'Fair enough. I shouldn't try to coerce you, Angus. It isn't fair.'

'No,' he sulked. 'It isn't.'

'But they'll be a while, won't they? Coming in with the clothes and everything? Can't you get on with my notebook until they get here?'

Angus sighed. He really fancied this woman. And her old man was a good sort, despite what everyone said. 'All right. I'll give Donald a call and get him to give me a heads-up when they've delivered to him.' The thought of Angus with a head up was rather amusing in itself. 'Best I can do.'

Jacquie patted his gloved hand.

'Oops,' he said, sliding it off. 'No touching, now.' The pictures that went through his mind were best kept to himself.

'Sorry, Angus,' she said. 'I'd better be off anyway. Give me a ring if anything turns up?'

'Sure thing,' he said. 'I've got your mobile number.' And he reeled it off, number perfect.

'My word, Angus,' Jacquie said, appalled. 'How very...'

'Amazing. I know. I've got that sort of mind.'

Jacquie had been going to say creepy, but amazing would do. 'Right. Bye then, Angus.' And she

266

was off down the stairs at a steady trot, trying not to listen for footsteps behind her.

Sylvia Matthews kept glancing across at Maxwell in the front seat of the police car. The hapless uniformed man in the driver's seat was trying desperately to keep up with the narrative, complete with actions, that Maxwell was delivering in his usual inimitable style. He appeared to be miming bringing a string of flags out of his backside now – surely, that couldn't be right. She turned back to the queasy row in front of her; they couldn't all have seen the body, could they? And anyway, to listen to the more rational of her colleagues, it really wasn't gory at all. But being a teacher was a two-way street; they taught the kids Reading, Geography, Social and Life Skills, Maths, and the kids taught them how to be whiny, needy and melodramatic. Ah well, she had a jumbo pack of Nurofen and it was amazing what they could achieve, given with the right amount of confidence.

Pansy Donaldson was watching Maxwell too. That poor policeman, shut up in a car with that madman. He appeared to be pointing to his bottom now; the depths to which that man could sink were simply unbelievable. Whatever could his buttocks have to do with the case in hand? She had watched him leave the room on many occasions, and, as far as she could see, they were nothing to write home about. Totally disgusting. No wonder the youth of today were sinking in depravity.

'Pansy? Mrs Donaldson?' She could hear someone calling her name from a long, long way off. 'Pansy? Are you all right? You were grinding your teeth.'

She came to with a jump. 'I'm terribly sorry, Mr Diamond. Miles away. It has turned into quite a day, hasn't it?'

Diamond was staggered at the woman's take on life. Quite a day? Yet again, his school was embroiled in some seedy crime scene. Yet again, Maxwell seemed to know more than simply being on the spot would really explain. One of them would have to go soon, or Diamond knew he would be booking a one-way ticket to the funny farm. He made do with, 'Yes, indeed, Pansy. It has turned into quite a day. I'm going back to school now. I've checked with the police.'

'I'll come with you, Mr Diamond. You will need help, the Press, that sort of thing.'

He passed a weary hand over his face. 'I'd just like some time on my own, Pansy, to tell you the truth. Perhaps you can go and visit Nicole in the hospital. See how she's doing? Would you do that for me?'

She couldn't recognise a brush-off if it bit her on the leg, thought Helen Maitland, overhearing the exchange. But if the result of that was an afternoon blissfully Pansy-free, then she was all for it. She stepped forward. 'You're looking rather peaky, Headmaster.' He flinched. Maxwell seemed to be catching, rather like Swine Flu or the moronic interrogative. 'Can I give you a lift? I brought half the PE Department with me this morning. I'm sure they would be happy to drive your car back to school for you.'

Legs looked across to where the PE staff were seeing who could hang upside down from a tree for longest without losing consciousness. They had more paint on them than Seven Ex Pea after an interactive art class. The space not taken up with paint was covered in mud. His car was a BMW, with beige leather seats. Pansy, hearing Helen's offer, was looming nearer. Filthy seats versus Pansy. Pansy versus filthy seats. 'What a kind offer, Helen,' he said. 'I would like that, thank you.' He fished out his keys and she took them over to the PE gang, who whooped and jumped in the air, crashing stomachs together and giving each other extravagant high fives. Bill Grogan got the keys and would be driving. Diamond groaned, but he was still confident that he had made the right decision.

Helen glanced across at the police car. Maxwell was clambering out, and was saying a few last words to the policeman. She called him over and he came at a loping run, close to the ground, looking left and right. 'It's all right, Max,' she said. 'It's only me. You can relax.'

He looked crestfallen. 'It's the clothes. I just don't seem to be able to shake it off.'

'I'm just giving Mr Diamond a lift back to school,' she said brightly, doing the best Joyce Grenfell Maxwell had heard in a long time. 'Would you like to join us?' She tried to ignore the sound of two grown men who should know better giving vent to instantly suppressed groans; working together was bad enough. Travelling together was beyond the pale.

'I'd love to,' he said.

269

'I'd love to,' said Diamond, just that second later.

'Right, then. My car's over there. If you'd like to let yourselves in, I'll just let the police know we're going.'

'No, no,' Maxwell said. 'You two get in the car. You know how hopeless I am at all this clicking business. Give me a good old-fashioned key you can turn, that's what I say. I'll just tell the DCI we're going.' And he walked off normally, to Helen's relief, to where Henry Hall was standing with a small clutch of constables.

'DCI Hall,' he said, formally. 'Mr Diamond is feeling unwell and Helen Maitland and I are going to take him back to school, if that's acceptable.'

It wasn't really acceptable for anyone to leave the site, with an unidentified body hovering over them, so to speak, but Hall was always glad to see the back of Maxwell. He would often enough have to engage the man's brain, but he preferred to do it where there was no one else to see.

'That's absolutely fine, Mr Maxwell,' he said, keeping it equally formal. 'We may have to be in touch later.'

'I quite understand,' Maxwell said and, only just resisting the urge to salute, went back and got in the back of Helen's car. 'Let's go, then,' he hissed, in the manner of a bank robber in a getaway car.

Helen released the handbrake and eased slowly away from her parking space. 'Leighford High, then,' she said. It was halfway between a statement and a question.

'Hmm. I need to pick up Surrey,' Maxwell said,

'but then I'll be off home, Headmaster, if I may. I've got to pick up my emails at home.'

The two people in the front of the car turned round to stare at him, in Helen's case much to the detriment of basic road safety. He gestured her to turn back before he would respond.

'I expect that surprises you, but I'm not as much of a dinosaur as you all seem to think. I am perfectly adept at surfing the superhighway,' he said, hoping he had got at least one of the phrases right.

'Well done, you,' Helen said. She would believe it when she saw it. She changed the subject. 'Did I hear that Doreen thought she had seen the dead guy somewhere before?' she asked Maxwell.

'She said so, yes. But I think we all know the general standard of Doreen's short-term memory.'

'Yes,' Diamond piped up. 'Every morning, she brings me coffee, milk, two sugars and a Snickers bar.'

'Every morning,' Helen said. 'That's good, then, isn't it? If she never forgets.'

'I'm borderline lactose intolerant and a single peanut could kill me,' Diamond said. 'My digestion has never been the same since ... the incident.' He could never bring himself to refer in any more detail to the mass attempt on the lives of his staff by means of poison. It was true that he had never been the same since. But then, he hadn't really been the same before.

'Perhaps it's a really cunning attempt on your life, Headmaster,' said Maxwell, from the back.

'I'm sorry, Max, if I don't laugh,' Diamond said. Maxwell wondered why he was bothering to apologise just this one time. What about all the million others when he had failed to crack a smile? 'The whole thing is still very painful for me. I get nightmares, you know. It's all very unpleasant.'

'Sorry, Headmaster,' and for once, Maxwell actually meant it. Helen caught his eye in the rear-view mirror and he could tell from her eyebrow position that nasty things would happen if he didn't shut up. The rest of the journey went by in silence, broken only by Maxwell's sighs as he thought of something he knew he would be better off keeping to himself. Like, where were the missing girls? Who was the dead man? Why on earth had Diamond ever appointed Pansy Donaldson? How had he managed to go this long without rechristening her Pansy Potter, the Strongman's Daughter, beloved of schoolboy *Beano* readers in the Fifties?

Halfway up the drive of Leighford High School, Helen pulled up and turned to Maxwell. 'I'll let you out here, Max, shall I? Handier for the bike sheds?'

'Thanks, Helen,' he said, attempting to hop out but finding that his legs had more or less seized up. 'Ooh, paintballing is a young man's game, I'm discovering.'

Helen opened her door and came round to help him out. 'I told them there should be an age limit,' she said. 'I'm thinking of poor Mavis here, as well as you.'

'What do you mean, as well as me?' Maxwell was aghast.

'Well, when she goes, you'll be the oldest

member of staff.' Having extricated him and made sure that he was basically in working order, she got back into her idling car and drove away, round to the car park at the rear. He stood and watched her go. He didn't feel like the oldest member of staff. Some days he didn't feel older than Nolan. His feet dragged for more than one reason as he went round the building's corner to the bike rack. Surrey was safe and sound, every speck of rust intact. He could leave it wherever he liked and for some reason no one ever stole so much as a screw.

He swung his leg over the crossbar, but something didn't seem quite right. He looked down and found, to his surprise, that his leg hadn't gone anywhere, but was still firmly attached, via his foot, to the ground. He stared at the offending limb and, by concentrating really hard, managed to swing it just high enough to straddle the bike. Pushing off was another challenge which it took some time to achieve, but finally, he was on his way home.

It was a strange feeling, skimming through town, that no one whose doors Maxwell passed knew of the events in Paintballers' Wood as the Press would soon no doubt name it. No one? No, that probably wasn't true. *Someone* knew. The same someone who had broken a man's neck and dumped him in a ditch like an old supermarket trolley.

Surrey hissed around Fletcham's Corner and Maxwell joined the rest of society by breaking the law and riding on the pavement, just long enough to get past the roadworks.

A lollipop person was risking instant death by stepping into his path at the head of a string of tots from St Ivel's or whatever that snobby little prep school was called. Jacquie had been talking about sending Nolan there, but purple wasn't really the lad's colour.

Missing girls and a fly-blown corpse. Even before he reached the Flyover and the road to Columbine, Peter Maxwell was looking death in the face again.

Chapter Sixteen

It was déjà vu all over again. There was a little old lady camped out on his doorstep. But this time, it was Mrs Troubridge. She clambered to her feet when she eventually focused on him, using the hedge for leverage as he wheeled Surrey to a halt.

'Mr Maxwell,' she said, accusingly. 'I was beginning to think you were trying to avoid me.'

Maxwell managed to look shocked. 'Mrs Troubridge, I am hurt and amazed.' He was certainly amazed; as far as he could see they had been very successful in avoiding her.

'Perhaps it's just me,' she said doubtfully. 'Here's your post, by the way.' She handed over a mangled sheaf of envelopes. 'Mostly junk mail. But I'm sorry, Mr Maxwell, I digress. I've been very stressed since yesterday, as you can imagine. Not to say significantly out of pocket. Children eat so much, don't they?'

Mrs Troubridge's non sequiturs usually came straight out of left field, but this was odder than usual. Had Nolan been popping round for midnight snacks? Had she found footprints in the butter? He decided to ignore his instincts and actually chase this particular intellectual hare. 'What children, Mrs Troubridge? Nephews? Nieces?'

'No, Mr Maxwell.' Her little brow was furrowed at his stupidity. 'The girls who are staying with me. Well, I couldn't leave them outside, could I? I know it is officially spring, but really, the weather can be so treacherous. And you were so busy yesterday, what with that ... business with your cleaning lady. Problem with wages, was it? Something of that nature?'

'No, Mrs Troubridge, no. But ... these girls. Who are they?'

'They talk so quickly, Mr Maxwell. And mumble as well. It's so hard to understand what they say, an–'

'Mrs Troubridge!' Maxwell bellowed in her ear. It was so loud her hair seemed to blow back like a dog with its head out of a car window. 'What girls?'

'They call each other Zee and Lee. I don't know if they are their names; girls can be so odd, can't they, Mr Maxwell?' It sounded like a plea.

'Girls are always odd, Mrs Troubridge, in my experience. Are they still with you?'

'Oh, yes. They didn't get up until gone twelve. They seem to be quite upset about something, Mr Maxwell, and they wouldn't tell me where they lived or anything. But I knew that if they wanted to see you, it must be something important.' She looked down at her feet and Maxwell felt a seminal moment approaching. 'You are someone you feel you can trust, Mr Maxwell. You and Mrs Maxwell are the first people I would come to if I was a girl and I was in trouble.' She looked up at him and for once she didn't look truculent or argumentative. 'I'm glad you live next door.'

Maxwell could believe there was a time when Mrs Troubridge had been in trouble – but a girl?

Never. There was only one thing to do, and Maxwell did it willingly. He bent down and put his arms round her and gave her a hug, as hard as he dared, because she always looked as if she might break. 'Mrs Troubridge,' he said, after a moment.

'Yes, Mr Maxwell?' Her voice sounded muffled, from her face being pressed into his shoulder.

'Can you help me up? My back seems to have gone.'

'What do you want me to do?' she asked, beginning to sag under his weight.

'I'm not sure. Jacquie usually just puts her knee in my back and pulls on my shoulders. But you're in the wrong position for that, I suppose.' Was it his imagination, or were they sinking lower?

'I really can't hold you up any longer, Mr Maxwell.' Even in extremis, Mrs Troubridge was always formal. Her knees buckled and slowly, like a mighty redwood giving up the ghost in a forest after hundreds of years of life, the combined edifice of Maxwell/Troubridge fell onto the path, his arms still locked around her shoulders. They lay there for a few moments, each individually checking off limbs and finding them still, nominally at least, in working order.

'Well, that was one way of doing it, Mrs Troubridge,' Maxwell said at last. 'What happens now? You are lying on my arm and I am lying on my jacket, so I can't get up. You?'

She gave a few experimental tugs. 'It's no good, Mr Maxwell,' she said. 'You seem to have my skirt quite entangled in your bicycle clips, let alone the fact that you have somehow got your watch strap caught in my cardigan.'

It wasn't the time for small talk, but it seemed churlish to just lie there in silence. Maxwell was racking his brain for a comment that would not sound too flippant but which would not draw immediate attention to their plight when he heard the blissful sound of Mrs Troubridge's front door opening.

'Hello?' He called. 'Julie? Leah? Is that you? I seem to have fallen on Mrs Troubridge. Can you give us a hand?'

The door closed again. For pity's sake, he knew they were having a hard time, but really! They surely couldn't intend just to leave them there, locked together like some kind of mating ritual from one of David Attenborough's more racy programmes? The door opened again and this time was followed by the sound of footsteps on the path. Then kind hands were disentangling them, hands under the armpits hoisted him expertly to his feet and then he could see his rescuers. Julie and Leah indeed, fit and well. In a trice they had Mrs Troubridge on her feet and were dusting her down and kissing her old cheeks and making her chirrup with pleasure.

'Mrs T,' Julie said. 'We'll be back shortly. Just got to talk to Mr Maxwell for now.'

'You are an angel,' Leah said, giving her a gentle squeeze. 'We won't forget this. Honestly.'

'Oh, girls,' she twittered. 'It was nothing, really. Nothing your own grannies wouldn't have done.'

There was a moment's pause while they both pictured their grannies. They shook their heads in unison. 'Nope,' Julie said. 'Our grannies wouldn't

278

have done this. Just you, Mrs T. You're a doll.'

She tottered away down Maxwell's path and up her own, looking a little dishevelled but otherwise none the worse for wear. The girls turned to Maxwell, who was holding himself up as best he could by leaning on the door-frame. It was against all the rules, but he would have to lean on one of these girls while the other opened the door. Perhaps if he just eased himself over to one side it would be enough.

'Can you see the keyhole?' he asked through clenched teeth.

Leah peered round behind his shoulder. 'Just about,' she said. 'Where are your keys?'

'In my pocket,' he said. 'The one half way down my leg.' This was a relief. At least anyone seeing her forage would not get the wrong idea.

'Got it,' she said. 'Right, brace yourself, Mr Maxwell. We're going in.' The key refused to turn. 'Is this the right key?' she asked.

'There's a knack,' he grunted. 'Lean over to the left. Pretend you're left-handed, that's the secret.'

'You'll have to lean over a bit more, Mr Maxwell,' the girl said. 'OK, there, that's got it.' The door swung open. 'In we go.'

'Can you get up the stairs, Mr Maxwell?' Julie asked.

'I have a method,' Maxwell said, trying to move his mouth only slightly, so as to not jar his back. 'It's not pleasant viewing, though. Best plan is if you go upstairs and put the kettle on. I'll join you as best I can.'

The girls went reluctantly up the stairs, glancing back anxiously at Maxwell as he slid down the wall until he reached a stair about four up the flight. Leaning on the wall and bracing his back, he edged up the stairs as though negotiating a snow chimney halfway up an Alp. He'd get there, by hook or by crook. Perhaps a crook would help, under one arm. Perhaps a Stannah stairlift. The girls went into the kitchen and started making tea.

The mug was steaming on the coffee table when Maxwell arrived, hot and sweaty from K2. 'Thanks, girls. I need that now.' He leant forward as much as he dared and picked up the mug in both hands. 'Ah, the cup that cheers, but doth not inebriate.'

'That's tar water, Mr Maxwell,' Julie said. 'Background to the Industrial Revolution, Year Nine.'

'You lovely girl,' Maxwell said approvingly. 'But I shouldn't be pleased with you, all things being equal. Where the hell have you been? They've practically had the dogs out.' Only now had he remembered to haul off his hat. The cycle clips would have to wait.

'We haven't been gone long,' Julie protested. 'I thought people had to be missing for over twenty-four hours before the police took any action.'

'An adult, yes. Even a teenager if they are the disappearing kind. But you two – one of you misses the dentist, the other leaves her young sister in the lurch. It just wasn't you, if you can see what I mean.'

'That's ridiculous,' Leah exploded. 'I made sure my mum would be there for Anneliese. She promised.' Silence from the other two said more than words. 'Oh, don't tell me. I know I shouldn't trust her, but you have to sometimes, you know?'

'I didn't even remember the dentist,' Julie said. 'So I certainly didn't do that on purpose.'

'So,' Maxwell said, leaning back gingerly, 'neither of you meant to disappear in a sheet of fluorescent sparks. You just meant to slide into the background for a while.'

'That's right!' Leah said. 'We left our phones on the bus, but we pushed them to the side of the back seat, so probably they haven't been found yet.'

'You didn't by any chance leave your diary, did you, Julie?' Maxwell asked casually.

The girl went white. 'I've lost my diary,' she said, her voice deep with tension.

'I found it,' he said. 'It was down the seat on a bus I was on this morning. No phones, though.'

'You didn't ... read it, though, did you?' she asked anxiously.

'I didn't have the time, but in fact as soon as I knew it was a diary, I wouldn't have read it anyway. But I'm afraid I have bad news. I gave it to my wife, who as I understand it is handing it in to forensics.'

'Oh. My. God.' Leah turned to Julie in a mock dramatic way. 'They'll read your diary.'

Julie jumped to her feet and fetched her friend a stinging slap across her face. 'Don't you laugh at me!' she screamed. 'They can't read my diary. They mustn't read my diary.'

Maxwell struggled upright and sat, listing badly to the right, on the edge of his chair. 'Julie, calm

281

down. Both of you, please.' They were both crying, storms of hysterical tears. He knew that this was not just for the lost diary, or for the slap, but for the weeks and months of stress which they had been going through. 'I'll ring Mrs Maxwell and try to stop the diary being read. I don't expect for a minute they will be dealing with it yet; they found a dead body up at the paint-balling centre this afternoon and that will be taking precedence.' He winced and eased himself into a more comfortable position.

'Is that why you're dressed like that?' Leah asked, with a sniff, watching his image become clearer through her tears. 'I did wonder.'

'Aren't you a bit, like, old for paintballing?' Julie added.

Maxwell looked thoughtful. This was the second time in just over an hour that he had been reminded how old he was. The difference was that Helen knew how old he was; these girls probably thought he was about seventy. 'I didn't think so, before I went,' he said finally.

'A body, though,' Julie said. 'Not a teacher?' There was a bit of dread, a bit of hope in her voice.

'Not that Mrs Donaldson, in the office?' There was just hope in Leah's voice.

'No,' Maxwell said. 'No to both of those options. The man is a stranger, we think. Certainly nobody recognised him. Well, except one of the dinner ladies.'

'Not Doreen?' Julie asked. 'Only, if it's Doreen, she's as mad as a cake. She can't remember an order, from you saying it, to her picking up her spoon.'

'I'd heard that,' Maxwell said. 'But she seemed quite sure, even though she couldn't remember any details.'

'I wonder who he is?' Leah said. 'It's quite sad, isn't it, that he was just lying there and nobody knew? Or cared.'

'Yeah,' echoed Julie. 'I wonder who he is.'

'We'll soon know who he is,' Jim Astley said breezily to Henry Hall. The police surgeon for Leighford was not known for his bonhomie. His wife drank and was no longer welcome on the social circuit. Had anyone asked him, as a keen young houseman, what his ambitions were, he would probably have said an expensive private clinical practice and a K by the time he was forty. That was nearly twenty years ago and none of it had happened. Instead, here he was, reduced to slicing up dead people to try to put them, somehow, back together again. He was standing in the ante-room to the post-mortem suite and was gloving up prior to getting up close and personal with John Doe. 'Donald is in there now doing the fingerprints. We'll run those through the system and we'll be sure to come up with the answer.'

'You seem very sure that he'll be in the system,' Hall said. It was his experience that most dead bodies were just dead bodies. They weren't wanted criminals, famous people or even someone who once did a bit of shoplifting. They were just a person who happened to be dead.

'He is,' Astley said smugly. The doors crashed back and Donald squeezed through. His years of MacDonalds and KFC had made him twice the man he once was and the scrubs had an upsetting gap at the back where they didn't quite meet. Several feet of pale and meaty Donald were on view. Hall tried not to look. 'Tell Mr Hall why we know our man is in the system, Donald.'

'You tell him,' Donald said sullenly. 'It was only me that noticed, after all.'

'Oh, he's got one on him this afternoon and no mistake,' Astley said, quite fondly, as if Donald was a slightly recalcitrant pet. 'Well, *Donald* noticed when he stripped our chap off that he had very few bumps and bruises, which to be honest had me surprised. It's not easy to break someone's neck and not at least bruise an arm or anything. But I digress. One mark that was very clear was on the right leg. Ankle, to be precise. The old talocrural joint. There was a kind of scuffing, as though he had worn something heavy and slightly loose around it. There was also some damage to the bottom of the fibula, as if, well, as if...'

'For God's sake,' said Donald, who hadn't eaten for half an hour and whose blood sugar was correspondingly low. 'He's been wearing a tag and someone levered it off. That's how we know he's in the system.'

'Well, if you wanted to tell it, Donald, why didn't you just go ahead in the first place,' said Astley testily. Even pets begin to irritate after a while.

'A tag?' Hall said. 'You mean, this guy is on a curfew, something like that? ASBO?'

'That or working from an open facility,' Donald said. 'Tags are really common, these days. I'm just running the prints now. We'll be able to tell you who he is in about ten minutes. IDENT1 is foolproof.'

'Well,' Jim Astley said. 'This won't get the cause of death identified.' He pinged the cuffs of his gloves and shouldered his way out of the room. 'There are *some* things a machine will never be able to do.'

'Broken neck,' muttered Donald.

'I'd say so,' Hall agreed.

'He likes to be thorough,' muttered the Fat Assistant. 'We'll be up to our knees in internal organs unless I get in there. Can you hang on until the result comes through, Mr Hall? It will print out there.' He pointed to a fax machine on the bench.

'How many minutes did you say?' Hall asked.

'About two, now, by normal standards,' Donald said. 'In fact, I can't think what's keeping it.' He barged the doors open and was gone.

Hall stood there, wondering what to do to while away the time. Two minutes wasn't long if you were in your own office, sitting at your own computer, in front of your own TV. But sitting in someone else's ante-room, with the strange smell of preservatives, disinfectant and fried chicken in the air, he found it hard to relax. He stared out through the windows of the double doors and watched as Astley and Donald, working, against expectations, like a well-oiled team, started their first preparations for the post-mortem. Astley pulled the microphone down towards him and Hall knew what he was saying, although the sound barely reached him at all. He was giving

285

the date, the time, his name and credentials and Donald's name and credentials. He was so lost in thought that the ring of the fax phone made him jump.

He turned, to see the paper start to emerge from the bottom of the machine. It was quick; not like the fax at the nick, which still used heat-sensitive paper and took an age to print out the simplest thing. The image emerging was a set of ten prints across the top, too small to be useful but there as a reminder of what the fax was about. Below, a stark line. 'Prints not on database.' Hall looked at it, amazed. Donald and Astley might look like a couple from a children's Sunday morning cartoon, but he had never known them, particularly Donald, miss their guess. He tapped on the glass and Astley gestured to Donald to go over and see what the nuisance DCI wanted.

Hall was waving the piece of paper in the air as Donald barged through the doors.

'Ah,' said the assistant smugly. 'Who is he, then?'

Hall held up the paper in front of his face, like a yashmak. This made him even more difficult to read than usual, with only his blank lenses in view. Donald leant forward and his lips moved soundlessly. Then, he reacted.

'Not found? *Not found!* What do they mean, not found?' He stuck his head round the door and called to Astley. 'This bloody system needs a bloody good kick. They say he's not found.'

'Not found?' Astley repeated.

'Gentlemen,' Hall said. 'Please stop saying "not found" over and over. I could have done with a result as much as you could, but the man who knows says he's not on the database, so we'll have to go back to first principles. At least his face isn't marked; we can do a photo.'

'But...' Donald refused to accept what was being waved in front of his nose. 'He was wearing a tag. He *must* be on the bloody database. It's their sodding system. It's crashed or something.'

'I think we'd know, don't you?' Hall said mildly. 'Wouldn't they say that the system was currently unavailable, something like that?'

'This isn't a bloody car insurance comparison website,' Donald howled in frustration. 'It's a national – no, *international* – police database. It can't crash, freeze or otherwise not work. It *can't* be wrong, but it is. He was definitely wearing a tag.'

Astley tried to calm his mountainous assistant. 'Donald, perhaps we made a mistake. Perhaps the marks are from something else.'

'What?' spat the man. 'What something else?'

'Well, a friendship bracelet?' hazarded the pathologist. 'Something like that.'

'If you give friendship bracelets that leave that kind of mark,' Donald sulked, 'I'm glad I'm not friends with you.'

Astley was a little crestfallen; he had always thought they got on quite well, all things being equal. 'Can you give us a while, Henry? I think we need to do a bit more work on this. We're obviously going to have to identify this chap the hard way.'

'But that's stupid,' Donald burst out. 'He *has* to be on the system.'

'I'm heading off back to the station, now,' Hall said. 'If you get anywhere, can you let me know?'

'Of course,' Astley said over his shoulder, shepherding Donald back into the PM room. He grimaced at Hall and nodded towards Donald.

Hall turned and made his way back to some fresh air. He realised he still had the fax in his hand and he thoughtfully folded it and put it in his pocket. He was the last person to think that Astley and Donald were always right, but they were right ninety per cent of the time and for him that was enough. He would have to make a few calls back in his office; there must be someone who could unravel this – it would just be a matter of finding out who they were.

At Columbine things had taken a strange turn. The girls, having established that Maxwell would contact Jacquie as soon as he could and that he was all right, no, really, *really* all right, had gone back to spend the rest of the afternoon with Mrs Troubridge. She was, apparently, really cool and had some brilliant stories to tell about when she was a girl. Only, she called it 'gel' and they'd had a few minutes the previous day when nobody knew what anybody was talking about. Maxwell encouraged them to take supplies – there was no need to antagonise the old girl further than strictly necessary.

The front door slammed down below and Maxwell eased himself back gingerly in his chair. Just a few minutes, perhaps, not sleeping, just resting his eyes. His back pain had reduced to just a dull roar, and by sitting back in the chair twisted round to one side, he could just about get on with it for now. He exhaled slowly and tried to relax. The warm sun coming in through the large window was soothing and spoke of nicer days to come. He let his mind wander, to walks he had taken with Jacquie and Nolan and without them, a different child prattling at his heels, a different pair of eyes looking up into his.

Metternich padded softly in and lay out-stretched in the printed yellow panes on the carpet, dusty with sunlight and warmth. Maxwell had only ever had one cat and that cat was Metternich. He had come to him through a weeping sixth former, years ago. The girl had a sad story to tell; her cat had had kittens, but they would all have to die that night in a bucket of water if she couldn't find homes. Maxwell, living alone in bachelor austerity didn't need or want a cat, but somehow he found himself that evening the proud vassal of a scrap of black and white fur. It was only when the cat had Maxwell's heart firmly under its white and pink hand – Maxwell could never call it a paw, especially when the Count was listening – that he discovered that the kitten scam was played out every year and almost every member of staff with a kind heart had a sibling of Metternich's ruling their house.

In a rare moment of affection, Metternich bared his canines at Maxwell in what the man chose to believe was a smile. What the cat believed was nobody's business. The room slowly relaxed into a somnolent doze.

Suddenly, Metternich was up and out of there. That blasted plastic thing which his people held to their ears for hours on end was shrilling. Maxwell jumped too, and was still softly cursing with pain when he pressed the green button and the caller was in his ear.

'Mr Maxwell?'

'Yes.' It came out as a sibilant groan.

'Mr Maxwell. It's Doreen. You know, up at the school.'

'Yes, Doreen. Hello.'

'Are you all right, Mr Maxwell? You sound a bit funny.'

'Nothing a course of intensive physiotherapy won't put right, Doreen, thanks for asking. How may I help you?'

'I've remembered where I saw that bloke, the dead one.'

'Really?' As a rule, Maxwell would have sat up to attention, but it was clearly out of the question.

'It was with Edna. At the staff Christmas dinner. At the Horse and Groom, you know, out Tottingleigh.'

'Edna? What staff Christmas dinner at the Horse and Groom? I only remember one mince pie and some British Sherry in the staff room.'

'Oh, that would be the teachers' do. No, the ancill'ry staff have a good do, families and everything. We don't always do the Horse and–'

'Yes, Doreen. Lovely. Edna?'

'Edna! You know, Mr Maxwell, *Edna!* Your cleaner at school.'

'Oh. Mrs B.'

'Umm, yes, that's right. We call her Edna, of course.'

'On account of that being her name. Yes, fair enough. Who is he, then, Doreen?' A sick feeling was beginning to form under Maxwell's ribs.

'That's the trouble, Mr Maxwell. I can't really remember. In fact, thinking about it, he might not have been *with* Edna. Perhaps he was just sitting next to her.'

'Was his name Colin?'

'That's right, Mr Maxwell. However did you know that? I remember, because it was like that black bloke, that general in a war sometime. I can't remember which one... Coe-lin. Like that. Not Colin, like we'd say. Edna's sister always was a bit posh, not that I've met her that many times. I remember–'

That was rather unlikely, given Doreen's usual form, but Maxwell was never impolite except on purpose. 'Doreen, you've been amazing. I'll let Mrs Maxwell know straight away. But, can I ask you something?'

'Yes, Mr Maxwell?' Doreen sounded nervous. She'd just about emptied her head for the moment.

'How did you get my number?'

'Oh, Mrs Donaldson has everyone's number on her database.'

'I daresay she has, but how did you get it?'

'It's pinned up on the wall in the office. Haven't you ever noticed it? On that big board along one wall.'

Maxwell closed his eyes and tried to picture the scene. The trouble he had was that whenever he tried to imagine the office, Pansy loomed so large, both really and metaphorically, that he couldn't see beyond her. 'I'm sorry, Doreen, I haven't.'

'Margaret in photocopying was fiddling for ages. She had to have a sandwich in her room, she was so pushed for time.'

Maxwell knew that Margaret's output was somewhat ad hoc, giving twenty copies where two hundred were required, and once accidentally setting the machine to produce five thousand copies of the school play poster, but surely one copy of the staff phone numbers couldn't have been that big a job. He hardly dared ask. His brain was beginning to lay down tracks and he didn't want to catch the train that was running down them. 'Why was the job so big, Doreen?'

'She had to copy all the staff details, numbers, addresses, emails, and then the same for all the kids. It was a really long job. She had to make sure they all fitted on the page and everything. Mrs Donaldson wanted them big enough so she could see them without getting up. It takes up a whole wall. I can't believe you've never noticed it.'

Maxwell's mouth was dry. With difficulty he said, 'You've been a brilliant help, Doreen. See you Monday. Ciao.' Somehow that seemed the most appropriate sign off to a dinner lady.

'Oh, yes, right. OK, Mr Maxwell. See you Monday.' He could be a terse old bugger when he wanted to, she thought. Still, that was one job jobbed, and she trotted out of school with a clear conscience.

Behind her, in the back room of the main office, where she had been using the phone, a pair of eyes watched her from the darkness. Things were getting a bit out of control. Threads would have to be pulled. Favours called in. And, if necessary, murders committed.

Another day. Another dollar.

Chapter Seventeen

Donald had told Angus that he had about an hour, in his opinion, to work on the diary before the cohorts arrived bearing scrapings, Sellotape samples and various insects to pore over. It hardly seemed worth starting, with just an hour to spare, what with the preparation of the cabinet, the labelling of the tubes and all the thousand natural shocks forensic scientists are heir to, but he had the choice of that or an hour of paperwork from a previous case. No real contest.

Angus gave the case a number, one which he had taken out of circulation some time before to give him wiggle room for occasions just such as this. He printed out a whole load of bar code labels and moved over to the cabinet, slightly pressurised to keep what was in there in there, and keep his own dandruff out. He opened the diary at the first page. The outside was so compromised now that it wasn't even worth addressing. He swung the lens across so that he could pick up any visible objects before he swabbed the page. He liked this kind of work; in his own life, outside in the world, there could be no bigger slob than Angus. He liked his friends, he liked his drink, he liked his baccy to be wacky, but here, in the cool, calm quiet of the lab, he could let his mind wander into the realms of the other Angus, sent to save the world. That bit of him was soaring over the rooftops when something caught his eye and brought him down to earth with a bump.

It was hard to scan a page of writing without sometimes focusing on the writing. It was rather untidy, often leaving the lines, and the ink was smudgy, as if it had got wet. He had been told it was a diary, but there were no dates, just breaks to show different days. Sometimes the ink was a different colour. Then, one line got his attention and he had to keep reading. After that the swabbing and other analyses seemed unimportant.

'He came into my bedroom again last night. He says he will kill my mum if I tell. I've heard all about this, it's on the telly in an advert and they're trying to say it never happens. But it must do sometimes. He's a doctor. He could kill her and no one would know. And then he'd have me all to himself, all the time.'

The blood was pounding in his ears. Surely, Jacquie must already know the contents of this diary. But no, he rationalised. Jacquie was a good policewoman. She knew procedure. He was the first person ever to read the contents of this diary. And like Jacquie, he knew the right thing to do. He calmly closed the sliding door of the cabinet. He peeled off his gloves and went into the office. He dialled Jacquie's number from his capacious memory.

'Carpenter. I'm driving, can I call you back?'

'Jacquie, it's Angus.' To hell with formality at a time like this. 'This diary.'

'Hold on.' Faint sounds of an indicator clicking and a handbrake being applied came to him down the line. For God's sake, woman. Health and Safety be blowed. 'Right.' She was back on the line. 'Angus. The diary.'

'I've read a bit.'

Jacquie's heart slowed and her breathing went quiet. Every bit of her was concentrating on what he would say next. She felt a breakthrough coming on. 'Come on, Angus. What did it say?'

He told her and listened to the silence. 'Are you still there?'

'Angus, you are my favourite person in the whole world. I'm about halfway at the moment, between you and the nick.'

Please turn round, Angus begged her in his head. Come back and congratulate me properly. Angus's daydreams could be very vivid.

'I think I'll go on, though. I don't think the DNA and the rest is important now. Can you copy a few pages and fax them to me. Better still, email them. You've got my email? It's–'

'Got it.'

'Yes, of course you have. Right. Could you do that for me, Angus?'

His skin prickled. 'You know for sure who this guy is, don't you?'

'Oh, yes.'

'And he's got something to do with all this texting, emails and that.'

'What do you know about that?' Was nothing confidential in this place?

'IT guys. Lunchtime. You know how it is.' Cyberspace. The last frontier. Angus and the others often boldly went there.

'Fair enough, I suppose. We're all on the same side, after all.'

He could tell she was not listening to herself. But he enjoyed the matey 'we' for what it was worth. 'Well, Jacquie,' he risked another lapse of formality while the going was good. 'I'll get on with that scan and email, shall I?'

'You're wonderful,' Jacquie said. 'I'll make sure you get credit.'

It was only after he had put down the phone that Angus realised that meant all sorts of pain coming down the line. Requisitionless jobs. Bar code numbers being used against regulations. Reports not done. He sighed. It was almost worth it.

Jacquie sat for a moment, digesting Angus's news. Could the answer really be so simple? She shook herself. Why not? This wasn't an episode of some ridiculous TV cop show, with twelve murders one by one in the same town. In fact, there was only one dead body knocking around at the moment and that was surely just a coincidence. Her coincidence muscle gave a twitch – she and Henry both refused to acknowledge coincidence, whilst accepting that it usually reared its head at some point in most investigations. She was about to turn the ignition when her phone rang again. She looked at the screen and a smiling Metternich looked back at her. Home. So Maxwell had got back OK. That was one more box in her 'things to worry about' list that she could tick.

'Hehlooooo.'

'I assume from your merry response you are not in the nick, dear heart?'

'No, I'm not. What's the matter? You sound strange.'

'I'm having you burnt at the stake first opportunity, woman,' he said. 'My back is playing me up. How can you possibly tell over the phone?'

'My secret. Anyway, sorry to hurry you, but is this a check-in call or do you have actual news, because I must get back to the nick?'

'I have news as well, but it isn't very good, I'm sorry to say.'

'Go on. Do I have to write it down?'

'Well, it comes in several parts, but I think you'll remember it all without recourse to papyrus.'

'Is it good news and bad news?'

'In a way. I've found the girls. And I know who the dead man is. I suppose they both come under the good news banner, but only just. Julie is hysterical that we have found her diary and the dead man is Mrs B's lost nephew.'

'What?' Jacquie jumped and lost her grip on the phone. She could hear Maxwell talking as she fumbled in the footwell to find it.

'...so that was where they'd been all night.'

'What? I'd dropped the phone.'

'The girls. They'd been at Mrs Troubridge's. That's why she kept coming round.'

'Poor old soul. She must have thought we were trying to avoid her.'

'Weren't we?'

'Fair comment. Why were they with her?'

'They came round to see you. I would love to think it was me, but I hope I'm a humble man and the finer points of Castlereagh's foreign policy probably have relatively little interest for them.'

And, thought Jacquie, despite the regard and love he was held in, he really *was* a humble man. 'Why me?'

'You're a police person. They were ready to tell all about their problems, I'm assuming.'

'Well, I doubt that, sweetheart. Because I've just had... I don't have to tell you this is a deadly secret thing I'm telling you.' It was a statement, not a question and one she'd made a thousand times before.

'Of course you don't. Everything you say is considered a secret. Always has been.'

She thought back to all the times over the years when he had dropped her in it up to her earlobes but decided to let it pass. 'Well, I took the diary for analysis, DNA and the rest, you know, to Angus in Chichester. In case it would help us find out who might have taken them. If they had been taken. He started to swab it and all the other things they do, but he couldn't help reading as he did so.' She stopped.

'Don't keep me in suspenders, Woman Policeman. What did it say?'

'No need to quote, Max. The drift is... Julie is being abused by her stepfather. Usual threats. Kill her mum if she tells, that sort of thing.'

'Oh, no.' Maxwell's groan came from the pit of his soul. 'Poor little girl. I said, didn't I? A poor little girl.'

'Yes.' Jacquie's voice was soft. 'Are they with you now? I'm assuming they're not.'

'No. They're next door. They and Mrs Trou-

299

bridge have bonded in some bizarre and unexpected way. They're probably coercing the old neighbour to change her will in their favour.'

'Well, keep it that way if you can. We need to keep tabs on them now.'

'Do you think the stepfather is also sending the emails and texts?'

'That's what I don't know. He's a busy man... I know everyone thinks they are, but he really is – hospital, all that. I don't see how he could do it. But it's a tempting scenario.'

Maxwell thought for a moment. 'I don't think he is, you know. He's controlling her by threats and coercion in the home. There's no need to embroider it.'

'He may just get a kick out of it. I must say he is the most horrible, controlling...' Jacquie ran out of words she cared to use on an open network.

'I know, hon. But I think an open mind would be best on this one. But, in other news ... the body.'

'How did you find out about that? I hope you're not basing this on a family resemblance or anything so vague.'

'No, Doreen, one of the dinner ladies, rang me and told me she'd seen him with Mrs B.'

'So, not definite, then.' Doreen's lack of mental acuity had had the Maxwell dinner table in hysterics many a time.

He gave a small chuckle. 'I know. Poor old Doreen. But, no, I think she may have it right this time. I mean, think about it. Colin goes missing. A man resembling him turns up dead in the area.

300

He had been holed up with Mrs B before he got caught for this particular crime.'

'Which was?'

'Some computer thing, I gather.'

'Max! For heaven's sake. Computers! I ... I... Did you not put two and two together?'

'Why ever should I?' He was rather nettled. 'The damn things are everywhere. I might just as well suspect the guy who comes to mend the dishwasher. That's all done by microchips now.'

'Oh, I'm sorry.' She wiped her hand over her face. 'It's been a long day. Too much information. I'll get back to the nick and find Henry. He's in charge of the murder investigation. He'll probably be in touch. Can you stay at home for a bit?'

'I'd be hard-pressed to do anything else, dearest. I can only move my legs if I watch them. My back has seized up completely. I fell on Mrs Troubridge earlier. It could have been quite unpleasant. No, it *was* quite unpleasant.'

'Max, you're whittering. Fell on Mrs Troubridge, indeed. I'll ring you later.' And she was gone.

Maxwell put the phone down on the arm of his chair. He half turned, as best he could, to Metternich, who had slunk back and was sitting in the doorway, making significant glances towards his food dish in the kitchen. 'I did fall on her, didn't I, Count? Were you watching? Clearly not, as you're not laughing. And you can forget any food. Unless you can open that pouch yourself, my lad, you're getting nothing.' He relaxed back into the chair and grimaced. 'Count?'

The cat chirruped helpfully.

301

'Am I getting old, do you think?'

It was something the cat had been chewing over himself lately, that and the shrews of Juniper Lane. He was either getting on a bit, or the game was sprightlier these days. Best not discuss it and perhaps it would go away. He wandered over and sank his claws into Maxwell's leg. Unless he had misunderstood the drift of a *Discovery Health* programme he had caught a few minutes of the other night, pain in a different place could be helpful in certain circumstances. It was hard to tell from the yelling and writhing it caused; people! He'd never understand them if he lived to be one hundred and forty in what humans for some odd reason referred to as cat years. What other kind of years were there?

Jacquie got the car into gear and back into the traffic before any more calls could come in. She was only about twenty minutes away from Leighford nick now, given a following wind, and she had a lot to share with Henry. She wasn't sure how much weight to give to the news about the identity of the body. Doreen was notoriously flaky, but it seemed too much to believe that she would choose to identify the dead man as someone known to be missing, by a mere fluke. She would deal with that one quickly, though. She was so looking forward to dragging that pompous pig Melkins in on child sex abuse charges that she really wasn't too bothered about anything else. If it cleared up the text abuse as well, so much the better.

Before she realised it, she was at the nick. The

Doblò wasn't exactly a Ferrari, but it covered the miles OK and there was more room for the accumulated Maxwell rubbish in the back. She retrieved her laptop from beneath a pile of crisp packets and toys on the back seat, flipped it open and logged on. As usual, the dratted thing was taking an age to boot itself into life, so she closed it and let it do its thing while she went up to the first floor and Henry Hall's office.

She tapped on the door. 'Yes?' Obviously his day wasn't going too well. She stuck her head in and saw that he had loosened his tie. This was usually a sign that a case was solved. So why the long face?

'I've got a bit of news that you might be interested in, guv,' she said.

'Oh, make it good news,' he said. 'I'm a bit fed up with the other kind.'

She sat down, with her computer on her lap. 'I've just had Max on the phone...' she began.

'Jacquie, I really mean it when I say I only want good news.'

'I'm not saying this is cast in stone,' she told him, 'but Max thinks he may have a lead on who the dead man is.'

'Really? And is that because he has an unusual birthmark in the shape of a ferret which turns out to be a gravy stain? Something like that?'

'Have you had a hard day, Henry?' Jacquie asked kindly.

He did something totally unexpected and took off his glasses to rub his eyes. 'No worse than usual. I'm sorry to be rude, but Astley and his performing gorilla have rather annoyed me today.

First, they say they will identify the guy in no time because he was wearing a tag at some time. Then it's – oh, sorry, we can't identify him, his prints aren't on file. They just don't provide the service these days. DNA won't be ready for days and when it is, it's only any help if it's on file and if his prints aren't on file...well, you can see where this is going.' He put his glasses back on and tightened his tie knot. 'Anyway, you were saying. Max thinks he knows who the man is?'

'It's not that he knows, but that someone who thinks they recognise him has been in touch. And I have to say, Henry, that your talk of a tag has made my short hairs rise a bit. This man we're talking about has absconded from an open prison.'

Hall leant forward. 'What? When?'

'Last weekend, as far as I can tell. He's the nephew of our cleaning lady and she asked me ... well, she asked Max–'

'So, she hasn't identified the body, as such?'

'No. But someone who knows her, one of the dinner ladies at school, was at the paintballing and saw the man's face.'

'The dinner lady was at the paintballing?' Henry was intrigued in spite of himself.

'It was some team-building thing. Legs – you know, the Headteacher – wanted all the staff to go.'

'So, how does the dinner lady know your cleaner?'

'Mrs B works up at the school as well.'

'So why wasn't she paintballing?'

'Good question. Too much common sense, I

expect. Anyway, Doreen – the dinner lady – went away and thought about it and then rang Max and said that she thought it was Mrs B's partner for the Christmas dinner.'

'A while ago.'

'Four months, guv, that's all. I know Doreen's not the brightest noodle in the wok, but she can remember that far back.'

'I'll look into it.' Henry pushed himself back from his desk then paused. 'Your computer is blinking.'

'Oh, yes, sorry. I have some more news. The girls have been found safe and well.'

'Where? Don't tell me. Max knows where.'

She sat silently.

'Well?'

'You said don't tell you.'

'You mean they really are at your house?' Hall had not really expected that to be the answer.

'No. They're next door. With Mrs Troubridge.'

Hall screwed up his eyes and pictured the woman. Small, wizened, mad as a box of frogs. Not the typical child abductor, though. His head was too full for this. 'I'm not going to ask for details, Jacquie. This was always more your job than mine. Anything else?'

'Yes,' she said triumphantly. 'This!' she opened the laptop and signed into her emails quickly. She turned it round so that Hall could see the screen.

Hall adjusted his glasses. The varifocal idea was still not second nature. He read out the email. 'A family will be almost overcome by death. The red red ones will knock down the red one.' He looked up at Jacquie. 'Should I recognise this?'

Jacquie jumped up and went round behind his desk. 'Sorry,' she muttered. 'Wrong email. That was one that Max got at home. I forwarded it to myself for later. Umm ... this is the one I meant to show you.' She stayed behind him to read over his shoulder.

Angus had attached the scans separately and when they were opened the two read silently as Hall scrolled down the page. When they had finished, she went back and sat down. He closed the laptop thoughtfully. 'I assume you know whose diary this is,' he said at last.

'Yes. It is the diary of Gregory Melkins' step-daughter, Julie. One of the missing girls.'

'We know that for certain? How did we get hold of it?'

'Well, we know that her diary is missing, that she slapped her best friend when she realised that someone else might read it.'

'And we got hold of it...?'

'Umm, Max found it down the back of a bus seat.'

He looked at her from behind his blank lenses. She started to whiffle.

'Well, he was going to the paintballing on the bus. Haha, Nolan and I thought it might be amusing. Well, he found this and gave it to me. At the paintballing.' She started to run out of steam. 'When I was there.'

'Yes, why *were* you there? And with some vampire girl, or something.'

'Maisie. Yes, she was helping me with the email and text thing. She is a very nice girl, in fact. She

306

goes to the same school as Yvonne's kids. Her boyfriend works at the paintballing place and ... well, we heard there was a dead body and...'

'Jacquie, I say this without any unpleasant motive. You have got to stop expecting Max to be every dead body we find.'

She hung her head. She didn't want to say it out loud. He's not as young as he was. He shouldn't be cycling, paintballing, fossicking about after bodies left and right. He shouldn't even be teaching. There were knives, guns, infectious diseases. *Stairs*, for God's sake. They had wasted enough of his life already, what with her not being born early enough. She wanted to have as much of the rest as she could. She just said, 'I know, guv.'

'Not to worry. I do understand.' And oddly enough, he did. He had seen that the maddest teacher in town had made his favourite sergeant happier than even the laughing policeman, and so, if only for that, he liked the man. 'The find has good provenance, at least. It wasn't some drunk foraging in a bin. But even so, it's not enough for an arrest. We'll have to get prints or something off it.'

'In hand, guv.' She realised that perhaps she should have wrapped that statement up a bit. She had clearly circumvented normal procedure.

'Angus?' Hall raised an eyebrow.

'He tries to be helpful,' Jacquie muttered.

'Wait for prints,' Hall said. 'Give Angus a call and say I will requisition in retrospect.'

Jacquie couldn't help Maxwell springing into her head. She heard him say, as a retrospective of his own, in full Michael Palm mode, 'Nobody expects the Spanish Requisition.' She tried to concentrate on her boss.

'When you have definite identification that the diary is hers – perhaps you could ring your neighbour and ask Julie to describe it, just to be sure. *When* you have definite identification, we can pull the stepfather in. Give him something to do over the weekend.' He almost gave her a rare smile. 'Well done, Jacquie. And well done to Max. Meanwhile, I'll contact Jim Astley with the other news and we'll see if we can give this body a name. Do you have your cleaning lady's number handy?'

'I do, but...' Jacquie looked at the clock. 'You'll probably just catch her at Leighford High School. She'll be finishing up in about half an hour, so you'll have to be quick.' She jotted the number down anyway and got up to leave. Hall handed her her laptop across the desk.

'That email Max had – a bit weird, isn't it?'

'It is odd. He hasn't had any texts today, at least. I've been carrying his phone.'

'Texts?' Hall was yet again in the dark.

'He's had just the one. We're not jumping to conclusions yet, especially now that we've found the girls. The email is from Nostradamus.'

'What, the pot noodle guy?'

'Not exactly. Sixteenth century seer, got most things wrong, but various web loonies can find anything in his prophecies – you name it.'

'Oh, I know the kind of thing. And the world to an end shall come, in tumpty tumpty tumpty one. One size fits all.'

'Exactly. It's Quatrain 19 from Century eight.'

'You seem to know an awful lot about it,' he said, without thinking.

'Well, Max has...'

'...got a book on it. Of course he has. Even so, it sounds... I can't quite put my finger on it. It reminds me of something.' He shook his head. 'Never mind. It will either come to me or it won't.' He reached for the phone. 'Good luck with Mr Melkins. Keep me in the loop. I'd rather like to be involved in this one.'

She went out and as she did, heard Hall say, 'Squad car to Leighford High School.' What she didn't hear him say, because she had closed the door was, 'Calm down, Dave. No, we're not going to arrest that mad bugger Maxwell.'

Chapter Eighteen

Wheels were turning, but with glacial slowness. Angus was on to it, Astley was on to it, Donald was on to it. Then, as if everything hadn't got bogged down enough, the entire intranet system of the Leighford nick gave a hiccough and a shrug and closed itself down. Anyone passing at that moment would have heard a whole building shout 'What?' at once, followed by the kind of profanity which the general public would prefer their policemen not to use. 'Evening all' it most certainly was not. And coppers the length and breadth of a south coast town were sticking pins into wax models of Bill Gates.

Henry Hall had gone out to interview Mrs B with the intention of getting an identification of the paintball body. He had caught her just as she was winding up the cord of her Hoover, going home at the end of another day moving the Leighford High filth from one spot to another. He had been gentle with her. He had sat her down. He had waited while she dried her tears. The description had made it pretty much a foregone conclusion, so that he felt able to give Astley and Donald a while to make her lost nephew a bit more presentable before she had to make the official pronouncement. Tomorrow would do. For today, she had calls to make, arrangements. Colin's mother had to be got to Leighford somehow, put up in the spare room. She felt better with something to do; the only concession she made was to accept a lift home in a squad car. As long as she could sit in the front – her neighbours were nosy bastards and she didn't want to give them any more ammunition. She still wasn't sure who had shopped their Colin to the fuzz in the first place.

With nothing to do until the IT boys had done their bit, Jacquie took the opportunity to go home, if not early then at least in daylight. She picked up Nolan and got back to Columbine in time for supper. The lad was exhausted and fed up with his stitches. He stomped up the stairs and ignored the cat, always a sign that the best medicine would be a quick spaghetti on toast and bed. Maxwell was lying in a strange position in his favourite chair, but his eyes were open and moving, so no cause for alarm.

'Hello, dears,' he called. 'Don't mind if I don't get up.' He *had* gone to a good school.

Nolan, taking no hints at this advanced stage of grump, and with the advantage of a good run-up, leapt onto his lap. Maxwell jack-knifed, flinging the boy to the floor. There was a small pause, before the screaming began. Jacquie scooped the boy up, with little sympathy. 'Did I tell you in the car that Dads had a bad back?'

'Yes.' The boy's face was set in injured pride mode.

'So, did I say be careful? Not to hurt him? No jumping or gouging? No feet tickling and running away?'

'Yes.' The boy wriggled in her arms. 'But I want

to play.'

'Yes, mate,' Maxwell said, trying to sit a bit more alertly. 'But I've hurt my back, you see. I fell on Mrs Troubridge.'

Nolan's eyes were like saucers. 'You fell on Mrs Toobidge?' He looked up at his mother. 'You didn't tell me Dads fell on Mrs Toobidge,' he said accusingly.

Jacquie looked alarmed. 'I didn't think that Dads had really fallen on her,' she said. 'I think I thought he meant ... well, I'm not sure now what I thought, to be honest.'

Maxwell twisted his neck round to look at her. 'When you've worked out what the other meaning might be,' he said acidly, 'you might care to let me know.'

She went over and knelt at the side of his chair. She smoothed his hair. 'I'm sorry, Max,' she said and dropped her head onto his shoulder. Then she looked up again. 'Was it ... was it very funny?' She tried not to laugh.

'By all accounts,' he said smartly. 'Now, clear off, woman. Feed your child. And your cat. Then I suggest you go round next door and see if the squashee is all right and that the girls are settled. I'm assuming they won't be going home?'

'Well, Leah is free to, of course, except that there are child protection issues, since her mother didn't turn up until nearly three this morning and then absolutely bladdered in the company of two naval ratings she had met in a club.'

'Oh, so the fleet's in,' Maxwell remarked. He sang a few truncated bars – 'I'm Popeye the sailor man. Poop. Poop.' Pooped he most certainly was.

'Indeed. And Julie's dad hasn't replied to any calls as yet. That will turn out to be quite complicated, I think. Henry has asked me to wait for confirmation of the diary before I bring our man in. But if Julie is safely here, then that's fine.'

'Have the parents been told that the girls are safe?'

'Yes. But no details. It was interesting that Leah's dad was just totally relieved. Julie's parents wanted her back immediately as if she was a lost handbag. Tough luck on them.'

'Off you pop, then, sweetheart. Sooner you're gone, sooner you're back.'

'I'll just get Nole's supper and then go round if you'll mind him.'

'No problem, as long as he will sit still. He's got ants in his pants tonight.'

'He'll behave. He just didn't understand.' She turned to the boy, who had plonked himself down in front of the television and was engrossed in a programme about seaweed. Two thousand channels and nothing to watch as always. 'Nole, come and get your supper. Then you can talk to Dads for a while when I'm next door.'

He got up with an easy grace that Maxwell could only envy. The boy looked up at his mother. 'Is Mrs Toobidge flat, Ma?'

'No, darling, not flat. But I'll have to check she's all right.'

'Did you get her any flowers?'

'Oh, babes, I forgot. Why don't you go out into the back garden, see if you can pick her something? She'd like that. Some primroses, there are a lot along the back fence. Careful down the stairs, now.'

Maxwell lay back and closed his eyes, letting the family prattle wash over him. He felt that he could actually sense each bruise as it popped to the surface. It was one thing to be not covered in paint after paintballing. It was another to be black and blue all over. He began to snore quietly.

Nolan clambered up the stairs clutching some sweaty primroses, a few dandelions and some grass. Jacquie arranged them in a jam jar and knew that Mrs Troubridge would be bowled over by them. Nolan could have presented her with a bouquet of dog poo and it would have received pride of place.

She put the boy in front of the television with his plate of pasta on toast and a boxed drink. She made extravagant shushing gestures and crept out of the room. Maxwell slept on. Metternich sashayed up to his Boy and nosed the spaghetti experimentally. Blecch! He had learnt over the years that Nolan occasionally had some quite good stuff on his plate, but today was not one of those times. He sneezed and scrubbed his nose with a paw. Nolan shushed him and slurped up the spaghetti, a strand at a time. He liked the way it whipped round and smacked him gently on the cheek. It was fun to try and guess which side would get the last slap. Even Metternich seemed to be enjoying the fun. Finally, with all the tomato sucked out of the toast and all the juice squeezed out of the box, the cat and his Boy slid quietly out of the room and left the poor old geezer to his snooze.

Soon, there were few sounds in 38 Columbine.

Quiet snores and mutters from the sitting room. The sound of tomatoey fingers being sucked in Nolan's room and the furtive licking as Metternich tried to clean the Boy up a bit. Really, the youth of today – no standards. And the beeping of a very old computer in the study, trying to tell someone in the only way it knew, 'You've Got Mail.'

Jacquie knocked at Mrs Troubridge's door and, when it was flung open a few moments later, could only step back in amazement. Mrs Troubridge had had what had to be described as a makeover, as there was no other word for it. And yet it was a makeover from a parallel universe. Somewhere underneath the shading, the eyelashes, the lip liner and the hair gel was a little old lady having a whale of a time.

Jacquie recovered quickly. 'Mrs Troubridge! You look amazing.' She held out the flowers. 'These are from Nolan.'

The old woman took them as though they were orchids and inhaled deeply. 'Primroses,' she said. 'The smell of spring, I always think. These and bluebells.' She then stood in the doorway, waiting for Jacquie's next move. 'You haven't come to arrest the girls, have you?' she asked nervously.

'Of course not,' Jacquie laughed. 'But I would like a word with them, if I may. I've brought some biscuits and a few essentials. I know how girls can eat.'

'My word, yes,' Mrs Troubridge agreed. 'But I like to see a healthy appetite on a girl. None of this faddy nonsense. Come in, Jacquie. Come in.'

She ushered her neighbour up the stairs.

Jacquie was always amused by the differences between her house and Mrs Troubridge's. Once, they must have been identical, but now they looked as though they had been built in different centuries. Maxwell may be an historian, but his tastes in furniture ran to comfy and squashy, his taste in colours muted and earthy. Mrs Troubridge preferred to live in an era in which her grandmother would have been comfortable. Huge darkbrown furniture loomed out of corners. There was a stuffed dog on the hearth; this creature had given Nolan nightmares for weeks when he realised it was, as he called it, a real empty dog, not a toy. There was an odd smell, comprising old lady, cabbage and just a hint of gin.

The girls were a bright spot in the fusty lounge, sitting on the floor surrounded by bottles and tubes. Leah looked up as the two women came in. 'Mrs Maxwell,' she said calmly, as though she had not been the subject of a county-wide search for over twenty-four hours. 'We hoped you would pop round.'

Julie didn't look up. Jacquie greeted them both, but then spoke directly to Julie. 'Do you want to have a private word with me, Julie?' she asked.

'No,' she said. 'What about, anyway?'

'Your diary?'

The girl looked up and her eyes flashed. 'Have you read my diary?' she said defiantly.

Jacquie thought fast and told what was, technically, the truth. 'No, I haven't.' But Angus has, she added in her head, for the sake of verisimilitude.

'Well, I don't give my permission,' Julie snapped. 'I want it back.'

'It's the weekend now, Julie,' Jacquie said. 'The offices are closed until Monday.'

'I don't believe it,' the girl said. 'Police offices don't close.'

'The diary isn't with the police,' Jacquie said. 'It's with forensics. They thought it might help to trace you. They're just swabbing it for DNA. They're not interested in what it says.' She crossed her fingers at this blatant lie. Behind her back, Mrs Troubridge saw her do it, but was uncharacteristically silent. She had become fond of the girls in her care, as she considered them to be, and had identified Julie as the one more in need of help.

Julie relaxed perceptibly. 'Are you sure?' she asked doubtfully.

'Absolutely. I'm just here to check you are all right and also to ask Mrs Troubridge if she wouldn't mind keeping you another night.'

Mrs Troubridge was torn. They were lovely girls, but so expensive to keep. Jacquie saw her indecision.

'Obviously, there is a contingency fund for this kind of occasion. You are, in a way, Mrs Troubridge, *in loco parentis*.' And loco is dead right, she thought to herself, but fondly. The little woman swelled with pride.

'I would be delighted, Jacquie,' she said. 'Or,' she added roguishly, 'since this is official, perhaps I should say Detective Sergeant Carpenter.' She grinned broadly.

'That's sorted, then,' Jacquie said. 'And I have

317

another favour. Mr Maxwell seems to have done something to his back...'

'He fell on Mrs Troubridge,' Leah offered.

Jacquie looked at her. It must be true, then. She hurriedly turned to Mrs Troubridge. 'Are you hurt?' she asked, possibly a little belatedly.

'I won't pretend it wasn't very uncomfortable and embarrassing at the time,' she said, through tight lips. 'But no harm done. What favour?'

'Could you have Nolan for me tomorrow? I'm not sure his father's back would be up to it and I–'

'Oh, say we can, Mrs T,' Leah said. She was missing her little sister. 'It would be great.'

'Yeah,' Julie said. 'He's a great kid.'

'We'd be delighted,' Mrs Troubridge said. 'We could take him for a walk, perhaps. To see the bluebells.'

Jacquie thought quickly. She was grateful that she had not had to finish her sentence, because the obvious end to it would have been '...have to arrest your stepfather first thing, Julie.' But on the other hand, it wasn't such a good idea that the girls should be seen in public. Mrs Troubridge, in her new sensitive mode, saw her problem.

'We can cut down the back lane at the end of the road. We'll be at the woods in no time and no one will see us, except the odd dog walker. I'm sure it will be lovely.'

The girls, who would rather have been next door with the Wii and all the trimmings, nodded all the same. She was such a sweet old girl and her breakfasts were to die for. 'That will be lovely,' they said. 'We can take a picnic.'

'Oooh, girls,' the old lady said. 'No sitting on

318

the wet grass. When I was a gel, I remember...'
The girls hunched closer. They loved her stories.

Jacquie took the opportunity to sneak back down the stairs and to look after her crocked husband. They would be good to go all night. She couldn't wait to see what Mrs Troubridge would look like by the next morning. She had a feeling there were more makeovers in the pipeline. She went into the sitting room at 38, all ready to describe the new-look Mrs T. Maxwell was sleeping like a baby, relaxed at last. Upstairs, Nolan was also sleeping and, with rather more reason, he also slept like a baby. Jacquie made herself a sandwich – beetroot, peanut butter and hummus, only allowed when there was no one there to see – and poured herself a beer. She covered Maxwell over with a throw from the other chair and turned out the lights.

Upstairs in her bedroom, with the beer and the sandwich on the bedside table, the curtains drawn and the TV on low, she mulled over the day. A distant beep from the study became part of the background hum and, only slightly beetroot stained, she went on watching a rerun of *War Games*. She knew that the film was more than twenty years old – so why did Matthew Broderick still look the same to this very day? And could a hacker really get into the Pentagon computer? Why did this seem important? Why did she always forget until it was too late that beetroot gave her wind? She slid down into the bed and, stretching across the unaccustomed space, she slept.

Maxwell was still in the armchair when day and

battle broke. He woke up with a jolt which brought stars to his eyes and he realised anew that he hadn't been to bed. He had, though, 'dropped back', as the Maxwells had it: that is, he'd woken up once and gone to sleep again, and he suddenly had sharp memories of the first time.

Little Nole had been dancing around until his mother hushed him, shouting 'Picnic! Picnic!' like he'd won the lottery. He'd planted a slobbery kiss on his father's cheek and vanished in the company of his mother, who seemed as pleased as the Boy. Metternich may have the cream (he usually did) but it was Jacquie who said 'Gone arrestin'' with a smug satisfaction only usually seen when Dirty Harry was pointing his Magnum at somebody.

Maxwell checked the sitting room clock as he groped for the Nurofen. Ten to ten; the bleeding time.

On the telly, they wore flak jackets and struck at dawn, smashing through front doors with those heavy metal things while half the SWAT team watched the back. In reality, Jacquie and Matt Carter, looking like a couple of Jehovah's Witnesses out on their Saturday morning swoop, ambled up the path to the house in question.

'Mr Melkins,' she said, flashing her warrant card as he opened the door. 'I am Detective Sergeant Carpenter. This is Detective Sergeant Carter.'

'I know perfectly well who you are,' Melkins told her. 'Is there any more news?'

'Oh, yes,' said Jacquie, wide-eyed. 'The news is that I am arresting you on suspicion of child abuse. Do you have a coat or a wife you'd like to bring? Sergeant Carter will read you your rights on the way to the station.'

Melkins' eyes darted fire. 'I know my rights,' he assured her. 'I have the right to a lawyer.'

'And you have the right to remain silent. Let's start with that, shall we?'

Jim Astley didn't do Saturday mornings. Whenever he could and there was a 'y' in the day, he was to be found on Tottingleigh Golf Course, slicing little white things through the cloudless blue of a perfect picnic day. So it was Donald who did the honours at the morgue, dutifully pulling back the green sheet that covered the dead man. And it was he who saw the little, suddenly old, lady hold her hand to her mouth and sway a little until DCI Hall caught her and led her away.

And it wasn't Colin Russell's mother who finally identified him on the slab; she had lost her nerve and had asked her sister to do it. It was Mrs B, who did for the Maxwells and up at the school.

It must have been mid-afternoon when Maxwell's doorbell rang. The tablets had kicked in by now and he could just manage the stairs. Love him dearly though he did, please God don't let this be Nole back already from the picnic, otherwise he'd have forgotten all about Dads's back and demand endless renditions of 'Stop the cavalry' complete with bouncing on the knees. He was relieved to see that it didn't look as if DCI Hall would relish the same treatment.

321

'Henry.' Maxwell said. 'To what do I owe the pleasure?'

'I've just come from the morgue, Max,' he told him.

'Don't tell me,' Maxwell smiled. 'You need cheering up.' He ushered the man in. 'Tea? Coffee? Yard of ale?' Maxwell still had enough flexibility in his spine to make a moderate sweeping gesture with his arm. 'I'd offer you Southern Comfort but I suspect you're on duty and I'm not sure the sun's over the yard arm by very much.'

Hall declined it all and sat down. 'What can you tell me about a Colin Russell?' he asked.

Maxwell blinked. 'I don't think I can tell you anything about him, can I? Who is he?'

'Mrs Bee said she'd told you all about him. And I wouldn't like to think that you're not helping police with their inquiries.'

'Oh, *Coe*-lin! Sorry, yes. Mrs B's nephew. I didn't know the surname. He *is* our corpse in the copse, then?'

Hall nodded. 'What exactly did Mrs Bee tell you? She was a little less than coherent with me. Seemed to be speaking in sound bites.'

'Yes,' Maxwell nodded. 'You need practice to manage Mrs B. Well...' He dredged up the memories. 'Colin, sweet boy and apple of the family's eye and so on, was doing bird in Ford Open Prison, but he had done a runner. Mrs B, of course, wouldn't have it; her Colin wouldn't do that sort of thing.'

'It looks as though she may be right, doesn't it?' Hall said grimly. 'We're waiting to find out how long he had been up at the paintball copse, but

322

the money is on almost a week.'

According to Mrs B, he had been missing since last weekend.'

'Well, forensics will confirm that for us.'

'What I don't understand, amongst many other things,' Maxwell said, 'was why you couldn't identify him. I mean, he does have a record.'

'Good point. It seems young Colin had a bit of a way with computers. He had been put away for fraud connected with some software he had developed.'

'Yes, Mrs B told me about that. No details, but he had taught her to use a computer rather well.'

'He used a false name and sold the software rights to a load of different companies. One of them had CCTV. Also, and this was where he was unlucky, two of the managers from where he had sold the rights happened to be golfing partners and also a bit loose-lipped on the industrial espionage front. So they got him, bang to rights.'

'But that means he has a record, surely. Prints, DNA, that kind of thing. I do watch TV, you know. *CSI*. The police procedural never lies.'

'Well, it frequently does,' Hall corrected him, 'but we won't quibble about that now. What Colin had done was to leave his name in the prison system, but wipe his prints and DNA, personal description, all that. He kindly did it for all his friends on the wing. Leaving his name was a stroke of genius; that way, all his prison records remained on the system, so that the officers could update him, book visits and everything. But from outside, he was invisible.' Hall sighed. 'Clever.'

'So he really was a computer whizz?' Maxwell asked. 'Only, Mrs B tends to deal only in super-latives and it's sometimes a little difficult to judge.'

'Oh, no, he was clearly very talented in that way. The software he had designed was never discussed in court; apparently it is still subject of a legal wrangle between all the people he sold it to – but it's bound to be a workable product. I don't think he was naturally bent.'

Maxwell had a thought. 'Where was he work-ing, on licence? Asda? An estate agent?'

Hall barked what may have been a laugh. 'You might like this. He was working for a software company.'

'What?' Maxwell leant forward and was pleased that his back just gave a warning whimper rather than going into a complete spasm. 'I had no idea he had access to computers. Have you linked him at all to this texting and emailing problem?'

Hall looked thoughtful, then shook his head. 'No. No need to pursue that, anyway. Unless Jacquie has been very unlucky, I think she may have someone for that today.'

Maxwell was between a rock and the usual hard place. He couldn't let Hall know how much he and Jacquie had discussed. But he really didn't think that Melkins was the man for all the other problems. He settled for a simple 'Ah.'

'Jacquie is like the Mounties,' Hall said. 'She always gets her man.'

Maxwell tried and failed to picture Jacquie in a rather strange hat and a scarlet coat, wrassling a bar and stirring her coffee with her thumb. It wasn't a picture that came easily to him, but he agreed with the general principle. 'Let's hope you're right,' he said.

'For the record,' Jacquie said clearly into the tape-recorder, 'interview commencing one-thirty in the presence of DS Carpenter and Carter, Mr Gregory Melkins and...'

'John Whitby,' the brief filled in, adjusting his glasses and straightening his tie. Jacquie noted that the man looked six. When lawyers start looking younger than policemen...

'Tell us about Julie,' Jacquie said.

Melkins looked at her. Then at the brief, who nodded. 'My stepdaughter,' he said, 'currently attends Leighford High School.'

'Is that it?' Jacquie asked.

'What more do you want?' Melkins snapped. 'Her bra size?' The silence was tangible.

Jacquie sat back. Leighford CID, one; child-molesting bastard, nil. 'That's rather an odd question,' she said.

'Look.' Melkins came the heavy. 'First, my stepdaughter goes missing, which by the way you people didn't really seem to take very seriously; then you say she's safe, but you won't say where. And now you're charging me with child abuse.'

'You haven't been charged yet,' Jacquie reminded him.

The brief nodded.

'Does your stepdaughter keep a diary, Mr Melkins?' It was Matt Carter's turn.

Melkins looked at him. 'I really have no idea,' he said flatly.

'Well, allow us to enlighten you,' Jacquie said. 'She does. It's a rather frilly, girly thing, all pink with a kitten–'

'You can't believe a word she says!' Melkins shouted. 'The lying little bitch! Whatever's in that diary is a pack of lies. I never touched her! Never!'

He was on his feet now, trembling and looming over Jacquie. He barely felt his lawyer's restraining hand on his sleeve.

'For the record,' Jacquie said, 'Mr Melkins is ... at one-thirty-four ... using intimidating body language.'

'Greg,' the brief called his client to one side. 'If I may just have a moment, Sergeant?'

'For the record,' Jacquie said, 'Mr Whitby is conferring with his client.'

She and Matt Carter sat stony-faced while the whispering on the far side of the desk hissed this way and that. At the end of it, Melkins sat down, avoiding everyone's gaze.

The brief cleared his throat. 'My client wishes to state that he has had sexual relations with his stepdaughter, that these have not been with her consent, but there has been no penetration.'

'So that makes it all right, does it?' Carter asked.

Melkins' eyes came up level with his. 'What do you know about it, you moron? There she is, night after night, swaying her hips, putting her make-up on, leaving her bedroom door open. I'm only human, for God's sake.'

'Let's leave God out of this, shall we, Mr Melkins?' Jacquie suggested. 'Tell us about the texts.'

'Texts?'

'And emails. The "I know what you've done" business.'

Melkins frowned at her, then at the brief. 'I haven't the faintest idea what you're talking about,' he said.

'Don't you?' Jacquie asked. 'We shall, of course, be checking your PC – at home, at the hospital. And your mobile phone.'

The doctor threw the thing onto the desk with a clatter.

'For the record,' Jacquie said, 'Mr Melkins has just volunteered his mobile phone.'

'I certainly have,' he hissed. 'I'll put my hand up to interfering with Julie, but you're not going to pin every unsolved crime on your books on me. Not by a long chalk.'

And there was something in the way he said it that made Jacquie realise the interview was over, even before she spoke the words into the microphone. She should have been happy. She had a result. She'd got her man. And yet, it somehow didn't all tie up. Not quite. There was still something missing and she had to know what it was.

Maxwell was still mulling over the image of Jacquie arresting a clutch of lumberjacks single-handed when Hall suddenly spoke. He had been trying to remember what else he wanted to speak to Maxwell about and it had finally come into his head. One of these days he would master the re-minder gadget on his mobile phone, but until then he had to rely on his increasingly leaky memory.

'I know what I was going to ask you,' he said. 'What did you make of that strange email, the "red red ones" thing? Have you had any more?'

Maxwell sat up straighter. He hadn't really thought about it in the last twelve hours, wrapped as he had been in his personal world of pain. But Henry was right. It was strange. He could believe all sorts of things, but not that Nostradamus had predicted this. And he hadn't checked his emails since that message had arrived. 'I wondered if Jacquie had discussed it with you,' he said. 'I can't make it out. I was assuming the family overcome by death was ... well, was mine. Although that is very ancient history, I suppose, for anyone but me. There is literally no one left alive now who was affected by it, except me. That's a sobering thought, Henry.'

They sat in silent contemplation for a moment, of the passing of time, the fragility of human life. Henry had sat at the bedside of his dangerously ill wife within the past year. He had got her back, but it had been touch and go; he could only imagine how Maxwell had felt, still felt, sometimes.

Maxwell pulled himself back to the present. 'But I realise now that it probably refers to Mrs B and her family. But what the "red red ones" can mean, I have no idea. Old Michel de Notre Dame had a rather sideways view of the world. He's not talking about Communism, that's for sure. Or Native Americans.' They had a little silent mull. Henry liked these moments with Maxwell. The man may be perceived by many to be a meddling old idiot, but he didn't speak when speech wasn't called for. And his brain was the best that Hall could tap into. 'Sorry,' he said suddenly, making the DCI jump. 'You asked if I had had any more. I haven't checked. Would you like to look now?'

'Is that ... all right?' Hall was aware that Maxwell wasn't exactly a major player when it came to computers.

'Henry, that was a nice thing to say,' Maxwell said, reading his mind. 'But I'm not quite the total moron that people believe me to be. I can read my own emails. I can send them, too, pretty reliably. I don't like forwarding, attaching, all that stuff. But I'm fine on the basics. No, the problem here is me negotiating the stairs, but if you're willing to go at my speed, we'll manage. I'll tell you what would be a good idea. If you go into the kitchen and make us a drink. Everything is out on view, so you'll be all right, I'm sure. That way, I can get a head start and we won't have to make small talk while I take it a step at a time.'

'Good idea,' Hall said, who had been beginning to regret his refusal of a drink when he had arrived. 'Coffee?'

'Tea for me,' Maxwell said. 'But have what you prefer.' He went to the foot of the stairs and started the climb, painfully lifting one leg onto the bottom-most tread. He listened carefully. Hall seemed to be busy with mugs and kettle, so he sped up; not much, but a little. He didn't have anything to hide, but he just wanted to read the message before Henry.

In the kitchen, Henry Hall clattered the mugs, but not so much as to be unable to hear what Maxwell was doing. He smiled secretly to himself

329

– the only type of smile he ever allowed – when he heard the relatively swift footfalls on the stairs. It was what he would have done himself; grabbed a chance to read the email before anyone else. A horrible thought struck him; were he and Maxwell becoming more alike? He suppressed a small shudder and got on with making the tea.

In the study, the computer had gone to sleep. Maxwell knew, from what others said, that their computers did this and a light tap on any key had them buzzing and alert again. Maxwell's computer needed banging, shouting, pleading and cajoling, but eventually it woke up and he found that the email page was already there. There were two unopened messages for him, both from unknown senders. He clicked on the first one.

'The ancient work will be accomplished,' it said. 'And from the roof evil ruin will fall on the great man.' He recognised this for two reasons. It was the wording of the text. And it was a quatrain he frequently quoted to his classes when they were discussing the Kennedy assassination. But it was only half of the verse. He racked his brain for the other half. He would have to look it up. He clicked on the other message. He had hesitated before doing it, because this was marked in the subject line – 'For Henry Hall'. Even so, he wanted to see it first.

'They will accuse the innocent, being dead, of the deed. The guilty one is hidden in the misty copse.'

This was the second half of the quatrain. Century 6, if he recalled it right. But that didn't really matter. It was how it impinged on now that

330

counted, not what some mad French pot-head wrote years ago. He was shocked he could even think that, it was an insult to history, but it was sadly true.

He heard footsteps on the stairs and Henry Hall came into the study carrying a tray. The mugs matched. There was sugar in a bowl, milk in a jug. This domestic angle was a new side to the DCI and Maxwell was impressed. Still holding the tray, Hall looked over Maxwell's shoulder.

'Hang on a minute,' Maxwell said. 'There are two. You need to see them in the right order.' He clicked on the first and then, glancing over his shoulder with some difficulty to check that Hall had read it, clicked on the second.

Hall put the tray down on the window sill and pulled up a stool. 'Put the first one up again,' he said and Maxwell obliged. 'I don't want to worry you, Max,' he said, 'but I would advise you not to go out ... well, until we've caught this joker.'

'Why ever not?' Maxwell was astounded. As a rule, Hall could be relied upon to down play drama and excitement. And here he was recommending a virtual house arrest, however much it was self-imposed.

'Well, read it. "The ancient work will be accomplished." That's history, surely, ancient work. "And from the roof evil ruin will fall on the great man." Now, I don't want to make you big-headed, Max, but you know that is one of your nicknames at school. And no doubt in other places as well.' Although not where I work, he added silently to himself. Different nicknames there altogether.

'Henry. I'm blushing. Do you mean ... well, I

assume you mean someone will, what, throw something at me from a roof? Drop something on my head?'

'Yes, I do. I do mean exactly that.'

'But, why?'

Hall prepared to count on fingers, but first he said, 'I know that lots of these things were not planned, Max, it's just the usual case of you being in the right place at the wrong time, but our murderer doesn't know that. Our murderer, and our texter, I'm beginning to think.'

'Really? One person?'

'One person or one group of people.' He held up his thumb. 'You have been approached by a couple of the girls involved, who then disappeared.' Index finger. 'You turn up at the paintballing, when the body is found.' Little finger; Maxwell found it quite endearing that DCI Henry Hall, Leighford nick supremo, couldn't count on his fingers sequentially. 'The girls turn up, at or near your house.' Ring finger. 'Your cleaning lady turns out to be related to the dead man.' Middle finger. 'Actually, I don't have anything for that finger, but you see where I'm going with this.'

'Let's recap, Henry.' Maxwell's thumb went into the air. 'Of course I was approached by the girls. I am approached by girls, and may I add here for completeness, and to avoid any charges of sexism – or worse – by boys as well, all the time. It is my job.' Index finger. 'I was at the paintballing with the entire staff of Leighford High School, all four thousand of us, against my will.' Middle finger, triumphantly held up. 'I didn't know the girls were next door for almost twenty-four hours and anyway, isn't that just more of the thumb point?' Ring finger. 'I know my cleaning lady is related to the dead man, but I had to be told by a dinner lady from the school.' Pinky. 'And I do have something for this finger – someone is having a bit of a poke at me, because I stick my head over the parapet. I don't know who the murderer is, I don't know who the texter is, if they are one and the same or not. But I do know who is sending me these emails and it is someone at Leighford High School who wants rid of me for her own twisted purposes.'

'She?'

'Yes. I'm almost certain it is either ... well, I'll get a bit more certain than almost before I name her, if that's all the same to you, Henry. But I'm being very uncivil. Let's drink our drinks and you tell me who *you* think it might be.'

Hall passed him a mug of perfectly brewed tea. It would be a cold day in Hell before he confided fully in Peter Maxwell. But he was prepared to humour him up to a point. Maxwell took a sip and raised an eyebrow in praise. 'Well,' the DCI said. 'I think that the whole thing is linked because Colin Russell was a computer geek and the texter is a computer geek.'

'Why?' Maxwell thought he knew, but wanted to make sure that Hall was on the same track before making a complete idiot of himself.

'It's just a feeling I have,' Hall admitted. 'It's not easy to get phone numbers – mobile phones, that is. These girls are giving out their numbers in some kind of forum where they are accessible, if not to all, then to someone who can get deeper into the records than the users expect. A mediator in a chat room, someone like that. Someone who has greater access.'

Maxwell was impressed. 'My word, Henry,' he said. 'I'm impressed.

'Thank you.' Hall sipped his coffee. 'Unlike you, I don't think your emails and … one text, was it?' Maxwell inclined his head. 'Yes, I don't think they are unconnected. I would be interested to know who you think it is, for that reason.'

'We'll have to agree to disagree, Henry. Let's just stick to the emails, shall we? Perhaps we can dig something out using those.'

Hall recognised a brick wall when he walked into one. 'Right. Can you click on the first one? I need to get it absolutely right.' The mail appeared on the screen and Hall leant forward, pulling on his lower lip and humming quietly. 'I just can't…' Suddenly he sat back and almost fell off his stool, coffee slopping everywhere. 'Sorry, Max. I've got it. I've got it.'

Maxwell was patting at the coffee pools on the essays waiting to be marked on his desk. It had probably improved them; he just hoped Eleven Jay Ell Vee would agree.

Hall pointed at the screen. 'What is Colin Russell's hair colour?'

'Well, poor lad. Ginger.'

The red one.

'Ah. And "red red ones"?' Maxwell needed more confirmation.

'You won't know this, but … did Jacquie mention a colleague whose kids are getting texts, well, the girl is?'

'She did say ... Yvonne Thomas, is that right?'

'Yes.' Hall didn't even bother to take up this blatant case of breach of confidentiality. 'Twins, they are. A boy and a girl. Josh and Amanda. Nice kids on the surface, but a bit weird, like twins sometimes are. Josh would do anything for Amanda. Especially if Amanda is being targeted by some bloke, possibly with paedophile tendencies. He's a big lad. Sporty. Strong.'

Maxwell took a deep breath. 'Red hair?'

'Red hair.' Hall chugged back his remaining coffee. 'I've got to go, Max. I've got to get on with this now I've thought of it. I hope you don't mind; I'll probably have to bring Jacquie in on this. You didn't have plans?'

'You know better than that, Henry. The Maxwells don't have plans when the game is afoot.'

'Umm...?'

'Sherlock Holmes.' Maxwell helped Hall out of his confusion. 'Don't you worry. You go off and arrest the children of the damned. I'll see Jacquie when I see her. I hope you don't mind if I don't see you out. You could be here for hours.'

Hall was already halfway down the stairs. Seconds later, Maxwell heard a distant slam as he left the house. Twirling gently in his old swivel chair from side to side, Maxwell clicked from one email to another. 'Henry, my old mucker,' he muttered to himself. 'I really, really think you're barking up the wrong tree.'

Chapter Nineteen

Saturday night in Columbine. The sun had just gone down on a pretty average, warmish, damp- ish, cloudyish, sunnyish British spring day. Nolan was in bed, full of more E numbers than he had eaten in his whole life until this day. Metternich was having a last-minute groom before going out on what he euphemistically called 'the Town' – in fact, the overgrown bit along the footpath behind the houses, where the valley voles were fatter. Mrs Troubridge was also in bed; girls' nights in were all very well, but at her age, a few went a long way, so Julie and Leah were watching tele- vision in her retro lounge. The television had the tiniest screen and the worst reception that they had ever seen, as well as for some reason only receiving five channels, more BC than BBC. They knew that next door, just through the wall, Maxwell was stretched out in front of a flat- screen, HD-ready, Sky-receiving TV and wished they had the nerve to go and hijack it. But they had known Mad Max now for over five years and knew their boundaries.

Maxwell was loyally waiting up for Jacquie. He was doing it in the comfort of his own bed, though. He hadn't spent many nights in a chair, and he had no intention of scoring two in a row. Possession was nine-tenths of the law. These things could become a habit.

He was not the kind of father who ignored his child and so, even though his mind was full of other things, he had fed, amused, bathed and bedded his one and only. He had closed the door of the boy's bedroom with the feeling of a job well done. What Jacquie would say the next day when she found that Nolan still had his trainers on, he would discover when the time came. Until then, he was satisfied with a job well done.

He heard a click two floors below. This must be Jacquie, home from the daily grind. Her footsteps on the stairs were slow and dragging and Maxwell suddenly felt bad about being in bed while she had been working all day. He leapt gingerly to his feet and ended up meeting her on the landing. 'Good day, hon?'

She shrugged. 'So-so. Put a child molester away, I hope. First stages of, anyway. Bad side of that, I'll have to tell Julie that I know what's in her diary and her family has been ripped to shreds. Henry has got the Thomas twins in a council facility, notionally accused of murder. Their parents are in shock. Yvonne is on a million prescription drugs, just to stop the screaming, really. If I never see anything like that again, it will be too soon.' She sat on the bed and covered her face with her hands. He sat beside her and rubbed her back. There was nothing he could say, not really. Telling her that he thought Henry was wrong wouldn't help at all. 'I kept seeing Nolan, that's the thing.' She raised her head. 'Our little bloke, innocent as the day is long, banged up for something he couldn't possibly have done. Because, they haven't done it, Max.

Those kids wouldn't hurt a fly.'

He let out a long breath. Thank goodness for that. Now he could speak without getting the flak. 'I know,' he said. 'I see why Henry might jump to that conclusion, but I think he's being led that way by the real killer.'

She looked up at him and scrubbed the tears from her eyes with the back of her hand. She looked like a tired and slightly grubby schoolgirl. 'How do you mean?'

Maxwell gave her a kiss on the nose. 'I'm going to run you a bath. You go and get a couple of drinks and I'll meet you in the bathroom in a minute.'

She sighed and stretched. 'That sounds lovely. Candles?'

'I'm afraid you've been reading too many lifestyle magazines. And what that bugger Johnny Depp aka Inspector Abberline was doing, soaking thus in *From Hell* as he pursued Jack the Ripper, God only knows. Candles are rubbish in a bathroom, the steam puts the flames out and since I will be sitting on the loo in lieu of anywhere else, the only place to put them will be the window sill, in which case...'

'I get your drift. Southern Comfort?'

'As big as the great outdoors, if you would. Just as you Mounties like them.'

'Pardon?'

'Train of thought. See you in a minute.' He went into the en suite bathroom, as being further away from Nolan and less likely to wake him up. He loved his son, but tonight was no time for playing Sink the Bismarck, no matter how much

Metternich would approve.

When Jacquie was ensconced in the bubbles and they had chinked glasses together, she got back to the point. 'So you think Henry is wrong?'

'I think I'm prepared to go further. I *know* Henry is wrong. What happened was, he got so excited about the red red ones, that he ignored the other two emails I showed him.'

'You've had more? He didn't say.' She sank lower and her breasts disappeared at one end as her knees appeared at the other. It looked like a Paul Daniels trick for the late night cabaret circuit.

'Yes. Well, one really, in that they are the two halves of one quatrain. And very lazy. I use it quite often at school.'

'You teach Nostradamus? Don't you get complaints?'

'I would if I did, but I don't. It crops up when we cover the Kennedy killing. When I debunk the coincidence theories and other stuff that the kids get off the net and trot out at me.'

'Well, go and get them, then. You open the mail, click the printer icon...'

'If you please, madam, I am quite capable of printing an email. Quite often, anyway. But I don't need to. I know it. The first half says, "The ancient work will be accomplished and from the roof evil ruin will fall on the great man".'

Jacquie surged up out of the water, a mini tsunami flowing in all directions. 'Max! Surely, that's a direct threat to you! Is Henry doing anything? Protection?'

'Darling, darling, calm down. You weren't this interested when I got this as a text.'

Jacquie had the grace to look contrite. He had certainly tried hard enough to tell her about it. But stuff, police stuff, important stuff kept getting in the way.

Maxwell patted her and then dried his hand on her hair. 'Don't fret, heart. Back in the water this instant or you will chap. Yes, Henry sees it as a threat. No, he isn't doing anything because it would be stupid. And he also isn't doing anything because he thinks he has his killers. So, stop it. The second half, which came as another email says, "They will accuse an innocent, being dead, of the deed. The guilty one is hidden in the misty copse".'

'And what do you take that to mean?' She sipped her drink.

'Well, what I'm *supposed* to take it to mean is that the twins – who have already been set up in the first email, don't forget – will put the blame on Colin Russell, the man in the ditch. He was, after all, found in a copse – although it wasn't misty when he was found, it no doubt is at dawn or thereabouts.'

'"Supposed to mean"? So you don't think that it is what happened. That the twins will try and blame it all on Colin?'

'What's to blame? Colin was guilty, if he was guilty of anything, of taking money that wasn't his. I don't think he is behind the texting and emails and how can he be guilty of the only other crime – his murder? It's hard to break your own neck and leave yourself in a ditch, no matter how determined you might be.'

'It isn't Melkins, either. He's a nasty piece of

work, but he definitely hasn't done anything except molest Julie.' She took a big gulp of her drink. 'I didn't think I'd ever hear myself say that.'

'I know what you mean, sweetness, don't worry. No, I think a lot of hares have been started today and I just hope Henry can put things right with the twins' parents. It's not the sort of thing that goes towards good staff relations, is it?'

'Their dad's a copper as well.'

'Henry really knows how to do it – he doesn't often mess it up, but he certainly doesn't do things by halves when he does.' He leant forward to turn on the hot tap for her. 'I'm assuming you are at home tomorrow.'

'Yes,' she said, with no room for quibbling. 'I've done no shopping. There's absolutely no food in the house.'

'Why don't we take Mrs Troubridge and the girls out for a Little-As-You-Can-Eat-Carvery-Only-£3.50 at the Weasel and Ferret? I think we all deserve a treat.'

She flicked some foam at him. 'I think we all deserve more than a piece of string and a plastic Yorkshire pudding at the Weasel and Ferret, but I agree with the principle. That would be good. But a lie-in, first, please.'

He stood up and reached into the airing cupboard for a big, fluffy towel – one of the forty-two she owned – and held it up for her to step into. 'Your wish is my command, oh best beloved.' He wrapped the towel round her. 'I would carry you to the bedroom, but you have to remember my Old Trouble.'

'I can walk, just,' she said, just making it to the

341

bed. 'Swing my legs up for me, there's a thing.' He did as she asked and went back into the bathroom for their glasses. 'I've put your jamas on the towel rail,' he said. 'They're nice and warm.'

But answer came there none. DS Jacquie Carpenter Maxwell was fast asleep.

Maxwell counted them in at Columbine and he counted them out at the Weasel and Ferret. They made a strange-looking family group, but Maxwell was strangely proud of his little brood as they trooped into the Family Dining Area. Mrs Troubridge was twittering with pleasure; it was years since she had had Sunday lunch anywhere other than in front of her own television and her festive mood had somehow rubbed off on everyone. If anyone noticed that Jacquie was watching the roofline with more than usual zeal, they were too polite to comment. Six roast dinners – leftovers in a moggy bag for the Count – followed by six really-still-half-frozen toffee puddings later and they were on their way back home. Scrabble for six, won inexplicably by Nolan and with no help from anyone, except possibly Maxwell, followed and a perfect Sunday was complete. No one mentioned phones or emails or anything electronic or otherwise cyber. Not even Jacquie had noticed the car trailing them at a discreet distance. Not even Metternich had noticed the bushes rustle down on the footpath behind the houses. Maxwell officially absolved Leah and Julie from school the next day. *Midsomer Murders* on the telly in the bedroom, Maxwell spotting that the antique dealer did it within minutes of the opening credits finishing, brought the day to a proper close. Jacquie closed her eyes on her world with a feeling that, if she hadn't taken any steps forward, at least she hadn't taken any steps back.

'Nolan!' Jacquie was calling from the bottom of the stairs. 'Don't make me come up there.'

'All right,' he called back. 'I won't.'

'You asked for that one,' Maxwell remarked, from his place at the kitchen table. 'You have to learn to stay one step ahead, don't ask any closed questions and always be prepared for the answer you don't want.'

'All good interviewing techniques,' she conceded.

'And also damned fine strategy for dealing with Year Ten,' he said. 'I've always said we do the same job.'

'If I did your job, I'd be in a strait-jacket. And if you did mine, you would have retired by now.' The words were out before she heard them coming.

Maxwell took another bite of toast and chewed thoughtfully. 'Ah, the R word. It seems to be spinning around in the air at the moment. Whenever I see Legs I always feel it is what he wants to say next. I know Pansy and Nicole would like me gone.' He gave her an assessing look. 'And what about you?'

She considered lying and then decided that would be counterproductive as well as pointless. 'I worry about you.'

'I know that. But do you want me to retire?'

'May I plead the Fifth on that?'

'No.' A one word answer was so rare from her husband that she had to take notice.

'All right. Since you ask. I would love to have you at home. I know you have a million things you'd like to do – writing, modelling, gardening.' The last was just a hopeful addition, but it didn't get past him.

'They say everyone has one book in them, so that might be true of me. The modelling can always do with a bit more time. I've ignored the gardening crack – you will have your little joke. But, would you like me to retire?'

'Oh, Max. Give me a break. It's Monday morning. Nolan is still in bed–'

'No, I'm not,' came an irritated voice from behind her. 'I'm here, waiting for my breakfast.'

She spun round. 'Darling, I'm so sorry. I didn't see you there. You came in very quietly.'

'Metternich's teaching me,' the boy said, reaching for his milk. 'He's very good at it already.'

'I understand the second lesson is how to lick your own–'

'Max! That's enough. You can't retire, anyway. You're only four.'

'And a half.' The Head of Sixth Form laughed and stood up from the table. 'Can't wait for you two today. I need to be at school early.'

'I was going to drop you today,' Jacquie said. 'Because of ... well, you know. Your back.'

'Fit as a flea,' he replied, doing a few running steps on the spot. 'I only missed doing the Marathon because I'm so busy with marking. Anyway,' he kissed his wife and son on their respective

344

heads, 'time's a-wasting. Abyssinia.'

''Sinya,' Nolan called, Coco Pops going everywhere.

'Love you,' Jacquie said, but quietly. 'Take care.'

Maxwell had made the same journey on the same bicycle, give or take the odd spare part, for nigh on a century, or that was how it felt. He no longer took any notice of his surroundings and often got to Leighford High wondering if he had, perhaps, run down and slaughtered whole squadrons of small children, old ladies, or it might even be missionaries going about their lawful business in his path. He had discussed this one morning with another cycling teacher, a nice lad from the Geology Department, and had been reassured that he was not the only one to worry. The thing to keep in mind, he had been told, was that should he in fact decimate whole swathes of Leighford's population, he would certainly notice, if it was only because of the blood on the mudguard.

He was quite glad, therefore, to discover from firsthand experience that this was true. Except that he was the potential victim, not the slaughterer. He was swinging wide on the final turn as he so often did, coat flying, hat on his head by sheer willpower alone, when he heard an engine behind him. An SUV of unnecessary size and horsepower was coming up behind him on the turn and it was only by a mad twist of the handlebars and a flying leap onto the verge that he wasn't squashed like a bug. The vehicle, having turned into the drive of the school, did a screaming U-turn on its handbrake and sped off the way it had come.

Maxwell lay on the verge counting his limbs by twitching them one by one. Everything seemed to be present if not correct and he rolled over carefully to survey the damage to Surrey. Again, everything seemed present and correct. He clambered to his feet, not such an easy task without Mrs Troubridge to depend on, and was dusting himself down when a breathless voice called his name. He looked up to see Nicole Thompson jogging round the corner, sweat-bands on her wrists and some serious-looking trainers on her feet.

'Max! Are you OK? I saw that. He looked as if he was aiming straight at you.'

'Did you get a number? A description?'

'Sorry, Max.' She was alongside now, fresh as a daisy, not a drop of sweat anywhere. He wasn't surprised. He often found that seriously ambitious people weren't built quite the same as the common herd. 'All I saw was a bloody great car nearly run you down. Are you sure you're all right?'

'Yes, yes. Just a bit shaken. I'll just walk Surrey into the bike shed. Erm ... Nicole?'

She was shocked. He had called her by her real name. 'Yes, Max.'

'Not a word about this, if you don't mind. I don't want to worry people.'

'Well, I think someone ought to know. Your wife, for instance. Isn't she a WPC?'

'Well, a detective sergeant, as a matter of fact.' He felt petty but he hated it when women tried to belittle other women to make themselves feel more important. And whatever else he knew about Nicole Thompson, she liked to feel important. 'But you're right about the woman bit. No, really, she doesn't need to know. And, to be honest with you, Clara, I've got so many bruises because of Friday, she'll never notice.' He saw her stricken face. 'I am so sorry, really I am. What was I thinking? Are you totally recovered? From the shock.'

She smiled, but it was rather wobbly. 'They kept me in until Saturday morning. Apparently I was in acidotic shock. Hyperventilation. My heart was a bit–'

'Irregular? Pounding?'

She nodded.

'That's me getting out of bed in the morning,' he laughed. 'But you seem better now.' That wasn't particularly true, but he didn't think that she would welcome being told that if she was going to be this fragile about finding a not terribly upsetting body of a complete stranger, then she wasn't going to do so well working in a cut-throat job in a school where everyone was out to getchya.

'Well, I've got some tablets,' she said. 'In case I feel, you know, wobbly again.'

'That's good,' Maxwell said, patting her shoulder. 'Mother's little helpers.' He had been quite a Stones fan for a day once. He held out a hand and made a small bow. 'Shall we?'

And the dinosaur and the IT girl walked up the drive to face another Leighford High day.

Maxwell was having a quiet ache in his office during what people laughingly called a 'free' period when the door crashed back and Sylvia Matthews stood there, armed with some rubbing liniment and, therefore, dangerous. 'Peter Maxwell, what are you playing at?'

'I'm sorry, Sylv,' he said mildly. 'I have no idea what you're talking about.'

'You certainly have,' she said menacingly. 'You came off your bike today and you have kept it to yourself.'

'I knew you'd come up here with that horse ointment,' he said. 'Do you remember the last time you used that on me?'

She looked at her feet and muttered something unintelligible.

'I beg your pardon?' he leant forward, cupping an ear.

'I may have been a little over-generous. It may have trickled down ... somewhere it had no business,' she said. Her straight face cracked and she laughed out loud. 'You were so funny, Max. I've never seen anyone run round my treatment room at head height before.'

'It was extremely painful, I'll have you know, Nursie, and I won't have you near me with that stuff. I took a small tumble because some imbecile driving a car the size of a small town nearly crushed me. But I'm all right and Surrey's all right, so no harm done.'

'Car?' Sylvia looked puzzled. 'I heard you'd just fallen off.'

Maxwell looked even more puzzled. 'But ... wait a minute. Where did you hear this?'

'Nicole. From IT.'

'I know where she's from. Hell. What have I

done to her that she's always out to get me?'

'Max. Just because you're paranoid...' Sylvia began.

'Yes, yes. Good joke, but I'm too annoyed.' He gestured for her to sit down and, closing to her, took both hands in his. 'Sylv, listen to me. I was riding in...'

'...on the wrong side of the drive...'

'...if you say so, and this huge, I really mean it, a huge car came off the road, where it had been going in the same direction as me, and deliberately tried to clip me. I twisted out of its way and instead of carrying on up the drive, as it had started to do, it turned in front of me and took off back in the way it had come. It nearly got me in the turn as well. Then, a couple of minutes later, while I was still checking that everything was in working order, Nicole Thompson comes trotting up and tells me how dangerous the car's driver was, how she had seen everything. How...? Sylv, she wasn't even sweating. She had jogged to school, and her hand was as dry as a bone.'

'Not everybody sweats a lot, Max. It's still quite chilly in the mornings.'

Maxwell ignored her and the train of thought he had been following. He stored that one away for later. And then she goes round school telling everyone I fell off. I am assuming she is implying that in my geezerhood I just stopped pedalling and fell sideways onto the verge. That the balance of my mind, etcetera, etcetera. Is that right?'

Sylvia squeezed his hands. 'Pretty much on the button, Max. I'm sorry. The woman's a bitch. I'll tell everyone...'

349

Maxwell hitched back in his seat, releasing her hands. 'Don't bother, Sylv. Really. If people want to believe her, then they'll believe her. And they all know she's a bitch anyway. But, whatever the reason for my hitting the deck, you can clear off with that stuff. I still get the pain in wet weather.' He adjusted himself, Frankie Howerd to the life, and shooed the nurse away. She gave him a tap on the shoulder and left the room, waving as she went. He didn't look up. His head was full of threads, waving this way and that, and he was trying to make them all come together. He sent up a small prayer to St Fiacre, patron saint of knitters, and then went over to his desk. He fished under it and brought out his laptop and switched it on. While he waited for it to lurch into life, he pulled a pad and a pen towards him. In an historian's world, the old ways are best.

He had cross-hatched the page into columns. They hadn't got headings yet, but he felt better having something to work with. He was just about to start filling in some boxes when the phone rang.

'Ahoy, ahoy.' Mr Burns to the life. He hoped it was Pansy; it always annoyed her when he answered the phone in any way other than the guidelines she had printed out and glued to each desk.

'It's me.' Jacquie, in the office and therefore being eminently sensible and also, to judge from the level of her voice, quite sneaky.

'Heart. How the devil are you?' He kept it light-hearted. If some busybody had seen fit to let her know about his fall off his bike, he wanted to scotch that little rumour before she got going.

'Max, I'm going to ask you something which I'm pretty sure you won't know the answer to, but I'm going to ask you all the same.'

'Well, that sounds sensible, my little currant bun. Good use of everyone's time.' There was a knock at the door and he held the phone away from his face to call, 'Come in.' Alice stood there, tiny and frail-looking, and he motioned her to come in.

'Sorry?'

'No, just talking to Alice. Go on.'

'If you've got someone there...'

'No. Go on. I can still talk even though I am looking at Alice.' He smiled encouragingly and she crept further into the room.

'Have you heard of a site on your intranet called itsgoodtotalk, where the kids can take part in chat rooms anonymously?'

'Any reason?'

'It's up and running in Maisie's school. Which means the Thomas twins are part of it. I think it might have a bearing.'

'Oh, yes, good thinking. But you're right that I'm not the man to ask. Hold on.' He pressed the phone to his shoulder. 'Alice. Do we have a thing called it's good to talk here at school?' The effect was electric. Alice jumped as though he had hit her and ran blindly out of the room. He looked at her in amazement and slowly put the phone up to his ear. 'I've just asked Alice,' he said.

'And?'

'I think the answer is yes. Can I get back to you later?'

'Max? Max? Are you there? What's wrong?' But the phone was down and he was on the warpath.

Pansy Donaldson had heard the news from Nicole that the mad old bastard had fallen off his bike. Surely now Diamond would be getting rid of him. He was a Health and Safety issue now. Old people falling over all around the place. Students might fall over them. Bacteria might settle. They could be victims of Swine Flu. The school would have to be closed. She could hardly contain herself, such was her glee. Thingee found the whole thing most distasteful, especially when Pansy's dewlap started to sway. She rang Maxwell's number to warn him of the impending doom of a final visit from Pansy, but she was too late. The school manager – or seeker after world domination, as Maxwell preferred to think of her – had met the Head of Sixth Form at the top of the stairs.

'Mr Maxwell!' she hailed him as though he was half a mile away, the odd errand-running child turning to stare at her.

'Mrs Donaldson. Not precisely the person I was looking for, but, by God, in a pinch you'll do.'

'I beg your pardon, Mr Maxwell?' She bridled and set everything a-sway again. 'What can you mean?'

'I'm going to clean up this town,' he menaced. He had no physical characteristic in common with Lee Van Cleef, but to hear him you wouldn't know it. 'You can start by going downstairs and taking that ridiculous wall of information down.

352

You can then go outside and, careless of Health and Safety requirements, you can set fire to it.' Maxwell shot a fiery glance at the errand-runner, who promptly vanished.

'But, Mr Maxwell, I need my information.'

'You ludicrous woman,' Maxwell spat, his famous gentlemanly behaviour hanging by a thread. 'Have you any idea how many rules you have broken by having all that up in public? Does the data protection act ring any bells? When I can be randomly rung by a member, no matter how well meaning, of the kitchen staff because my number is three feet high on your wall, what does that tell you? When small girls are driven to nervous breakdowns because their email addresses and mobile phone numbers are on that self-same wall, does that make you proud?'

She was, for the first time in many years, totally speechless.

'Don't just stand there,' Maxwell snarled. 'Do it.'

She turned and went down the stairs like a slinky, with one part naturally following the other due to gravity. He watched until she reached the bottom of the stairs. She turned and looked up at him, with malevolent eyes, watching him until he turned away.

Maxwell took a folded piece of paper from one pocket and a pen from another and made an extravagant tick. 'One down,' he muttered. 'One to go.'

Maxwell pounded up the stairs and proudly paused at the top. Not even slightly out of breath, although he had to be far above the tree-line. He slipped one hand inside his jacket and counted his heart beats. Steady as a rock and well within the normal for his age. This was an assumption on his part as he neither knew nor cared what that normal count might be. He shrugged his jacket to fit his suddenly macho shoulders better and marched along to the IT Department, tucked away in what had once, when Leighford High and the world were young, been the smokers' room. This was an irony Maxwell had enjoyed, as the smokers could hardly manage the stairs.

He threw open the door and was met by two pairs of puzzled eyes. He nodded. 'Mike. Ned. Any idea where Nicole might be?'

Mike paused from his task of printing out the postage labels for his eBay sales. 'I think she went down to see if she could see Mr Diamond. I don't know what about.' He smirked at Ned, who dipped back to his magazine.

'I think I know why she's down there. I just want her up here. Now.'

'I don't see how I can do that, Mr Maxwell,' Mike said, still smirking.

'Ring her up,' Maxwell said. 'I can't imagine that she doesn't carry her mobile at all times. Just because the kids are banned from it and the staff discouraged, doesn't mean that you guys, the IT crowd, have to obey the rules, does it?'

Ned cracked first. 'I'll text her, Mr Maxwell. In case she's in with Mr Diamond.'

'Ring. Her.' Maxwell was close to losing his temper. He didn't turn green and burst out of his clothes but there were grown men out there in the real world who still went pale when they remembered the day he had lost it with them.

'Ring who?'

Maxwell turned gracefully, grateful that he didn't fall over. That manoeuvre was always a tricky one. 'Clara. Lovely to see you. I think I have a bone to pick with you.'

'Do you? Boys, if you would go and ... I don't know. Do something useful with the mainframe. There's always something.' She smiled coldly at them and they scraped their chairs back and left in a hurry. She waited a moment before opening the door they had slammed behind them. 'Mainframe's on the ground floor,' she reminded them. 'Back of the library. Sorry,' she corrected herself, 'the old library. The book store, you know.' Sheepishly, they walked slowly down the corridor and she watched them to the head of the stairs. She went back into the room and, smiling at Maxwell, offered him a chair. 'How can I help you, Max?' she asked him.

'You're very cool, Clara,' he remarked.

'I try to be,' she said. 'My outburst on Friday was very out of character.'

'Yes, why did you get so upset? If you didn't even know the man?'

'It was so sudden. I hadn't had anything to eat or drink. I was a bit disoriented. It's not what I usually do, running around in woods and things. I just ... overreacted.'

Maxwell crossed his legs and leant back. Nicole sprang forward.

'Don't do that, for God's sake. Those idiots have got almost all these chairs booby-trapped.

355

It's like working with children.'

He rearranged himself carefully and, with nothing dreadful happening, continued his questions. 'You knew him, though, didn't you?'

'I have never ever in my life seen that man before Friday. I see him now, though. Every time I close my eyes.'

'Did you know he was a computer buff?' he pressed.

'Max. I don't know the man. He could be a trapeze artist for all I know.'

'He was Mrs B's nephew, you know. He had been hanging around Leighford for a while before he was arrested and sent to prison for computer fraud.'

'Not so much of a buff, then, if he got caught.'

Maxwell looked thoughtful. That was something he hadn't considered. He had been unlucky, that two of his marks had known each other, and they had him on CCTV, but surely, he should have had contingency plans. 'You've got a point there.' He recovered himself. 'But that's not all. Why are you going round telling everyone I fell off my bike?'

She just sat, looking at him and tears slowly welled up in her eyes. She shook her head and finally said, 'I don't know.'

'Is that it?' He almost sat back in amazement. 'You don't know. You tell Pansy Donaldson that I fell off my bike, so she goes around treating me as if I am a leper who might give oldness and madness to the whole school and all you can say is you don't know why you did it. Can you at least give a hint?'

By now she was weeping real tears and it took some time for Maxwell to restore the room to order. Eventually, with a screwed-up hankie in one hand and a fistful of Maxwell's jacket sleeve in the other, she told her story.

'I'm trying to get a new job, Max. I need a new job. I can't stay up here with these idiots for one more day. They do nothing. They know nothing. Every time I ask them to do something, I end up doing it myself. The only thing they ever took on when I asked them to was the internal chat room. It was invented by some guy, at another school, I think it was. Anyway, I asked Ned to do that and he seems to have taken it on board. It's working, anyway. I check the activity from time to time and it seems to be very popular. Not so much lately, but I think it will pick up again after exams. But, anyway,' she gave a huge sniff, 'I know there's talk of an HR job and so, I thought that if I showed an interest, you know, in people's welfare, then perhaps... Max, I'm so sorry,' and she threw herself into his arms in new paroxysms of tears.

By bracing his legs at the last minute, Maxwell managed to prevent them both going over in an unseemly heap. He patted her, he made comforting little noises and, eventually, he managed to reach over her shoulder and call Sylvia Matthews. Without going into detail, he managed to palm off the hysterical IT girl onto the matron and slip away. Cogs had been whirring, threads had been ravelling and now the fabric was almost complete. Just a few more passes of the shuttle and he would have the whole thing sewn up.

Mavis would be so proud.

He clattered down the stairs again, past his own mezzanine floor and on, through the foyer and past the dining room. A small huddle of cooks impeded his progress. He tried to dodge round them, but suddenly they were hanging from his clothing and asking him things. They were like piranhas – small and singly quite harmless, but powerful in a school.

'Mr Maxwell, have you heard?' One broke off from the mass. 'About poor Doreen? We're having a whip round.'

His heart contracted in his chest. 'What about Doreen?' His own voice seemed to come from terribly far away.

'She was waiting for a bus this morning and a car mounted the pavement. She's lucky to be alive. She's in Leighford General with two broken legs.'

'What sort of car was it?' He asked the question but he knew the answer.

Mad Max, what a character. They knew he was fond of all the staff, well, with some major exceptions, but he would come out with silly questions. 'It was one of those great big things, with the bars on the front. Silly, I call it, in town.'

Maxwell dug in his pocket and hauled out a note. He pressed it into the nearest hand and dashed off down the corridor. Blimey! He might be mad, but twenty quid – that would make the final haul almost twenty-one pounds if they were lucky.

With an exceptional turn of speed, he hurtled down the long corridor across the back of the school. He heard snatches of lessons Doppler as he hurried past. He could see the double doors at the end of the corridor that marked, in happier days, where the library had once stood, hushed and cool, lined with books and filled with silent children. Now, it was a ghost of a library, not even a Learning Resource Centre, the librarian (or Learning Resource Centrifuge) long gone to finish her days shushing old men in the reference section at the main library in town, trying to get used to the long days and the residual smell of wee.

He pushed the doors open and called. 'Mike? Ned? Are you here?'

There was no answer, but he somehow felt, in the dusty dark, that he wasn't alone. He twitched aside a blind at the nearest window and let in a shaft of light, which didn't quite reach across the room.

He could see two huddled forms over by the mainframe cupboard, but they were still almost in darkness and he couldn't see what they were doing. 'Mike? Ned? Answer me.'

'No.' A husky voice answered him. 'We don't want to talk to you, Maxwell. Go away.'

'It's no good, lads,' Maxwell said. 'I know what's going on. There are a few gaps. Can I try them out?'

'Why not?' The voice was somehow odd sounding. Generic. No one's in particular.

'Who am I talking to?' he asked.

'Woo hoo. You must be stressed,' mocked the voice.

'That was a really bad sentence. Don't you mean, to whom am I talking?'

'That would be better,' Maxwell conceded. 'But I'm allowed a few mistakes, surely? We're all allowed that. I don't expect you meant to kill Colin. It just happened by accident, is that right?'

'Nope,' said the voice and Maxwell suddenly understood. It was coming through a voice changer. And the reason the silhouettes looked strange was because they were wearing Troopers' helmets, from the original Star Wars movies. 'It was deliberate. He was rubbish. He could write any program you could imagine, and then he couldn't sell it to save his sorry life. The last one he did...' The laugh was horrible, metallic and harsh. 'It would have made us millionaires. But, poor old Col, he has to invent something that only crooks would want. Dodgy geezers. So we couldn't ask too much money. So we had to ask for it again and again. And we got caught. Well, *he* got caught. And now, of course, sod's law, the blokes that shopped us, they've come out of the woodwork, going through the courts to get the ownership. So we could have been legit after all.'

'But why kill him?'

'Stupid sod, did a runner from Ford and came here. Wanted to come clean all about it. Well, I'd found another use for it meanwhile. So he could bugger that. So,' Maxwell saw the shoulders shrug under the bulky head, 'I just twisted his sorry neck for him.'

'What had he invented?' Maxwell asked.

'Only a program that could hack into anything you like. From the bank on the corner to the

360

Bank of England. Weapons. Money. You could do what you like.'

'And what do you do with it?' Maxwell could hardly stop himself from adding – you dirty-minded little pillock.

There was an evil-sounding chuckle. 'I have my bit of fun. With all the girls and their little secrets. I've got them running. I'm doing it local for now. I like to see their faces when I'm out in town, at a club. I like to think they're scared of me, without knowing me. It's,' he gave a lascivious wriggle, 'good.'

'Look, Ned,' Maxwell said. He thought it was time to make it personal. 'I know it's you. Mike, you're safe. I'll help you.'

'Mr Maxwell,' said the voice. 'How did you work out it was me?'

'Not hard,' Maxwell said, creeping closer and closer, not taking his eyes off the two. 'You quoted from Nostradamus, and I taught you all about that when you were here at school. Then there's the time I put you in detention for bad grammar. And I know you never forgot that, so you picked me up on it just now. Then, Nicole told me you ran the school intranet chat room. So QED.'

'Ah, Mr Maxwell, you're too clever for me.' One figure rose to its feet and to Maxwell's horror the other one fell sideways and lay splayed on the floor. 'Catch me if you can.' He dashed out through the fire exit at the back of the room and Maxwell could hear his feet on the stairs.

Maxwell gave chase, pausing as he saw the body at the open cupboard. He hoped he wouldn't live to regret it, but there was something about the position of the neck which told him that there was no point in stopping to check if he was alive. He tore up the first flight, but by the second was relying more and more heavily on the banister. By the top of the stairs, his lungs were screaming for air and he had to stop, hands on his knees, to try to force some breath down into his chest.

He took the force of the blow across the back of his shoulders and went down as if poleaxed. Somehow, he still had enough energy left to roll sideways, so the next strike missed him and clanged onto the top step. He heard his assailant hiss as the vibrations travelled up his arms. The weapon clattered down the stairs as the pain made him open his hands and drop it. At least they were now equal, or as equal as two men could be when one was not exactly known for his sporting prowess and was thirty-odd years older than the other.

'Well, Mr Maxwell,' the voice grated through the helmet. 'It looks like hand-to-hand. I'll let you get up. It's only sporting, after all. Not like running you down in a car or anything.'

'That was you?' Maxwell said, struggling to his feet. 'How did you manage that?'

'Easy. Bike in the back. Park down the road. I've been doing it all year. People tend to ask questions if you drive a thirty-five thousand pound car on nine thousand pounds a year.'

'Good point.' Maxwell was walking towards his man, getting him further away from the head of the stairs. 'And why the Nostradamus?'

'Like you said,' the voice calmly explained. 'You

taught it to us at school.'

'No, Mike, I didn't,' Maxwell said. 'I didn't start doing that lesson until Ned had left.'

'I'm not Mike,' the electronic voice said. 'I'm Ned.'

'Come on, Mike,' Maxwell said, walking inexorably forward. 'Not only are you taller and broader than Ned, you have a row of labels stuck to your left sleeve, ready to stick on the parcels you've been packing. And it is, after all, *Michel* de Notre Dame, not Edouard. Take the helmet off, now, there's a good bloke, and let's talk.'

Slowly, the man raised his arms and pulled off the helmet. He stood there, a crooked grin on his face, his hair standing on end, with the headgear under his arm. 'There's nothing to talk about, Mr Maxwell,' he said. 'We're alone up here, I'm taller than you, fitter than you, younger than you. In a minute, I'm going to rugby tackle you and then toss you out of the window. Like the man says, evil ruin will fall on the great man. Well, the Great Man will fall, that's good enough. Then, I'll be out of here, into my nice big car and away. It's not as if I don't have enough money.'

He never even heard the whish of the laptop through the air as Pansy Donaldson prepared to bring it down on his head. And the rest was silence.

'Pansy,' said Maxwell, as he stepped over the fallen murderer to give her as near to a hug as he could manage. 'I never knew you cared.'

Chapter Twenty

'Max? What are you doing up there?' Jacquie called up the stairs. 'Supper's on the table.'

'Just coming,' Maxwell replied. 'Just sending an email.' He looked proudly at the totally typo-free document on his screen.

Dear Mr Diamond,

I would be grateful if you could accept this letter as my official request for early retirement. I have given this matter a lot of thought and, of course, recent events have rather tended to concentrate my mind. I do, of course, realise that further meetings will be necessary, but as tomorrow is the last day for requesting retirement for this school year, I have chosen to send it in this way; I hope you will find it acceptable. And I would like to thank you for what you have done.

Yours sincerely,

Peter Maxwell

Right, now what was next? Yes, check address. Diamoj at all the usual offices. Click. Send.

The message disappeared as the logo of a little envelope faded into the background. Maxwell literally rubbed his hands together with the pleasure of a job well done.

Early evening in Brazil is a beautiful moment. The sun kisses the tops of the mountains with a beautiful peach blush just before it sinks out of sight. Exotic birds call from the treetops and the monkeys shout their raucous 'goodnight' calls from every bough. The smell of blossom and sun-warmed fruit fills the air. A lovely evening. Watch some bastard spoil it.

Hector Diamoj arrived home from work and walked through his still-cool house, scratching a thigh and rubbing some of the dust of the day from his tired eyes. He tapped his computer into life and perched on the chair, waiting for his emails to load. *Madre de Dios!* More spam. If this maxwep didn't stop sending him this English rubbish soon, he would have no choice but to report him to his internet provider. Hover over the delete icon. Click of the mouse. And that would be that until the next time.

Midnight in Leighford is a beautiful moment. And at 38 Columbine, as Peter Maxwell cuddled into the warm back of his lovely wife, he smiled in his sleep. No more getting up early to go to school. No more marking. No more kids. No more...

The publishers hope that this book has given you enjoyable reading. Large Print Books are especially designed to be as easy to see and hold as possible. If you wish a complete list of our books please ask at your local library or write directly to:

Magna Large Print Books
Magna House, Long Preston,
Skipton, North Yorkshire.
BD23 4ND

This Large Print Book for the partially sighted, who cannot read normal print, is published under the auspices of

THE ULVERSCROFT FOUNDATION